The Hair Mavens—
Book One

She Does Good Hair

Terri Gillespie

What others are saying about . . .

The Hair Mavens (Book One)

She Does Good Hair

She Does Good Hair captured my heart and funny bone. Gillespie weaves colorful characters, lively, spot on dialogue, and romance that sizzles with a poignant tale of forgiveness and redemption. A winning combination.

Cathy Gohlke, best-selling and award winning author of *Saving Amelie, Band of Sisters* and *Promise Me This*

Terri Gillespie's *She Does Good Hair* is a creative, fun, and touching story that will grab hold of your heart from the first page. I loved the cast of colorful characters and the well-drawn setting. Terri has a gift for writing crisp, entertaining dialogue and for creating a story that rings true with depth and meaning. Come along and enjoy the ride. You'll love the Hair Mavens!

Carrie Turansky, award-winning author of *The Governess of Highland Hall* and *The Daughter of Highland Hall*

ISBN 10: 1500319406
ISBN-13: 978-1500319403

To my beautiful daughter, Rivka, who inspires me.

"Do not plead with me to abandon you,
to turn back from following you.
For where you go, I will go,
and where you stay, I will stay.
Your people will be my people,
and your God my God.
Ruth 1:16 (TLV).

ACKNOWLEDGMENTS

Every book is more than words on a page—each word carries passion, hope, and experience. That's a lot packed into each word—which is why having others to share in that burden is so important.

Those who know me know my passion for unity. The most beautiful story of unity is the Biblical story of Ruth and Naomi—Jew and Gentile, one in faith, love, and community.

My thanks to the following people who not only believed in me, but also believed in this modern day Ruth and Naomi parable and are living testimonies of Jew and Gentile, one in the Messiah Jesus: my dear friends Cathy Gohlke and Carrie Turansky, who began as writing friends and have become sisters of the heart; ACFW Crit1 buddies, especially Cynthia Ruchti, and Julia Scudder Dearyan; My StoryCrafters friends, especially Joyce Magnin; my writing mentors Angela Hunt and Marlene Bagnull; the ladies of Salon Bella Gente, especially the owner Kathleen McGehean, and my miracle-working hairdresser, Sharon Hatala; my Congregation Beth Yeshua family, especially Debbie Chernoff, Barbara "Bobbi" Fox, Mindy Salkind, Melissa Goldner, Teresa Maguire, Danielle Chernoff, Rhona Epstein, and Debbie Finkelstein; my friend Daniah Greenberg who continues to challenge and inspire me to greatness; and my mom Phyllis Macalady, sisters Alicia Macalady and Phyllis Wilson, and sister-in-law Laurie Macalady. And a shout-out to The Hair Mavens Team Leaders—thanks, ladies!

A special thanks to the Messianic rabbis in my life who have both inspired and taught me what true unity can look like: Rabbi David Chernoff, Rabbi Jason Sobel, Rabbi Eric Tokajer, and my dear brother in creativity, Rabbi Michael Wolf.

Thanks to my true love, my husband, Bob who has stood beside me to encourage, behind me to push, ahead of me to lead, and beneath me to carry me when I didn't have the strength for one more step. I love you, P-Man!

And then there is the One who is responsible for planting this passion within me. It is His passion, because it was and is His prayer (John 17)—unity between Jews and the nations. Why? Because when that happens, the world will know who He is! He is Yeshua—ישוע—Jesus—Jésus—Gesù—Jesús—يسوع‎—and His Name goes on to all the nations of the world.

My prayer is that this book will not only entertain, but also enlighten. So the world may know . . .

.

1

Wrapped in the warmth of affection and admiration, Shira Goldstein exited her Beverly Hills salon into the perfectly beautiful sunny day. She turned and blew kisses toward her clients who had pressed their faces against the salon window like children in a candy store and she their Willy Wonka of beauty.

With practiced grace, she slid her sunglasses on as she looked down Rodeo Drive. There. Her transportation waited for her at the curb.

From the black stretch limousine, a handsome driver exited, wearing a black tux and crisp white shirt, which matched his perfectly whitened teeth and olive complexion. Like a performer from *Dancing with the Stars* he salsa-ed her to the back limo door and opened it.

"Thank you," Shira purred.

The driver winked and said in a squeaky feminine voice, "Shira, I'm dripping."

Shira blinked. The handsome driver dissolved into the back of Mrs. Sally Phillips's soppy wet head.

The warmth of embarrassment wrapped itself around Shira's face. She had just broken Élégance Salon and Spa's number one rule: Keep the client happy and *dry*.

"Shira, I said I'm dripping." Mrs. Phillips' nasal, East Coast accent confirmed that Shira's Beverly Hills fantasy didn't match reality and her client was not happy. Were Sally's forehead not recently Botoxed it would be creased with irritation.

"I'm so sorry, Mrs. Phillips." *Stop the daydreaming already. You're not in Beverly Hills. Yet.*

Shira repositioned the thick black towel at the nape of her wealthiest client's neck and gently massaged. A little trick she'd learned to help patrons

1

return to their blissful place when interruptions like this occurred.

A quick glance at the mirror confirmed that Mrs. Phillips was in the zone. Her eyes were closed and her head lolled freely with each knead of Shira's experienced hands. She let out a moan of pleasure. Everything was good again.

Shira chewed her bottom lip. She'd waited five years for this moment. More than a month ago, over lattes and oatmeal scones, her boss Veronica Harrington had shared the news of finalizing her plans to open another salon in Beverly Hills. The rest of the Manhattan staff had only learned about it a week before.

Back then Veronica had all but promised that Shira would be the manager of the newest Élégance Salon and Spa. Still, she had invited any of the staff to apply for the position. No one else had dared to apply for the position except—

Nigel.

As if reading her mind, Nigel flounced past her. His ability for annoyance was only matched by his sneakiness—like some well-dressed mosquito taking dives at her, sucking every drop of her confidence. He walked toward the shampoo area and pointed a bejeweled finger at the shampoo girls. A chorus of them harmonized, "Oh, Nigel!"

Everyone loved Nigel. Maybe Shira would have liked him more if they weren't competing for the same job and she didn't have to constantly clean up after his mistakes. Although he was a genius at the "Mac-Daddy" blow-dry.

No offense to Nigel, but she'd given the past five years of her life to Élégance, and he had only arrived nine months ago. Veronica couldn't possibly give the job to him.

Nigel knocked on Veronica's office door then went back to *schmoozing* with the girls. Veronica's door opened. Like a high-fashioned jack-in-the-box, her upper torso appeared, followed by a willowy hand that motioned to him. Nigel rolled his neck, straightened his tie then strutted into Veronica's inner sanctum.

Once the door shut, Shira returned her focus to the nearly comatose Mrs. Phillips in her chair. She fingered the strands on top of her client's head. Yes, her triple foil job was flawless. The perfect balance of butterscotch-blonde and Monroe-platinum highlights with chocolate-brown lowlights had created follicle drama. Better than natural.

Shira grabbed her Ecru serum and pumped a small amount onto her palm. Rubbing her hands together until a deliciously soft layer of silk proteins covered them, she smiled. Mrs. Phillips' cuticles would practically radiate healthiness once she finished. She worked it into the hair, especially on the blond streaks, then combed it through.

She opened her station's drawer.. Inside, laying on gold felt were her

Kamisori shears—lined up by size—like a surgeon's tray. She chose the correct instrument for this cut, inserted her fingers into the brightly colored handle, and became one with the scissors. The pleasant-sounding snips of her favorite tool effortlessly shaped and trimmed a chic masterpiece.

The time flew as quickly as her fingers. It wasn't until she had walked Mrs. Phillips—expertly coiffed with color-dimension the envy of every stylist—out the door and locked it for the night, that Shira realized Nigel was still in Veronica's office.

She patted her gurgling stomach then checked herself once more in the mirror. Despite another ten-hour shift, her Crisis104 suit didn't seem the worse for wear. She buttoned the jacket and smoothed a palm over the matching skinny pants. Very Audrey Hepburn. Classically feminine, yet professional—Veronica's mantra.

It was nearly eight o'clock, and New York's premium salon still buzzed with activity. Everyone from the cleaning staff to stylists had hung around for the official word. Who would earn the coveted promotion to the Beverly Hills salon? Who would get to rub bony shoulders with stars?

Shira sipped her third mocha-mint latte, which had long gone cold. Still, it gave her shaking hands something to do. She probably should have eaten today, but her stomach had knotted like a chignon since before the sun peeked through the tall buildings around her apartment.

"Quit pretending you're nervous." Fawna, one of the shampoo girls—and her best friend—punched her arm and walked away.

"Ow." Shira rubbed the throbbing "love-pat" and studied Fawna's long blonde hair with mega-shimmering highlights swishing from side to side—another testimony of Shira's color-genius. Fawna looked over her shoulder. "You know you got the job, Goldstein!"

Although others had whispered this to her throughout the day. Shira still wondered why Veronica would even consider Nigel. Not only could he not manage his way out of a Gucci bag, but he'd only graduated from the London Hair Academy nine months ago. Nigel left all the paperwork for Shira to do. Yesterday she'd actually seen him scribble some guy's phone number on the color inventory sheet then tuck it into his suit pocket, where she'd later rescued it. Imagine running out of Chestnut Brown or Edge of Night Black? There'd be chaos on the streets of Manhattan.

A giggle bubbled to the surface and turned into a snort. Several people glanced her way. She covered her mouth and faked a cough. She turned toward her station and—oh, great—spotted another silver strand taunting her. Yes, like her father, she was prematurely going gray. Sam Goldstein hadn't given her anything in years. Except his silver curse, that kept giving.

What is taking Veronica so long?

She plopped onto her leather styling chair. If there were any chance God would listen to her, she'd actually pray right now. Thoughts of Aunt

3

Edna back in Pennsylvania praying for her produced a wisp of gratitude that swirled around her heart, warming it. God would surely listen to her aunt. She was a saint—if Jews had saints.

Nice to know she had a few people who cared. Veronica, Fawna, Aunt Edna, and, of course, Alec. She wiggled her naked ring finger. Surely this promotion would finally motivate Alec to say the magic words.

Stop it, Shira. You just pumped up the nervous volume.

Shira jumped out of the chair and tried to walk out the panicky energy. Aunt Edna would say she had a bad case of *schpilkis*. Her heels clicked on the marble floor as she paced toward the front of the salon. The floor-to-ceiling windows framed the city lights and the busy foot and street traffic like a travel poster for the powerful and influential. She would miss the rhythm and excitement that was New York, but it was time to move on.

Shira rubbed the smooth paper coffee cup against her cheek.

Muffled laughter erupted from Veronica's office. Like a red-hot curling iron it seared Shira's already twisted insides. The door opened to Veronica's melodic scales and Nigel's loud theatrical staccato. The schpilkis hit a new level.

Something cold and wet ran down her pant leg. In her tightened fist was the crushed paper cup. She glanced down. The sticky contents had produced an ugly brown stain—like a caffeinated oil spill—down her cream slacks. Her eyes traveled up to see Veronica and Nigel in front of her.

"Shira, love, have an accident?" Nigel brought his fingertips to his mouth and shook his bulbous head, barely stifling a giggle.

She ran back to her station to grab some tissues. With quick frantic strokes she tried cleaning her pants. Instead she left a trail of tissue dandruff. Veronica came up behind her and handed her a towel.

"New suit?"

Their eyes met. Shira hoped to read sympathy in the smoky gray, but something more like amusement sparkled.

"Yes." Try as she might, Shira couldn't stop her lips from quivering. Her Crisis104 pantsuit—the Dad-Forgot-My-Birthday-Again outfit—looked the way she felt. Ruined.

Nigel snickered. His response renewed her annoyance. She mustered up an angry glare then shot it in his direction.

"Don't get your knickers in a twist, girlfriend." He tugged on a cuff and adjusted the lapel of his Ralph Lauren suit. "Veronica, love, meet you at Savoy?"

What?

"Yes, Nigel," Veronica nodded toward him. "Run along."

Shira turned toward the woman she had trusted with her future. Veronica glanced down at her gold alligator-skin flats. Her friend's pale cheeks colored.

Oh, the betrayal. Shira had helped Veronica pick out those shoes.

Nigel pranced through the salon lifting his arms and pointing to his head. "I got Beverly Hills," he bellowed.

Someone let out a moan. Shira realized it had come from her. Her heart pounded against her chest, wanting out of her body. To run somewhere safe.

A crowd formed around Nigel. The shampoo staff took turns hugging him. Squeals and laughter fell like verbal balloons and confetti. Shira watched as her best friend Fawna looped her arm through his and planted a kiss . . . on his lips?

Shira blinked. The scene before her turned soft and fuzzy. Everyone seemed to move in slow motion. *Was this a dream?*

"Shira?"

Was someone calling her? Veronica's face moved into Shira's view. "Dear?" Veronica wrapped her arms around Shira and tried to guide her away from the celebration.

Except Shira's legs had turned to rubber and all she could hear was a strange ringing in her ears. She glanced back toward the swarm of well-wishers.

As if on cue, they stopped talking and stared at Shira. Everything went dark—

"You fainted?" Alec's sonorous voice pulsed through Shira's head.

"Yes, Alec. Could you please reduce the decibels? You know what happens when my blood sugar gets too low." She massaged her temple preparing for the next blast. "Then I quit."

"Are you crazy?"

"Thanks for your support, Alec." Shira stomped across the living room's hardwood floor toward the shopping bag containing Crisis112's booby prize. Like a junkie needing a fix, she reached into the Saks bag and pulled the Chanel sweater from the tissue wrapping. She rubbed the pink cashmere against her cheek. Soft as a Phyto hair conditioning.

In the words of Coco Chanel: "A girl should be two things: classy and fabulous." What could be more fab than this sweater?

"What did you buy for this disaster?"

She shoved the sweater behind her back. "What makes you think I bought anything?" Her face heated. What was she doing? Alec couldn't see her.

He cleared his throat.

She brought the sweater back around and held it up. "It's beautiful, Alec. The yummiest pink pullover with—"

A familiar tuneless hum came from his end. Alec was bored with her, had tuned her out, and was at this moment—most likely—admiring himself

5

in a mirror.

Alec Hudson knew he was gorgeous. How many times had women thrown themselves at him, when Shira stood right next to him?

"So Nigel got the job," he said.

The modicum of peace from her purchase evaporated. Was it only a few hours ago she had admired herself in the mirror at Saks? The lusciousness of the sweater had helped her overlook the stains on her pants—and her life.

A burning in her nasal passages meant tears wouldn't be far behind. She pinched the blemished area of her pants. Nigel got the job.

"Yes." She hugged the sweater, trying to soak in its perfection as she walked toward the window, the floors creaking with each step like a mournful "no, no." Surely this crisis had altered the space-time continuum. She peeked through the blinds at the busy street.

No. Life went on, despite hers ending.

Her sigh frosted the glass. The city scene blurred as pools formed in her eyes.

"Did Veronica give you a reason?"

Shira moved to the couch, the cloud of pink safe on the coffee table. "She said his 'profile' was a more suitable demographic for Beverly Hills." She lay down and rested an arm over her eyes. The tears finally released and streamed into her ears.

"What the heck is that supposed to mean?"

"He's British, a London Hair Academy graduate, and gay." She sniffed. "I'm domestic and dull. He's imported and intriguing."

"And he's a college graduate, right?"

Shira winced. "Yes." Nigel had completed his business degree. Now she had her father's voice buzzing in her head. *You'll never amount to anything without a degree.*

"So you really quit." Alec puffed out a breath. "Think that was a wise thing to do?"

Another stream rolled into her ear. *No, but I was humiliated in front of the whole salon. Doesn't anyone care about that?* She wiped the tracks of disappointment with the back of her hand.

"You know what, babe? It's gonna be okay," Alec said. "Because Veronica is gonna beg you to come back."

"Think so?" Shira sniffed and chewed on her fingernail.

"Of course I do!" He snorted. "She can't run that salon without you. You know as much about the business as she does."

Veronica did say that. That she depended on Shira. Right now she was needed in New York.

"She'll probably give you a bonus to come back. You'll see."

"She was pretty angry when I left." Shira pushed herself up to a sitting position. This felt good, Alec coming to her defense.

"Come on. Your clients will stampede her office. All those designer shoes at her door and she'll do anything you want."

A giggle dribbled from her.

"That's my girl."

How did he do it? She could take on the world now. Except that there were no tissues around. She rubbed her nose on her silk blouse sleeve.

Good thing Alec wasn't there. And good thing the sweater was out of harm's way.

"Babe, we'll just put our plans for California on hold for a while."

Their plans. Shira stared at her ring-less ring finger.

"The audition for the play went good. I probably got the part," he said.

"That's great, Alec!"

She stood and stretched. Alec's recent birthday gift drew her toward the fireplace like fresh-baked brownies. She leaned on the mantle and ogled the expensively framed photo of him. A small spotlight was positioned above. She clicked the light and instant marquee.

"When will you know something?" Shira traced the outline of his lips and gazed at his ice-blue eyes before stepping away.

"Arnie says the director loves me, so any day, I'm sure."

"It's about time your agent worked up a little sweat on your behalf." A gurgle came from Shira's stomach. She walked toward the kitchen.

"So what about heading to the Savoy for a late dinner?" he said.

Shira skidded to a stop. "No!" The last people she wanted to see were Veronica and Nigel—not yet, anyway. "Um, let's try a new place."

"Sure, babe. You wanna call Fawna to see if she'll meet us?"

"No. I prefer to have you all to myself this time, Alec."

He paused.

Apprehension landed on her shoulders like an old smelly blanket. She cringed. *Don't ask. Don't ask. Don't—*

"Babe, the underwear commercial shoots tomorrow, so can you, uh, you know, spot me for tonight?"

"Yeah. Sure. Whatever." So he was a little short right now. With the commercials and the play, he'd be discovered soon. And, who knows, he might soon support her as Hollywood's newest heartthrob.

"You're the greatest. Pick you up in an hour?"

"I'll be ready." She ended the call, retrieved the sweater, and sprinted back to her bedroom. Possible outfits rolled in her head like a slot machine in Atlantic City.

By the time Alec was due to arrive, Shira's bed and floor resembled the aftermath of a Loehmann's sale. But she didn't care. The perfect outfit had risen from the heaps. She examined her reflection in the full-length mirror. She hadn't starved herself enough to get into a size two, but a four wasn't bad. The pink sweater and the new blonde highlights she had added last week brightened her chocolate-brown eyes. She dabbed a layer of gloss on her full lips and blew herself a kiss. She was ready to *par-tay*.

Call Aunt Edna.

Shira turned around, expecting to see someone. Where did that come from?

Aunt Edna? That was the last thing she needed. Drawn back into the clutches of small-town America? She didn't think so.

Still, a cup of Aunt Edna's hot cocoa sounded pretty good. With mini-marshmallows. Some sympathy? A hug?

But it wouldn't only be a cup of cocoa or hugs. It would come with strings, like sermons, God-agendas, and good old-fashioned Jewish guilt.

She could imagine her aunt's perpetual effervescent voice saying, "Shira, come work in my salon."

Doing granny hair? She wasn't that desperate.

The buzzer rang. She jogged to the security system by the front door and pressed the intercom button. "Yes?"

"Hey, babe. I'm here."

Her Prince Charming had arrived.

"I'll be right down." She grabbed her leather jacket off the hook, then her new Chloe bag and keys.

The phone rang.

Shira's heart did a flip-flop. Maybe it was Veronica. She rummaged through her bag and grabbed her cell.

Aunt Edna's smiling face appeared on the screen.

The theme from the Twilight Zone played in her head as she sent the call directly to voicemail and placed her cell in her pocket. A barb of anxiety pricked her conscience. She shook it off, her hand on the cold metal knob.

Was Alec right? Would Veronica eventually call?

Shira shrugged, then chuckled as she opened the door. Of course she would call. As Alec said, Veronica needed her.

If he were wrong, Shira would have to do granny hair.

Once again the room spun around Shira like a vortex. Only this time the sensation was self-inflicted. She stumbled toward her living room and hit her shin on the end table.

Why hadn't she stuck with her usual glass of wine? Why? Because Alec called her a peasant and made her drink some concoction one of his bartender friends had dreamed up.

Alec. The *schlub* had abandoned her for some of his actor friends. Catch you later, babe. Humph. She bought him dinner, picked up his bar tab and what did she get?

A belch sent shock waves around the living room. Shira's hands flew to her mouth.

She kicked off her heels and shook out of her jacket as she swayed toward the bathroom. Her phone clunked to the floor. The message light flashed. *Veronica.*

The music was so loud at the bar she must have missed her call. A new intoxication, one of excitement now energized her.

"She's not angry with me after all. Thank you. Thank you." She tapped the screen to get to the list of last calls. "Alec, you handsome man, you were right." The list of recent calls names appeared. "I forgive you for being a jerk and—"

Only Aunt Edna's name. Some older calls. No Veronica. No job. No—

Shira grasped her stomach and bent forward.

Not only was the room spinning but now she felt like she was riding in the backseat of a rollercoaster. Her hands covered her mouth.

Minutes later, Shira sat on the cold tile floor, her head resting on the toilet seat. The song of regret played in her head. She'd heard its pounding tune too often these days. It wasn't just tonight's episode; it seemed her whole life was out of control. The more she tried to manage her life, the more it seemed to tangle.

Why did this keep happening to her? She pulled herself up and rinsed her mouth at the sink, avoiding her reflection in the mirror. How was she going to get out of this mess?

Entering her bedroom, she walked over the piles of clothes she'd left earlier and stood before the mirrored closet doors. The image before her didn't look like a fabulous and classy career woman. She looked pathetic.

She needed a hug.

A hug. Shira slid open the closet and dropped to her knees. Somewhere, buried in the back was a large white box Aunt Edna had mailed her last year for Hanukkah. Her aunt had called it a long-distance hug.

There it was. She felt a surge of urgency as she lifted the lid. Fingers pawed through the crisp blue tissue paper. A fuzzy white robe with matching fuzzy slippers. Probably from Walmart, but she didn't care.

Shedding her designer clothes, she slipped the soft cotton onto her body and cinched it loosely around her waist, then thrust her feet into pillowy softness. All she needed was a box of chocolates, a couple hours of soaps, and she'd be fine.

A contented sigh pushed through her once tensed body. She scuffed her way into the kitchen and tugged open the refrigerator door, the condiments rattling, "Will you ever cook again?" and looked inside. She passed the take-out graveyard to grab an Evian,. then twisted the cap as she shut the fridge door with her fluffy backside.

Maybe she should listen to her aunt's message? No. It was probably her annual Rosh Hashanah guilt call anyway. I'll make brisket and pineapple kugel. As if.

But her stomach called out, *yes, feed me brisket and kugel.*

She pointed to her abdomen. "Traitor."

No, she wasn't up for the family shame game this year. Especially now that she was officially a failure and everything that her father had predicted. Who knew where she would be in a few weeks? One thing for sure, it wasn't back in Philly.

She didn't care how beautiful fall was in the little town of Gladstone. She wasn't coming back. Not for brisket, not for kugel, not for a heaping serving of guilt with a side of regret.

She sipped and turned off lights as she shuffled to her bedroom. On her dresser was the worn leather journal. It was time to log in today's crisis. The discolored pages almost moved by themselves to the last crisis. Crisis111—car splashed mud on new shoes and purse. Shira turned her ankle to better inspect the gold ankle bracelet from Macy's. Fitting payback.

After logging Crisis112 and the booby-prize—the sweater—she paged through the old book. Even the journal was in response to a crisis.

Crisis One.

The familiar gate to Shira's heart clanged shut. She slammed the book closed and threw it on the dresser. It slid to the floor, landing upside down, its pages crumpled like her heart. She snatched up the book, something floated to the carpet.

A photo. Shira dropped to her knees.

Mom. The picture was taken before her mother's last round of chemo, almost fourteen years ago when she was twelve. Dad snapped it when Shira and her mother had shared a happy moment—back when they were a family. She lovingly held the photo and traced her mother's face with her finger.

Their hair blew together into one happy twist of brown—foreheads touching, laughing—a cherished moment caught on a flimsy slip of photo paper.

Shira cinched her hug a little tighter. She'd call Aunt Edna in the morning.

2

Harriet Foster took the last drag of her cigarette, then glanced once more down the sidewalk toward The Hair Mavens Beauty Shop.

Where was Edna? Thirty years of Ms. Always-on-Time, and the last month she'd been late three times. May as well get this show on the road. Harriet exhaled the menthol smoke as she bent toward the public ashcan in front of Delicious Bakery.

"Good morning, Harriet!"

She turned to see Bob Henry, Edna's insurance guy.

"How are you this fine crisp autumn morning?" he said. He clasped his hands behind his back and took a little bow.

Harriet straightened her shoulders. She couldn't help feeling like Queen Elizabeth whenever Bob flowed with poetic genuflection.

She worked to hide a smile, then dropped the ciggy into the ashcan. "Good, Bob. How about yourself?"

He gazed up at the sky—or maybe his modest "Bob Henry Insurance" sign above the bakery. She couldn't tell. "Can't complain. Can't complain." He shifted his gaze toward Hair Mavens. "Edna late?"

"It would appear so." She readjusted the strap of her shoulder bag then grabbed the bakery's metal door handle. *I'm burnin' daylight here, Bob.*

"Well, I won't keep you. Have a wonderful day." He unlocked the door leading to his second floor office, then twisted back toward Harriet. "That blue blazer looks mighty pretty on you, Harriet."

She admired her jacket for a second, a thank you ready for release, when—poof. He was gone. His faint footsteps on the stairs the only evidence he hadn't simply vanished into thin air.

Warmth radiated from her stomach all the way up to her cheeks. She smoothed her hand down the cotton navy blue blazer from Target. Nearly

11

forty bucks it cost her, but undoubtedly worth it.

She patted the back of her stiff beehive to be sure there were no errant hairs, then opened the heavy glass door. The familiar scents of cinnamon and gooey, sweet concoctions welcomed her as she entered Delicious Bakery. Nonni wore her usual white uniform. Her long salt-and-pepper hair was pulled into a braid that reached nearly to her behind—the last remnant of her hippie days. Harriet would love to get her hands on those thick, coarse tresses. For sure she'd start with coloring it.

"How's it going, Harriet?" Nonni rested her sturdy forearms on top of the glass display case, her chin barely coming to the top. "The usual?"

"Yep."

Nonni snatched a waxed paper sheet with one hand and shook a small white bag open with her other. Then with practiced grace she delicately pulled one cherry cheese Danish from the tray and placed it in the bag. She repeated the process with another Danish then set the bags together.

She filled two large Styrofoam cups from the coffee urn. "So where's Edna?"

"I'm not sure. Late start again, I suppose." The coffee's rich toasted aroma made Harriet's mouth water.

Nonni nodded as she pressed the plastic lids firmly in place. She opened another white bag and packed the coffees, a couple of the little containers of real cream, sugar, and red stirrers. There was something comforting about watching her movements. Like a ballet or something.

As Harriet paid with exact change, Frank walked in with a tray of pecan sticky buns. Their deliciousness was almost good enough to change from her and Edna's regular choice, but if it ain't broke . . .

"Hey, Harriet." Frank looked around. "Where's Edna?"

"Hey, Frank." Harriet pulled out her I LOVE NEW YORK key ring, then readjusted her purse. "She must be running late." Again.

Frank winked as he slipped the tray into another case. "See ya tomorrow."

Balancing her bags and purse, she walked three doors down to The Hair Mavens. Her keys jangled merrily as she unlocked the shop door. Before entering, Harriet took an affirming glimpse around at downtown Gladstone—all one block of it. This was her town. She couldn't help the mushy feeling of sentiment and familiarity. Just a few steps from anything she needed. Grocery store, dry cleaners, bakery, Chinese restaurant, pizza shop, florist, bank, and even a fancy-schmancy antique shop she'd never been in. And Edna's place, the heart of this borough.

Harriet reached in to turn on the lights, relocked the front door, and dropped the keys into the pocket of her black work pants. Hair Mavens wouldn't be opened for another hour and a half.

Today was Wednesday, the day she cut and styled and touched-up the gray roots of Edna's thick chestnut brown hair. But if Edna didn't get her rear end out of bed, that wasn't going to happen.

"I'm here!" Harriet craned her neck toward the back of the building.

No answer.

She placed the Danish bag with one of the coffees at the first station, Edna's place. Always neat, combs in the blue disinfectant jar, product arranged by order of use and brushes in her drawer. Her scissors and razors lay out by height on top of her roll-away cart like a surgeon's tools. A few photos of Edna with her niece and brother—the brat Shira, and the freeloader, Sam—were neatly framed and mounted next to the mirror. A Boston fern with a small Israeli flag planted in the soil finished her décor.

A few steps to Harriet's station, second chair. Everything was pretty much the same as Edna's except Harriet's pictures were postcards from her clients. Exotic places she'd never see.

No plants. The fragile little things hated her—seemed they'd rather die than allow her to take care of them. Like a lot of people in her life.

Next to Harriet, Beulah's cluttered counter was pure chaos with photos, news clippings, and stickers plastered all over her mirror. It was a wonder Beulah could see to work.

The last station belonged to Kathy-the-Mouse. If Harriet were a cop or something, she'd call it nondescript. No personality—like the Mouse. She wasn't interesting enough to be a mystery.

Harriet's scrutiny traveled back to the picture of Shira, Sam, and Edna together at a park. Smiling faces hid selfish hearts. Her jaw tightened, her molars grinding. She had ripped down her photos of Shira years ago.

Shake it off, old girl. This was what happened when there was too much quiet, too many thoughts and memories.

She marched back to the break room, shrugging off her blazer as she went. Harriet stroked the crisp cotton before hanging it up. Her cheeks warmed again as a half-smile exercised her facial muscles. That blue blazer looks mighty pretty on you, Harriet. How long had it been since a man gave her a compliment?

A quick examination of her black smock hanging next to the blazer revealed more droopy threads and bleach marks. Rats. Better drop it off at Wang's Cleaners tonight. After two years, the Wangs were used to repairing the evidence of a real workingwoman. Women. Edna knew what it meant to give everything to the job and to her staff—like the smock with her name in hot pink.

Edna. Where was she?

Harriet opened the door leading up to Edna's apartment on the second floor. "Edna, come on girl. Get the lead out!" She puffed out a frustrated sigh.

Even though it wasn't her turn to make coffee for the clients, Harriet grabbed the glass carafe and filled it at the sink. While it brewed, she ambled back to her station for her special beverage. After pulling off the lid, she doctored it with cream and sugar, then poured it into her Beauticians 'do It Better mug. She didn't mind the chips in the porcelain or the broken handle she had glued back on who knows how many times. This thing was a collector's item.

She plopped into her chair. It moaned as she swiveled around to the mirror. Leaning closer, she checked her makeup and beehive. A pout formed on her face. She remembered when it was eight inches high. With the bleaching and years of teasing, the mound had shrunk three inches in the last thirty years. A real shame.

The nicotine craving niggled. She yanked open her station's drawer to pull out a pack of ciggies. A quick jiggle torpedoed the next cigarette, which she adeptly lipped and removed from the pack. She slid the lighter out of the pack's cellophane cover and flicked once, twice. The flame hit the tip with a faint crackle.

There we go. A nice long drag. The calming smoke flowed down to her lungs and then up through her mouth and nose. Her reflection soon clouded as she exhaled.

The steam from the bakery coffee merged with the smoke, a perfect complement to her morning routine. After a careful sip, she reviewed the day's appointments in her mind. Mrs. Garaciola—wash and set. Mrs. Maynard—cut, wash, and set. Mrs. Brown—blue rinse, wash, and set. Harriet shrugged. Every day was pretty much the same. Just the way she liked it.

Anything—or anyone—out of that order made her hair frizz. And at the top of Harriet's I-hate-it-whens were late people. Like Edna was today and yesterday and Friday. The irritation drove her out of the chair. She bowed toward the shelf and grabbed one more sip then a deep drag on her ciggy. Edna didn't like Harriet smoking in the apartment so she left it smoldering in the ashtray.

Retracing her steps through the break room, she entered the stairwell. By the time she had reached the top of the stairs her lungs cried for mercy. Her legs throbbed.

That's what she needed this morning. Another reminder of the twenty pounds she'd gained over the past couple of years.

Take a deep breath, Harriet. She's your best friend. Don't bite her head off.

Harriet knocked.

No answer.

She knocked again then placed her ear on the dark-stained wood. "Edna, it's Harriet." Her heart did a flip flop. No sounds came from the apartment.

Her heartbeat picked up. With a shaky hand, she fished into her pants pocket for the keys.

Calm down, old girl. One more knock, just in case she's in the shower or something.

Silence.

The door made no sound as she let herself in.

"Edna?"

The place was dark, the curtains still shut.

"Edna, are you here?"

Something felt wrong. Yet nothing was disturbed in the kitchen or dining room. As usual, neat and orderly. The old clock on the sideboard ticked like a dripping faucet.

Harriet's feet lurched as though her legs had turned to stumps. She made her way through her friend's living room toward the bedroom. The hallway was dark, but she could see the bedroom door, partially open. A few steps to the opening, she hesitated.

The shakiness had shifted from her hands to her knees. She reached for the glass knob. It was cold to her touch.

"Edna?" Her heart hammered so hard it felt like it would jump out of her chest. She wanted to go back downstairs.

Streams of sunlight filtered through the blinds like sparkling jewels. The pale blue walls of the bedroom spoke of Edna's calm presence. There she was in bed, eyes closed, with a slight smile on her lips.

Oh, she's still sleeping. Harriet exhaled loudly. Relief loosened her tense muscles. She turned on the overhead light.

No movement. Her muscles tensed again.

"Edna?" her voice croaked. "Honey, it's time to get up."

Harriet stood gazing at Edna's beautiful, peaceful face, and even as her mind comprehended, her heart refused to believe it.

She reached toward her, drawn to the kindness and compassion that always seemed to emanate from Edna. Harriet longed to touch, but instead took hold of the cordless phone from Edna's nightstand and dialed.

One ring. Two rings.

"911. What's your emergency?"

"Please hurry. My friend—" How strange. Her smock was wet. Harriet reached up to her face to find rivers of tears. She gazed at Edna again. Her chestnut brown hair curled on top of her pastel green pillowcase like delicate vines. Those long, graceful fingers rested on top of her open Bible. She looked so beautiful, so content.

"Ma'am? Are you there?" The disembodied voice jarred the peace in this room.

"M-my friend, Edna Goldstein. I think she's dead."

3

Oy. Shira's head felt like someone had shoved a year's worth of gym socks into it. No doubt her breath smelled like it.

She rolled out of bed, slipped her feet into the comfy slippers, and cinched her polar bear robe around her.

As she walked into the bathroom, reality hit like a bowling ball to her gut. She grabbed a scrunchie from the basket on the counter and pulled her sleep-tousled hair through its loop. Tired eyes glared back at her from the mirror. She pointed her finger at her reflection. "Shira, you have to call Veronica."

After removing the night's coating from her face and teeth, she left the bathroom feeling less like a science project gone awry. Her cell's tiny message light blinked like a beacon from the coffee table. She shook her hair and tightened the robe belt.

She'd call Aunt Edna, eventually.

Growling noises emanated from her mid-section. Her mind inventoried the fridge as she made her way to the kitchen. Aha. There was some leftover roasted vegetable pizza from Antonio's. Coffee would have to wait until she walked the few blocks to Starbucks.

Yesterday's fiasco replayed in her head as her breakfast reheated. The humiliation stung as much today.

She could go to another salon. For years Fidel from Gooding's had tried to hire her away from Veronica. She rubbed her temples. The thought of starting over in someone else's salon and fighting for top stylist again only made her want to crawl back into bed. Most of her clients would follow her there, but Shira didn't like how that felt—as if she were stealing from Veronica, the woman who had invested years of beauty savvy into her.

Then again, if Shira waited too long the other stylists at Élégance

16

wouldn't feel a drop of guilt stealing her clients. If they hadn't already. She chewed her thumbnail.

What she really wanted was her own salon. Like that would happen now. Her timeline for her own premium salon had dashed out the door with her when she lost the promotion and quit her job.

Her floppy slipper tapped the floor. She shrugged her shoulders.

She had to go back.

The micro dinged. The perfect punctuation to her revelation. As she pulled the steaming, droopy breakfast from the oven, a hot piece of eggplant dropped onto her slipper and bounced to the floor.

Bending over to pick up the errant vegetable, she saw that the pristine white fuzziness was now marred with tomato sauce. Wiping it with the napkin only spread the mess. Oh no. She shook her head.

Don't make such a big deal, Shira. You have a bigger mark—to your reputation—to fix.

The first hot bite of her "breakfast" burned the roof of her mouth. She spit it out.

A craving for an oatmeal scone triggered a plan. She'd stop at Starbucks and pick up Veronica's favorites, maple oatmeal scones and mocha-mint lattes. No way her boss could stay mad if she came bearing gifts.

She pitched the once-upon-a-time pizza into the trash.

Her fashion mind kicked into hyper-drive as she headed for her bedroom. No argument, the perfect outfit was the Crisis107—Alec-stood-me-up-on-New-Year's-Prada suit. This was serious business, after all. She pumped her fist in the air. She could do this.

The song, "You're a Mean One, Mr. Grinch" interrupted her mission. No need to check the caller ID—it was her dad.

Wait. Sam Goldstein picking up the phone, to call her? Aunt Edna was pulling out the big guns to get her home this year.

Oh, well. She may as well get this over with. "Hey, Dad, what's up?"

Strange noises, like moans and a crowd of voices, came from the phone.

Her heart flopped. "Hello?" No response. "Dad?"

"Shira? It's Daddy."

He hadn't referred to himself as Daddy since she was twelve. "What's going on?"

"Honey." He took a deep breath. "Honey, I have bad news."

Someone yelled, "Be careful with her!" It sounded like the Beehive. "Dad, is Harriet with you?"

"Shira." He paused as if his brain wasn't working. "Harriet's here. The paramedics are leaving now. Shira, honey, Aunt Edna died."

What?

"She must have passed away in her sleep. Harriet found her this morning."

No. That wasn't right. She had to return her aunt's call. She hadn't listened to the message. The message her aunt left last night. No!

Shira threw the phone. It hit the wall and landed on the couch. Her legs wobbled. She dropped to the floor like discarded trash.

A sound rumbled through her chest and broke out like a howl.

Seconds, minutes later her eyes opened. She had no idea how long she'd been lying in a heap on the hardwood floor— A tinny voice called her name.

The phone.

She crawled to the couch.

"Hello?" Her voice sounded like it had been dragged through gravel.

"Shira! Oh thank You, God." Her father was crying. "Shira, are you okay?"

"I . . ." She swallowed. Her throat felt like jagged glass. "I'm fine." She forced herself to stand, then propped herself against the wall as though it were her only support. She wanted to crawl back into bed . . . wearing Aunt Edna's hug.

"Shira, I'm coming to get you."

"No." Her spine stiffened. Since when did he care? "No, Dad. I'll take the train. When is the funeral?" She took a few steps toward the bedroom but fell back on the floor like a rag doll.

"Are you sure, honey?"

That's right. Make your conscience feel better. Then you can justify to your God how you are a wonderful father. "I said I'm fine," she huffed. "When is the funeral?"

His disappointed sigh released another torrent of guilt. She shoved back its familiar current by remembering all the rejections of Daddy-dearest.

"Rabbi Joel is here. He says tomorrow at four."

Tomorrow at four. Once again Shira wished she wasn't Jewish. That she had more than twenty-four hours before the finality of throwing a shovel of dirt on the plain pine casket containing the last person in this self-obsessed world who truly loved her.

"She'll be buried at Har Yacov, next to my parents and your mom." He choked back a sob.

The tears returned. *Why do you hate me, God?*

". . . the shiva will be at the house."

"Fine. I'll let you know when I arrive." She kneaded her forehead. "Can you pick me up at the train station?"

"Of course I'll pick you up. Why would you—"

Click.

No, thank you, Father. The double portion of Jewish guilt was more than she could handle right now. Besides, there was something she needed to do.

She thumbed the phone screen to access her voicemail. She leaned back against the wall to listen to the only message: "Shira, dear one, did you get the promotion? I've been praying God's will for you. Rosh Hashanah is coming up. I'm making brisket and your favorite pineapple kugel."

A bittersweet chuckle mingled with her tears. She chewed on her fingernail.

"It's been three years since you've been home, Button. And I miss hugging you. Your old room is waiting."

Visions of frilly pink curtains that matched her comforter on her canopy bed.

"There are all sorts of new, interesting people at Beth Ahav. There's one in particular I'd like you to meet. Call me back soon. I love you, Button. Your daddy sends his love, too. Kiss-kiss. Hug-hug. Bye-bye."

The voicemail recording informed her that the message was over and asked what she wanted to do next.

Shira hit replay.

4

Beulah Montgomery knew Sam's conversation with his daughter hadn't gone well by the deepening lines of grief on his face.

"She hung up on me." His face glistened with several hours of tears. He held Edna's kitchen phone toward Beulah. She hung it up.

Beulah swallowed back her distress. The devastation that had settled on Edna's brother nearly buckled her resolution to keep it together.

Sam appeared more like a wounded little boy than the successful engineer and pillar of his congregation. His thick black hair was disheveled from running his fingers through it. She rested her hand on his back.

Standing beside Sam was Rabbi Joel, the leader of Sam and Edna's congregation. His eyes were moist and compassionate.

"Well, it figures the brat would pull one of her shenanigans," Harriet said.

Sam's arm stiffened beneath Beulah's palm. "Harriet, please," she said.

"Yeah. Whatever." Harriet took another long drag, looked away, and blew out more toxic fumes.

"Let me fix you a cup of tea, Sam."

Edna's handsome sibling was tall. Beulah's head only came to his chest, but she led him like a toddler to a kitchen chair. He sat obediently.

"Thanks, Beulah."

This was what Beulah did best, minister to others in the mundane tasks no one seemed to think of at times like this. But in this case, she fought against losing herself in grief. Edna was her best friend. Her prayer partner. Her sister in Jesus.

The person who saw her.

Beulah opened the cabinet to retrieve one of Edna's Rejoice in the Lord coffee mugs, the ones she had given her friend two years ago for her birthday. She closed her eyes tight, forcing back the emotions she wasn't ready to handle. No one else was stepping in. She had to. Harriet, who normally ran the show, had plopped herself into a chair and made no gestures to help.

"Rabbi, would you like a cup?"

"No thanks, Beulah." Rabbi Joel Davidoff squatted next to Sam and took the grieving man's hands in his. "Sam, this is a great loss to you—to all of us." He nodded toward Beulah, then Harriet. "Your sister—as was your beautiful wife, Aviva—was much loved by everyone."

Sam pulled one of his hands away to cover his eyes as great heaving sobs poured from him. Beulah's nose and eyes burned. She focused on the rabbi's black suede yarmulke on top of his dark brown hair. Once, when Edna was out sick, she actually had the privilege of trimming his hair.

Oh my, Beulah. What a thing to think about. Still, it was better than focusing on the ball of barbed pain rolling around within her.

"But God will see you through this, Sam." Rabbi Joel glanced at Beulah, giving a silent invitation for her to join him in prayer. He adjusted his prayer shawl to keep the fringes from touching the floor.

Beulah was honored the rabbi had invited her. Since her husband's stroke, she had attended services with Edna regularly, even though she was Baptist.

She stood behind Sam and laid her palms on his bobbing shoulders as Rabbi Joel began to pray.

"*Avinu Malkeynu*—our Father our King—from the beginning of time You knew this day would come. But for those of us here who have known and loved Edna, this is a shock and a great loss." The rabbi took a ragged breath.

"Yes, Lord," Beulah said.

"We need that *shalom*, that peace, that surpasses all our understanding as You keep our hearts and minds in the Messiah *Yeshua*—Jesus. Abba, please give strength, wisdom, and discernment to Sam at this time. As Shira is returning home, Lord, we pray that she would sense your love in a powerful way. Protect her as she travels from New York. May there be reconciliation with Sam . . . and with You, Father. In Yeshua's name. Amen."

Beulah whispered her amen.

A sweet peace filled the room despite the occasional snuffle and nose blowing. It dawned on Beulah that Harriet was quiet. She looked over her shoulder toward the living room. Harriet was gone. *Oh no, Lord.*

Beulah squeezed Sam's shoulders then resumed making tea.

Sam needs to go to Shira.

Gooseflesh rippled over Beulah's neck and arms. In all her years as a Christian, Beulah had never heard the Lord's audible voice, but she knew His voice in her spirit. She was certain—it was Him.

21

Still, did this poor man need to deal with his daughter's anger right now? Yes, if God said so.

"Uh, Sam," Beulah said.

Sam wiped his face with his palms. "Yeah?"

"Sam, I sense the Lord is saying you need to go to Shira."

He stared down at his lap. "I felt the Lord was saying the same thing while Joel was praying." He roughly wiped both his eyes again with his forearm. "I was sitting here thinking, how will she ever know and trust our Heavenly Father's love, when she's never trusted mine."

His revelation impressed Beulah. Edna and she had prayed for many years that Sam would learn how to reach his daughter after years of his neglect. Beulah reached over and gave Sam's shoulder another squeeze.

Rabbi Joel stood. "Sam, if you need anything, anything at all, call me."

Sam rose. "Thanks, Joel. Thanks for rushing right over." They embraced hard, slapping each other on the back.

Beulah looked away. The chair where Harriet had sat appeared alone and out of place—like her. She wrapped her arms around her waist, walked to the door, and stood on the landing.

If only Harriet had stayed. They could have shared this grief together.

The question Beulah had avoided all morning crashed like a giant wave as she finally gave herself permission to weep. "Oh, dear Lord, what will we do without Edna?"

5

Harriet had never seen anything like that before. She shook her head.

Leaning against the door, she locked the deadbolt. They had talked to God as if He were right there in the room with them. But, she had to get out of there. For some reason, it made her feel exposed, raw.

She dropped her heavy, purple purse on the coffee table and peeked at the oven clock. Almost six. Was it really still today?

She'd spent hours at the salon calling everyone to let them know about Edna. She'd cancelled all the appointments for the rest of the week.

Her stomach rumbled. Clutched in her hand were the white bags. For some reason she had grabbed both of the Danish off their station counters. She lifted the little bags spotted with stains from the fatty pastries and stared at them. Inside the wrinkled paper were their usual breakfasts. She opened one and peeked inside. A familiar whiff of sweetness . . .

Crushing the bags, she took a few steps, and stumbled against her recliner.

Edna had died. Her best friend had died.

She dropped into her recliner's worn seat. The bags dropped to the floor. She didn't care. The smell now made her nauseous.

The tall, leather customer directory stuck out from her purse. Each of The Hair Mavens's clients she had spoken to had been shocked. Some had cried. Sometimes she cried with them. After four hours she had packed up her stuff and was about to leave when she realized she hadn't called Kathy-the-Mouse.

It had been the kid's day off. When Harriet broke it to Kathy, she had made this high-pitched sound and slammed the phone in Harriet's ear.

When Harriet had tried Kathy again, to give the synagogue's address for the funeral, the weirdo hadn't picked up. She had had to leave it on the machine. Who knew if the Mouse would show?

She scratched her chin. "I'm beginning to think she's one sandwich shy of a picnic." Harriet spoke out to the empty room. What did Edna see in the girl to hire her?

A crushed, empty pack of cigarettes sat next to her purse. She patted her blazer's pockets searching for another pack. Nope. Normally there were a couple packs in her purse. Heck, they were all over the house.

Several strands of blonde hair clung to the blazer—her new blue blazer. When had Bob-the-insurance-guy complimented her? Had it only been this morning? It seemed like years ago.

Reaching forward to grab the straps, she pulled her "suitcase" into her lap. She needed a smoke bad. Rifling through all the junk, she finally found a loose one—a little bent, but she didn't care. Once lit, she shoved back the Naugahyde recliner and let the nicotine do its thing.

She clapped twice, and the lamp over the chair turned on. Something shiny caught her attention. A framed photo rested on its back. Her purse must have knocked it over. She righted the picture.

Edna's face. Slender, creamy complexion, doe brown eyes with thick, brown hair and a few grays at the temple. Must have been before Harriet had started coloring it out for her friend. Harriet took a deep drag.

Harriet was at least twenty pounds heavier than Edna back then. More now. She shrugged. Her beehive was at least an inch taller than it was now. Seemed life had a way of pressing down on a person.

Edna was gorgeous. She could have had any man, but she was too daggone dedicated to that freeloader brother and his brat. Never had a chance for a life of her own.

Still the brother had been pretty torn up today. Served him right.

The pic had been taken at the brat's graduation from one of the fancy-schmancy salon schools in New York. She looked away.

She snuggled deeper into the recliner finding the indentations that fit her body. When she had locked up the shop tonight, she had had the strangest sensation—a bittersweet realization that she was now the new owner of The Hair Mavens.

How would she do it without Edna?

Tears hammered at her eyelids. She pressed her fingertips against them. She'd just keep them closed until the flood went back where it came from.

Maybe she could pray. How did she go about doing that? She was Catholic. 'Course she hadn't been in a church—except for weddings and funerals—in eighteen years. Eighteen years in March.

Not since Ray had divorced her for his jail-bait secretary. She'd been pretty mad at God since then. Edna dying sure wasn't endearing her to Him now.

But when she had heard Edna's rabbi praying . . . she still didn't understand what she had felt, but she thought she might have liked it. Maybe, maybe not.

And Beulah was right there praying with him. She wasn't even Jewish. Wasn't she a Baptist? The rabbi had seemed to know Beulah pretty well. Why?

She had stood there in Edna's living room like a fool, holding onto the stupid smock like it was a kid or something. But it was like she was holding a part of Edna. If she held on real tight— It was all wrong. Just wrong. She wanted to go right up to the three of them. Join them.

She flicked the ashes into the ashtray next to the picture. Nah. Coming home was the best thing.

Edna is—was the most decent human being she had ever known. How many nights had Edna stayed up with Harriet because Harriet couldn't sleep without Ray?

Who'll stay up with me tonight because I lost my best friend?

She took another drag, her lips trembled. Edna had stayed with Harriet in the hospital after the miscarriages. Three of them before the doctors took out her womanhood. Ray had only visited.

Harriet huffed. He had probably stayed the night elsewhere.

In the thirty years of their friendship, Edna had become more like family than Harriet's family. She owed her friend more than she could ever repay. But she'd certainly try. She took a long drag then blew the smoke straight up to the ceiling.

"I'll do you proud, Edna. I'll take good care of The Hair Mavens."

6

"I love you, Button."

Shira hit the "one" on her phone to replay the message again.

"Shira, dear one, did you get the promotion? I've been praying God's will for you. Rosh Hashanah is coming up. I'm making brisket and your favorite pineapple kugel . . ."

Wrapped in her "hug", Shira lay in her bed, listening to Aunt Edna's phone message over and over again. She knew she had to pack. Call the travel agent. Get ready. But more than anything she hungered for her aunt's voice, her touch, her smile. The pit of guilt deepened, threatening to yank what little hold she had on comfort. Aunt Edna's peaceful tone was like strong arms keeping Shira from falling into that abyss.

". . . It's been three years since you've been home, Button. And I miss hugging you. Your old room is waiting."

Every morning, from the time Shira was thirteen until she went to college, Aunt Edna's "Rise and shine, Button" had greeted her.

Then "I love you, my Button" comforted Shira each night before she had welcomed the sleep of innocence.

"There are all sorts of new, interesting people at Beth Ahav. There's one in particular I'd like you to meet. Call me back soon. I love you, Button . . ."

Before the sentimental garbage about her father played, Shira thumbed the replay key. She grimaced. Her ear hurt. The phone had been sandwiched between her pillow and head for hours. She wouldn't change her position, no matter how much it hurt. It was foolish to think it, but she was afraid if she readjusted to a more comfortable spot she might lose her aunt. Instead she pulled another tissue from the half-empty box in front of her.

After an unladylike, but satisfying honk she gently laid the crumpled ball on top of a small pyramid of tissues she had built.

The wait between replays was excruciating.

"Shira, dear one, did you get the promotion? I've been praying God's will for you . . ."

Call waiting beeped. She reluctantly raised her head enough to check the caller ID.

Alec's handsome face appeared on the screen.

"Hello?"

"Babe? You sleeping?" He sounded like he was calling from outside. An angry blast came from a nearby car—was it from the phone or outside her window?

"No." Shira grabbed another tissue and held it to her nose as a new flood of fluids commenced. "Alec, I called you . . ." she looked at the clock on the nightstand, ". . . five hours ago."

"Yeah, babe, well," He cleared his throat. "I had a long meeting with Arnie. He met with the director and producer, and they're asking me for a call-back. It was great. You should have been there. I'm one of two they're considering for the part."

He was talking fast. He always talked fast when he lied. She didn't care.

"Alec, I need you." A sob welled up. She managed to choke out, "My aunt Edna died."

"Who? Oh yeah, yeah, the lady with the hair salon."

The lady with the hair salon?

"Shira, babe, you there?" He cleared his throat again. "I'm real sorry to hear about your aunt."

"Alec, I need you here, now." She drew her knees up and hugged them to her chest. "Please?"

"Aw, babe, I'm real sorry. Remember, I have the audition—the call-back?"

In the silence, the traffic noises reminded her that life had gone on where he was.

"Listen, babe, it'll take an hour, two tops, and I'll be right there."

She'd have to settle for that. "Okay. Thanks, Alec."

"Chin up, babe. I'll be there soon. Maybe we can grab a bite and take in a movie."

Had this man been raised by moles? "Alec, I don't want to see a movie." She sat up and punched the air with her fist. "The woman who raised me after my mom passed away just died! I need you!"

"Sure, sure, babe. You got me. What was I thinking? I'll be there by eight, nine at the latest."

"Fine." She lay back down.

"Love you, babe."

"Love you too." She guessed.

She disconnected. In the quiet, the pit beckoned her to the edge again. She fumbled with the phone to resume her connection with Aunt Edna, even though by now she had memorized every word of the message.

"Shira, dear one . . ."

The security buzzer sounded. Alec?

He had been close by after all. He had a change of heart. He did love her.

Shira rushed to the door. Flowery thoughts of his love drove back the darkness. She practically fell on the intercom button. The phone still in her hand, she whacked it against the wall. "Alec?"

"Shira, honey, it's Dad."

Dad? Here?

She didn't think she could take another emotional outburst. "What are you doing here?" She cringed at the roughness in her voice.

"I'm here for you."

A whimper escaped. "I don't need you." *That didn't sound the least bit convincing.*

"Shira, let me in."

Her finger developed a mind of its own and hit the buzzer.

Within seconds there was a knock on her door. She peeked through the peephole. Her dad stared right at her, causing her heart to somersault.

After releasing the two deadbolts, she opened the door then took a step back.

The man before her wore grief as wide and deep as hers. She realized there was someone else who felt the serrated knife wound this loss had produced. She needed to share this grief. More than that she needed a—

His strong arms pulled her to his chest then with one arm, directed her head over his heart.

He hugged her tight. She pulled her hands to her chest like she had done when she was little. The phone dropped to the floor.

Shira stashed two giant shopping bags on the backseat floor of her dad's Lexus. Her face heated as she felt more than saw him staring. He had to think she was crazy.

They had pulled off the Garden State Parkway for a coffee break. Which was what her dad had purchased. She, alas, had purchased two Eagles sweatshirts, matching ball caps, a couple pair of sunglasses, and whatever else had caught her attention in the gift shop. She couldn't remember. She slammed the car door, settled into the front passenger seat, and buckled in. The shopping choices at the New Jersey rest stop were pretty slim. It would have to do until she could run to King of Prussia Mall where she could fulfill her Crisis113 properly.

Awkward silence permeated the car as her dad merged back onto I-95.

She didn't know what to say to him. The last significant conversation they had was an hour ago when he had loaded her suitcases into the trunk. Initially they had both been lost in their own thoughts. Now it felt different. Maybe her dad was trying to find a diplomatic way to ask if she was nuts.

The headlights illuminated trees on the side of the highway. Turning her head to the right, she watched as those same trees became dark silhouettes. She bit her lower lip. How did her father know she wouldn't have been able to make it back on her own?

He had said the Lord told him. Whatever. Why couldn't God have told him that she had needed him fifteen years ago when her mom died? She folded her arms across her chest. Years of neglect weren't negated by this atypical show of parental concern.

No. This was simply an anomaly due to Aunt Edna's death. Why read anything more into it?

She turned toward her dad. His profile in the nighttime setting felt familiar. He glanced her way. They made brief eye contact. He smiled then redirected his focus to the road before she could return the smile. He'd aged since she had seen him last. Tired eyes. Deep lines of grief wrapped like parentheses around his mouth.

She supposed now was as good a time as any to set the ground rules for this visit. "Dad, I want to stay at Aunt Edna's apartment."

When he didn't respond, she snuck a peek at him.

"You don't want to stay at the house, in your old room?" He didn't look at her but squeezed the steering wheel.

"It hasn't really been my room since I was thirteen." The statement was true, but the reminder of his neglect probably hadn't given him warm fuzzies.

His jaw clenched. Her body tensed as she waited for the usual digs about her inconsiderateness.

"Not into the Seventh Heaven posters anymore?" He cocked his head and gave a lopsided grin.

"No, not for some time." She released a quiet sigh.

He reached over and patted her hand then returned it to the steering wheel.

"Thanks for understanding, Dad."

He nodded. "I'll pick you up at about nine-thirty then?"

"Sure."

No argument. No guilt.

This was new. She wondered how long it would last.

7

Nyet, nyet, nyet. No, no, no. This cannot be true.

Kathy Smith paced back and forth in her living room like a tiger in a cage from the zoo. She glared at her nails. She had bitten them since Harriet had called. The cuticles bled. If Edna could see what Kathy had done, Edna would have hugged her and said, "Do not hurt yourself, honey."

She put her hands in her pockets and sat on the metal chair.

Despite being dressed, ready to go before the sun rose, she couldn't bring herself to open the door. Every time she touched the knob, her tummy felt sick.

Edna was dead. What would she do now? Who would she talk to? Edna was the only one who knew . . .

8

Harriet paused on the sidewalk. "So, tell me again what a shiva is?"

Beulah had explained it to Harriet earlier, but frankly, Harriet hadn't been paying much attention.

Beulah closed her eyes, finger inches from Sam Goldstein's doorknob. She sighed and turned toward Harriet. "It's a Jewish tradition. After a funeral, friends and family come to the bereaved's home to support them."

"Oh, like a wake?"

Beulah withdrew her hand and wrapped it around the strap of her purse. "In some ways." She tilted her head a little and pursed her lips. "I think shiva is Hebrew for seven. So for seven days family and friends help the mourners cope with the grief. The mourners are supposed to sit and allow others to minister to them—food, prayer, cleaning—whatever they need. That's why they call it sitting shiva."

Oh, great. She had to wait on the brat and the freeloader? For seven days!

"Harriet?" Beulah touched Harriet's arm.

Had Harriet said that out loud? "What?"

"We are the mourners." Beulah lowered her head to stare at Harriet from the top of her eyeballs. "Edna counted us as her family."

Harriet straightened her shoulders and looked away from Beulah's determined gawk. What was she? A mind-reader? How did Beulah know all this Jewish stuff anyway?

Edna, Sam, and Shira were the only Jewish people Harriet had ever known. Today she'd met more Jews than she could count. Her German mother must have rolled over in her grave.

Beulah reached for the doorbell. "Ready?"

Harriet nodded.

Shira sat next to her childhood best friend, Cari Abrams-Lowinger, holding her hand. She hadn't seen Cari in three years. Yet Cari had treated her as though the gulf of time never happened—or that Shira hadn't purposely neglected their relationship.

Shira squeezed then released Cari's hand. Cari was a casualty of Shira's separation from life there.

Well-wishers packed her father's two-story Philadelphia Main Line home. Thankfully, Cari knew Shira's issues with crowds, especially this crowd. All afternoon Cari had been her buffer from the suffocating and draining attention. Her polite diplomacy had kept the steady stream of people moving, with minimal contact with Shira.

A half-eaten plate of pineapple kugel rested on the floor under Shira's chair. Someone's well-intentioned efforts—unfortunately it tasted like wallpaper paste, and further reminded Shira of her loss. *I'm making your favorite pineapple kugel* . . .

Harriet with her ancient bleached-blonde beehive and that other lady who worked at her aunt's salon stood before Shira. The lady—she couldn't remember her name—bent over and gave Shira an awkward hug. Shira straightened her jacket and looked away.

Someone harrumphed. She didn't need to see who it was.

Seconds later the duo walked into the dining room. Cari had done a good job of moving them on. Miss Beehive was still as cranky as ever—and evidently still loved her sweets. She had just snatched a fistful of cookies from the table. The less Shira saw of Harriet, the better.

Shira turned her attention to Cari's beautiful red hair with natural golden highlights.

"You know, Care-bear." It felt good to call her friend by her nickname. "I've tried to duplicate your hair color over the years." Shira stretched out one of the curls to examine it. Cari kept her head still but watched Shira.

"Never was able to do it." Shira released the curl. It sprang back to its original shape.

"That's because God did it." Cari winked.

Whatever. "You don't straighten it anymore. I'm glad."

"Why fight it?" Cari shrugged a shoulder. "I love your blonde highlights—very Hollywood." She rested her chin on her fist. "You know Shirry, I was always jealous of your brown hair."

Shira held a hunk out to Cari. "Be my guest."

She slapped Shira's arm and giggled. The squeaky twitter caused a few frowns in the room, but Shira didn't care.

"Well, at least we were both blessed with freckles," Cari said.

"I'm not sure blessed is the word I'd use."

"Excuse me, Mrs. Lowinger?"

The teenager standing in front of Cari seemed familiar.

Cari grabbed the young woman's wrists. "Shirry, do you recognize this beauty?"

Shira shrugged.

"Shira. Come on." She twirled the poor girl around as though it would make it easier for Shira to figure out.

"I give up, Care."

"It's little Melly." She lifted and lowered the girl's arms like a puppet.

Shira did a double take. "Melissa? Melissa Cohen?" It couldn't be.

"Yes, Ms. Goldstein." She blushed and gave Cari a please stop plea.

Ms. Goldstein? Now Shira felt old. Really old. She had babysat for Melly—changed her diapers, for goodness' sake. "How old are you now, Melissa?"

"I'll be eighteen in June." She blinked then raised tear-filled eyes. "I loved Aunt Edna, Ms. Goldstein. I'm so sorry for your loss." She extended her right hand to Shira.

Her slender fingers had the youthful softness women spent fortunes to recapture. "Thank you, Melissa. And you can call me Shira, you know."

Her tiny frame, dark brown hair in a pixie cut, and pink sweater dress reminded Shira of a fragile china doll.

Melissa glanced toward the front door. Her parents waited there. "I have to go."

Shira vaguely remembered talking with the Cohens earlier. They waved to her.

Melissa kissed Shira on the cheek. "It was good seeing you."

Cari rose and gave Melissa a hug. Shira watched the young woman walk into the warm embrace of her parents. A glob of emotion stuck somewhere between her heart and throat.

"She's one of my students," Cari said. "You know I'm teaching at the private girls' school, right?"

Shira shook her head. "I feel very old."

Cari leaned toward Shira and whispered, "Is that a Prada outfit?" She pinched the sleeve of Shira's black suit jacket.

"Yes. Very impressive, Care."

"Hey, we get Vogue out here in Philadelphia too, you know." She waggled her eyebrows. "Besides, I need to keep up on the latest styles so I don't come across as a dummy in front of my best friend."

Shira wasn't sure why, but Cari's comment stung.

Aaron Lowinger, Cari's husband, was in the kitchen talking with a tall guy with curly brown hair. Shira had missed their wedding last year. She was supposed to have been her friend's maid-of-honor, but Shira had been in Paris at a hair competition. The awful truth was she hadn't wanted to come back. What had she been thinking?

"Sorry for not being there for your wedding, Care-Bear." She couldn't even look at Cari. Her chest burned with shame.

"Yeah." Cari stretched out her legs and scrunched her shoulders before relaxing. Her eyes clouded with more tears. "I won't lie. That was rough, Shira. You're my best friend."

Present tense.

"So how's married life?"

Cari blushed. "Wonderful." She gazed lovingly at her husband and sighed. "He's amazing." She looked at Shira and smiled. "You know Aunt Edna played matchmaker with us, right? Of course she would have denied that." Cari seemed to have trouble swallowing, then sniffed.

"I seem to remember something about that."

At that moment Shira missed Alec. She missed him, but was angry too. *Sorry, babe, I can't come. I have to wait for Arnie's call.* That had really hurt.

She wondered what Aunt Edna would have thought of him. Although he could charm the scales off a snake, her aunt wasn't taken in by fancy talk. Maybe she was afraid to introduce him. Maybe because she could see through the phony façade he sometimes put on. Maybe—

Her naked ring finger glowed like a beacon of loneliness. Where was a good man like Aaron for her?

Matchmaker, matchmaker, make me a match . . .

Brown penny-loafers appeared from nowhere, inches from her feet. Someone cleared his throat. Shira looked up.

"Excuse me, Shira?" A tall man with light brown eyes and the deepest dimple in his chin stood before her.

"Yes?" Shira tried to keep her mouth from dropping open.

"My name is Jesse Fox. I was Aunt E—that is, Edna's attorney." He pulled up a metal folding chair and set it in front of Cari and Shira. "I'm so sorry for your loss." They briefly shook hands. Nice, strong, dry grip.

"Hey, Care." He bent forward and hugged her before sitting down. Shira caught a whiff of his aftershave. Spicy. Very nice.

"Hey, Jesse," Cari said.

Shira's peripheral vision captured Cari giving her a smirk.

Resting his arms on his thighs, Jesse's amazing orbs drew Shira's focus to a lock of curly hair that had fallen across his forehead. "Shira, your aunt left instructions to read part of her will at the shiva. Could you please remain after *Kaddish?*"

"My aunt has, had . . . you're her lawyer?" His words were beginning to sink in.

"I'll let you two talk." Cari stroked Shira's arm then left.

Cari returned to her soul mate. Aaron wrapped his arm around her waist and drew her close to whisper in her ear. Shira ached with a gnawing emptiness.

"Cari tells me you two grew up together," Jesse said.

Shira swallowed. "Yes." She folded her arms and crossed her legs. "How do you know Cari?"

He leaned back and crossed his leg bringing the ankle to his knee. Striped socks. She'd try to not hold that against him.

"I've been a member of Beth Ahav for the last two years."

There are all sorts of new, interesting people at Beth Ahav. There's one in particular I'd like you to meet.

She pursed her lips then smiled.

"Did I say something funny?"

She switched her focus to her folded arms. "So, you've been at Beth Ahav for two years?"

"Yes. I'm a partner in Abe Liberman's firm."

"You're a partner? In Abe's firm?" Also a member of Beth Ahav—and her father's best friend—Abe had never trusted anyone enough to make them a full partner. Jesse couldn't be more than thirty, thirty-five. "I'm impressed."

She casually peeked at his ring finger. No wedding band. Bad, Shira. What about Alec? "So, I guess you know my father, Sam?"

"Yes, for eight years." His tapped his heart. "He's been like a father to me since I moved here from Virginia."

Shira tensed. Like a father, huh? Must be nice. She clenched her fists. "So what did you do in Virginia?"

"I was an assistant DA."

She lifted her brows. "That's impressive."

"Not really. There was a herd of us. I got tired of all the politics." He ran his hand through his brown locks.

Oh, to have the natural curl he and Cari had.

Rabbi Joel stepped into view behind Jesse. As she shifted her gaze toward the rabbi, Jesse looked over his shoulder.

"Rabbi?" he said.

"I'm sorry, Shira, Jesse. I wanted to start the Kaddish soon. Edna had made special arrangements for Jesse to first lead us in worship."

"Excuse me. I'll be right back." Jesse jumped up.

Shira watched him until he disappeared around the corner. Where had he been all her life?

No signal. Beulah closed her cell phone and dropped it into her purse. Her hand went to her brow then covered her mouth. She searched the crowd in the dining room for Kathy. Not there. She stepped outside onto the patio. She wasn't there either. Now she'd lost track of Harriet, and Harriet had made her promise to not leave her side.

Kathy hadn't made it to the funeral. Harriet relayed a few minutes ago—before she had lost her—that Kathy wasn't dealing well with Edna's death.

The poor dear was such a strange, fragile little thing. Edna was like her mother.

Beulah struck her palm to her forehead. *You goose, you should have picked her up and taken her to the funeral yourself. Dear Lord, please help Kathy. And help me know what to do.*

Sam's home phone had been ringing off the hook, and Beulah didn't feel right tying it up to try Kathy again. Maybe if she went outside she would get a better signal.

Setting her purse on a dining chair, she opened it wide and sifted through the jumble. Holding both straps, she bounced the purse up and down. This always worked with her keys . . . *Oh, you goose, Beulah.* The cell wouldn't make a jangling noise.

"Hey, Beulah."

She looked up. "Hi, Jesse." They hugged. He kissed her cheek.

"Lose your keys?" Jesse had his guitar and, frankly, Beulah would rather talk about that right now.

"Well, uh . . ." She gave him a lopsided grin. "It appears that way, doesn't it? But actually, I've misplaced my cell."

"Here, let me call your cell from mine." He carefully rested his guitar against the wall. "You should be able to hear it and see the light."

"I've already seen the light." She chuckled despite the corniness. He did her the courtesy of smiling. Nice boy.

He dialed her number. She heard a muffled "Hallelujah Chorus." She moved brushes, books, hair spray, and heaven knows what else until she finally found the evasive little thing, under her pocket Bible.

She gave Jesse a peck on the cheek. "Thank you so much."

He retrieved his guitar and embraced it. The guitar released a musical sigh of affection. "Are we going to have singing?"

"Rabbi Joel asked, well actually, Edna requested I lead worship before Kaddish."

"Edna requested?"

"Yes. Strange, huh?" he said. "I don't know that I've ever been to a shiva—Messianic or otherwise—with worship."

"Edna had her own way of doing things. She loved your voice, Jesse." She tapped his arm. "I'm so scatterbrained sometimes that I'll probably be late for my own funeral."

Jesse smiled. "You coming?"

She lifted her cell in the air. "I just need to make a quick phone call and I'll be right in."

"Okay. Don't forget about the meeting afterward."

Beulah wound her way through the crowd to the front door then stepped outside. A cool breeze blew a few strands of her shoulder-length salt-and-pepper hair into her mouth. She picked it out, then opened the cell and held it up as she walked. By the time she found the elusive signal, she was across the street from Sam's house.

She pressed the seven key a few seconds, activating the speed call to Kathy. The students in her Sunday school class had helped her program all the phone numbers. Only eight and they were computer geniuses.

As the automatic dialing beeped she searched the street. Cars were parked on both sides. No wonder the house was packed with people.

Oh. Was that? Yes. Kathy. Purse squished under her armpit and phone to her ear, Beulah ran down the sidewalk. *Beulah, goose, you don't need the phone now.*

She folded it then shoved it into her jacket pocket. As she approached Kathy, Beulah waved. Kathy waved a handkerchief then brought it to her glasses. She leaned against one of the cars.

Kathy must have weighed all of a hundred pounds—soaking wet. She wore black slacks, a white button-down shirt, and a black cardigan sweater. Her dark corkscrew mane was roofed by a black *sur la tête*. It reminded Beulah of her great-grandmother's flapper hat. Beulah couldn't help thinking how stylish Kathy looked—and how out of character with her usual unkempt appearance.

Kathy finished wiping her glasses then slipped them back on. The thick black horn-rimmed frames covered the most beautiful violet eyes. It was rare anyone got more than a glimpse of their exquisiteness. Either the glasses were on or she hid behind walls of hair.

Twisting her handkerchief, Kathy grimaced and dropped her head as though in pain. Beulah gradually stepped closer, afraid Kathy might take flight. The young woman glanced at Beulah briefly then returned her attention to the ground.

"I was worried about you, Kathy."

She rubbed her ear on her shoulder. "I am sorry, Beulah."

Beulah could barely hear Kathy's weak response. "We missed you at the funeral, sweetheart."

Kathy turned her head away. "I was there."

"You were?"

"I was standing in the back. I left before everyone stood up." She pointed toward the end of the street. "The bus left me off there."

Beulah gently gathered one wall of Kathy's hair and placed it behind her ear, then took the opportunity to stroke the poor thing's back. How bony it felt. "How are you doing?"

"I woke up this morning and thought yesterday was a bad dream." She stared at Beulah, her youthful forehead creased. "I called the shop, hoping Edna would answer the phone, but the message said she died. She died. Edna is dead."

The handkerchief twisting became more frantic. Kathy bent then straightened her knees. Beulah couldn't tell if Kathy intended to run or faint.

"Beulah?" Panic etched something frightening on Kathy's face. "What am I going to do? What am I going to do?"

Capturing Kathy's jumpy hands, Beulah moved her head until they made eye contact. But only briefly, as Kathy's eyes roved from side to side—as though she watched for some predator. Beulah squeezed Kathy's fingers. "The first thing you are going to do is take a breath." She gently shook her hands. "Breathe."

She took a shallow breath.

"Okay, good. Another one."

After a few minutes her body relaxed, although she continued to clutch Beulah like a life preserver in stormy seas. "Kathy, this is hard, very hard. We all loved Edna. She is—was an important part of all our lives." Beulah worked hard to swallow down her grief. She had to be strong for Kathy.

Kathy watched her, unblinking, like a lifeless doll.

"God will get us through this."

Kathy's eyes darkened, like a shade had been pulled. The sudden shadow on the young girl's countenance sent what felt like a herd of spiders loose on Beulah's skin. "Kathy?"

"I do not believe in God, Beulah."

Beulah tried not to gasp. "Well, Kathy, dear, I do believe. And I'll just have to believe Him enough for the two of us right now." She managed a wobbly grin then kissed Kathy's hands. Kathy appeared to stare right through Beulah. Then blinked. The tiniest trace of a smile appeared. At least Beulah hoped that was what she saw.

Beulah decided to go for broke. She hugged Kathy. It was like hugging a new sapling. The ineffective deed did nothing more than throw Beulah off balance so that she twisted her ankle, dropped her purse, and phone, then bumped Kathy's little hat.

As she picked up her phone she noticed the time. "Kathy, we need to go inside—"

"I cannot." She bit her bottom lip and shook her head rapidly.

"Why?" *Lord, what on earth happened to this child?* "Well, sweetheart, we will have to go in eventually. Edna wanted you, Harriet, me, Sam, and Shira—that's Edna's niece—in a small meeting with Jesse. You remember Jesse?"

Her focus never left Beulah. "Yes."

"Well, it will only be us. You want to know what Edna wanted to tell us, right?"

"Yes."

"Okay. I'll make you a deal. You and I will wait out here until everyone else leaves, then we'll go in and find out what Edna wanted to tell us. Sound good?" Beulah forced a smile for Kathy. More than anything, she wanted to be in the house with Edna's family. To worship the Lord and find comfort in the fellowship.

Kathy closed her eyes and sighed. "Thank you, Beulah."

Beulah exhaled. *Thank you, Lord.*

Oh, no! I left Harriet alone with Sam and Shira!

9

Harriet gripped her gargantuan purple purse so tight against her chest she could barely breathe. Where was Beulah?

Fortunately, the couch was close to the door. She was going to give Beulah a sizeable chunk of her mind—Beulah had promised, *promised* to stick by her.

And she had missed the whole Kaddish-thing so Harriet had no one to explain all the stuff to her. The room was packed with people singing, crying, and . . . it just too—

The singing-lawyer-kid had left the room to find his briefcase, so now she was stuck with the freeloader and brat. Sam and Shira emitted enough tension between them that Harriet could have lit a cigarette. And what she wouldn't give for one, now.

She swiveled on the leather couch to peer out the living room window. Where was she?

She snatched glances at the brat. She looked pretty bad. Probably on drugs or something. Harriet had heard from her clients about those designer drugs kids were on.

Shira hadn't moved from that expensive chair since Harriet arrived. Like the brat was the queen of England or something. Harriet figured for what Shira paid for that outfit she was wearin', a family could have been fed for a year. It was a disgrace to Edna's memory. All the good stuff Edna did for the poor. Sheesh.

Harriet shifted her position on the couch, which created an awkward sound on the leather. Shira stared at Harriet then quickly looked away. The kid took another tissue from the table next to her chair.

Harriet hoped the brat was suffering. She had hurt Edna more than a few times. Edna had cried buckets for that ungrateful kid. Harriet couldn't stand to see her friend cry—she had tried to hide it from Harriet, but she knew.

Another wave of tears shoved its way out of Harriet despite her promise not to cry in front of the two people who had caused Edna heartache. She opened her purse to retrieve the rolled-up tissues. She practically stuck her whole head into the opening to blow her nose and dab her eyes.

Sam-the-Freeloader cleared his throat. Harriet shifted her attention to him. He had tried to be hospitable, but he had to know she was on to him. She pulled her purse tighter against her chest.

His selfishness had kept Edna from having a life. She was always doing for him like she was his mother. The big baby.

Once Harriet got the salon, she wouldn't have to see his sorry face again. "Harriet?"

Harriet jumped up, bumping her purse off her lap and onto the floor.

"I'm sorry for startling you," Sam said as he picked up her purse.

Cough. "You didn't startle me." Harriet straightened her shoulders and snatched her purse from him.

"Can I get you a cup of coffee or tea?"

Cough. "No, I'm fine." Cough. "Thank you." Cough again.

"Are you okay?" He reached toward her. She fought the urge to slap him away.

"I'm—" Another cough "—fine."

Harriet got these coughing spells once in a while. They were more than a little embarrassing. She tried holding it in, but it burst out of her like an avalanche.

Sam helped her up from the couch, causing her purse to hit the carpet, and a pack of cigarettes tumbled out. How poetic.

She bent over, still coughing. It was possible she could bring up a lung with this round. She was seeing stars, which meant she wasn't getting enough oxygen. Now her ears rang.

"Jesse, get some water!" Sam passed a handful of tissues to her.

She pressed them to her mouth. Like lava rising from a volcano, she felt the bile rising up her throat. *Oh, God, please don't let me throw up.*

The brat watched from her throne, half sitting, half standing. She must really be enjoying this.

Jesse handed her a glass of water. It was warm. *Oh, thank you, God. How did he know to do that?*

After taking a shaking sip, she hacked some more. Another sip. Followed by a little less hacking.

Somehow she had ended up sitting on the floor. She avoided looking at anyone and wished they would find someone else to help. A few minutes later she was able to pull more air into her lungs. But the deep breaths were painful.

The front door opened. "Harriet? Goodness. Are you all right?"

Perfect timing, Beulah. Where were you when I needed you? "Yeah, yeah. I'm fine." Frankly she was sweating bullets and had given her Depends a good workout, but otherwise just peachy. Harriet tried standing up, but her knees gave out and her bottom hit the carpet again. Did she need to get on all fours and crawl to the couch?

Sam snaked his arm around her. Her face heated as he hefted her to her feet with a pronounced grunt. She mumbled, "Thanks." and bent to pick up the spilled items from her purse. Jesse and Sam both knelt to help her. She didn't think she could handle all this niceness.

"Harriet, I need to freshen up a bit. Will you come with me?" Beulah's kind offer to Harriet probably hadn't fooled anyone, but Harriet appreciated it nonetheless.

"Kathy?" Jesse walked toward the Mouse with his hand extended. "Do you remember me? I'm Jesse Fox."

So the Mouse made it after all. The kid's eyes darted toward outside then to the floor. She wondered if she'd bolt.

This was getting interesting.

10

Shira had barely caught her breath from Beehive's drama, when another scene unfolded. Who was this Kathy-person? Who was she to Aunt Edna?

There was something about her that seemed off. She had a vague sense that she knew this woman, and it annoyed her like a stubborn knot. She shifted in her chair, then got up. What she needed was to stretch her legs and find somewhere quiet where she could think. Once Cari left, she had felt like a lone comb that had fallen under a dresser.

The fresh air called to her and she followed.

"Shira, honey." Her father reached toward her. "Don't go too far. We'll be starting soon."

She nodded then turned for the door and the freedom from the intensity of it all. It was all too real. Aunt Edna was gone.

She watched from the front porch as the last of the cars pulled away from her dad's house. A gust of wind blew a few strands of hair and the branches of the Japanese maple a few feet from her. She gathered her hair and twisted it into a knot at the base of her neck.

The maple leaves were beginning to change into the bright red she had always loved. Even as the tree prepared to shed its leaves for the barrenness of winter, there was such striking beauty.

A memory landed gently in her mind. Aunt Edna sitting on her bed, stroking Shira's head and humming a song. Her sobbing had silenced in the quiet of Edna's love. Her father had been unable to tuck Shira in after her mother's funeral. She'd heard his cries to God and had been frightened. But there was dear Edna. Always there. Loving her.

She wrapped her arms tightly around her waist.

Another memory surfaced. A few years ago, during one of her aunt's news-from-the-family calls, she mentioned hiring a new stylist. *I hired a new girl, Button. She's just a slip of a thing, but, oh my, what talent.*

At the time, Shira had wondered how talented a new stylist could have been to want to work in her aunt's old place. Truth be told, Shira had felt a twinge of jealousy with Edna's glowing report of the talented "little slip of a thing."

That would explain the Kathy-person. But didn't explain why she seemed familiar to Shira.

"Honey."

Shira turned. Her father held open the door.

"We're ready."

Once Shira had settled into her chair, she glanced at Kathy. *What is that she's wearing?* The slacks, Shira was certain, were Marc Jacobs. A few seasons old, but expensive. Cheap glasses and a chic hat. The sweater, seemed to have been someone's discarded hand-me-down.

Jesse set his briefcase on top of the glass coffee table and thumbed the combination to open the lock. Now that the reading of the will was about to happen, it dawned on Shira that she had no idea what Aunt Edna would leave her. Her old bedroom furniture, canopy included? Maybe the beautiful string of pearls from *Bubbe* Golda, Edna and her father's mother? What if . . .

"We're back."

Harriet followed the woman—Beulah?—back into the living room. "So sorry to keep you waiting," Beulah said.

"No problem, ladies." Jesse nodded toward the sofa.

All three women from The Hair Mavens sat together on the leather couch. Shira thought they resembled magpies on a telephone line—Harriet, Beulah, and Kathy. Were they as nervous as she was?

Her father patted her knee as he walked by. Other than the touch, she felt nothing. He took the other wingback chair that only a few minutes before had held Cari. She wished her friend were still there.

Jesse stood next to the coffee table. Shira's heart skipped a beat. He glanced down then looked deeply into Shira's soul. Tears appeared simultaneously on both their faces. He palmed his eyes. *If he breaks down, I'm leaving.*

He chuckled and shook his head. "Well, sorry, everyone. I certainly blew the professional persona." He exhaled a "woo." "Before I read the will, let's say a quick prayer. We're all a little nervous."

Shira couldn't help rolling her eyes. Between the funeral, Kaddish, and the thousands of promises that people were praying for her, she'd had enough prayers to last a lifetime.

No sooner had she finished her mental complaints, than everyone said their amens.

Certain her pounding heart could be heard around the room, Shira made a concerted effort to appear the cool and professional one.

Jesse sat toward the end of the leather loveseat, his long legs pressed against the coffee table. With the speed of a turtle on Xanax, he repositioned his briefcase next to him on the loveseat. He fingered through some files like he had all the time in the world.

Just get on with it! Shira wrapped her arms around her waist and squeezed.

"This reading is unusual." Jesse ran one hand through his thick hair. "Edna requested two separate readings. Tonight's reading is for her family—"

Jesse nodded toward her and her dad, then swiveled his body toward the magpies on the couch.

"—which includes Harriet, Beulah and Kathy as her 'family of the heart.'"

Shira might just gag.

"Tomorrow's reading is for friends." Finally, he pulled out a stapled packet with blue paper on the back. He cleared his throat. "'I, Edna Naomi Goldstein, being of sound mind and body . . .'"

Beulah's feet bounced, despite all her attempts to quiet them. She couldn't imagine what Edna would feel so compelled to leave her. Their friendship and fellowship were two of the most precious gifts she had—and that was taken with Edna yesterday, when she went to the loving arms of her Messiah.

"'And to Beulah Kay Montgomery, I leave all my jewelry, except my mother's pearl necklace set.'"

Beulah gasped.

"'I wish I could see your face, my sister.'" Jesse glanced up from reading and smiled.

Beulah felt a blush forming on her cheeks, which quickly spread to her neck. *Jewelry? Why, the only jewelry I've ever worn is my wedding band from my dear Wilbur.*

She swallowed. "This is too generous. Too much." Her voice was little more than a whisper.

Jesse smiled—a twinkle appearing in his eyes. "She said you'd say that. She wanted you to have as much 'too much' as possible."

The only clear thought Beulah had was that she must stop by the nursing home and tell Wilbur.

Jesse went on speaking about Edna. His voice faded into the background as a memory of Edna wandered in. Edna and she had visited Wilbur on the past Sunday. Beulah noticed that her friend wore a small diamond-chip Star of David necklace. Its elegance and beauty were in its simplicity.

45

"Is that new, Edna?"

She looked down and lovingly stroked the star. "No, I've had it a number of years. I felt like wearing my *Magen* David today." She sighed and stared off into the distance. "Just a little reminder for me that Yeshua is my shield and my strength."

"'And to Kathy Smith, I leave my dinette and living room set, as well as all kitchen utensils and everyday china. Also, my bedroom set. My brother, Samuel, and Jesse will help you move these items into your apartment.'"

Beulah felt Kathy's body go rigid.

Kathy covered her mouth and shook her head. "No." She whispered. "No. It is too much."

"Whatya mean, 'no,' kid?" Harriet's face showed no compassion. Beulah wished she could scold Harriet, but she was afraid any confrontation would shoot Kathy out the door like a cannonball.

"Kathy," Jesse said. "Edna knew you'd respond the same way as Beulah." He winked. "In fact, she wrote, 'Kathy, dear one, stop shaking your head and accept this gift from God, for it was He that inspired me to do this.'"

A small gasp came from Kathy. She paused long enough that Beulah thought she had accepted the sweet gift. But, the young woman resumed her head shaking.

"These things should go to family, not to me."

"Kathy." Everyone transferred focus to Sam. He bent forward. "My sister wanted you to have these things, because you were family to her." His deep voice was kind and soothing—like Edna's.

Beulah rested her hand on Kathy's shoulder. "Kathy. She loved us very much. We should be grateful that she thought of us in this way. Don't you think?"

Kathy untwisted her handkerchief and pressed it to her face. Then she proceeded to bend over and rest her head on her knees.

Beulah looked at Harriet. Harriet's chin had practically embedded itself into her neck.

Harriet scooted further from the Mouse and eyed the door. Edna was one of the most non-drama people she knew. Surely her friend—wherever she was—was appalled at all this nonsense.

She needed a smoke—real bad.

"'And to my friend, Harriet Rose Schmidt Foster . . .'"

Here it is. Harriet's heart raced like a greyhound at Philly Downs.

"'I leave the sum of ten thousand dollars to be used how you see fit. I hope, my dear friend, you finally take that trip to Europe you've always talked about.'"

Ten thousand dollars? But what about—

"'And to my Button, my heart, Shira Elisheva Goldstein, I leave The Hair Mavens Beauty Shop, the remaining contents of the salon and apartment, and my red 2005 Mini.'"

No!

Shira gripped the arms of the chair and pushed forward. *What?*

Several gasps came from the sofa, but Shira couldn't take her eyes off Jesse.

He continued reading. "'It is my hope you will remain here and operate the shop. Transform the old girl into a place of beauty, style, and love. My mavens, Harriet, Beulah, and Kathy will help you. I have enclosed specific instructions concerning—'"

"Shira?" Harriet sounded like the Wicked Witch of the West. She stuttered something unintelligible and pointed at Shira.

Shira could have sworn steam spewed from the top of her beehive like Mt. Vesuvius.

"Aren't you moving to Hollywood or something?"

How did Beehive know about—

Beulah reached over Kathy and held Harriet's arm.

"Harriet, this is not the time or place." Beulah rubbed the fuming woman's hand. "Edna knew what she was doing."

"We'll see." Harriet harrumphed and crossed her arms.

Jesse cleared his throat. "If I can proceed."

Harriet swatted the air and rolled her eyes. "Whatever."

Jesse raised his eyebrows and seemed to appeal to her dad. He nodded.

"'Also, the beneficiaries of my life insurance policy are Shira and Samuel Jacob Goldstein and Jesse David Fox. The amount of two hundred thousand dollars, minus legal and filing fees, will be equally distributed between them.'"

Shira's head suddenly felt too heavy for her neck. The room seemed to fade and the proverbial ringing started in her head. She watched her father bring his palms to his face and weep. She didn't know what to feel.

The Hair Mavens is mine?

11

Shira crossed the threshold of The Hair Mavens Beauty Shop—her salon. Proof of this incredible fact was the thick manila envelope pressed against her heart. Jesse had only moments ago handed it to her before she exited his warm car into the cool evening. She waved toward Jesse who still lingered, the engine idling. If he had had his way, he would have accompanied her inside, but only after he had searched every corner of the premises to ensure nothing evil lurked, waiting to pounce on her.

He lowered the passenger window and leaned across the console. She stepped back toward the car and rested her hand on the door. "Try to rest as best you can, Shira. My card is in the envelope. Call me anytime." His eyes misted. "My deepest sympathies."

She nodded then stepped back and lingered on the sidewalk until the taillights of his white Volvo sedan had disappeared into the night. A sedan. She had not figured him for a sedan—rather more the sports car type, maybe, with a convertible top.

After relocking the front door, she switched on the remaining interior lights. The fluorescents flickered and clicked into their annoying hum as they struggled to light the salon.

She kicked off her pumps and stuffed them in her hobo bag, then set it on one of the reception area chairs. Every fiber of her being was spent. She sat next to her bag. The vinyl cushion hissed. Her toes wiggled their gratitude for being set free.

Quiet.

The salon seemed so empty. As though its life had been drained out like a pool at summer's end. It missed its owner. Memories of Aunt Edna flooded Shira's mind in a jumbled wave of emotion. She groaned and shut her eyes tightly. *No.* She breathed heavily as she labored to shove the images away. Fortunately, she was well practiced in shutting off unwanted emotion and still being able to function—to do her job.

Glancing at her watch, she wondered if a decent store was open after ten. The need to buy—something, anything—was irrational, but she didn't care.

She inhaled and placed her feet on the frigid linoleum. What was she thinking? It was definitely too late. It didn't matter anyway. Hadn't she promised herself a trip to King of Prussia? She could wait a few hours and make the twenty-minute drive up there tomorrow. A sigh released. Just the thought of walking the shiny marble floors, carrying a new treasure, loosened the tightness in her muscles.

In the meantime, she would do her job.

Could she succeed here? The opportunity was there. The real question was, did she want to succeed in the small town of Gladstone? Or should she sell the place, as is?

Taking a few steps into the salon, she spied Harriet's smock flung over her chair. Somewhere deep inside her gut, anger rammed its way out. Shira couldn't wait to fire the Beehive—and the rest of the so-called mavens.

She stepped back. Did that mean she was staying?

How could she? Her life was in the Big Apple, not Smallville. Alec was there. Her apartment. Maybe even her job at Élégance.

She could always let Beehive manage the place. The thought made her gag. No way.

One thing for sure, time was of the essence. Tuesday she'd need to re-open the salon and generate some revenue, which meant four days to find a lawyer—check that, she had Jesse—locate a banker and architect, and then review the salon's current client records.

She rubbed her temple. Two days of crying had generated a colossal headache. She needed a nice, cool bottle of Evian water. Did her aunt have anything like that stashed in her fridge? Her dad had dropped her off so late the previous night she had gone straight upstairs to the apartment and fallen asleep on the couch.

Whatever her final decision, she had to determine her assets.

Where did she begin? She hadn't really looked at the place in three years. Her peripheral vision spotted a cobweb in the corner next to the restroom.

As exhausted as she was physically, her mind suddenly kicked into high gear. No way she'd sleep now. It was as good a time as any to perform a preliminary inspection.

Clutching the envelope tighter, she stepped toward the reception desk then ran her hand across the black Formica countertop. The cramped cubicle contained a chair, a built-in shelf holding the phone, various office paraphernalia, and a large appointment book, its pages curled and stained with coffee spills. It seemed ages ago that she had felt so proud to manage this area.

Photos of her with Aunt Edna were taped everywhere, like some shrine.

The scruffy old penholder—the one she had made in Shabbat School out of an old soup can and scraps of pink-flamingo wallpaper—threatened to yank her back to the tender spot she didn't want to go.

"Enough, already!" She cried out. "Do what you know how to do." Straightening her shoulders, she dimmed the switch to her emotions then grabbed a ballpoint.

Swiveling back toward the reception area, she clicked the pen. This was where new clients were either "wowed" or sent running to the competition. Five stackable reception chairs were assembled against the front window with magazines scattered on three of the seats. Sun-bleached pink curtains with a scalloped valance made of wood, painted in black enamel paint, topped the large picture window. She wrote on the front of the envelope. New chairs and draperies. Get rid of the wacky valance.

Using the pen, she pushed back the dusty fabric. Painted in black and hot pink script on the picture window was The Hair Mavens Beauty Shop. The traditional "glamour" decal of a caricatured woman stared mindlessly onto the sidewalk. She released the curtain to cover the eyesore.

To the right of the chairs was the coat closet. She opened the paneled door, which released a musty odor monster. She turned her head and sneezed. Someone's abandoned light blue sweater hung on one of a dozen or so wire hangers. Ironically, the vacuum sweeper was surrounded by a bevy of dust bunnies.

Next to the closet was a long mirror hung vertically over a pink shelf holding a discolored white coffee maker, Styrofoam cups, and packets of sugar and non-dairy creamer. She shook her head. They probably still used coffee in a can. A nice espresso machine with real cream and Demerara sugar were essential. She added that to the list.

The door to the small powder room hung crooked. She swung it back and forth, causing it to groan like something from a bad horror film.

Verdict? She could almost feel the gust of wind as women ran for the door.

Re-do the reception area. As if she needed to write that on the list.

Against the restroom exterior wall sat the manicurist table. At least, she remembered it had been that. She pushed aside an array of magazines—and she used that term loosely, for most were grocery aisle rags—and eventually found the black surface. Did Mavens even have a dedicated nail tech? All stylists were trained to do manis and pedis, but it was always best to have someone who only did nails.

She inhaled. The acrid offense of cigarette smoke, perms, and other chemical odors assaulted her nose. Wasn't there some ordinance prohibiting smoking indoors? A new ventilation and air purification system was a must—hadn't anyone ever heard of secondhand smoke?

SMOKE-FREE ENVIRONMENT! IMMEDIATELY! She underlined immediately and added another exclamation mark that punctured the envelope.

A glance toward the yellowed ceiling tiles revealed more effects of Harriet and age. She puffed her cheeks and expelled air.

Redirecting her attention toward the left wall, she studied the heart of Mavens, the four stylists' stations. Also constructed of the black Formica, the counters were packed with the tools of the trade—if one was styling in the 1980s. The four black vinyl and chrome styling chairs were tattered and rusting. Aunt Edna's station, first in line, was neat and organized. Photos of Shira with her dad and news clippings about her various awards were placed in a long narrow frame. A lump formed in Shira's throat. Her body longed to pause—to touch.

She bit her bottom lip. *Focus.*

Harriet's station, she hated to admit, was also neat and organized. *Yuck.* Except for the disgusting half-smoked cigarette in an ashtray and a full, curdled cup of coffee in that atrocious mug. She grabbed the ashtray and threw the whole thing in the trash.

The next two were as different in appearance as right and left. One was a cacophony of disorder, the other starkly uncluttered.

She ran her finger over the counter. Sticky with hair spray and dust. Despite the overall organized appearance, it needed sandblasting to remove the layers of aerosol lacquer and grime.

Each station had a black plastic trolley cart that acted as a kind of boundary. She opened one of the drawers to shove in a few dangling perm rods.

Her pen was poised in position to add more tasks to the already growing list. She exhaled loudly. Was anything salvageable? She wrote that down.

To the right were the three shampoo stations. A filmy gray residue coated the black fiberglass bowls. The trigger-back chairs were also black vinyl, also tatty and torn. She tapped her chin with the pen. *I wonder.*

She approached the middle chair and attempted to recline the back. Clank. It plunged backward too far. Still broken from when she had worked there over ten years ago. She shook her head. Replace chair. She scribbled out the line. Replace *all* the chairs.

The black Formica shelving behind the shampoo bowls was a disorganized mess of gallon shampoo and conditioner bottles, white towels, and pink floral plastic shampoo capes. A tall plastic philodendron had dust balls hanging from it like some bizarre Christmas tree.

She fingered the white towels. Thin. Rough. Some even threadbare.

Down the center aisle for all to see were two antiquated helmet hair dryers, their plastic brittle and broken, posted atop black platform base chairs, all scuffed. The scruffiness continued along the base to the cracked and yellowing linoleum under her feet.

The walls were painted a Pepto-Bismol pink. Pink and black—how eighties can you get, Aunt Edna?

Framed posters of hair models—with styles she doubted any of them could handle—lined the walls.

Her chin dropped. It's just too, too schlocky for words.

Once this place had been her playground. Her refuge. "The most beautiful-est shop in the world," she whispered.

As she walked toward the overcrowded supply room, she yawned. The day had at last caught up with her.

No more. Her brain had officially shut down. Before cloaking the problem in darkness, she took one more peek at the salon. She was delusional. The place was a lost cause—why even try to save it?

She opened the door to the stairwell leading up to the apartment, switched on the light there, and turned off the salon lights.

The door to her aunt's apartment—her apartment, if she chose to stay—was closed. Moving the package under her arm, she dug into her purse for the keys. After unlocking the door, she felt for the light switch and flipped it on.

She stalled, grasping the keys. Once she entered, it was final. Aunt Edna wouldn't be in the kitchen stirring a pot of hot cocoa. She wouldn't be singing in her bedroom as she dressed for work or services. Shira licked her lips and tapped her foot. Just do it already, Shira.

She pressed the package against her chest and entered the apartment. There was some peculiar sense of comfort, holding it close to her heart like this. Perhaps it was because Jesse had alluded to there being a letter from Aunt Edna to her, as well as the legal papers. Something more tangible than the saved voice message back in New York.

"You're really gone, aren't you?" Her voice barely penetrated the emptiness. "What were you thinking? Giving Mavens to me?"

"Can you believe it? I own my own salon." Shira walked around the kitchen, tethered to the ancient wall phone. It hadn't taken long for the anxiety to hit her. The upsurge of overwhelmed-ness and all alone-ness had her doing something she thought better of—calling Fawna.

"Yeah, that's cool." Fawna seemed distracted. She knew her friend didn't get to bed before one or two a.m., sometimes not at all. So she hadn't been sleeping.

"I wonder where my missing boyfriend is." Shira sat on the kitchen table like she had as a kid. "I just left my third message on his voicemail."

"Oh, Alec?" Fawna coughed. "He's at rehearsal."

Shira peeked at the oven clock. Midnight. "This late? Wait—" She hopped off the table. "He got the part? How did you—"

"Yes. Isn't it exciting? I mean it's not the lead or anything, but it's a pretty important role. He's the fourth murder victim in the third act—"

Shira chewed her thumbnail. Suddenly Fawna was energized. Like the pink bunny beating her drum, Alec, Alec, Alec. Warning bells, the size of the Liberty Bell, clanged in her mind.

"What's going on, Fawna? How is it you know where my boyfriend is?"

She grunted. "I'm here, Shira. You're not."

Shira's tongue felt frozen to the roof of her mouth.

"By the way, Nigel left for California today."

Ouch. Was her friend trying to stab her in the back? *No.* This was more like a frontal attack.

"Good for Nigel."

"Veronica is still really angry at you."

"Good for Veronica." This conversation had deviated down a path Shira didn't want to go. "Oh, hey, Fawna, I need to get going. Long day and all. You know, just buried the most precious woman in my life, inherited a salon, my whole life is up in the air, and I'm a little tired."

"I—"

Click.

If she weren't so devastated by Fawna's lack of girl-friendliness, she might have enjoyed the hang-up. Instead, all that tumbled out were sobs mixed with "I thought you were my friend."

She rubbed her eyes and nose on her sleeve. Her blouse had turned into a soppy mess. Tissues. Normally Edna had a plethora of tissue holders strategically positioned throughout the apartment. She sprinted to her old bedroom. On her white desk was the pink flamingo tissue holder she had begged her aunt to buy on a trip to Florida. Its black spindly legs were ridiculous looking. She laughed as she grabbed a handful from the body of the fowl.

After giving an unladylike honk, years of accumulated *chatchkes* drew her attention. Everything from porcelain ballerinas and more leggy flamingos to snow globes and pink and blue ponies cluttered shelf after shelf. She lifted one of the snow globes that contained the Seattle space needle. Her dad had surprised her with the treasure from the gift store high atop the city. It had been their last family vacation. She tipped, then righted it. The glittery snow fell like fairy dust.

The phone rang. She wasn't up to any more conversations. Even if the call was from Alec. She blew her nose again. After a few more rings, the prehistoric answering machine kicked in.

"Shirry?" Cari's sweet voice filled the room like butterflies. "Are you there?"

Shira slid across her bare mattress to grab for the pink princess phone on the nightstand. "Cari?"

"You're there. Is it too late for me to call?"

"Yes— no—I mean, it's not too late." For you. Shira had no way of stopping the streams of tears and decided she didn't want to.

"How are you doing, Shira?"

"Not very good, Care-bear." She barely choked out the words. "Too many memories here."

"I'm coming over."

Shira coughed, trying to dislodge the lump in her throat. "No. Don't you dare." As much as she wanted Cari's company, she knew it was too huge of an imposition.

"Stop it, Shira. I'm coming over." Shira could hear Cari muttering something to Aaron.

"Cari, don't come over." She sat the on bed. "But you can stay on the phone with me for a while."

Cari sighed. "I can do that."

"Thanks." Shira stood and took the phone with her. Fortunately, her aunt had installed a mile-long phone cord that let her walk around the entire apartment.

"What happened at the reading of the will?"

"I'm the new owner of The Mavens." Where was the bedding? The closet?

"Wow." She blew air through her lips like a horse. "Shira, how do you feel about all this?"

Finally. Someone who cared. Her hand rested on the brass knob to her closet.

"Honestly, I don't know." She opened the door.

A face stared back at her.

Shira screamed and jumped back. Her feet tangled themselves causing her to fall on the bed. The phone hit the floor. *What in the world?*

Bending down to retrieve the phone, she peeked at the wide-eyed face.

"Miz Suzie-kin." Shira set down the phone and reached for the head. "For goodness' sake." She pulled down the mannequin head with real human hair and hugged it. "I can't believe it."

"Shira! Are you okay?" Cari's voice called from the floor.

Shira couldn't help laughing. She picked up the phone and held it to her ear with her shoulder. "Sorry I dropped you. I almost had a heart attack."

"You gave me one."

"I found Suzie-kin." She set it on the desk before going back for the plastic pro-case with all the curlers, scissors, rods—well, everything she had needed to practice wash and sets.

"No way," Cari giggled. "I can't believe your aunt kept that."

"What do you mean? Every stylist still has her first mannequin head, doesn't she?"

"I don't know. It's kinda creepy, Shirry."

She made a stab at smoothing down Suzie's wild hair. "She's a mess. What in the world did we do to her?"

"I think that was our experimental stage."

"She bears a resemblance to baby orangutan—on a bad hair day."

They laughed, hard. She wiped the moisture from beneath her eyes. These tears were good tears.

"Care-bear, thanks for calling me."

"Of course." She exhaled. "So tell me, what are you going to do first?"

Harriet flung her purse onto the couch, spraying half its contents around the room. She kicked off her shoes. One hit the end table and almost knocked the lamp off. The other landed on the desk to her left.

The nerve of that brat! She fisted and trembled and growled. "Edna, what were you thinking giving The Hair Mavens to that, that person?"

What she needed this instant was something to calm her down—a smoke. She stomped through the living and dining rooms toward the kitchen. The well-stocked ciggy drawer next to the sink had what she needed, and she needed it bad. She jerked the handle, pulling the drawer completely out. Packs of ciggies, lighters, and books of matches fell out onto the floor. Great, just great.

She dropped the drawer and bent over the sink, gripping the edge of the counter. Her reflection glared at her from the window.

This couldn't be happening. She pounded her fist on the kitchen counter. "Edna, why?" She spoke to her reflection, as tears squeezed their way out and down her face. "Why did you give the shop to the brat? How could you do this to me?" She breathed in through flared nostrils.

She rubbed her nose with her forearm. "Harriet, get a grip. She was your best friend. You can't be mad at her." She scoffed. "You could never stay mad at her."

Straightening, she grabbed a paper towel from the holder. After a quick blow of her nose and rough swipe of her eyes, she bent to grab one of the fallen cigarette packs and a lighter.

She'd figure out this mess. If she could shut off the waterworks and think, the solution would present itself. She shoved her foot against one of the dinette chairs, pushing it back from the table. Her fingers shook as she peeled open the wrapper and pulled out a cigarette.

"This isn't as bad as it seems, old girl." She lit the end and took a deep drag. A few coughs followed. "Think it through."

The nicotine kicked in, taking some of the edge off her raw emotions. "Fact is Shira hates Gladstone. She's most likely moving to Beverly Hills to manage the fancy schmancy salon she went on and on about with Edna."

Did Edna know that when she wrote the will? Surely she must have. The woman had planned her whole funeral, right down to the songs. If that lawyer kid was to be believed.

Harriet propped her right leg onto another chair. So what would Shira do with Hair Mavens? Sell it? Of course she'd want to sell it. Or maybe lease it out. Either way she wasn't going to want to hang around here and run it. With Edna gone, there was no one the brat cared a whit about—nothing to keep her here.

Oh. "I get it, Edna." She pointed to the ceiling, a trail of smoke following. "You wanted me to use the ten thousand dollars as a down payment toward the shop."

She drew on the cigarette. Why hadn't her friend said so in the will? She exhaled smoke through her mouth and nose.

Edna couldn't think of every situation. She was good, but she wasn't clairvoyant.

Harriet flicked ashes into the crystal ashtray she kept on her dinette. Would Shira stick around long enough for Harriet to find a new beautician? Even if the brat bailed on her she'd make sure no client went without service. And if Shira decided to do the right thing for once, then Harriet would be big enough to work with her.

As the smoke billowed around her, the fog in her mind finally lifted. It was simple, really. She'd call a truce and offer to buy or lease the shop on Tuesday when they re-opened.

The Hair Mavens would be hers—as Edna intended—and she'd never have to deal with Shira Goldstein again!

Beulah knelt by her bed. "Thank You, Lord. Thank You that You are in control." Her kneecaps popped in the quiet of her bedroom.

"I'm scared—I admit it—please forgive me." She tightened her folded hands and brought them to her forehead. "Wilbur is sick again. He was paler than usual tonight when I visited him. His eyes were even more dull and lifeless."

Her husband hadn't shown any signs of recognizing her or their son, Tom, since his second stroke. "Please, Lord, he needs Your healing hand."

She shifted her hands to her lips and held them there. Was Wil still inside his mind, held captive by paralysis? He didn't give any indication—any hope—that he was in there. Not a flutter when she spoke. Nothing. Sometimes she wanted to share her burdens with him as they did in marriage. However, if there was an inkling of the possibility that he was still there, she didn't want to upset him—especially when there was nothing he could do.

Instead she had enthusiastically talked about "visiting" with Edna's family. How good it was to see Shira after all these years and that Edna had given Harriet, Kathy, Shira, and her lovely gifts.

How foolish she had felt going on and on. As if her heart hadn't been broken at the gravesite of her friend. At the gut-wrenching reality that she would have to find a new place to work now that Mavens belonged to Shira.

She glanced at her fingers. They were red from clenching them so tightly. She unlocked and wiggled them to get the circulation flowing. What was she going to do?

Placing her palms on top of the bedspread she continued her prayer. "I need this job, Lord. Wil's pension is not enough with all the medical costs. I know Edna's heart for The Hair Mavens, but giving it to Shira when she hates Harriet, and doesn't even recognize me after fifteen years."

Chapped fingers dug and tugged into the blue chenille fabric. A groan pushed its way out of her as though it had the force of an exploding volcano.

"My friend, Lord." Sobs intensified within her and spilled into her words. "I miss my friend! What will I do without her? I'm alone and scared. Edna saw me.

"There's no one who sees me now. I'm this invisible—"

I will never leave or forsake you.

She released a long sigh.

Shaking her head, she let go of her tight grip and shifted to a more comfortable position on the carpet then rested her head on the side of the bedspread. The chenille's fuzzy texture pressed against her cheek.

"I'm sorry, Lord. Forgive me. You're here. I'm not alone. You see me."

She finally granted herself permission for the tears to fall freely. There was no need to be strong for anyone right now. With each wave of tears God's peace floated in around her. It reminded her of the weekend she and Wil had spent at the Jersey shore. They had floated on rafts holding hands, basking in the warmth of the summer day.

The chimes of the grandfather clock played. She checked her watch. One a.m. Goodness, gracious, she had been sitting there for an hour.

"You have a real treasure up there with You, Lord." Her voice was raspy and worn, yet her heart was refreshed. She felt grateful.

She palmed off the tears from her face, a yawn working its way out.

Edna's greatest desire was for Shira's relationship with the Lord and with her father to be restored. She and Beulah had spent many nights on their knees praying for them.

She drew her knees up to her chest and wrapped her arms around them. It would be an honor to continue that intercession for both Shira and Sam.

Without taking off her clothes, she climbed into bed and pulled the covers up to her neck. Fresh tears glided down her cheeks, but these were good tears. Thankful tears.

"Thank You, dear Lord, for Edna's friendship these past years. Thank You for a friend who truly saw me." She turned on her side and brought Wil's long-unused pillow to her, hugging it tightly.

"And as for The Hair Mavens, Father, Your will be done."

12

Shira dumped the bags from the official Crisis113 booty—as opposed to the junk from the rest stop in Jersey—just inside her aunt's apartment. She shoved them against the wall with her foot next to the cheap plastic bags. The living room now resembled a museum of retail—from the ridiculous to the sublime.

Nevertheless, the trip to the mall had been successful. This shopping endeavor truly honored the seriousness of Crisis113. Shiny, practically frame-able sacks brandishing names like Michael Kors, Lush, Coach, and even Williams and Sonoma held extravagant treasures. These things she would inventory later when she logged them in her journal.

Now what most interested her was the one item nested in tissue paper within the crisp white Williams and Sonoma bag. If she was going to finally read Aunt Edna's letter—and for some reason she had procrastinated until that day to do so—then she felt something chocolate was in order.

She lifted the red and white striped canister from the bag and hugged it tightly. Chocolate mint cocoa. Yes, that would do nicely. After placing the tin on the counter, she opened a lower cabinet door and found the cocoa pot her aunt had traditionally used on chilly winter evenings. It was neither chilly nor winter, but Shira craved the warmth all the same. She read the directions. Milk?

She tugged open the refrigerator. Please let there be milk. The fridge was packed with fresh veggies, fruit, and various ingredients that her aunt would have been able to pull together into a grand banquet in minutes. Surely there was—yes! She grabbed the carton of organic skim milk and checked the expiration date. Still good.

Minutes later she whisked the mint-infused chocolate shavings into the warming milk. The heavenly scents intensified with each second she stirred.

She stuck her nose closer and sniffed. *Yum. For goodness' sake, I'm cooking!*

"Aunt Edna, you would be proud of me." She did a little happy dance, the silly kick-out steps they had done together when they wanted to celebrate.

Eventually the mixture rippled and bubbles popped, indicating it was ready. With a flick of her wrist, the flame extinguished. Her ambrosia was ready to drink.

The everyday stoneware was to be given to that Kathy-person, but she got to keep Bubbe Golda's gorgeous china. Which was the perfect vessel anyway. Standing before the glass-front china cabinet in the dining room, she admired her inheritance. Her grandmother's exquisite Welmar china from Germany had hand-painted pale pink flowers in waves of light green background on uneven scalloped edges reminiscent of flower petals. She pulled the cabinet door's small brass knob. It stuck a little, gently vibrating the treasures inside. Carefully, she lifted a cup and saucer and carried it to the kitchen sink to give it a rinse. Who knew the last time her aunt had used the good stuff? Passover, maybe?

Taking careful aim, she poured the hot chocolate into the spacious cup. With a contented sigh, she set the cup and saucer on the table and sat in the cane back dining room chair. A few familiar squeaks greeted her as she made herself comfortable.

The envelope containing the will and Aunt Edna's letter sat before her. Her list of to-dos had marred the outside with her wishes and desires for the salon. What were Aunt Edna's wishes and desires?

She blew across the thin rim of the cup and took a sip. "Pure heaven!" she whispered. Setting the cup back onto the saucer, she brought the package closer. Why was she hesitating? Her heart pattered as though she had run up the stairs. She rotated the cup, examining more of the pattern.

She had heard the stories of her family so many times growing up. Her Bubbe's mother—her great-grandmother—had shipped the china and other valuables to a relative in New York. After *Kristallnacht*, the family felt certain things would not improve for Jews—even though they were believers in Jesus.

Fortunately, Bubbe's parents had shipped her off to those same relatives, or she most likely wouldn't have survived . . . which meant neither her father, Aunt Edna, or she would even be there. The rest of the family in Germany was eventually murdered in the camps. The ultimate crisis.

Big globs of tears spotted the manila-colored paper. She took a mouthful of the sweetness in an attempt to remove the bitterness of these memories, but the warm brew stuck in her throat like mud. She cleared her throat.

Her stomach rumbled. A quick glance at her watch confirmed that it was close to dinner, and she hadn't eaten since the scone with her

Starbucks. Wasn't there a Chinese take-out place a couple doors down? She could—

Shira, you can't put this off any longer. After another sip for strength, she opened the package. Butterflies flitted from organ to organ inside her. Jesse had said there were specific instructions about the salon. Did she really want to know what more Aunt Edna had to say?

Yes, she did.

The contents fell with a thump from the package. She removed a large binder clip holding everything together. On top of the legal documents was a cream-colored envelope with her name written. She recognized her aunt's graceful handwriting. Shoving aside the legal gobble-de-goop, she ran her finger under the flap then pulled out the letter.

There were two pages—that was all. The date was almost to the day of her death . . . two years ago.

Dearest Shira,

If you're reading this letter, then I'm at this very second in the presence of our Heavenly Father and our Messiah and Savior, Yeshua. I'm rejoicing, but I know those I leave behind are grieving. Please do not grieve long, Button. God has much in store for you and—

Shira grimaced. Even though she wasn't surprised God would be brought up in anything coming from her aunt, He was still the last person she wanted to hear about—or from. He had already taken too many of the people she loved. Who cared that Yeshua and Aunt Edna were partying up there?

—please know you are not alone. Believe it or not the mavens will be there for you.

What was that supposed to mean? She took another taste from her cup—the liquid had cooled. It needed a warm up.

I left you The Hair Mavens, dear one, but I also leave you the mavens themselves. You cannot separate them from the salon, because they are the salon.

The paper wrinkled as her grip tightened.

Enclosed are three contracts. One for Harriet Rose Schmidt Foster, one for Beulah Kay Montgomery, and one for Kathy Smith. Jesse can explain them to you in detail, but essentially these women must stay with the salon. Any changes and improvements you make to Hair Mavens will be with the mavens as active participants.

No! She shuddered as though some malevolent entity had entered the room. This couldn't be what her aunt had intended all along. She shook her head as her fist squeezed.

As I write this, I can see you shaking your head and getting angrier by the second. Button, this is for the best. I've prayed long and hard about this, and I know this is the right decision—

She crushed the letter to her temple.

Was this some cruel cosmic joke? God had told Aunt Edna to do this to her?

She dropped the crumpled letter and scattered the contracts searching for Jesse's business card. He would know what to do. Where was that card? She shook the envelope. It tumbled into the cup of chocolate. She growled then rescued it.

Shoving out of the chair, she stomped to the kitchen's wall phone and punched in Jesse's cell number. She patted her chest, trying to calm her rapid heart, but the first ring rattled her nervousness more. The second ring. She glanced toward the contracts strewn across the table. Wait. Didn't Jesse draft these documents?

"Hello, Shira."

Words. She needed words to let him know—

"You . . . you traitor." Her voice churned with as much venom as she felt.

"You read the letter, I take it." His voice was calm, which fueled her anger even more.

"How could you?"

"I am, was Edna's lawyer. It's what she wanted."

She punched the air—since he wasn't there in person. "What am I supposed to do now?"

Jesse sighed. "I don't know, Shira. Maybe you need to decide if you want the salon or not."

Pressure surged through her head. "I want the salon, Jesse. I don't want them." She kneaded her forehead.

She began pacing, but the cord tripped her. Kicking it out of the way, she had half a mind to venture into Aunt Edna's bedroom for the cordless.

No, she wasn't ready to go in there yet. She backed up against the wall.

Silence.

Had he hung up on her? "Hello?"

"I'm here." He puffed out a bit of air on his end. "Shira, I'm still at work and will be here at least a few hours more. How about we meet for lunch tomorrow—my treat—and we'll talk then?"

She slid down the wall until she sat on the floor, one arm resting on her knee. "I don't know if I can sleep, Jesse." Her fingers combed through her hair. "I need a drink."

"Shira, you don't need a drink."

Oops. Had she said that out loud? Whatever.

"Where should I meet you, Jesse?"

"How about we meet at my office at one and I'll drive? Do you remember how to get here?"

"Of course." How would she get there? *Right.* She had inherited her aunt's cute red Mini. She hoped it wasn't a stick. It had been a while since she had driven one.

"Be sure to bring the envelope with the contracts and deeds. We'll review them then."

"All right."

"Shira?"

"Yes?"

"I'll be praying you have a good night's sleep."

Normally when she heard the *p* word, her mind numbed. For some reason something else welled up inside her. What was it? "Thanks, Jesse."

She must have been more tired than she thought.

The sounds and smells of Philadelphia's Broad Street reminded Shira of a toned-down version of Manhattan. It felt good to be back in civilization. She and Jesse emerged from the parking garage into the bright crisp autumn day. A gentle breeze ruffled her ponytail and Jesse's curly mop.

Most of her morning had been spent figuring out what to wear. She hoped her appearance would partner favorably with her well-designed arguments against Edna's ridiculous requests. She was still angry with him for not immediately disclosing Edna's restrictions. Well, sort of angry. She had slept well and it was a beautiful day . . .

She had settled on the classic Alexander McQueen light tweed dress. The pencil skirt with the wide black leather belt accentuated her small waist and long legs. Wearing it made her feel so Audrey Hepburn. The legal papers had fit nicely into her Michael Kors black patent leather satchel.

"I hope you like this restaurant. It's one of my favorites." He nodded toward Broad Street's sidewalk.

Placing his hand gently on the small of her back, he guided her into the flow of pedestrian traffic. Shivers rippled through her body.

"Right here, Shira." He opened the glass and black metal door, then steered her inside a small reception area. Paneled in light maple with a diminutive waterfall nestled in a copse of tall bamboo, Shira admired the exquisiteness of the tiny space.

"Welcome to The Blue. May I help you?" A young, trim, and attractive hostess made eye contact with Jesse and gave him a sensuous smile.

Shira felt certain her nails were morphing into talons. The chick better watch it.

"Yes, ma'am, two for lunch please." He gave her an innocent no-teeth grin—like something he'd give his mother or sister or some old lady.

Was this man for real?

As the hostess lifted two leather-clad menus, she noticed Shira. She leveled a strong stare at the hostess while readjusting her purse onto her shoulder. The woman lowered her eyes.

"Right this way, please." She parted a dark blue curtain and nodded ahead.

It may have only been Shira's imagination, but the hostess seemed to have cooled a few degrees to the proper professional tone. Much better, missy. She and Jesse entered the main dining area.

"Wow." Shira whispered.

She hadn't expected such simple grandeur. Tall ceilings. Most of the walls had light maple tongue-in-groove paneling. The main wall behind the bar had two massive built-in sections of blue-glass tile. The sunlight danced off the tile giving the effect of motion, like moving water.

The wall facing the street had four ten-foot high canvassed photos of waves. Below the prints were booths. With the gentle lighting, the overall appearance of the restaurant was like an underwater refuge.

The hostess ushered them to an intimate table for two next to the window.

"I'm sorry, ma'am," Jesse said. "This is a business meeting. Could we have a booth on the mezzanine level, please?"

Shira felt her cheeks warm. The hostess nodded. Shira didn't miss the smirk on the girl's face.

They followed her up the stairs to a table overlooking the main dining area. The view was pleasing, but disappointment continued to grow in Shira. Business meeting? *Shake it off, Shira.* It was a business meeting after all. They tucked themselves into their respective seats and accepted the menus from Miss Smirk.

"Enjoy your meals."

Jesse gave her a great toothy smile. "Thanks, ma'am."

The only semblance of a smile from Shira was tight-lipped and what she hoped would be interpreted as dismissive.

"How about we order first, Shira, then discuss the contracts after we eat?"

Business. Just business. The disenchantment spread like an oil spill.

"Fine." How easily she had slipped into a more intimate mind-set with

Jesse. She needed to watch herself with this man. Alec already had claims on her, after all. Yes, the boyfriend who still hadn't returned any of her messages.

Their waiter took her order of roasted beet salad with mixed greens, goat cheese, spicy pecans, and white balsamic dressing. Instead of merely relaying his order, Jesse chatted with the waiter, adding another layer of discomfort in Shira, and the sensation of feeling left out. Which didn't make sense—she barely knew the guy.

She redirected her interest toward the dining area below and caught a glimpse of a few designer outfits she liked. *Hmm.* She wondered where they had shopped. Never knew when the next crisis would arise. Lately, they came pretty regularly for her. Which reminded her, most of the Crisis113 items were still in bags on the living room floor.

"I'll have the grilled sirloin burger—medium rare—with Portobello mushrooms and the fries." Jesse handed his menu to the young man.

She chewed her lip while watching Jesse take a drink from his water. His lashes were so long and curly. He smiled. How would they fill that awkward time before the food was delivered and their business meeting officially began?

"So, Shira," he began, "don't you hate that awkward time of small talk before the meals arrive?"

She laughed. Jesse did a marvelous job of engaging her in light banter and funny stories. Before she knew it, their meals were set before them.

There was something about beautifully presented food that always put her in a good mood. Taking a forkful, the savory and sweet flavors awakened her taste buds with delight.

The time went by quickly as they ate and chatted. She poked at the last beet in her glass bowl. "So, Jesse, it seems you were close to my Aunt Edna."

He set down a fry. Those light brown eyes drew her in again. "I loved Aunt—your Aunt Edna."

Sadness clouded their eyes at the same time. Shira stared at the remains of her salad. "She was amazing." The *was* lodged uncomfortably in her throat.

Jesse reached for her hand. "I know she loved you, Shira."

She raised her eyes toward his.

"You were all she talked about. I feel I know you." His lids lowered briefly, those long lashes brushing at his cheeks. "Between your dad and aunt, I knew I needed—wanted to meet you."

Her heart fluttered in a strange way. It was more than attraction, for clearly she was developing that for Jesse. This was sweet and new and something she wanted to learn more about.

He looked at his plate. "You are blessed, Shira, to have two people who love you and care for you like that."

She huffed and withdrew her hand from his. The sweet mood evaporated like a raindrop on a hot pavement. Jesse's brows rose.

"Don't romanticize my relationship with my family." Her face heated.

One nicely muscled shoulder lifted. "I know your childhood wasn't perfect, Shira. Your dad has shared with me that he made many selfish mistakes after your mother died."

Her father admitted to making mistakes? Still, she didn't know how she felt about her dad talking about her or their family issues with a stranger. What was she supposed to do with this?

"My mother died too. When I was ten." He exhaled softly.

This time she reached for him. He continued to hold her hand securely.

"She died of a broken heart, I think. Or maybe she gave up and didn't want to fight the cancer anymore." He gave her a sad, lopsided grin. "My father is an alcoholic. He was very abusive, physically and emotionally, to my mother and me."

Under the table, she crushed her linen napkin. Physically abusive? She didn't know what to say. Her childhood hadn't been as bad as that. Her father had neglected her in his grief and was insensitive to a young girl's emotions, but he'd never struck her.

"He kicked me out of the house at thirteen with just the clothes on my back." He shook his head and scrunched his dimpled chin. "Great way to enter manhood, huh?"

"Jesse, I'm so sorry." So neither of them had their bar or bat mitzvah— their Jewish rite of passage to adulthood. Her lack was because her father couldn't bring himself to think of anyone but himself, but Jesse's was because he was homeless. She felt a tear escape down her face.

He bent forward and tightened his hold. "Don't be sorry, Shira. It was the grace of God."

Familiar anger pushed to the surface, her instinctive response to religious platitudes. She tugged from his hold, but he held firm. Eyes with such sincerity latched onto hers like a lifeline. He laughed quietly. "Yeah, I didn't think so at the time either. But the night he threw me out, I stumbled upon a church concert in the park and met Pastor Horace Smith and his wife, Hope." He took a deep breath, released it, and grinned.

She realized she still held hers.

"The Smiths unofficially adopted me. They took me in that very evening." His eyes sparkled and danced. "Can you imagine? A total stranger, tattered clothes and sporting a real shiner."

Trying to imagine the clean-shaven, successful man seated before her as homeless and abused raised questions in her mind. How did he overcome such challenges and remain so, so innocent? So kind?

"Horace and Hope were sensitive to the fact that I'm Jewish. Neither of my parents was religious. I only visited the synagogue for cousins' bar and bat mitzvahs." He swirled his glass, the last remnants of ice faintly clinking.

"The Smiths already had a deep love for Jewish people and Israel. They taught me what it meant to be Jewish." He paused and slowly shook his head. "Pretty amazing, huh? Christians teaching a Jew how to be Jewish?"

Little rivulets of tears trailed down his face. "Every day they told me what a blessing and treasure I was to them and how I would make a difference in the world. Every single day." He wiped his face with his napkin.

I love you, my Button. Hadn't Aunt Edna tried to make her feel special? "What a wonderful family, Jesse."

He nodded. "The Smiths helped put me through college and law school. Eight years ago, they learned of the Messianic Jewish conferences in Pennsylvania and encouraged me to attend."

She willed herself to not roll her eyes. All her life she had been forced to attend those conferences. She had rejected her faith and the conference with all the emotion of a seventeen year old . . . nine years ago.

"That's where I first met my later-to-be partner, Abe Liberman. He was the one who introduced me to your dad and Aunt Edna."

Her stomach dropped. Had she attended the conference instead of staying home they could have met? The delicious meal she just finished soured.

"Shira, it was like a dream. I was back with my Jewish people again, and we all shared a love of our Messiah, Jesus, Yeshua." He slipped his other hand under hers to form a cocoon of warmth. "When I finally moved here two years ago, it was like coming to the Promised Land."

She looked away and swallowed. "That's nice for you, Jesse." The words came out with more disdain than she had intended.

Withdrawing his hands from hers, he placed them in his lap. The loss went straight to her heart.

"Sorry, Shira," he said with a shrug. "I didn't mean to go on like this."

"Don't apologize, Jesse. Your story is touching. You seem to know so much about me. I like learning more about you." But she could sure do without all the religious stuff.

The waiter appeared and cleared away their dishes. He asked if they wanted to view the dessert cart. Shira didn't know Jesse well enough yet to indulge in chocolate in front of him, so they ordered coffee.

Once the china cups were filled with the aromatic brew, she pulled the package—with the offending contracts—from her bag.

"Ready to get down to business, I see." Jesse waggled his brows.

"Shira, I'm telling you, you can't fire them!" Jesse lightly pounded the table with the sides of his hands. Their coffee sloshed against the sides of their cups.

An hour had passed and she was no closer to getting her way than when they had started. They were on their fifth cup of coffee and both feeling the caffeine. He placed his elbows on the table and ran both hands through his hair. He had done that a lot in the last sixty minutes.

"Jesse, none of them fit into the redesign of the salon." She extended her hands, palms in. "Aunt Edna said to bring the place up to date—"

"She also said you can't do it without them."

It was her turn to muss her hair. She groaned.

"Listen, Shira. We're at an impasse. The fact is unless these ladies commit a serious infraction or they quit on their own, the mavens stay."

That's it! Her body straightened.

"What?" He cocked his head and squinted. "What's going on in that head of yours?"

"You said it. Unless they quit on their own." She grabbed the contracts.

"You're going to force them to quit?" He pointed to the documents. "I can't condone that, as your lawyer—"

"No." She pulled the papers back from his reach. "No, I'm not necessarily going to make them quit. It's just with all the changes I'm planning they won't want to stay." She tapped the contracts on the table to straighten them into a neat stack, then gave him her it-will-be-fine smile. "See?"

"Shira, I think you underestimate your aunt's friends."

She lifted one hand, wrist and palm down, and waggled it from side to side. "Listen, I know salons. I worked in Manhattan, for goodness' sake. I'd wager none of them have done a foil job since beauty school."

Her hand crept toward his, then stopped. "I know Gladstone is a small town, but we are only three miles from the wealthy Main Line of Philadelphia. I had clients in New York who traveled ten times that to come to Élégance."

"What if they can keep up with you?" Those eyes, filled with integrity, tried to melt her resolve again. "What if they capture your vision and want to help?"

She pursed her lips and shrugged. "Won't happen."

"What if it does?"

"Then I'll deal with it when it comes." She reached down to grab her purse.

"You'll support them?"

As if. She placed the paperwork into one of the side pockets of her bag.

"Shira, can I trust you to do the right thing?"

She exhaled and averted her eyes toward the dining room below. *Oh, cute shoes.*

"Shira, look at me." He sounded like her father.

She huffed then shouldered her bag. "Yes, Jesse. If by some miracle they do learn, we'll all become one big happy family."

His thumb and forefinger circled her chin and gently jiggled it. At his touch, something akin to magma ran through her.

"I have your word, Shira?"

She couldn't help smiling.

"Do I have your word?" His chin lowered.

Mm, that dimple was so cute. "Yes, Jesse." She fluttered her lashes.

"Good. You won't be sorry, Shira."

Huh, it wouldn't be she who was sorry. *Watch out mavens. Your days are numbered.*

13

Harriet clutched her purse strap with both hands against her shoulder. Maybe this wasn't such a good idea. Try as she might, she couldn't take the last few steps to Delicious Bakery. The alternative for her was to open Mavens, but she definitely wasn't ready for that.

Her second cigarette nearly finished, she knew stalling wouldn't change anything. But her chest ached like a dump truck had plowed into it. She glanced over her shoulder, half expecting to see her friend. It had finally sunk in.

Edna would not be meeting her to pick up their cherry cheese Danishes today . . . or ever again.

She groaned. Would everything she did today remind her that Edna was gone?

"Good morning, Harriet." Bob-the-insurance-guy seemed to have appeared out of nowhere.

She placed a hand over her revved heart. "Hi, Bob." Like it had a mind of its own, her hand repositioned itself behind her head to smooth any errant strands from her beehive.

He adjusted his round wire-rim glasses and glanced at his feet. "Harriet," he said and shifted his gaze toward her. "I'm so sorry about Edna."

She had never noticed how blue his eyes were—like a spring sky. "Thanks, Bob." A new wave of emotion built inside her. She didn't think she could handle the pressure in her chest without exploding. Looking away, she broke their connection.

He bit his lower lip. "I saw you at the funeral."

"I didn't see you. Why didn't you—"

"You were pretty busy with Beulah and the rest of the Goldstein family." He sniffed.

"Bob." She touched the sleeve of his tweed sport jacket then quickly withdrew it. What else could she say?

His hands traveled behind his back before he made his customary little bow. "You know, Harriet, I could sure use a donut and coffee. How about you?"

She inhaled a ragged breath. Her lower lip trembled. "Yes, Bob. I could too."

He opened the door and placed his hand lightly on her back, allowing her to enter first.

The bell jingled. Nonni turned. "Oh, Harriet!" She cried and ran around the front display case to pull her into a warm embrace. "I can't believe she's gone."

They both blubbered—right there in front of the sugar cookies and breakfast treats.

Frank's burly arms materialized and wrapped around both of them. His tears united with theirs. Harriet glanced over her shoulder. Bob stood a few inches away, blowing his nose in a handkerchief. She removed her arm from Frank's shoulder and tilted her head toward their little weeping group. Bob shuffled over and rested his arm on Harriet's shoulder and the other on Frank's.

A decidedly strange huddle—two old hippies, an insurance guy, and a washed-up beautician.

"Thanks again, Bob." Harriet leaned over and gave him a quick peck on the cheek. He blushed. She felt her own cheeks heat. *I do declare.*

"You are most welcome, Harriet." He lowered his chin and peered over his glasses. "Please call if you need anything."

"I will." Raising the two bags of cherry cheese Danishes and the cup of coffee as a kind of salute, she turned and headed down the sidewalk toward Mavens.

Somehow, sharing that time with Bob, Nonni, and Frank had given her strength for her impossible mission—making peace with the brat—a.k.a. Shira. And then working out an arrangement for her to take over The Hair Mavens.

As she inserted the key into the lock, she glanced back toward where Bob and she had stood talking. Bob waved. Her face heated. He's still there. Hopefully, she was far enough away that he couldn't see her blush.

Another peek confirmed he was watching her. The warmth washed over her like a warm summer day. She nodded and waved back. He waved again.

Inside the shop, she relocked the door and flipped on the lights. She almost went to the window to see if Bob was still standing there, but thought better of it. Instead, she looked around the place.

It was so quiet. And empty. She groaned. The first day back to work and she felt as disconnected as the Scarecrow in the Wizard of Oz, when those creepy monkeys had ripped him apart.

She set the bag with the extra cherry cheese Danish on the reception desk. It was intended to be her peace offering to Shira. Bob had paid for it—for everything. A new flush of warmness reached her cheeks at the memory.

The little devotional calendar on Edna's station still showed Wednesday, the day she— Harriet flipped the pages to today's date. Tuesday, the first day of their workweek, had always been planning day for Edna and her. How ironic that Harriet was planning to take over her best friend's business.

With her coffee and bag situated at her own station, she grabbed the smock off her chair and headed to the break room. She held it to her cheek a few seconds as she walked. It wouldn't matter if the thing wore into a frayed, threadbare rag, she would never stop wearing it. And pity the fool who tried to take it from her.

Shedding her purse and jacket, she slipped her arms into the sleeves and smoothed the front.

Back at her station, she peeled the lid off the Styrofoam cup to pour the coffee into her 'do It mug.

Oh. She froze. The coffee from last Wednesday was still in the cup. She had never cleaned it out, because . . .

She grabbed the counter with both hands. *Easy, old girl. Don't lose it again.*

After washing the cup, she poured the fresh coffee and took a sip. The Danish bag sat on the counter before her, reflecting itself in the mirror. She swallowed an unexpected sob.

Suddenly, she wasn't hungry.

Shira startled at the slam of the salon door. Ms. Beehive had arrived. Harriet had to be making that racket downstairs on purpose—just to annoy her.

She yawned. Right now Shira felt like she was back in college, pulling an all-nighter, but instead of researching and writing a term paper, she was in the throes of planning what could be her new and improved life. Chewing on the end of her pen, she was reminded again that her aunt had no computer anywhere on the premises and that her pink laptop was back in New York.

Three hand-written pages lay before her on the table, a pile of wadded-up paper at her feet. Somewhere between draft three and the final draft, she had made the decision to stay in Gladstone—to give this thing a try.

A separate legal pad contained the growing list of items she would need to bring back from her apartment. The final entry, she had written, Alec?

She sighed. He still hadn't returned her calls. At some point she had stopped leaving messages and let it ring until his voicemail kicked in, then hung up. Did he think she was desperate? Probably. She was beginning to feel that way.

She tried to imagine him helping her pack boxes and load them into a truck. *Hah.*

From nowhere, an image of Jesse holding a large box and smiling at her formed in her mind. Hmm. It took no imagination to see him doing any act of kindness. In fact, it seemed like a normal thing for him to do.

After their meeting, she recognized the need to tackle the maven problem with more finesse. She figured a meeting at the end of the day to review her business plan was the most professional approach. She stretched her neck and rubbed the small of her back.

It was eight thirty. Aunt Edna's, that is, her first appointment wasn't until ten, so after she jumped into the shower, she'd run to the printers and use one of their computers to enter all her notes and print enough copies for the mavens and Jesse.

She stacked all the papers on the table then stretched her arms above her head. She felt old. She was twenty-five-ish and closing in on thirty.

Shedding her pajamas as she made her way toward the bathroom, she wondered if her gym had a branch around Gladstone. Jesse obviously worked out. Maybe he could give her the name of his.

Jesse. Despite the heated discussion they'd had at lunch, he was right. If she came in like a steamroller with all the rules first thing that morning, it would throw off everyone's game and the clients would suffer. He was so wise.

She opened the bathroom door. The giant pink flamingo's beady black eyes stared at her from the shower curtain. She pulled her tank top over her head and threw it at the silly thing. It billowed slightly but rested unaffected by her assault.

Turning on the faucets, she waited for the water to heat. The bird's blank stare bothered her. It reminded her of something. She remembered when her room was filled with the leggy pink and black birds.

The Pepto-Bismol pink and black décor in the salon suddenly registered.

Oh no. Hadn't it been her brilliant idea? Her head fell into her hands. She groaned.

The shower curtain—her idea. The flamingo décor in her room—her idea. *Aunt Edna, wouldn't it be so cool to have hot pink and black as the Mavens' new color scheme?*

Shira had happy-danced her aunt around the apartment after they had installed the new curtain and the matching pink carpet, toilet cover, and pink and black towels. The current towels appeared relatively new. That meant Aunt Edna had kept the same décor on purpose?

Steam billowed over the curtain. She stepped into the shower and allowed the pressured water to pound her scalp. Eventually, she had outgrown the flamingo design but hadn't really cared about changing it. By her senior year, all she had wanted to do was to get out of Gladstone and head to New York. Her father had imposed his will on her to get her business degree instead.

After squirting shampoo into her palm, she rubbed them together to get an even layer and applied it to her scalp.

At eighteen, she still had an annoying remnant of neediness for her father's approval. She had attended two semesters at the University of Penn. Yes, instead of fulfilling her own plans to enter the elite salon world, she had waylaid those dreams for his alma mater—even her aunt had questioned that decision.

It was during her first weekend home from college that Aunt Edna met her outside the shop and covered Shira's eyes for the big reveal. When her aunt had removed her hands and the mavens cried out, "Surprise!" she wasn't prepared for the "new and improved" Hair Mavens—a washed in Pepto and black. Everyone had been so excited. She hadn't had the heart to tell her aunt how bad it looked.

She bowed her head against the cold tile, suds flowing down her face and into her eyes. Her stomach knotted and burned. How could she have forgotten her aunt's kind gesture? Had Aunt Edna held on to the design specter to honor Shira? She bumped her head against the wall.

Shira, you are such a brat!

14

Beulah's hand trembled as she pointed to the coffee maker. "May I get you a cup of coffee, Mrs. Talbot?" She took a discreet peek at her watch again. Ten-twenty. Where was Shira?

Of all Edna's clients, Mrs. Talbot was the most finicky. In her seventies and very wealthy, she could go to any one of the exclusive Main Line salons—something she had reminded Edna of every chance she could. And always in that shrill, nasally voice.

Mrs. Talbot pursed her lips and scoffed. "I've been waiting here for twenty minutes. I told Edna I would never put up—"

A chorus of gasps came from the salon floor, followed by a silence so dense it was suffocating. Beulah had stifled her own, but clearly everyone was shocked by Nellie Talbot's insensitive remark.

Beulah watched Nellie Talbot's blue-painted lids drop and her chin quiver. Beulah turned around. The busy shop looked like a snapshot. Hands were frozen in mid-air and every horrified reaction was aimed in Mrs. Talbot's direction.

Beulah rushed to Mrs. Talbot's side and placed her hand on the old woman's shoulder. She gazed up at Beulah with dewy eyes.

"I-I'm so sorry, Betty. I didn't mean anything by that." Her voice was hoarse and damp. "I loved Edna." She covered her face with her slender fingers, overloaded with expensive rings.

Now was probably not a good time to remind the woman once more that her name was not Betty. Deep, shaky intakes of breath told her that Mrs. Talbot was crying, but not a sound emanated from her petite frame. Beulah sat in the chair next to her and wrapped her in a hug. Mrs. Talbot leaned into Beulah's embrace and finally released soft sobs.

Dear Lord, please comfort Nellie Talbot. She's like the rest of us, mourning the loss of our friend.

"Beulah?" Kathy's delicate voice interrupted the silent prayer. She extended a box of tissues toward her. Beulah pulled several and passed them to the grieving woman. She mouthed a thank you to Kathy, who nodded and walked back to her station.

Harriet stared at Beulah intently for a few seconds. Beulah couldn't read her friend's expression. Finally, Harriet lifted her chin and returned to rolling Mrs. Brown's hair.

The front door opened and Shira stumbled in. Her perfect hair was windblown, her sunglasses had slid down her nose, and a few papers floated to the floor.

"Oh." She straightened her posture, shrugged back her shoulders, and pinched off her sunglasses. "I'm so sorry to be late." She bent over to pick up the loose papers. Her big purse hit her on the head.

Mrs. Talbot raised her head from Beulah's chest, clutching the tissues to her nose. She squinted at Shira.

At some point Beulah was certain Shira would notice the door was still open, but she had the sense she wasn't the one to tell her.

Honk, honk. A car screeched to a stop in front of the salon and honked again. Several scalawags hung out the window and whistled—then called out inappropriate phrases.

Erect and undoubtedly annoyed, Shira grabbed the door with force and swung it shut. She looked around her in time to see she had an audience and stopped the door from slamming. Her smooth skin had mottled an angry pink.

Oh, how Beulah wanted to burst into laughter. Instead, she bit her lower lip hard and looked at her shoulder. Mrs. Talbot snorted into her tissue. Beulah heard several attempts by clients to cover their chuckles.

"Having a bad day?" Harriet's raspy voice wasted no time in casting the first stone.

Beulah winced. She watched the two women's reactions—like volatile tennis players. Shira lobbed a long hard glare in Harriet's direction. Harriet shrugged then reached for her cigarette and took a puff.

Shira's eyes narrowed. One side of her beautifully painted mouth shifted up into a sneer.

Uh oh, Lord, this emotional match is about to get ugly.

"Mrs. Talbot. Please forgive me for being so late," Shira said while still focused on Harriet. When she had pulled her glare from Harriet to the lady-in-waiting, her eyes softened. "Please allow me to treat you to a complimentary Dead Sea mud mask for your inconvenience. It will make you feel ten years younger."

A miraculous change occurred in Mrs. Talbot's demeanor. Like a child hearing school had been called off due to snow, she practically bounced in her seat. "Why, I would love a mask!" She handed Beulah her soppy tissues without a glance. "I didn't know you did mud masks."

"Yes, we do." Shira transferred her papers to one hand and extended a perfectly manicured hand toward Mrs. Talbot. "Step right this way to the first chair, and I'll be with you in a moment."

Evidently charmed, the once weeping woman took Shira's hand and allowed the young woman to lead her to Edna's chair. Once settled, Shira entered the reception booth and dropped her purse and papers in the cubicle. She eyed the bakery bag on the counter and snatched it.

Beulah spied Harriet. An uncharacteristic aura of vulnerability had settled on her face.

Shira peeked inside the bag, rolled her eyes, and tossed Harriet's peace offering into the trash.

Uh oh.

She threw it away. That brat! Every muscle in Harriet's body had tightened into pin curls of tension. Her eyes were glued to the trashcan where her peace offering had been tossed like so much, well, rubbish.

"Ouch," Mrs. Brown whispered.

Harriet looked down. In her fist was a hunk of her client's snow-white hair. She'd yanked poor Mrs. Brown's thin hair so far that Mrs. Brown's chin pointed up. Releasing it, the old woman's head bounced forward like a worn rubber band.

Harriet's face heated. "Sorry about that, Mrs. Brown." She gently squeezed her scrawny shoulders.

Lifting fingers gnarled by arthritis, Mrs. Brown patted Harriet's hand.

The swirl of smoke from Harriet's ashtray beckoned her. She didn't need to be asked twice and took a deep drag, then pushed it through her nose and mouth. Repositioning the rat-tail comb, she sectioned a portion of hair. Choosing the small yellow roller from her curler tray, she wrapped the ends evenly, rolled it tightly to Mrs. Brown's head, and held it in place with a metal clippie.

Glancing at her own reflection, Harriet could see the anger sectioning off wrinkles on her forehead and around her mouth, and rolling them tightly against her face.

She had thought for sure Mrs. Talbot would have read the riot act to the brat. She had been twenty minutes late for the old lady's appointment. Twenty!

But no, the old phony had fallen for the young phony's bit about a mud mask. Since when did this place do mud masks?

Mrs. Brown groaned. Harriet eased back—without apologizing, she continued. If she weren't careful, her client would walk out bald and never return.

Just a few feet from Harriet, Shira and Mrs. Talbot giggled like two mean girls. No doubt they were gossiping about Harriet.

Shira had stumbled into Mavens like she was drunk or on drugs or something. Then she had thrown away the Danish.

She threw it away. It was like a slap to Edna's face. No respect.

Fine.

Two can play at that game.

Kathy's heart was running circles in her chest. Her fingers shook as she removed the roller from Mrs. Carmichael's hair. The stiff cylinder shape would be brushed and teased into her usual bob. Would it not be wonderful if she could brush away the last week—and Edna would be alive?

She shoved back her thick-framed black glasses. This is not good. Not good. She did not like how it felt in The Hair Mavens and wished she could leave and find a new place to work. But where could she go? No matter where she went, Edna would not be there.

Shira wanted to meet with Harriet, Beulah, and her after work. Her stomach felt sick the moment Shira announced the meeting.

Harriet had not been nice to Shira when she came in late. Then Shira had thrown away the bag of sweets on the counter, and now Harriet was very angry. Kathy peeked in Harriet's direction. Harriet had not stopped muttering and gnashing her teeth since Shira arrived—which made Kathy sweat.

Above all, Kathy hoped there would not be any yelling. Yelling led to bad things. Edna had been so peaceful. Now she was gone and Harriet would be louder because Edna was not there to calm her. Harriet was always angry at something or somebody.

Kathy watched Beulah in the mirror. She washed Mrs. Nolan's hair and smiled as her client talked. Beulah was peaceful, but Harriet was stronger than Beulah.

Laughter came from Shira and the crabby lady sitting in Edna's chair. It was crystal clear Shira did not like any of the mavens. Kathy could tell.

The last roller out, Kathy ran her fingers through the curls, loosening them before she teased and finished her client's style. She reached over to her counter and shook the hair spray can. Good. There was enough. Mrs. Carmichael liked lots of hair spray.

Kathy's glasses fell down her nose. The cheap frames did not last very long. She needed to find another pair at Walmart and have the nice lady put the clear glass in them again.

She glanced at Shira, who wore another Prada outfit. Kathy remembered wearing Prada—back in her other life.

The tension was so thick Shira could have parted it with a comb and braided it. Now that it was time to confront the mavens, she was nervous.

She reviewed the three-page manifesto once more as she sat in the reception booth. Behind her she could hear the mavens cleaning up. All day she couldn't wait to drop the bomb on them. Now . . .

Was she having second thoughts? Impossible. Especially with being the recipient of Ms. Beehive's snide comments all day long.

She glanced over the appointment calendar. Her first day taking over Aunt Edna's clients hadn't been as bad as she had thought. Thanks to practicing on Miz Suzie-kin, she wasn't totally inept with granny hair. At least after the first three or four appointments.

Shira had tried suggesting new, more flattering and youthful styles for the old ladies, but all she had received were no's—accompanied by polite smiles and barely concealed giggles. Only two people had wanted a blow-dry. No one purchased any products.

She stood then straightened her jacket as she faced the ladies. Beulah was finishing up her last client, while Harriet lounged in her chair smoking a cigarette. Humph. Not for long.

Kathy busied herself with sweeping up the crumbs from all the baked goods customers brought in today. Shira had never seen so many cookies, brownies, cakes, and pies in her life. The manicure table and break room were still stacked with them. She'd have to throw them all out before they attracted bugs or vermin.

A parade of old faces she hadn't seen since she was a kid had walked in carrying home-baked confections. She must have received more hugs and condolences than at the funeral and shiva—combined. It would have been nice to have Cari with her today helping her navigate the maze of emotions. Exhausting emotions. Maybe that was why she had lost a lot of her steam for the meeting.

She stepped toward the product rack next to the front door. It was the third or fourth time that day she had needlessly straightened the bottles and jars.

Beulah entered the tight reception space to collect Mrs. Lowendowsky's check.

"Shira, dear, your Aunt Edna was so proud of you." Mrs. Lowendowsky cupped her hand around Shira's cheek. A whiff of her cheap lilac perfume—the signature fragrance of the old—wafted around her.

Her wrinkled face reminded Shira of a peach-colored prune. She wondered if the salon should add *captique* to their line of services. A little dermal filling would do wonders for some of these women—make them feel special and younger.

"What a wonderful thing you're doing, taking care of her beauty parlor," she continued in her thin voice.

It's a salon. And it's mine now. "Thank you, Mrs. Lowendowsky."

The woman touched her stiff 'do then slid her ancient black purse to the crook of her elbow. "Beulah, thank you, dear."

"You're most welcome. See you in two weeks." Beulah hugged her client.

Shira followed Mrs. Lowendowsky outside. She could see the lady's scalp—still pink from her time under the dryer. She made a mental note to pick up Nioxin at the salon supply as she waved goodbye. Mrs. Lowendowsky would see thicker-feeling hair in thirty- to-forty days.

After locking the door and flipping off the exterior lights, Shira took a deep breath and exhaled. Showtime.

"Everyone?"

Three sets of eyes turned toward her. "Five minutes."

Kathy nodded. Harriet rolled her eyes. Beulah stepped up sweeping the hair around her station.

Five minutes later, Shira stood before the mavens holding her file folder containing the good news and bad news. The mavens sat in their respective style chairs, waiting. Harriet puffed away on yet another foul cigarette.

Shira attempted to clear the last of her sentimental emotions from her throat. "First of all, I know it surprised everyone that Aunt Edna gave me her salon."

"You got that right."

She chose to ignore Harriet's murmured insult even though it stuck like a hair-pick in the scalp.

"But obviously she had her reasons for entrusting her salon to me."

Harriet appeared ready for implosion.

The next comment stuck in Shira's gullet. She couldn't believe she was going to do this.

"However . . . ." If this didn't work she would kill Jesse. Cute or not, he was a goner. She swallowed. "Aunt Edna made provisions for each of you to remain at The Hair Mavens no matter what changes are made by me."

Harriet folded her arms across her chest and bobbed her head like one of those bobble heads. "Really?" She smacked her lips. "Is that so?"

Beulah rested her elbows on her knees, smiling. Kathy slipped her hands under her thighs and rocked like some mental patient. Somehow, they reminded Shira of those three monkeys. Hear no evil, see no evil . . .

She pulled copies of the contracts Jesse had given her on Friday. "These are your copies of Aunt Edna's contracts stipulating your bond with The Hair Mavens."

Beulah jumped up and extended her hand. She passed them out to the other two ladies with joy, like a teacher distributing good report cards to her students. Shira allowed them a few seconds to read over the simple, but annoyingly binding agreements.

"So, what I see here is," Harriet narrowed her eyes toward Shira, "you can't get rid of us."

With great restraint, Shira nodded. "True. You can, however, be dismissed should you commit an infraction against the salon's policy."

Harriet jabbed the contract toward Shira. "What is that supposed to mean?"

She raised her brows and smiled. "You break the rules, you go."

"That's baloney!" Harriet rose from her chair. Shira took a step backward.

"Harriet. Calm down." Beulah laid her hand on the old biddy. "Hear her out."

Beehive sunk back into her chair and grumbled something Shira couldn't make out. Like she cared anyway.

"Shira?"

Shira turned her attention toward Beulah who had raised her hand.

"Will there be new rules? New policies?"

"Yes." She opened the file folder and took out four copies of the three-page Mavens manifesto. She placed them on top of the folder. "First, it's apparent this staff needs reminding of Aunt Edna's vision for this salon. Apparently it has long been forgotten. Does anyone even remember the definition of maven?"

Harriet slapped the arms of her chair. "Are you kidding me?"

Despite the enjoyment Shira experienced seeing the Beehive get all stirred up, she considered her options for multiple exit routes in case Harriet decided to go for her.

"I believe the definition of a maven," Beulah said, smiling at Harriet, "is someone who is an expert at something."

"Uh, yes." Who was this woman? "Aunt Edna had called her salon The Hair Mavens because she wanted stylists who were knowledgeable of the latest hair and beauty trends and best ways to serve her clientele."

Beulah nodded her head in agreement.

"So?" Harriet drew her head back until Shira couldn't make out her chin. "What's your point?"

"My point is," Shira brought a fist to her hip, "when was the last time anyone here did a foil? Or used molding wax? When was the last time you attended a hair show or took the time to learn the new styles and products?"

Harriet guffawed.

"You find that funny?"

"Well, yeah. Were you asleep all day?" Harriet pointed toward the door. "Did you see anyone who walked through that door that would be interested in any of that crap?"

"No."

"So . . ."

Shira wished she could wipe the smug look off Harriet's face. "But what if someone did? What happens in five or ten years when most of your clients won't care about wash, set, and curls? The average age of our clients is well over seventy."

Beulah raised her hand again. She blinked several times.

"Yes?"

"Shira, I must agree with you—"

Harriet rose a few inches from her chair. "Beulah, are you nuts?"

Shira wanted to tell Harriet to shut up, but Beulah tapped the agitated behemoth on the knee.

"Harriet, like it or not, she's right." Beulah turned her chair toward Harriet. "Edna used to pay our way to the hair shows, but she had to drag us there. I know it's been ten years, maybe more since she tried. She finally gave up." She swiveled back toward Shira. "We got lazy, I guess, since there wasn't much need."

"Speak for yourself," Harriet said.

Shira had prepared for every possible pushback from these women. She hadn't a clue how to respond to affirmation.

"Shira, dear, tell us what your vision is for The Hair Mavens."

"You'll be sorry, Beulah." Beehive blew a stream of smoke in Shira's direction.

Shira had positioned herself behind the hair dryers to stay out of Harriet's path.

"This is pure, unadulterated horse poop. And there ain't no way you're gonna make us do this." Harriet paced up and down the aisle. "You expect me to smoke outside?" She shook the already-crumpled list at Shira. "You expect customers to smoke outside?"

"Yes, if you want to work here. Yes, if clients want to be served here." Shira folded her arms against her chest to hide the tremors in her hands. She supposed she wasn't as brave as she had thought. Or perhaps it was exhaustion. They had been going at it almost an hour.

"What about this?" Harriet flipped to another page and pointed to something. "No eating at our stations?"

"Correct. We have a perfectly fine break room in the back. Use it."

Harriet threw her hands in the air and let her list fly. Beulah grimaced.

Shira finally switched her attention to the mouse-like Kathy. She hadn't said a word. Unlike Shira, she hadn't hidden her shaky hands. It was a wonder she could even read the paper—it fluttered like a hummingbird. Her long neck had buried itself between her shoulders.

That nagging feeling returned. Kathy raised her chin as if reading something on the ceiling. She removed the hideous glasses to rub her eyes. That feeling increased. Where had she seen her?

Harriet finally bent over to pick up her list. She flipped to another page. "This." She pointed to the center. "This is ridiculous. We have a dress code now?"

"Of course. Makeup and hair styles that reflect our new image," Shira said with a shrug. "No one appearing like they just rolled out of bed." She looked in Kathy's direction.

Harriet yanked on her ratty old smock. "What about these?"

Shira rolled her eyes. "They are the first to go. I've ordered—"

"Over my dead body!" Harriet stomped toward Shira. She held the folder out like a shield and backed up.

"Edna bought these for us." Harriet pulled her collar out. "You remember your aunt? The owner of this establishment?" A vein on her forehead bulged.

Shira's face flushed, and at that moment her underarms were having a spring shower. "As I was saying, I've ordered specially designed half-aprons for styling. Also, I've ordered full aprons for coloring, with the salon's name stitched on them."

"They sound lovely, Shira, don't they, Kathy?" Beulah reached over and stroked Kathy's arm. Kathy lifted one shoulder. No change in her bland expression.

Beulah scooted out of her chair. She walked toward Harriet and Shira. "Harriet, our smocks have definitely seen better days."

Harriet crossed her arms. She transferred her angry stare to Beulah. Beulah didn't seem daunted. She rested her hand on the fuming woman's shoulder. "Wouldn't it be better to take our smocks home? Let them be a sweet memento of our friend? I'd sure hate to have to throw mine away because it's so worn out."

Beulah's diplomacy and soothing voice warmed Shira, but she needed to fight that sentimentality. She couldn't get attached to anyone—especially since she wanted these women out of the salon.

Harriet and Beulah exchanged some unspoken understanding between them. Finally, the stand-off ended. They walked arm in arm back to their chairs.

"Shira?" Beulah raised her hand. Shira couldn't help smiling.

"Yes."

"Will you be teaching us some of the newer techniques you learned at Élégance Salon and Spa?"

Shira studied Beulah's wide, smooth face. Her shoulder-length brown hair was nearly white and held back by two tortoiseshell barrettes—like a high schooler from the eighties. Her eyes reflected a delicate innocence. Yet there was strength and determination. She reminded Shira of someone . . .

Aunt Edna.

A lump formed in her throat. She opened her mouth to answer the question, but only a hoarse fragment came out. She covered her mouth with a fist and swallowed around the growing mass of sentiment.

Stop. Don't get attached to her.

What was going on? This was not going as she expected.

15

Beulah rolled down her window. "Well Lord, that wasn't so bad."

The night air refreshed her. This morning had begun as one of the top ten worst days of her life and ended with a sense of hope and excitement. She took in deep breaths and tapped her fingers on the steering wheel to the Marty Goetz CD Edna had given her on her last birthday.

"And you shall love the Lord your God . . ." Marty's amazing voice and lyrics always took Beulah to that place of worship.

"Yes, Lord. I do love You. Thank You for being present during the meeting with Shira. We sure need Your wisdom in the days ahead."

Beulah was no fool. She knew Shira planned to make major changes to Mavens—to transform it more like where she had worked in New York. She also knew the three of them did not fit into those plans.

Up ahead, Beulah spotted Shady Pines Nursing Home's rustic wood sign. She slowed down, turned on her blinker, then pulled into the parking lot. And there was a spot right up front. "Oh, thank You, Lord," she whispered.

The automatic sliding glass doors opened as she approached the entrance. The brightly lit sterile, reception area was generally quiet this time of night. She glanced at her watch. *Oh my, eight forty-five.* Visiting hours would be over in fifteen minutes.

She bent over the modular counter to see who was working tonight. Good, it was Franny. She loved her Jamaican accent.

"Hi Franny."

"Miss Beulah." She pointed to the large wall clock above her. "A little late tonight, *mon.*"

"We had a meeting at the salon." Beulah rested her elbows on the counter top. "So, how was my honey today?"

She gave Beulah a tight smile. "'Bout de same. He was a little more agitated this evening. He seemed to be in more pain so Doctor increased his meds." She shook her plaited head and laughed. "He not going to be much company."

Wilbur hadn't been much company in a long time. She walked the long stretch of hallway until she reached room 108. The door was ajar. The TV volume was low. Wil seemed more peaceful when it was left on a nature channel.

Her husband's familiar snore resonated in the room. She kissed him on the cheek, then smoothed back a lock of silver hair from his temple. She laid her purse on the end of the bed and pulled up the plastic molded chair. Despite the slackness of his right side, he was still a handsome man. After thirty-nine years, she loved him so. How she missed his humor, his bravery and natural romance. His touch. He could never resist touching her any time she was near.

She sighed. Wil's hand curled in a stiff awkward position from the strokes. She gently picked it up and laid it on her palm. "I'm so sorry I'm late, sweetheart." With her finger she traced the scar that ran from his ring finger up his arm to his shoulder. One of the many injuries from his years as a fireman.

"I had a meeting tonight." She stroked his hand. "It sure was a doozy." She chuckled.

Wil's face moved. Was that a smile? *No.*

"Anyway, I don't think Harriet is going to be very cooperative. Truthfully, Wil, Shira wants to fire all of us. But she can't."

She brought Wilbur's hand to her lips. "Know why?" She paused even though she didn't expect an answer. "Because Edna made provisions for the three of us. Praise the Lord. Shira can't fire us—unless we break her new rules. We can quit if we want to. But as long as there is a Hair Mavens, we have jobs." She laid his hand back on the bed and straightened the covers around him.

"Shira has all sorts of new-fangled ideas for the shop." She walked around his small room straightening things that didn't need straightening. She went to the window and opened the blinds. A haze surrounded the full moon.

"For some reason I'm excited. Shira can teach us so many new styling techniques. She'll most likely draw more young people into the shop, and that will make the place alive. Fun again."

She folded her hands and brought them to her chin. "Oh, Wil, I'm more excited than I've been in a long time." She looked over her shoulder in his direction. "It means I'll probably be working more hours, sweetheart. I'll check with Franny to see if I can stay a little later, or come a little earlier before I start work."

The tone announcing the end of visiting hours came over the PA system. She gathered her bag then kissed his forehead. "I'll check with her right now."

Optimism and purpose gave Beulah a little bounce to her steps as she approached the reception counter. Franny peered up from a file with a furrowed brow.

"Franny, would it be okay if I stayed another fifteen minutes or so?"

"Yeah, mon. Dat fine, Miss Beulah." She chewed on her lower lip.

"Are you all right?"

Franny stood with the folder. "Let's you and me sit in the lounge, Beulah. I need to discuss dis matter with you again."

Beulah's heart charged up into her throat bringing a warm flush to her face. She couldn't bring herself to look at Franny because she knew what the nurse was going to tell her.

"Miss Beulah, I need to talk with you about your husband's medication bills. You are *tree* months behind."

Shira flopped onto the couch and kicked off her shoes. She was spent. Done in. All she wanted right now was to run a hot bath and soak for an hour. The oven clock glowed nine thirty. Somehow it felt so much later.

The loud brrring of the kitchen phone jarred her tired bones.

Who in the world would be calling her on that thing? She rolled off the couch and trudged to the phone. No caller ID. Maybe it was Cari?

"Hello?"

"Shira? Babe, it's me." Alec, the-missing-boyfriend.

"Alec. Where have you been?" Without warning, she bawled.

"Hey. Hey," he said. "It's okay. I'm here now."

"No, you're not." She rubbed her nose on her jacket. "I left like a gazillion messages for you." She pulled out a kitchen chair and dropped onto it.

"Right. Well, babe, things have been crazy. Good crazy, but crazy. You know?"

He had no idea. "So Fawna told me you got the part."

"Yeah, yeah. I told you that. Didn't I?"

"No, Alec. I haven't spoken with you since last Wednesday." Irritation rode her tone like a cowboy.

"Right. Right." He cleared his throat. "So how are things going there?"

"Crazy. Bad crazy, but crazy."

He gave her that fake, distracted laugh. "Listen, babe, when are you coming back?"

Now there was something. She hadn't much thought about Alec in the scheme of all her plans. Strange. "I'm not sure, Alec." She twirled a strand of hair. "I may not come back."

"Ha-ha, real funny, Shira. Really, when are you coming back?"

"I'm serious, Alec."

"You won't last two weeks in that Podunk town. Besides, what about us?"

"What about us? Where have you been?" Her bundle of raw insecurities was too exposed. Anger, fear, and sadness tumbled together like so many socks in a dryer. "I needed you, Alec. Where were you?"

"Right here, babe, where you should be." His voice had a spiteful tenor. "It's not like you want to be there. How many times have you been back there since I've known you? Like nada."

At this point, she was glad he wasn't here.

"Listen, babe, pack up your junk and leave Losersville. Sell the place— make a couple hundred grand. Beg Veronica for your job. I happen to have it on good authority that she needs you, but she won't admit it. Plead on your hands and knees if you have to. You'll make three times what you could make there."

Something didn't feel right. She hadn't dated Alec for his compassion. But now, when she needed a little kindness, he was acting like a money-hungry jerk.

The call waiting beeped.

"Hold on, Alec. I have another call."

"Wait—"

She didn't wait. Really, she'd rather talk with a telemarketer than him. "Hello?"

"Shira, it's Jesse. I'm sorry to call so late."

Another wave of emotion crashed down on her. She attempted to shove it back. "It's okay, Jesse." Her voice squeaked. "What—what's up?"

"Well, I figured today was probably a little rough on you. Have you eaten?"

There was no way he hadn't heard the glob of gooey sadness. Further evidence—as if she needed more—that this guy was a mensch. "No, I haven't eaten. You're so sweet. But frankly, I'm too tired to go out."

"No, no. I brought Chinese."

Brought? She stretched the phone cord and glanced out the door to the small veranda. "Where are you?"

"On the sidewalk."

Laying the phone on the floor, she opened the door and leaned over the wrought iron railing. There he was. Her heart skipped. She couldn't have wiped the smile off her face with a sandblaster.

With his cell still against his ear, he held up a plastic bag. She waved. This must have been how Julia Roberts felt seeing Richard Gere in Pretty Woman. "You're an angel. I'll be right down."

She hung up the phone and turned toward the door when it rang again.

"Did you forget something?" she chuckled.

"Babe, you're the one who forgot something. Me."

Alec.

"Alec, something's come up. I have to go. I'll talk to you later. Bye." She hung up hard. Hoping her resolve got through to Alec.

She dashed to the stairs. *Wait. I must look like a bad hair day poster child.*

A quick detour to the bathroom was critical. She groaned at her reflection. Not much she could do with the fatigue that had run circles under her eyes. She finger-combed her hair as best she could and took off her jacket and threw it behind the shower curtain. The phone rang again but she ignored it.

A travel-size bottle of Scope rested on the sink. Twisting off the cap, she took a swig, swished it around then spit. After a cursory inspection of the bathroom for any unmentionables hanging about, she sprinted for the door.

She clomped down the stairs to the salon, the racket sounding like a herd of elephants. Reducing her pace a little—she didn't want to appear too anxious—she finally reached the door and unlocked the dead bolt.

There he was, her—uh, her lawyer. She rested her cheek against the door. "Hi, Jesse."

"Good evening, Shira." His gorgeous smile deepened the dimple in his chin. "I hope you like hot and sour soup, wings, and chicken fried rice."

"Are you kidding? It's my favorite." Funny thing, it really was her favorite. She grabbed the plastic bag from him. The amazing aroma of spices, onions, and soy sauce revved up her hunger.

"Excellent." He shrugged off his leather jacket.

Okay, this wasn't fair. He wore a Ralph Lauren white cotton button-down and jeans. *Leather jacket. White shirt. And jeans. Oh my.*

"You okay?"

"Uh, huh." She smiled like an idiot.

"Where would you like to eat?" He folded his jacket across his arm.

"Upstairs, I guess." Her feet seemed rooted to the linoleum, and she couldn't seem to stop grinning.

He extended his arm toward the back of the shop. "Lead the way."

A whiff of his spicy cologne encircled her. Now her knees were doing funny things. She pivoted to lead the way but ran smack into the manicurist's table. "Yowch!" She massaged her hip.

Jesse came up behind her. "Are you all right?" He took the bag from her as he lightly touched her shoulder. His brief contact seared through her blouse. *Steady, Shira.*

"Sure, I'm great." She rubbed her hip a few times as she limped forward.

"Oh, my gosh!" Jesse ran back outside with their dinner.

His abrupt departure unsettled her. Something akin to abandonment snaked into her mind. She didn't know if she should shut the door and call it an odd night or remain in the hopes this all wasn't some cruel joke.

In the distance she heard a car door slam. She swallowed and continued to stare into the darkness outside. *Please don't leave. Please don't leave.*

Footsteps on the sidewalk.

Jesse strode into the reception area. He held up a pink bakery box, grinning and completely clueless to Shira's journey into the pit of her emotions. "Almost forgot our dessert."

She didn't have the heart to tell him there were enough sweets for a month scattered around the salon. "What's inside?"

He winked. "It's a surprise."

Yeah? Like she needed any more of those.

Shira entered the apartment first and headed to the dining room to retrieve the good china. Jesse set the bag and pink dessert box on the counter. He opened the silverware drawer on the first try. *Hmm.* He knew his way around this kitchen.

The table was set with the Welmar china, the Waterford crystal, chopsticks, spoons, and paper and plastic take-out containers. Elegant and disposable—how eclectic.

She reached for the container of soup. Jesse covered her hand with his. "Shira, do you mind if I thank the Lord for our meal?"

Whatever. "Sure." She withdrew her hand and dutifully closed her eyes.

"Abba, thank You for this meal. Thank You for the good company. *Baruch ata Adonai Eloheynu Melech haolam, hamotzi lechem min haeretz, beShem Yeshua.* Amen."

As if thrown back into her childhood, she joined Jesse in the ancient Hebrew blessing. Apparently it would take more time to eradicate that Messianic influence.

Jesse beamed his approval. *Humph. Doesn't mean I'm going religious, buddy, so don't get your hopes up.* She gave a half-hearted smile.

As she poured the soup into bowls, Jesse dished up the fried rice. "So, tell me how the meeting went."

Her blow-by-blow account brought about a few raised eyebrows, but mostly Jesse nodded enough times for her to believe he approved of most of her conduct. Which, as much as she hated to admit, pleased her.

He pointed his chopsticks toward her as he finished chewing. "It sounds like Beulah has captured your vision, Shira."

She shrugged. "I think she merely wants to keep her job."

"Of course she wants to keep her job. It's more than that. She also wants to please and support you."

"Why?" She gnawed on a teriyaki chicken wing.

"Because you're her boss and her best friend's niece." He shoved another bite of fried rice into his mouth.

Shira expelled a disgusted breath. Why did he have to spoil this nice evening with his predictable rhetoric? "Jesse, you're not going to convince me that Beulah or any of the other mavens are good for the salon. This is not some plan of God." She snatched the rice container to see if any was left. Empty.

Jesse slid most of his rice onto her plate. "Listen, if you could only see beyond this need to prove to your dad—"

"Prove to my father? How dare—" She shoved her plate. "You know what? I'm tired, and I don't want to talk about this anymore. I appreciate the dinner, but I need to go to bed."

He latched his gorgeous brown orbs onto hers. "Sorry, Shira. I didn't mean to force my opinions on you."

"Fine. Do you mind if we call this a night?" She scooted back her chair and got up. He did the same then retrieved his jacket. He paused at the door, his hand on the knob. The Crisis bags—like a wobbly mountain of compulsion—lay as her accusers at his feet. His head turned only slightly in her direction before he opened the door.

Embarrassment, guilt, and anger churned in her gut as they walked down the stairs. *Just who does he think he is? My father?* The last thing she needed to do was prove herself to anyone.

You'll never amount to anything . . . How many times had her father thrown that little phrase at her while growing up? She didn't need Jesse's condescension. She didn't need her father's approval. All she needed was for Jesse to fulfill his role as her lawyer—not her conscience.

By the time they reached Hair Mavens' entrance she was ready to bite off his head. She gripped the handle and swung open the door, giving him as wide a berth as possible.

He clutched the collar of his leather jacket as though he intended to put it on, but hesitated. Instead, he covered her hand with his. She shivered and clenched the metal knob harder. "Shira, please don't be angry with me."

Too close. He stood too close to her. That yummy cologne.

Shira looked over his head, outside to the street, to the right . . . anywhere but at him. His other hand touched her cheek. She was helpless to evade his nearness.

"I didn't mean to offend you. Please forgive me. I wanted—"

Her head shortened the distance between them. Before she realized, their lips met. Hard.

At first he resisted. Briefly. He returned her kiss with his own intensity—as though her lips had become his dessert, and he hungrily devoured her.

She wrapped her arms around his neck. He moaned as he pulled her tightly against his muscular body.

Like a shipwrecked sailor, she was lost in the ocean of his kisses—long and short. Sweet and deep.

He pulled away for a moment to gaze at her, his eyes half open, dark full lashes shading them. She moved to kiss him again, but his eyes widened as though he'd seen a ghost.

"What have I done?" He disentangled himself from her and stepped aside. She stumbled forward, clutching the jacket over his arm for balance.

"Shira, I shouldn't have . . . I need to go. Please forgive me."

He ran out the door.

She stood holding the jacket—looking like an idiot to anyone who happened by—watching him sprint away from her.

Left again.

A picture flashed in her mind. The Bible story of Joseph and Potiphar's wife. The evil woman had made a pass at the innocent young slave. Rather than succumb to the temptation, he ran—right out of his cloak.

She gawked at Jesse's leather coat in her hand.

Great. Just great.

16

Kathy kicked and clawed. She tried to scream, but his grip was too tight around her throat. Yuri, help me! Edna!

Her eyes popped open. Panting, her body sweaty and tangled in sheets, Kathy sat up. Only a dream. It was only a dream.

She sat on the edge of the couch, forcing herself to feel the wood floor under her feet and calm her breathing. The way Edna had shown her.

Little by little her body relaxed until finally she released her grip on the sheets.

The nightmare had returned the day Edna died. Every night she battled that demon and woke in terror. She clutched her head. Without Edna to talk to, to hold her and tell her all would be well, she feared she would go mad.

The sun had not yet risen. She should get more rest for today. But if she slept, she might dream again.

An hour later Kathy paced back and forth in her sparse apartment like a trapped animal. The salon would not be open for three more hours.

Lightning flashed. She covered her ears, waiting for the boom that would follow.

Raindrops fell against her window like tears. She imagined Edna crying in heaven, wanting to return. But there was no heaven. Only the earth. The ground with the insatiable hunger for those she loved.

She reached for her coffee and tasted the strong brew. Today she would need all the energy possible. She brushed a piece of lint off her Marc Jacobs black slacks. It seemed a lifetime ago when she had bought them in New York.

But her pink blouse was purchased last night—from Walmart. Shira knew her designers—of that Kathy was certain. She smiled. Imagine how confused her new boss would be. Maybe Shira would ask her where she bought her outfit, and Kathy would say, "Walmart. I can buy you one if you want."

She squeaked out a giggle. But Kathy would never say this to Shira. Above all, Kathy had become a coward.

Maybe Harriet would save Hair Mavens. She was strong and loud and not afraid to talk big to Shira.

There were many men in the villages outside Minsk who had talked big. They were part of the Belarusian mafia. Her mama had held her near when they tried to speak with Kathy. The scary men had been fascinated by her violet eyes and cared not that she was only twelve. Somehow, her mother had found a way to come to America, but when she died, there was no one to protect her from Justin.

She shivered and wrapped an arm around her waist. The wood floors were cold against her bare feet. She did not care. It kept her feeling. Helped to keep the darkness from coming back.

There was no peace now. Edna had been her peace. Harriet would make the shop noisy, especially if she forced Shira out.

She squeezed her middle tighter. If Harriet did not succeed, then Shira would change Hair Mavens. She would turn Edna's shop into a place with no heart—like Gooding's. Three years ago she had been one of Fidel's top stylists. He was like Shira. Someone who cared more for money than people.

She could not work at Mavens if Shira won. But she had nowhere else to go. Did she?

The phone sat on the table by the sofa. Her hand gravitated toward it. She set down her mug and picked up the handset then placed it to her ear. The dial tone hurt her head. She could dial or hang up—either way the sound would stop.

How many times had she gone through these motions since running from New York?

Yuri would be getting ready for work now. Shaving. She could even now smell his clean scent. She missed him, but she was no longer what she had been. Did he miss her? Even if he did miss her, he would hate her . . . eventually.

She replaced the receiver and walked away.

The crack of thunder vibrated Harriet's bones like an electrical charge. That was close.

A ciggy rested in the *v* of her fingers as she drew back the curtains. Figured. Raining cats and dogs. *Great. Just great.*

Thanks to the brat, she would be smoking in a monsoon. And what about all their clients who smoked? Her old, neon-yellow rain slicker hung over the desk chair. It was ghastly ugly but would come in handy. She picked at a stain on the sleeve. All she needed was a hand-held stop sign and she'd look like a school crossing guard.

"Excuse me, ma'am. I need to cross the street," she mimicked a kid's voice.

Her wheezy chuckle turned into a cough. She grabbed her coffee and quickly took a swig. The brew paled in comparison to Nonni's. On the table was her half-eaten toast and jam—a poor substitute for her cherry cheese Danish. But she couldn't bring herself to go to Delicious Bakery alone.

Could she ask Bob-the-insurance-guy to go?

Nah.

Normally she would be at Mavens by now. She tapped the ashes into the ashtray. Her whole schedule was off. She and Edna would have been chatting over their coffee and pastries. Planning the day.

A lump formed in her throat. She took a long drag and held it until the nicotine kicked in. This line of thinking would get her nowhere. Better to focus on her battle strategies for the day. If the three of them stuck together—as long as Beulah quit brownnosing—they would run Shira out in no time.

Her plan of attack rested on the kitchen table next to various empty Ben and Jerry's containers, Tastykake wrappers, and a full ashtray. Shira's new policy was crumpled up in a ball in the corner of the kitchen somewhere.

When she first got home from the stupid meeting last night, she was kicking furniture and throwing pillows. After she broke one of her mother's Hummel figurines, she restrained herself. Which set her mind racing with an assortment of homicidal thoughts. That went on for a while—the time it took to polish off the chocolate-chocolate mint ice cream.

Then she had watched a Criminal Minds rerun and gotten a couple more ideas for how to get rid of the brat. Finally, she realized something constructive was needed to force Shira out of Hair Mavens. Ultimately this would have more lasting benefits, as she didn't want to spend her retirement in prison.

She returned to her command station to review her plan of attacks. The chair moaned as though complaining that her behind had returned. She picked up her Bob Henry Insurance ballpoint pen and clicked it. Locked and loaded.

Attack one: do not answer the phones. Beulah would probably have trouble with this one. She was forever running to answer the phone. Harriet didn't think Kathy had ever answered it, so no problem there.

She moved the pen down to the next paragraph.

Attack two: do not do the laundry. It had always been an unwritten rule at Mavens that whoever had free time would run a load of towels. Next to the front door was a beach bag of extra towels she would use when the shop ran out of clean ones. Once she met with Beulah and Kathy alone, she'd tell them to do the same tomorrow.

Attack three: do not sell product. Recommend products they can purchase from Walmart or Kmart. She laughed. This would really infuriate the stuck-up brat.

The rest of the ideas? She might have trouble getting goody-two-shoes Beulah to do them, things like erasing phone messages, or using too much shampoo and conditioner or color and peroxide.

Oh. Maybe even hide some of Shira's stuff. *Oooo. Good one, old girl.* She quickly jotted down the newest scheme.

The Mouse shouldn't give her a hard time. As long as neither of them prevented her from carrying out her plans, this should work. And if not, if she had to play hardball, there were other ideas she could pull out of her beehive. She chuckled.

Either way, Shira was history.

The burning in her stomach returned and caused her to swallow around a lump in her throat. The sensation had plagued her most of the previous night as she laid out her strategies. Was it guilt?

She sniffed. She had nothing to be guilty about. This all could have been handled in a civil way. The ten thousand dollars from Edna would have given Shira some nice pocket money for her trip to Beverly Hills. And then Hair Mavens would be safe in Harriet's more than capable hands.

Instead, the brat stole the salon right out from under her.

Yes. Shira was history.

17

"Hullo?" Shira fumbled the phone to her ear and managed to open one eye. It worked hard to focus on the flamingo wall clock on the opposite wall. Six-fifty-five? Five minutes before the alarm went off—she hated that.

"Shira, honey, it's Dad. Did I wake you?"

Her heart skipped. "What's wrong?"

"Everything's okay. I guess I should call for more than bad news."

"Dad, it's too early for jokes." She sat up and propped a couple pillows behind her. "What's going on?"

He cleared his throat. "I had a few minutes before I leave for the airport—"

"Where are you going?" Was that rain outside? She bent forward, trying to see through the mini-blinds.

"Have to meet some vendors in Toronto about a faulty landing gear mechanism."

TMI. Who cares about landing gear mechanisms? *Oops. Maybe I do.* "Well, have a safe flight. The weather is bad out there."

"Thanks, honey."

Silence.

"Dad, was there something else?"

He cleared his throat. "I wanted to check to see how you were doing."

"Why?" She stretched the word into several syllables.

"Jesse stopped by last night."

Her face heated as she pulled the covers up to her chin. She felt like she had been caught doing something wrong. Hmm, maybe that was more accurate than she liked. Did her father intend to ground her now?

"He was pretty shook up, honey. Also a little embarrassed."

Her father was taking Jesse's side? The old wall rose between them.

"And you are telling me this because?"

"He said he took advantage of you—"

She managed to restrain a belly laugh. "Well, that's one way of looking at it." *Actually, Daddy dear, I threw myself at him.*

"He repented to me."

"To you?" This wasn't funny.

"He said he apologized to you, and as your father he wanted to apologize to me."

"What a *schlemiel.*" She reached back, grabbed a pillow, and threw it at nothing in particular. It landed on her desk knocking over one of the snow globes. "Whatever, Dad."

"Are you angry?"

"Yes." She jumped out of bed. This conversation was better done on her feet. "Frankly, this is none of your business. Jesse and I need to work it out on our own as adults."

"Of course."

"I don't get why you called, Dad." She ran her hand through her tangled bed head.

He groaned. "This isn't going very well, is it?" He whew'd. "Shira, I apologize."

"Enough with the apologies." She plopped on the edge of the bed and rested her elbows on her knees. "Dad, truthfully, this is weird and really embarrassing. I'm not accustomed to you being a part of my life. You haven't been there for over ten years." She cringed a little—that had to have hurt his feelings. She nibbled on a thumbnail.

"And for that, I'm truly sorry, Shira."

Another apology. More words.

"I wasn't there for you. I was too wrapped up in your mother's illness and then the pain of losing her. It was selfish of me. I seem to be pretty out of practice as a father."

Wasn't that what Jesse had said to her at lunch last week? She rested her forehead on her palm and felt the sinus pressure of tears.

Her alarm went off. She startled, then groped for the alarm-off button. "Dad, do we really need to rehash this at seven o'clock in the morning?"

A roll of thunder drew her attention to the window. A real storm was developing. Fitting.

"Sweetheart, it seems like you'll be sticking around now—much to my delight. But it's time we come to terms with my being the world's worst father."

Images of Jesse, battered and homeless, came to mind. "You weren't the world's worst father."

"So, you're maybe goink to nominate me for 'Vatter of de Year,' mein doighter? Humm?"

A chuckle escaped. She'd forgotten how his hundred-year-old Yiddish man imitation had always made her laugh. She covered her mouth so a full-on laugh didn't sneak out.

"Shira, will you forgive me? Can we work together at figuring out what kind of relationship we can have?"

Her heart knew the answer. Her mind fought it.

"Yes," she croaked out. "And yes."

18

Harriet's plan was working better than she had hoped. She glimpsed her own reflection as she unrolled the hair of her second-best friend, Billie Mae.

So far she had managed to suppress the laughter, but she sure couldn't wipe the grin off her face. The brat had run around in circles all day. Right now Shira's usual graceful movements were choppy and awkward. Her normally perfect hair had odd poufs where she had run her hands through in frustration. Even without Beulah's cooperation—and Harriet was gonna need to have a long talk with that woman—Shira was showing definite signs of defeat.

Outside the sun shone. The storm had blown over before Mavens opened, so she had actually enjoyed taking little breaks to smoke in the lovely weather. One or two of her clients had joined her each time—and she had been a ready ear for their complaints at being relegated outside, too.

Those little jaunts also made it easy to fake not being able to hear the phones. Who would have guessed Shira's stupid no-smoking rule would have fit into her plan? She could kiss that Smoke-Free Environment sign on the door.

The shop was filled with people. Wednesdays were always one of Edna's busiest days. Harriet loved the sound of feminine conversations, hair dryers, and laughter. She pulled a fresh stick of gum from her drawer and snuck another peek at her reflection. *Edna, you'd be so proud of me.*

Shortly after she'd arrived this morning, she came upon another brilliant idea. While reviewing her appointments in the book, she jotted down Shira's Friday and Saturday appointments. She would call them tonight and reschedule them all for tomorrow—but not make the corrections to the appointment book. Shira thought she had been busy today? Just wait.

She took her time pulling the hard plastic curlers from Billie Mae's locks.

Next to Edna, Billie was her best friend—although Billie didn't always see eye-to-eye with Edna's religion. Still, Billie was a hoot, and she'd been doing her hair since before beauty school.

"You look like the cat that swallowed the canary, Harriet." Billie Mae stared at her in the mirror.

Warmth covered her cheeks. "Whatever do you mean?" Harriet diverted her attention to organizing her curler drawer.

"Uh huh." Billie's smock lifted as she snaked out her hand to grab Harriet. "So dish," she whispered, the smell of bourbon wafting around her.

Harriet's next appointment wasn't for thirty minutes; she could fill Billie in on the scheme outside—at her sanctioned smoking area, away from the salon. "Not here." Harriet whispered back. "After I finish you, we'll go outside."

Billie wouldn't mind waiting. She loved a good scandal and frankly lived the life of ease. Her friend seemed pretty relaxed right now. 'Course the bourbon she smelled on Billie might have something to do with that, too. All of this was fitting together, but she still didn't feel full cooperation from Beulah and Mouse. It would be good to have a co-conspirator like Billie. She could be pretty devious. Her gut did a flip-flop. Maybe that wasn't such a good idea.

She shrugged. Too late now—she'd already alluded to a scheme and Billie had taken the hook.

Beulah rushed behind her. "Sorry. Wil's doctor called." Everyone muttered words of comfort as Beulah exited.

Now Shira had no one to help with the phones. Even Harriet had to wonder if there was some divine intervention on her behalf. She chuckled.

Too bad Kathy worked today. Shira would have had to take all Beulah's clients. Still, to the Mouse's credit, she hadn't put up a fuss about Harriet's other sabotages. She was always in her own little world anyway.

She fished in her blazer pocket—she missed her smock from Edna—for her magic wand. The magical tool that did miracles on all hair types. It was a combination of comb and metal pick. Harriet had seen it demonstrated way back in the 1990s at one of those hair shows Edna had always been trying to get them to attend. The thing was vintage—so what if it was missing a metal prong. But with her know-how and this little baby, she was like a drill sergeant, making thin flat hair jump up and stand at attention.

"So, Billie Mae." Harriet worked her magic, beginning with teasing the curls stiff from gel. "Are you taking that trip to Cancun after all?"

She placed her hand with the big rock over her heart. "Oh yes. Patrick said we'd celebrate our thirty-fifth anniversary on the beach."

Forget doctors and lawyers—Harriet knew the truth—plumbing contractors were where the big money was. Billie Mae's husband had started with one truck. Now, everywhere a person looked there was a

Patrick Gallagher truck. He was right up there with Donald Trump.

"Thirty-fifth, huh?"

"Seems like yesterday." She gave a girlish sigh. "He still makes my toes curl."

Harriet was no prude, but she hated all this romantic nonsense. Maybe because her ex had made his secretary's toes curl eighteen years ago.

"You got yourself a good one, Billie Mae." She focused on her work and not the knot of emotion in the back of her throat.

"Oh, Harriet, I'm sorry." Billie craned her neck to look back at her. "Ray was a rat. You'll find a good one. You mark my words."

She grunted. "Ain't nothing worth anything out there for me." She lightly combed the top of the teasing then smoothed it over with her palm. "Besides, I don't want a man complicating my life. I like things the way they are."

Billie Mae lowered her chin and stared at her in the mirror. "Oh, really?" With a subtle tip of her head toward Shira, she gave Harriet a knowing smirk. "Just the way you like it?"

She tilted closer to her friend. "I'm workin' on that."

Billie Mae hooted.

Shira glanced in their direction. Those perfectly plucked brows knitted into a *v*. Harriet merely smiled at her, then she rested her chin on Billie's shoulder. They snickered softly.

"By the way, Harriet." Billie glanced from side to side, then partially covered her mouth with her palm to whisper, "I have an idea that will fix the brat's fanny."

Harriet leaned closer.

Shira's body shook.

Don't cry. Don't cry. Her fingers trembled so badly that this was her third attempt to roll the same section of hair on Mrs. Griffith's head.

It felt like high school all over again when the blonde, blue-eyed cheerleaders had whispered behind her back.

This day was right up there as one of the worst days of her life. She shifted her back toward the two cronies. *Don't let the Beehive get to you, Shira.*

The waffling tone of the phone broadcasted to the salon and the crowd of women waiting in the reception area, "Shira is overwhelmed and not able to do the job." She gripped the tail of her rattail comb and tried not to hyperventilate before dashing to answer it.

Please, I need help. The door opened. *No, please, not another client.*

Someone carried a huge bouquet of flowers. The colorful bundle shifted and the most beautiful face appeared. Cari.

"Shirry! Look what came for you." Cari's red hair and wide smile felt like a ray of sunshine. "I grabbed them from the delivery guy."

Shira's lower lip trembled—she sucked it in. "Care-bear." Her voice barely carried over the clamor of the salon.

"Want me to get that phone for you?" she said as she set the vase of flowers on the counter then stretched to reach the handset. "Good afternoon, The Hair Mavens. How may I help you?" Cari winked.

What had made Cari come by the salon? Shira wasn't going to question why—she was simply grateful.

Cari spent five hours answering phones, doing laundry, and sweeping up so Shira could work non-stop on her clients. If she believed in them, Shira would have said it was a miracle that Cari just happened to stop by.

She watched in awe as Cari finished entering an appointment in the book and hung up the phone. "Girlfriend, this place is happening." Cari lifted the cumbersome book to flip through several curled pages. They were nearly full.

"Thanks again, Cari." Shira finished blow-drying Betty Wilson's hair. The one client she had been able to convince to try something new. "Don't you need to get home to your husband?"

Her cherubic lips pouted. "He's in Texas on a business trip." She waggled her eyebrows. "I'm all yours tonight."

The salon was pretty much empty now. Beulah had finally made it back around four. Shira had wanted to ask if everything was okay, but then thought better of it. She didn't want to get involved—or seem like she was interested. Even though she was.

Fortunately, Cari had asked, so Shira had learned it wasn't a life or death emergency. Beulah had left with Harriet and Kathy nearly an hour ago.

Applying a light spritz to Betty's hair, Shira passed the large hand mirror to her. She swiveled the chair around so Betty could inspect the back.

Mrs. Wilson moved the mirror and her head until she got a good view. "Oh, Shira," she said, gently touching the back of her 'do. "Oh my. I love it." Shira turned the chair back around, allowing her client to further inspect her new style. She lifted and lowered her chin, then shifted her head from side to side to examine the simple layer cut. "It's wonderful. I've never had bangs like this before."

Good grief. It was only a razor cut. "I'm glad you like them, Betty. All you need to do after you shower is run some of this gel through your roots with your fingertips." Shira held up the ancient product Mavens sold—she couldn't wait until her Ecru order came in. "Then turn your head upside down and shake. For a dressier look use your hot rollers. I left enough length for you."

She unsnapped the styling cape, revealing Betty's colorful nurse's uniform. Shira had to admit it matched the woman's cheerful disposition.

"Well, I'm telling all my friends to come here." She scooted forward to step out of the styling chair then leaned closer to the mirror. "Edna said you've won all sorts of awards in Paris."

"A few." She smiled.

A slim, freckled arm slid around Shira's shoulder. "Don't let her modesty fool you, Betty." Cari pressed her face next to Shira's. "You just had your hair done by the top stylist of New York's crème de la crème."

Her impressed client scrunched up her shoulders. "My, my. All the girls on the pediatrics floor will hear about this."

Nurse Wilson left the salon with a spring in her step and a bag of the gel and hairspray. Shira swept up around her station. Cari folded another load of freshly laundered towels. After counting the receipts, preparing the deposit, and placing it in the safe, fatigue blanketed Shira's body. She cradled her head in her arms on the counter.

From behind, Cari massaged her neck.

"Care-bear, I don't think I'm going to be good company tonight." She didn't even try to stifle a yawn.

Cari stepped toward the flowers and sniffed them.

Shira had completely forgotten about them. How thoughtless of her for not even thanking her friend. "Cari, I'm so sorry for not thanking you for those—"

Cari placed her hands on her hips. "Shira, aren't you the least bit curious who sent you the flowers?"

Shira raised her head. "You mean you didn't?"

She shook her head.

Alec?

Shira gently parted the luscious bouquet. The complex fragrance of roses, carnations, and freesia charmed and revived her senses. The little pink envelope with the Petal Pusher logo revealed itself. As she withdrew the card, her heart beat a little faster.

> *Sorry, Shira. Please forgive me.*
>
> *Can we still be friends?*
>
> *Fondly, Jesse.*

Friends? Fondly?

Cari raised her palms and moved them back and forth rapidly—the universal Jewish sign for *Well? So tell me already.*

"It's from Jesse." She laid the card face down on the counter.

"Jesse?" Her hands went back to her hips. "And when were you going to tell me about this?"

"There is no this—er— That is . . ." She huffed. "Okay, I made a pass at him."

"What?"

"I kissed him."

Cari rested her elbows on the counter and propped her chin on her hands. "And did he kiss you back?"

The memory of his hungry lips sent tingles down Shira's spine. She flipped the card over. "Oh, yeah."

Cari pursed her lips. "You know he is the most eligible bachelor at Beth Ahav?"

Like I would know this? Shira shrugged.

"Well, he never dates. The single women over eighteen won't leave him alone. I don't think he's ever cooked a meal in the two years since he moved here because casseroles, briskets, and kugels show up on his doorstep with scented notes from wanna-be Mrs. Foxes." Cari's stare tried to probe Shira's thoughts.

"Your point?"

"Shira, he's never showed an interest in anyone before. The only people he hung around with were Aunt Edna, your father, and the people in the law office."

Shira raised her hands and lifted her shoulders. "I still don't get it."

"Awk!" Cari covered her eyes. "Shira, you've been in town a week and he's kissing you. Sending you flowers. He likes you—"

"Except he ran away from me like he was Joseph and I was Potiphar's wife. It felt like one of Rabbi Joel's bad youth group skits."

Cari threw her head back and laughed. And laughed. Annoyance shoved out Shira's lower lip. She squirmed as her friend bent over, holding her midsection.

At last, Cari calmed herself enough to wipe a few tears, then hold Shira's hands. "I'm sorry, Shirry. But I imagined him in a loin cloth, his curly hair flopping as he runs down the sidewalk." Another spasm of laughter erupted.

"Well, I'm not laughing." Shira pulled her hands from Cari's grasp. "It was humiliating. His leather 'cloak' is still in the closet."

A squeal erupted from Cari as she sprinted to the closet. She yanked out the coat, which increased her hilarity. A glare from Shira shut Cari's lips tight. She covered her mouth with the jacket attempting to hold in the giggles.

She's so cute. How can I stay mad at her?

With great flourish Cari returned the evidence of Shira's embarrassment to the closet.

"I don't know the last time I've laughed so hard." She sighed.

Shira gave her a half smile and tugged a red curl. "Can we change the subject, please?"

"Certainly." She dragged Shira from the reception booth, then pushed her toward the back of the salon. "I say let's order Chinese—"

"No!" Shira stopped in her tracks. "Anything but Chinese."

"Why? You love Chinese."

"Pizza is good. Order a cheese-steak pizza."

She shrugged and resumed pulling her. "Okay, you're the boss. I'll lock up, you go call."

After their pizza was delivered, they each sat on opposite ends of the couch with their feet touching in the center—the way they had done as teenagers. They balanced plates of pizza on their knees. The mozzarella cheese was thick and stringy, the way she liked it. "So how long is Aaron in Texas?"

Cari finished her bite before answering. "He'll be home day after tomorrow." She examined her pizza, then picked up a large clump of steak and popped it into her mouth. "You want me to come in tomorrow to help again?"

Shira laid her pizza back onto her plate and pushed against her friend's feet. Cari looked up. "You would do that for me?"

"Of course." Cari shrugged a shoulder and picked at her pizza again. "I won't be able to come as early as I did today. I have a faculty meeting, but I can be here around four. Is that okay?"

She swallowed. "More than okay. I'll pay you."

She tsked. "Don't be silly." Cari's attention was drawn toward a corner of the living room.

"Shirry?" She pointed her pizza toward the door. "What's in the bags?"

"I forget." And that was the truth, she was sorry to say.

Cari studied Shira with those green eyes. "You don't have to tell me if you don't want to."

"Honestly, Care, I bought the stuff a couple days ago. I don't remember." She tried to focus on her pizza. "I ran in and ran out."

She continued to stare. Shira knew that look. Her friend was trying to read her. Did Cari remember the Crisis journal? Shira squirmed. "Cari, you want to go through beauty supply catalogs? I want to get some ideas for remodeling."

She smiled before taking another bite of pizza. "Uh huh. Have an architect lined up?"

"Not yet. Frankly, I don't know where to begin except Google."

She shoved Shira's feet. "I have the perfect guy. He—"

"—goes to Beth Ahav, right?"

Cari chewed and tried to appear innocent.

"Fine. I'm desperate. Have him contact me."

She nibbled her bottom lip. Her friend was cooking up something else. "What? What's going on in that head, Lucy?"

"You know, Ethel." Cari giggled. "You really could use some help. Things are only going to get busier at The Hair Mavens."

"Any suggestions?"

"Actually, yes." Her rosebud lips stretched into a smile. "Melly."

"Melissa Cohen?" The kid she had babysat—changed her diapers?

"Yes. She's been applying for part-time jobs. As a senior, her class schedule is flexible for career-related jobs."

"She's not planning on college?" Melly had always been such a smart little thing.

Cari's eyelids dropped. "She missed a lot of school the last few years. College is not a viable option for her right now."

Shira shoved Cari's feet. "What are you not telling me?"

She bit her bottom lip. "Melly had leukemia."

Melissa? Cancer?

"It's okay, Shirry. She's been in remission for six months. Melly just needs some normalcy back in her life. She would love working for you."

Cari had a heart of gold. Shira's business sense said, no way. The last thing she needed was another complication. But her friend's hopeful countenance contended against her common sense. Besides, after everything Cari had done for her—especially this last week—how could she not take Cari's recommendation? "Have her stop by. I'll interview her."

Cari's smile did little to convince Shira it was the right decision.

Her friend tossed the last bite of pizza into her mouth and winked. "Sounds like a plan."

We'll see.

Beulah's stomach percolated waves of nausea. A stack of bills—nearly as tall as her mug—mocked her open checkbook on the coffee table, adding insult to injury for this perfectly dreadful day.

She flung herself against the couch. Another round of tears wrestled her desire for control. The living room walls and tabletops were filled with photos of her family in better times, and she tried focusing on the many blessings she had over the years. But her efforts only seemed to embolden the despair that tried to drag her into that dark place.

Next to her was the photo of Wil and their handsome son, Tom. She had snapped the photo as her men held up their string of fish. They had all been so proud and happy. A perfect day at the Jersey shore.

Right now, it only reminded her of her loneliness. She couldn't put it off any longer. She needed to call their son. Let him know his father had taken a turn for the worse . . . and his mother had bungled the finances so badly she might lose the house.

Wil's body was in the early stages of shutting down. The doctor had called her at the salon to come in for a consult. She bent forward to rest her head in her hands, unable to stop rehashing the events of that afternoon.

The doctor had sat back in his chair, his hands folded except for his pointer fingers. She couldn't help thinking of that old game, "Here's the church, here's the steeple, open the door . . ." She had fixated on his fingers because she had tired of watching his mouth move and not being able to understand a word he said. Her head had felt heavy enough to roll off her neck and out of his office.

It wasn't until Nurse Franny had firmly jostled her that she had been able to focus on the question. *Did my husband want resuscitation or any life-support measures should something happen?* She had collapsed in Franny's arms shortly after.

The thought of having to ask their son if his father ever spoke of such things crunched her belly tighter than a balled-up piece of aluminum foil. Wil had never discussed things like that with her. As a fireman, his life had been about rescue at all costs. Quitting at life made no sense to her. Would he even have considered this?

Lord, I'm not good at important decisions. Wilbur is the strong one. Tom, too. She wished Tom would move back to Pennsylvania. But she shouldn't be so selfish. He'd only been in St. Louis a year and seemed to love his new job and church.

The photo of him and his father—taken only a few weeks before the first stroke—rested on the end table. Their arms around each other, Tom so dashing in his police officer's uniform and Wil's gray hair blowing in the breeze, she had taken that photo as they stood at the foot of the St. Louis Arch.

The Montgomery men with the charming Montgomery smiles that drew women like flies. She had been blessed with a faithful, Christian husband. And equally blessed with a son so committed to the Lord, he waited patiently for the godly wife chosen for him.

That week had been so wonderful—filled with sweet memories. Helping Tom settle into a new apartment, meeting his precinct captain, meeting his new pastor, and discovering gooey butter cake—a find that had cost her a few pounds.

She rubbed the sides of those gargantuan hips. All she had to wear lately were size fourteen sweatpants. Even at this size, the elastic cut into her waist. It was only a matter of time before she bumped up to the next size.

She didn't think that's what Shira had in mind for her new dress code. *Sigh.*

There were no extra funds for nice black slacks and fashionable blouses. She struggled to make the mortgage.

An overdue notice peeked from the stack of bills. Wil and she had taken a second mortgage on the house to help Tom get settled. Wilbur did some teaching on the side to pay for that mortgage, but now that income was gone. If she could perhaps borrow a little from Tom, at least until she could get a handle on these bills . . .

She pulled herself up from the couch then aimed her body toward the wall phone in the kitchen. Tom needed to know what was going on with his father.

After dialing, the phone rang several times. "Hello." A female voice.

"Oh." Who would be answering Tom's phone at this hour? "I'm sorry. Is my son there?"

"Beulah?"

"Yes? I'm sorry, do I know you?"

"Beulah, it's Shira. Are you okay?"

Of course. She had instinctively dialed Edna's number. Beulah tried to manufacture a convincing laugh. "Silly me. I misdialed. So sorry to bother you, my dear. Have a great evening. See you tomorrow."

"Beulah—"

She thumbed the phone off and bumped her head against the wall. *Oh Edna, I miss you so much! Wilbur, I need you.* A ball of emotion rolled over her heart, knocking down all of her attempts at control.

Lord, help me not frighten my son. Help me to be brave. Taking a deep breath, she carefully punched in Tom's new number. After several rings, his voicemail answered. She listened to her son's voice that sounded more and more like his father's. After the tone, she left a cheerful how-are-you message and to call as soon as he could. She hung up the phone and rested her forehead on the receiver.

Who could she call? She needed prayer. No one at her church really knew what had been going on—Edna's death, Shira coming home. Besides, it was Wil that everyone was drawn to. She had simply been Wil's wife.

Beulah had known Harriet for nearly fifteen years, but Harriet hadn't even asked what happened when Beulah returned from the nursing home. Only Cari had taken her aside to find out if everything was okay. But she hadn't wanted to share her troubles with the sweet girl. This burden was too big for someone so young and uninvolved in her life.

She had hoped Edna's death would cause Harriet and her to be better friends. But Harriet's idea of friendship was drafting her into the terrible clash with Shira to take over Hair Mavens.

Poor Shira had enough to cope with—the death of her aunt and all the changes in her life. Now she had to contend with Harriet's pranks. If she continued pondering on the hateful things Harriet did to that poor girl, she'd only get angry and . . . I know what I need to do.

Her fingers found a strange satisfaction hitting the keys. The phone rang.

"Hello?"

"Shira. It's Beulah." Panic swelled. "Again."

"What can I do for you, Beulah?" She sounded tired. "Are you feeling okay?"

"I—I wanted to tell you," her voice trembled along with her hands, "that if you need anything at all, let me know."

A long pause. She scratched at a tear in the wallpaper.

"Thanks, Beulah. I appreciate that."

"And, Shira, you're in my prayers."

She sighed. "You're very kind."

"Well, I'll let you get some sleep." Beulah clutched her blouse, feeling her heart pound.

"Thanks for calling, Beulah. See you tomorrow."

"Good—" The click interrupted her goodbye.

Okay, Lord. I did it. I don't know how much good it did.

Her stomach growled. A glance at the clock on the phone explained why she was hungry. Almost nine. She hadn't eaten anything since before leaving for the nursing home at eleven that morning. A cold inspection of the freezer revealed a couple frozen dinners. She grabbed the nearest one then followed the directions.

The micro rotated her dinner, a hypnotic distraction as she waited.

The phone rang. The ring jolted her out of her trance. "Hello." She didn't recognize her monotone-voice.

"Mom? Mom, what's wrong?"

Tom. She shifted to her cheerful voice. "So good of you to call back, sweetheart."

"Stop it, Mom. What's wrong?"

Her face flushed with shame. "I'm sorry, honey." She was losing control, and she had so wanted to be brave for her son. "Your dad . . ."

"Is he—"

"No." She swallowed. "But the doctor said his body is beginning to shut down."

"I was afraid of that." His voice quivered. "How long?"

Were they really having this conversation? "He doesn't know for certain. It could be a few days, weeks, or even months."

"I'll go to Captain Holland tomorrow. Put him on notice that I'll need to take some time off."

"Tom?" She tried to steady herself by sitting on the dinette chair. "Tom, the doctor asked me a question. Did your father ever speak with you about a living will? Whether or not to resuscitate or place him on life support?"

His pause spoke before he did. "Yes."

"When?" She couldn't help her anxious pitch.

He cleared his throat. "Shortly after the first stroke. When he was still able to communicate. He doesn't want any extreme measures taken. I helped him fill out the paperwork. It wasn't in his file?"

"Why didn't he tell me? He never said a word to me." She slapped her palm on the table. "Why didn't you tell me, Tom?"

"I'm sorry, Mom. He made me promise. He knew you wouldn't let him go . . . even if he was already gone." His quiet sobs curbed some of her anger.

While her son took some time to digest the reality, she sent up a silent prayer. *Lord, I'm angry. This is my husband. Why wouldn't he include me in the most important plans of his life—his death? Help me to forgive Wilbur and Tom. I need a clear head right now, Lord. There's the matter of the house . . .*

She switched the phone to her other ear and wiped her tears. "Tommy. It's okay. You were only doing what your father asked."

"Mom, I really hoped and prayed it wouldn't come to this." He groaned. "I even put money down on a little house in Richmond Heights with three bedrooms so you both could visit."

She shut her eyes tightly. He had no money to spare. The microwave dinged.

19

Harriet finished brushing her teeth, rolled the lipstick over her lips, and then grabbed the lit ciggy from the ashtray on the sink. For the first time in days, she was excited to go to work.

Billie Mae had come up with the greatest idea. She puffed as she teased her hair, trying to imagine what other creative plots her friend had devised. This plan was genius. Billie Mae had contacted a few of her friends who went to another salon. That way, Beulah wouldn't be able to spoil the plan.

With one final glance in the mirror, she smiled through the smoky haze.

Today felt like a cherry cheese Danish day.

"Yeah, Billie. What cha got?" Harriet paced up and down the sidewalk outside Mavens, holding the cell phone to her ear.

"The good news. I got the two ladies to help us. Cornelia and Bernice."

Both of these ladies were in Billie's and her bowling league, back when Harriet's knees worked. They were loud and obnoxious. Perfect. "So what's the bad news?"

"Apparently Shira is booked for the rest of the week, and with Beulah and the red-head watchin' the appointment book, we can't sneak them in. So it ain't happening today."

"Well, when is it happening?" She took a deep drag.

"Tuesday," Billie cackled—Harriet swore her friend sounded more and more like the Wicked Witch of the West. "Cornie's appointment is eleven and Bernie's at noon."

"A double whammy, eh?" Harriet gave her own spasm of laughter.

"The Brat won't know what hit her."

Shira watched as Harriet sauntered in. She resembled Lex Luthor

112

carrying a case of kryptonite. *What's she up to now?* Apprehension coursed through her body like a wildfire. A quick glance at her reflection indicated that the dread had spilled onto her face for all to see—especially Beehive. She loosened her clenched jaw and forehead.

The phone rang. So much for calm.

"I'll get it, Shira." Beulah touched Shira's arm as she scurried by. Her thoughtfulness tugged at her heart despite her decision last night to not become attached to her.

Unintelligible mumbles came from Beehive's direction.

"Shira." Beulah held the phone against her chest. "A reporter woman from the Philadelphia Inquirer wants to speak with you." Her eyes were round as bagels.

She laid her scissors and comb on the counter. "Please excuse me, Mrs. Miranda."

"By all means, Shira." Her client clapped her hands. "How exciting."

Beulah handed the phone off and brought her fingers to her lips. Goodness. Such a fuss. "This is Shira Goldstein. How may I help you?"

"Ms. Goldstein, my name is Stephanie Simon. I write for the Lifestyle section of the Inquirer."

"Yes."

"Is it true you were a stylist at Élégance Salon in Manhattan?"

She swallowed. "Yes." Had Veronica spread the word that Shira had quit?

"What brings a top stylist from New York to Gladstone?" The edge to the reporter's voice seemed to suggest that this was the case.

"My aunt died recently. I inherited her salon here."

"My condolences, Ms. Goldstein." Her voice softened.

"Thank you, Ms. Simon." Shira rested her elbows on the reception counter. "May I ask how you heard about me?"

"Of course. Recently, my sister had a baby boy. While visiting her and my new nephew, the whole nursing floor was atwitter about a New York stylist working at a run-down beauty shop."

Hmm. Nurse Wilson had been true to her word—although she could have gone without mentioning the rundown part.

"*Mazel tov* on the birth of your nephew, Ms. Simon."

"Thank you." She cleared her throat. "Ms. Goldstein, I would like to interview you for this weekend's edition of Lifestyle. A story fell through, so I'm on a bit of a deadline. Could I come by this afternoon?"

Beulah watched Shira's face intently. "That would be fine, Ms. Simon. I have a full schedule, however. Would you be able to work around all the bedlam?" Shira gave Beulah a wink. Beulah responded with a little hopping dance.

"No problem for me." The gentle clicking of Stephanie's nails on some electronic device meant this was really happening. "Five-ish sound good for you?"

Shira glanced at the appointment book. Full. "It will be busy."

"Perfect. I'll bring my photographer and see you then."

After their goodbyes, Shira looked at a ready-to-burst Beulah. "They want to do an article about me and The Hair Mavens."

Beulah pulled Shira into a tight hug and released her quickly. "Shira. How exciting." Beulah practically skipped around the reception area. "Our little shop has never had an article written about it."

A small round of applause came from the clients sitting in styling chairs and under dryers.

It took some effort on Shira's part not to join Beulah's happy dance. "Well, before we get too excited, we need to clean this place up a little." What was she talking about? They needed a bulldozer. "Could someone run to Zaydie's and pick up some pastries?"

The door opened. The sun blinded her until it shut. Once her eyes readjusted, Melly's slender form stood before Shira like a visiting angel.

"Melly." Shira impulsively gathered the girl into a hug, which was so unlike her. She must be more excited that she'd thought.

"Ms. Goldstein." Her sweet young voice was like honey. "Mrs. Lowinger said you might be interested in a receptionist."

"First of all, call me Shira." She held the teenager's thin arms and looked into her large black-brown eyes. "Next, the job is more receptionist-shampooer-and-all-around-keep-this-salon-running-smoothly person. Think you can handle that?"

"If you teach me. I'll do my best." Her lovely face glowed.

"Then you're hired."

"I am? Really?" She grabbed Shira's hands and brought them to her cheek. "Oh, thank you, thank you, thank you."

Her gratitude stirred memories of Shira with her aunt Edna. She blinked a few times to keep a tear from escaping.

"Oh, Shira, when can I start?"

"Today. Now." Shira crossed her arms. "Can you stay?"

"Let me call my mom." She glanced toward Beulah. "Oh, Beulah, I'll be working with you, too? This is too magical."

A loud humph emanated from the Harriet territory. Who cared!

After Melissa cleared things with her mother, Beulah instructed her how to deal with the phones, the appointment calendar, sweeping up hair, and keeping the reception area tidy. Shira watched Melly tackle each task with youthful exuberance and gratitude. Shira remembered how excited she had been to merely hang around in the salon at that age. To know she belonged there.

Melly swept around Harriet's station, humming.

"You missed a spot." Harriet pointed with her comb to a few strands under her roll-away.

"Oh, Miss Harriet, I'm sorry." Melly bent down to drag the broom underneath. She straightened with a bright smile. "Thanks."

The old crab shrugged. Shira wanted to deflate her beehive.

Mrs. Miranda caught Shira's attention in the mirror as she put the finishing touches on her hair. "It's good to have young people in the salon again."

Shira squeezed Mrs. Miranda's shoulder. "Yes, it is."

The door opened. Cari entered with two more clients.

"Good afternoon, ladies." Her friend removed her sweater as she entered the reception area then hung it in the closet. "What's the good word? Any new gossip?" She rubbed her hands together and waggled her brows.

Beulah followed behind her freshly shampooed client. "Cari, the most exciting thing happened to Shira."

Shira winked at Cari, but her shaking knees belied the nonchalance. Truth was, she was frightened that Ms. Simon had already presumed she was some failure from New York who had nowhere to go but this rundown shop.

"I see her. She's coming." Melly's face flushed with excitement as she moved away from the front window.

"Calm down," Shira scolded, but her own heart had practically shot out of her chest. She checked her hair and makeup—for the umpteenth time in the last hour.

"Shirry, don't worry. You are beautiful as usual." Cari's arms folded across her chest. She manufactured an annoyed look, but Shira saw the sparkle in her eyes.

"Good grief. You'd think the First Lady was coming," Harriet said. She had created a cloud of hairspray around her client.

As the lacquered cloud dissipated, Shira gulped. That was the biggest, ugliest hair she'd ever seen on someone in this salon.

Great. Just Great.

Pozhalusta, ukhodityeh. Please, leave.

Kathy repositioned Mrs. Abernathy's chair so her own back was to all the activity. Just in time, because the clicking of the camera came her way. She lowered her chin so that her long hair covered more of her face.

Do not talk to me. Or take my picture. Please. I do not want a picture of me in the newspapers.

He might see it.

The new girl, Melissa, offered coffee to the reporter people. Kathy

115

watched in the mirror as the reporter lady and photographer returned to where Shira was working on Mrs. Dickerson's color.

Kathy exhaled.

"Harriet?" Kathy stepped into Beulah's area since Beulah was at the reception desk. She whispered, "How long do you think those people will be here?"

Harriet rolled her eyes and leaned nearer. She smelled like cigarettes and peppermint gum.

"They can't leave soon enough for me."

"Kathy? Harriet?" Melissa carried a tray of pretty cups and saucers. She recognized them. They were Edna's mother's china. Shira should not be using those here.

"Yeah, kid?" Harriet chewed her gum loudly.

"Would you like some coffee or tea?" She lifted the tray a little and smiled.

"No," Harriet said. "I would not."

Melissa shifted her gaze. "Kathy?"

Kathy felt bad that Harriet was rude. "Okay. Yes. Thank you. I'll take coffee, please." Even though she really did not want coffee now.

The young girl stared at Kathy. She quickly resumed rolling Mrs. Abernathy's hair.

"Would you like cream or sugar?" Melissa handed the cup to her.

Kathy was careful to not look at her as she took the cup. "No, thank you." But Kathy loved lots of cream and sugar. She could see the girl in the mirror.

"*Ustali*, Kathy?" she whispered.

Kathy sighed and nodded. "*Da*. I am very tired."

Her body froze. Oh, no. *What did I do?*

Melissa stared keenly at Kathy. "My grandmother came from Russia. It was the way you said coffee." She said this so quietly, not even old Mrs. Abernathy could hear. "I will not say anything. I promise."

Kathy scrutinized the girl's face. There was no craftiness like Harriet. There was no arrogance as she saw in Shira. No, her face was like Edna's. Peaceful. Her smile went all the way to her eyes.

She smiled then walked back toward Shira.

Melissa seemed nice. But could Kathy trust her? Could she ever trust anyone again?

"How many years were you with Élégance?" Stephanie Simon, dressed in a gorgeous linen Celine shirtdress, positioned the recorder on Shira's counter.

Somehow Shira had pictured Ms. Simon as stocky wearing a sensible suit and shoes, not the flowing feminine designer dress covering a model's body. Goes to show first impressions weren't always the way to go.

"Six years." She pulled a section of Mrs. Dickerson's shoulder-length hair at an angle and snipped the ends. What a lucky break Mrs. D had allowed Shira to try something new, instead of the usual bob.

Stephanie tap-tap-tapped on her iPad. "I placed a call to Veronica Harrington today."

A lump the size of a brisket formed in Shira's throat.

"She said you two had a falling-out of sorts."

"Yes, we did." She dropped a section of hair and retrieved it. "I'm very appreciative of all Veronica did for me. It was simply time to move on."

Stephanie nodded then glanced at her tablet to enter more notes. "She pretty much said the same thing."

Whew.

The reporter inspected the salon, starting from the ceiling. "Appears you have your work cut out for you here."

"Yes, I have big plans. The architect is coming on Monday." She caught Harriet's glare. "It's time to add a little Manhattan chic to Gladstone."

"I'm all for that," Stephanie muttered.

Shira grabbed the blow dryer and a one-inch round brush. With a practiced hand she shaped and dried Mary Dickerson's hair. The new blonde highlights gleamed.

Ms. Simon strolled past Harriet, Beulah, and Kathy's stations.

So far, the interview had gone well. Surprisingly well. She couldn't help the flutter of apprehension—Harriet had been strangely restrained. A few harrumphs and strategically placed coughs were the extent of her disapproval so far. It was too good to be true. Shira wondered when the other spiked-heel would drop.

Stephanie observed Harriet as another example of big hair materialized under a toxic cloud of hairspray. And another client was under the dryer, ready for the same treatment, Shira was sure.

Ms. Simon rubbed her chin as Harriet gave another unnecessary round of hairspray.

Please don't let her talk to Harriet.

Cari circled around Ms. Simon and stopped in front of her with a plate of pastries. The reporter's eyes lit up. "Are those from Zaydie's?" Her fingers hovered over the china plate filled with the Jewish bakery's best, waiting for Cari to give the correct response.

Cari winked. "Of course."

Stephanie moaned. "I shouldn't." But she did. Twice.

Cari moved on to the photographer, who sat at the manicurist's table noshing on the crudités. He dropped the baby carrot and swiped a couple macaroons.

Someone's cell rang. Everyone searched for their phones until the tone became recognizable—a metallic-sounding "Hallelujah Chorus." Beulah pulled her phone from her pocket. Her face turned a bright red. "I'll be outside if you need me, Shira." She shuffled out the door like a nun on speed. Shira huffed a small laugh.

Harriet led her styling monstrosity past Stephanie Simon as she popped her gum. "How's it going?" Harriet continued on toward the reception desk.

Ms. Simon raised her brows and pursed her lips.

Shira shrugged and gave a tight smile. Was Harriet about to sabotage the interview?

"Hello?" Beulah continued walking to the side of the building, the cell tight against her ear. What little traffic Gladstone had was always busy this time of day.

"Mrs. Montgomery? This is Allison Garvey, Weiskopf Realty." Her melodic voice sounded pleasant enough. "I understand you are interested in selling your home."

Her insides dipped like a roller coaster ride. "Yes," she squeaked.

"Excuse me?"

"I'm sorry. Yes. Yes, I need to sell my home." She took a deep breath. "My husband is in a nursing home and my son lives in Missouri. It's only me now, and I need to . . . downsize, is it?"

Miss Garvey's soft sigh communicated compassion—at least Beulah chose to think that. "I think I understand, Mrs. Montgomery. Are the medical bills piling up?"

She took a ragged breath. "Yes."

"Well, don't you worry—I handle this sort of thing all the time. How soon can we meet?"

"I'm off at six-thirty."

"How about I meet you at seven, your house?"

She gave her the address and said goodbye. Somehow, despite the reality of having to sell her home, she felt better. At least she was doing something.

Slipping the phone back into her jacket pocket, she reentered Mavens. The reporter and photographer were packed up and ready to leave.

Ms. Simon extended her hand to Shira. "Shira, thank you for accommodating us at the last minute."

Shira gave the reporter a beautiful smile as she shook her hand. The smile reminded Beulah of Edna.

"I hope you'll return for a style, my treat."

"Really?" The reporter transformed from professional to giddy. "I would love to."

Beulah slipped past the two women and headed to her station. Harriet shoved her arm and gave her a scowl.

Over Harriet's shoulder, Beulah watched as Shira linked her arm with Ms. Simon's. "Melly?"

Melly glanced up from the reception booth. "Yes, Shira."

"Please take care of Ms. Simon. Book her with me at her earliest convenience."

"I would be happy to."

Melly seemed to be fitting in nicely. She would be part of Shira's future at The Hair Mavens. Beulah hoped to be included in that future.

Who was she kidding? Without Edna, without Wil or Tom, she couldn't even take care of herself. She was about to lose her home. What did she have to offer anyone?

Allison Garvey slid the listing contract across the table. The pen in Beulah's hand quivered.

"Mrs. Montgomery, if you will merely sign at the sticky notes, I'll take this back to the office and enter it into the MLS tonight." She pulled several brightly colored sheets of paper from a file. "These are some excellent hints for open houses and showings. Simple things, like boiling cinnamon in a pan and laying out photos of the house in different seasons."

She continued chatting while Beulah's frozen hand held the Weiskopf Realty pen.

Beulah, you're such a goose. Just sign the papers. She steadied her hand and pulled the contract toward her. With a few strokes at the hot pink sticky notes, she signed off a lifetime of history.

Allison gently tugged the paper back, glanced at Beulah's signatures, and slipped it into a folder with her address on the tab. She glanced up and gave Beulah a compassionate smile, then placed her jewelry-laden hand over her bare fingers to give it a sympathetic pat. The sparkling diamonds reminded her that she had yet to examine the jewelry Edna had so thoughtfully given her.

"Mrs. Montgomery. Thank you for entrusting this important decision to me." She squeezed her hand. "I pledge to do my best for you. But truthfully, this adorable house will sell quickly. Even with your second mortgage, you should come away from this sale with a nice settlement. Then I can help you find a lovely condo."

After locking up and turning off the front porch light, Beulah walked back to her bedroom. The clear plastic shoebox Jesse had given her at the shiva sat on the top shelf of her closet. She stretched to pull it down, then set it on the bed.

Unexpected but quiet tears flowed as she removed the cover. Numerous jewelry boxes of various size and shape were packed into the container. With nervous fingers she lifted the first box and opened the tight gray velvet lid. Two beautiful pearl earrings peered up at her. She snapped the lid.

Pearls? Shouldn't these have gone to Shira? They must match the pearl necklace Edna had given her. She would put this box aside to give to Shira.

The next box was larger and covered in rich black velvet. She opened this box and sighed. It was the necklace. Lifting the box a few inches toward the overhead light, she marveled at the glimmer and shine from the diamond chips imbedded in the Star of David. Edna's Magen David—her Shield of David.

Such beauty and grace. It truly exemplified who Edna was. Could she ever be like her friend?

No. Why should she have such finery? She closed the box gently then laid the inheritance back in the container. Yes, she would pack all this up and give it back to Jesse.

What was Edna thinking?

20

"Quit calling me chicken." Harriet paced her living room floor, smoking like—well, she hated to admit it—like a chimney. "Knock it off, Billie Mae." That's what Harriet needed tonight, more humiliation. Why didn't she hang up on the biddy?

"I can't believe you missed out on an opportunity to really humiliate the brat." Billie Mae's raspy voice raised an octave to further grate on Harriet's nerves. "You had a reporter there and didn't do anything? Good grief, Harriet. Tell me you're not getting soft in your old age."

She was beginning to regret including Billie in her plans. "Listen, Billie Mae. If Shira gets bad press, then Mavens gets bad press. I'm not trying to destroy the place. I'm trying to save it."

"Whatever." Ice tinkled in the glass of whatever it was she was drinking. The slurred words would follow soon enough. "Sounds to me like you don't have the chops to do what it is you need to do."

"Listen, we just need to stick to the plan." Harriet flicked a long ash in the ashtray by her recliner and went back to pacing. "If I'm too obvious, I could lose my job. I ain't got a rich husband to support me."

"That's for sure." Her cackle sent a shiver down Harriet's spine.

Not nice. She faked a yawn. "Billie, time to get my beauty sleep. I'll let you know if anything new develops." *Not.*

"Okay, girlfriend. You do that." Another sip. "I expect to hear all the dirt tomorrow night."

"Sure." Harriet felt like Bill Murray in Ghostbusters—slimed. She wanted a bath. Hair Mavens needed her. Edna would have wanted her to protect it from becoming some cold, fancy-schmancy place no one in this town could afford. Edna couldn't have known Shira would try to change the place. Could she?

21

This Mini is so easy to park. I love it. Shira yanked up the emergency brake and turned off the ignition. Tonight had been a night of celebration—more of a G-rated version than she was accustomed to, but she, Cari, and Melly had had fun.

In a generous mood, she had sprung for dinner. Even though it was a quick dinner—both Cari and Melly had to get to the Friday Shabbat service—it was fun. There had been lots of laughter and reminiscing. She gave a happy, contented sigh.

On the passenger seat were her leftovers, wrapped in a foil swan, and her purse. She leaned over to collect it.

"Shira."

She screamed and jumped, knocking her knee on the steering wheel. *Ouch.*

Jesse stared at her through the side window.

"Are you crazy?" She massaged her knee. "If you were in New York and tried that, you'd be wearing mace."

"Please forgive me, Shira." He lifted his brows and made little effort to hide a smile. "I'm glad I'm not in New York." He opened the car door for her and extended his hand.

Against her better judgment, she took it. With his assistance, she slid gracefully from the small car. His hand was warm. Strong. Yes, this was a mistake. The shivers began at her fingertips then gushed through her body. She jerked from his grasp and walked around to the passenger side to retrieve her purse and food.

"What are you doing here, Jesse?" She glanced his way before reaching in.

"I came to get my jacket . . . and apologize."

Oh brother. "How many times do you intend to apologize for

something I did?" She slammed the car door and fumbled with the lock, then remembered the security system.

"I was a willing participant, Shira." His curly lashes lowered. "Very willing."

"And the running away, that was . . ."

"That was me doing the right thing for both of us."

Speak for yourself. "Well, I'm very happy for you." She clutched her items to her chest and felt the foil-wrapped quiche squish on her Ralph Lauren jacket. *Great.* "Heaven forbid that you should be 'unequally yoked' with this heathen."

How many times had Beth Ahav's youth leaders lectured about not dating unbelievers? Who knew she would have turned into one of those pariahs? She wondered if her picture was posted somewhere in the synagogue, warning single males.

She wouldn't have cared a whit about something like this two weeks ago. Why would she now?

"Shira, I would like for us to be friends." He stepped toward her.

Friends? A picture of a samurai impaling himself on his sword rolled like a movie in her head. The shiny sword twisted from side to side and up and down, ensuring that all the vital organs were eviscerated.

"Sure, Jesse. Why not?"

The loud clack-clack of her heels reverberated as she hurried toward Mavens. After several attempts to find the right key, she unlocked the deadbolt and stomped to the coat closet. Ignoring the inviting leather fragrance that had steeped in the closet for the last three days, she yanked the jacket, shooting the hanger like a missile to her shin. She bit the inside of her mouth to keep from crying out.

Jesse stood at the door, one arm resting on the doorjamb, running his hand through that brown corkscrew mane. Was he doing that on purpose? He had to know how yummy he was. Her legs were doing that Jell-O dance again.

Friends, Shira. Right.

She threw the leather beauty in his direction and pointed to the front door.

"See ya, friend."

"Abba Father, lay Your hands on me; Holy Spirit, set this captive free; from the chains that are holding me. Lay Your hands on me . . ."

Beulah hadn't attended Beth Ahav since Edna's funeral. It felt good to worship with her "second church" family. The days since Edna's passing had begun to weigh heavy on her. The salon, Wilbur, the house—she felt every pound on her shoulders.

The Davidic worship with the music and dancing in front of the sanctuary held such significance to her. She watched as the dance leaders gracefully led others in worship—men, women, and children—they moved in unity.

Edna and she had always danced to this song together. Side-by-side, hand-in-hand, in unity with the others in the circle. But tonight, the heaviness in her heart had sunk to her toes. She stood in the back row soaking in the music and lyrics, eyes closed.

Someone touched her shoulder. Jesse. He must have just arrived. He still wore his jacket.

They hugged tightly. She held his face. His expressive eyes seemed so sad. "Jesse? What's wrong?"

"I need to worship, Beulah. Could you come with me?" He took her hand.

She hesitated then nodded. He pulled her chair back so she could exit the back row without disturbing the others. They walked hand-in-hand to the large circle of people down front.

Rabbi Joel's wife spotted them and smiled. Releasing the hand of the person to her left, she opened a place for them in the circle. In seconds, she and Jesse picked up the rhythm of the group of worshippers. Cari and Melly were across from her in the circle. They exchanged knowing smiles.

She lost herself in the simple repetitive movement—two steps forward, then one step back. *Just like my life, Lord.*

After service, Beulah had joined Jesse and Sam, Shira's father for coffee and pie. The men could afford to indulge with pie this late at night, but the decaf coffee was good and plentiful, so Beulah was satisfied.

She and Jesse sat on one side of the booth and Sam on the other. The conversation so far had been light as the men waited for their desserts.

Jesse fidgeted with his spoon. "Sam, what are we going to do for Rosh Hashanah this year?"

"The Davidoffs invited you and me, Jesse. They said to extend the invitation to Shira, too. I'm sorry. With the trip to Canada, I forgot to tell you." Sam slapped his forehead. "Oh, Beulah, I forgot. You and Wil were always a part of our celebrations at Edna's. Oh my gosh . . . I'm sure there'll be room—"

A lump of emotion formed in her throat. "Don't be silly. I can't simply up and invite myself. It's fine. You go on ahead. The holidays are meant for family."

Sam stared at her intently. Beulah lowered her gaze to her lap.

He laid his hand on hers. "Beulah, you are family. Don't you know that?"

"That's right." Jesse swung his arm around her shoulder and pulled her against him. "I'm not going without you."

"Me neither," Sam said.

She coughed to camouflage the sob trying to escape. "You two. What am I going to do with you?"

The waitress lowered her tray with two scrumptious-looking pies. She took a sip of her coffee. "Jesse, you seemed troubled when you arrived at service."

He finished his first bite then wiped his mouth with his napkin. "I was. Am, actually."

"What's up, Jesse?" Sam laid his fork down.

Jesse cocked his head and exhaled loudly. "Your daughter, Sam."

Sam's fingers tightened. "Any more kissing?"

"What?" Beulah turned toward Jesse. "You kissed Shira?"

He ran a hand through his curly hair. "No and yes."

Beulah watched Sam's jaw tense. His whole body had tensed. He lowered his chin and leveled a look that resembled a papa-bear. "What does that mean exactly?"

"It means, no, there wasn't any more kissing. And, yes, Beulah, I kissed Shira."

Sam's body relaxed.

Beulah had a twinge of guilt, as if she were eavesdropping on a family discussion. Perhaps she should leave.

"So, what happened?" Sam took a small bite of his cherry pie, but his focus never left the young man's face.

"Well, I went to pick up my jacket before service. I had left it . . . uh, that night. And I asked her if we could be friends."

Beulah winced.

"What?" Jesse asked.

She smiled. "Most women—after they've been kissed—would be a touch put-out by that."

"Really?"

Sam paused between chewing. "Wouldn't you, if the roles were reversed?"

"Oh."

Sam and Beulah allowed Jesse to absorb this fact a little more. Jesse was such an intelligent young man, how in the world wouldn't he have seen this? Something else was going on here.

"Jesse?"

He shifted his gaze toward her.

"Honey, are you in love with Shira?"

22

Step on a crack, break your mother's back. Kathy had always hated that rhyme, but there seemed to be no way to keep it from going through her mind as she strolled to the Wawa convenience store. It had been one of the first nursery rhymes she heard the children sing in Brooklyn. She had been fifteen and too old for such things. But she had feared it might be true.

Mama had died of cancer soon after they had come to America. She wondered if she also had caused Edna's death by inadvertently stepping on the sidewalk incorrectly. Her awkward steps were worth keeping others safe.

The day was warm and full of sunshine—too warm for her jogging suit. But with her hood up, she was invisible. As she preferred.

The exact change she needed for the newspaper jingled in her pocket. Normally she did not buy newspapers. But today she must.

If she believed in the God that Edna and Beulah spoke so much about, she would pray that the article was not in the Sunday paper. Because if this story was good, more people would come to Hair Mavens. New people who wanted more styles like New York, and Shira would win.

But mostly she hoped there was no picture of her.

A man exited the front door of the Wawa and held it for her. She kept her head down and muttered a thank you.

The stack of newspapers was at the checkout counter. She waited behind three people buying coffee and wrapped sandwiches. The flavored coffees smelled good, but she had coffee at home.

Finally, it was her turn. She bought the paper, tucked it under her arm, and hurried the two blocks back to her apartment. The stone building was three stories high. She was willing to pay the expensive rent because of the security cameras everywhere. What little money she made was better spent ensuring her concealment than on designer clothes and shoes.

Her security code punched in, she waited for the clank, then opened the heavy glass door. The polished hardwood floors and warm lighting reminded Kathy of her beautiful apartment in New York. It was much nicer than this, but her income had been four times as much.

The paneled door to her apartment bolted, she peeked through the peephole. No one lingered in the hall. Sundays in the early morning were usually quiet.

She slipped off her sneakers and padded to the couch in her socks. Her coffee was still warm.

Time to find the story. She pulled the Lifestyle section, then gasped. The story of Shira and The Hair Mavens was on the front page of section G. Almost the whole page.

Her heart flapped wildly like a caged bird. The headline read "Manhattan Chic in Small Town." A big picture of Shira's face smiled above a caption that read, "Shira Goldstein, leaves Crème de la Crème for Small Town." There were smaller pictures of Cari and Melly, Beulah, Harriet and her client and . . . her.

The photographer had taken the picture from her back, but her face was exposed in the mirror's reflection. The photo was in color. Her eyes.

She threw down the paper. It floated to the floor as she paced.

This was not good. *Plokhoy.* Very bad.

What should she do? Maybe no one would see it. She picked up the paper. Yes, her violet eyes were visible—but barely. With the glasses she did appear somewhat different.

Anyway, who cared about the strange girl? People could only see the beautiful Shira.

She wanted to be pretty again. Wear makeup. Style her hair. She didn't want to be Kathy Smith any more.

"My name is Katya Stavropolsky." Her voice was clear in the stillness.

It had been three years since she had spoken her name out loud—to Edna, when she had told her story.

She wanted to be Katya again. But she wanted to be safe more.

Why did she have to choose?

Shira's kitchen phone rang, again. It was nearly noon and Shira was still in her robe. The phone had not stopped since eight-thirty when her father had called. After him, everyone who knew Edna's phone number—apparently a lot of people—had called to congratulate Shira.

Another brrrring. She laid her head on the kitchen table, raised an arm, and picked up the receiver. "Congratulations, you are caller number fifty. You win a free box of Dove bars."

"I love Dove bars, Shirry."

Now this was someone she wanted to hear from. She lifted her head. "Hey, Cari—"

"Shira, it's so exciting. You looked so beautiful. The front page of Lifestyle. Is that cool or what? Ms. Simon must have been very impressed with you. Oh, gosh, I can't believe the wonderful things she wrote."

"Cari, take a breath, girlfriend. You'll hyperventilate."

She laughed. "Don't pretend with me, my friend. You're pleased, and you know it."

Something familiar rippled up. Before Shira could stop it, a squeal popped out.

"I knew it," Cari squealed back.

Déjà vu—the day they were both asked to the senior prom. Hopefully, this would turn out better for Shira than that night.

"You know what this means, Shira?"

"People will want my autograph?"

She tsked. "You're going to have more clients than you can handle."

Shira hadn't had an opportunity to even think about the ramifications of such a positive story. "You're right." She puffed out air. "The architect is coming tomorrow, but my biggest problem is the mavens. I've got to step things up to get rid of them."

The silence on Cari's end surprised her. "Hello?"

"I'm here, Shirry."

"What?"

"I don't think your biggest problem is the mavens. I think you have a harmony problem."

"So, I'm off-key?" Shira's comment came out edgier than she had intended.

"You have the potential of a great group of women for your salon, Shira. Each has strengths. You need to—"

She slammed her palm on the table. "Harriet has nothing I need." Her face heated.

"You certainly don't need the *tzuris* she's been giving you. But you do need her consistency and ability to do granny hair."

"My salon will not be a granny salon."

"Maybe not, but it is now." She blew air through her lips. "Shira, you're the marketing expert. I don't have to tell you it's all about your demographics."

Yes, Cari, remind me I didn't finish my business degree.

"Even if—no, when—you pull men and women from the Main Line, you'll still have Aunt Edna's customers. You can't exclude them because they're old. It's not right, and it's not good business."

The thing Shira hated most about this conversation was that Cari might be right. And all this was beginning to sound a whole lot like Jesse's diatribe a week ago. She didn't care about doing the right thing. She wanted it her way.

It's my dream, not Cari's . . . or Aunt Edna's.

"Cari, I appreciate your support and enthusiasm, but ultimately this is my decision."

"Of course."

A rare moment of silence grew between them. Was Cari judging her? "So I suppose this means you won't have anything to do with this—with me—now."

"What in the world are you talking about?"

"You know, I'm not following Yeshua's ways."

"Shira, you're my friend. You'll always be my friend. Do I want you living the life of a believer? Loving Yeshua as He loves you? You bet. But what kind of friend would I be if I wasn't there for you?"

That stung. Cari probably hadn't meant it to. The disparity between Cari's actions as Shira's friend and her own were painfully obvious. Cari had truly been a friend. Shira hadn't. Shira gulped back a wad of guilt.

"Shira, I may not agree with you. I may even yell at you a time or two . . . like now."

Shira chewed her nail and sniffed.

"And there may even be some things I won't do for you. But I will be there for you. I promise." Her friend cleared the emotion from her throat.

"Care, can we please change the subject?" Shira felt the burn of tears.

"Shira, are you crying?"

Tears tumbled. "No."

Cari sniffed. "Me, neither." After a peaceful pause, she let loose her effervescent giggle. "So, Shirry, you want to go shopping, maybe? Aaron asked if he could go with us."

Aaron? Why?

Visions of designer stores in the mall disappeared the moment Aaron pulled his SUV into the local techie store. A little bird had kept him apprised of The Mavens' craziness, and he decided it was time to step in with some testosterone and technology.

First step, buy a much-needed computer for the salon. Although she had been severely reprimanded by Aaron for not allowing him to "build" a computer, he had graciously agreed to help her pick one out.

Build a computer? *As if.* Computers were to be purchased in well-lit, high-ceilinged stores with cute guys in polo shirts and chinos.

With her giant shopping cart that could house a family of four, Shira scampered through the aisles while the Lowinger lovebirds threw paper and print cartridges in. And—woo-hoo—a new cordless four-phone set, all with caller ID. According to Aaron, these were the highest-rated phones available. Shira believed him, since Cari said he spent his free time researching the best of every gadget and electronic equipment around.

Aaron had promised to set up a network on the cloud between the new computer and her laptop. That way she could access the best software, according to all his research, from anywhere—even with her laptop at Starbucks. Of course, she needed to retrieve her laptop from Manhattan.

"Shira." Aaron's deep voice belied his tall, slender frame. "I can order that salon software online when I get back and install it on Tuesday night. Do you want all the modules?"

Modules? Although she had used Élégance's software, she didn't know anything about the inner workings. "Do you think I need all the—whatever you called them?"

Cari hugged Aaron's arm. She was simply radiant as Aaron strutted his techie stuff. Aaron, however, looked at Shira like she was a four-year-old. "Well, you have the appointment module—"

"No more big, bulky, ugly appointment book." Cari pointed her finger at Shira.

He smiled sweetly toward his bubbly wife. "Yes. Then there's the customer module, which is the heart of your database. You can store anything from client's info to statistical info to the hair color you last used. You could send out mailers, texts, and e-mails."

"I like. I like. Go on." He'd researched all this for her?

He smiled. His eyes were really green, too. Their kids would be adorable. "Then the inventory and services module, the employees module, and the sales module."

"Whew. I'll take all the puppies." Élégance didn't have anything nearly as advanced. Shira couldn't help taking great pleasure in this.

Aaron squeezed Cari's shoulder and proceeded down the shopping aisle rattling off all sorts of techie jargon Shira didn't understand. To which Cari nodded her head, adoringly.

"Shira."

Shira searched right and left then turned around. Jesse. She hated that her first reaction was happiness. "Jesse," she said as coolly as possible, given her jelly knees. "Are you following me?"

"Had to pick up a watch battery." He held up his package.

She folded her arms. "I see."

"Congratulations on the great review."

"Thanks."

"You, you looked great."

Warmth traveled down her neck. "Thanks."

"I was going to call—"

Her heart fluttered.

"—to see when your dad and I could pick up Edna's furniture for

Kathy."

She was getting tired of this rollercoaster ride. "Sure. Fine. Whatever." She turned to push the cart away from him. Cari and Aaron were at the end of the aisle watching.

Jesse touched her elbow. "Shira?"

She stopped, but didn't turn around. "Yes?"

"I keep saying the wrong thing." He removed his hand. "What I know is that I have deep feelings for you. I hope we can be friends until we figure out what to do next."

How was she supposed to respond to that? "Jesse, you and my father can pick up the furniture this evening."

"Okay. Thanks."

From nowhere, Alec's handsome face flashed in her mind. His icy blue eyes could mesmerize any female out of diapers, yet Shira realized he paled in comparison to the man of integrity behind her. Jesse's strength of character, the respect he afforded her even when she wouldn't give it to herself . . . all of it.

Alec was subhuman compared to Jesse. But it would never work. Shira knew the rules. He couldn't date her and maintain the integrity she respected most in him.

She gripped the shopping cart handle then shoved away from this lawyer on a mission to save her . . . and drive her up the wall.

This lawyer who had stolen her heart.

23

Kathy's security buzzer sounded. She pressed the intercom button. "Yes?"

"Hey, Kathy. It's Jesse and me," Sam Goldstein said.

She pressed the lock release to the main door then ran to her peephole to watch for Sam and Jesse. Once the men entered the hallway, she opened the door. Although her stomach churned, she waved. "Thank you for doing this, Sam and Jesse."

Sam and Jesse were both dressed in jeans and T-shirts. Sam carried heavy work gloves and a tape measure.

"Hi, Kathy." Jesse wanted to hug, so she stood still to let him. "This is a great building."

Kathy let Sam hug her next.

He held up the metal tape measure. "We wanted to measure your doorways and bedroom to make sure everything will fit." He studied her bare living room. "You seem to have plenty of room."

Heat covered her face. This was why she did not invite visitors. Her bedroom had nothing but a few boxes. So little to show for her previous successful life.

After Kathy moved the boxes, Jesse and Sam carried the bed frame in pieces. They assembled it quickly. Next they carefully maneuvered a mattress and box spring and set them against the wall. Both were wrapped in plastic.

"Wait." She inspected the tags. "These mattresses are new."

Jesse left Sam to go back outside. Sam rested his hands on his hips. "Kathy, we had to throw the old ones away."

"I cannot pay for new ones."

"It's a gift."

Nyet. "N-no." She bit her top lip. "No, thank you. It is too much."

"I'll tell you what. You can cut my hair for the next year. That should about cover it."

He was Edna's brother and had kind eyes, but . . . "I do not cut men's hair."

"But I've seen Edna—"

"I do not cut men's hair."

Sam shoved his hands in his pockets. "I can't take the mattresses back today, and I won't have time tomorrow. It would mean so much to me if you would accept this."

Quickly calculating her lunch budget, she figured the bed would be paid off in about six months. "I will pay you each week for it."

He opened his mouth then shut it. "Okay. Deal." He held out his hand. Kathy pumped it once. A sense of accomplishment and peace flooded her.

Jesse carried two drawers from Edna's dresser. "You two strike an agreement?"

It was very late. Sam and Jesse had left hours ago. Kathy had unpacked all the kitchen things and put them away. For the first time in years, she would be able to cook more of her favorite recipes and eat on real plates, not paper. She loved the way the dishes brought color into the glass-front cabinets. The way the silverware drawer jingled when she opened it. She had washed and polished the glasses. They, too, sparkled from the cabinets.

Edna's comfortable living room was now in her apartment. Kathy tried to arrange the furniture the same way Edna had had it in her place.

The bedroom was as elegant as her loft in New York. The drawers of Edna's beautiful cherry wood dresser held her few belongings. She sat on the edge of her new bed and admired the two nightstands with the beautiful crystal lamps.

All of Edna's linens Kathy had washed in the basement laundry. It had been a long time since she had made up a bed.

Everything was fresh and clean.

Feelings she had not allowed in a long time visited as an old friend. Contentment. Perhaps even happiness.

The bed squeaked as she stood. Drawn to the handsome cherry wood dresser, she ran her fingertips over the rich dark wood. It was smooth under her fingertips. The mirror extended to the full length of the dresser. Kathy examined herself without the silly glasses—her hair pulled back into a ponytail.

It is you, Katya Stavropolsky. She hugged herself tightly.

Because of one woman, who had seen the fear and need in Kathy, her life had been saved. How had she ever argued with Jesse about accepting these beautiful gifts? How could she dishonor Edna's love and generosity— something Kathy could never repay—by not accepting it?

The things were not as valuable as what they gave her. That sense of belonging. That feeling of home. She looked up.

Thank you, Edna. Thank you for giving me hope.

24

For the last hour Steven Black, architect extraordinaire—according to Cari—had measured, sketched, shot photos, mumbled, and scratched his head. Initially, Shira had followed him as he explored every nook and cranny of the place, but he wore her out and she had the feeling she disturbed his flow with her questions.

She certainly appreciated his attention to detail and taking the time to understand her vision for The Hair Mavens.

While Steve-the-architect did his thing, she had been pulling phone messages off the answering machine. She was on message twelve of twenty-seven, and the phones were still ringing with new messages adding by the hour. It was good that the salon was closed on Mondays, or she would be there all night.

Only one weird message—a marriage proposal—the rest, so far, were new clients. Cari was right. She readied her pen over paper for message twelve. "Hello, my name is Sasha Hilton," said a sensual Lauren-Bacall-type voice. "And I simply must have an appointment at your quaint little shop. Please call me . . ."

Her appointment calendar was filling quickly. At this point, she actually wished the mavens did know more current styles—she could use the help. She was going to be pulling some long days. Which was fine since she had no life.

"Excuse me, Shira."

The dusty, bespectacled Steve-the-architect set his measuring tape and flashlight on the counter. "I'm about finished here." He flipped over the pages of his yellow legal pad. "Just a couple more questions."

"Shoot."

His shoulders slumped. "Is there any way you could gut the place and start from scratch?"

Don't I wish. "Unfortunately, no. We have to maintain service—at least, as best we can."

"I was afraid you'd say that." He grimaced. "I'll study the catalogs and trade magazines you gave me. Also, I have some ideas I want to research." He ruffled through a few pages. "It will take at least two weeks before I have a budget and model for you."

Her heart went pitty-pat. This was thrilling. "Okay. Sounds good." Now her feet wanted to do the happy dance. "I meet with the bank next week to complete the loan paperwork. My loan officer is waiting for your budget, but with Aunt Edna's insurance money and the salon as collateral, he doesn't see any problems."

Steve extended his hand. "I'm really looking forward to working with you, Shira. I'm very excited about this project."

She smiled. "Me too, Steve."

As she watched Steve-the-architect leave, bits and pieces of an old song Cari and she had sung as kids tumbled through her head. Something about burning ships? What had that been about? *Now I remember.*

Aunt Edna had explained how the early settlers didn't want to be tempted to go back to England if things became too challenging, so they burned their ships to force themselves to stick it out.

Time to burn my ship in Manhattan.

Beulah poised the scissors over her head. She exhaled loudly and studied yet again the trendy hair magazine on the toilet seat.

I can do all things through Christ who strengthens me. So, she should be able to cut her hair in this stylish bob.

Forty-five minutes later, she inspected her handiwork in the mirror. It was short, just to her jawline. Hunks of her shoulder-length white hair were all over the bathroom sink and floor. She had attempted the layering on the sides and back, and kept the front long. She'd need to rewet her hair to blow-dry it into something that resembled the magazine picture.

After another thirty minutes of wetting, blow-drying, and styling, her arms dropped in exhaustion. She grabbed the hand mirror and studied the back.

"I think I like it. It's certainly different." She swiveled her head from side to side. Okay, not too bad.

She shook her head to see if it moved like the magazine said it should. A wedge of hair fell over her eyes.

Her head dropped into her hands.

What was I thinking? It's terrible. I can't do anything.

Beulah parked in the grocery store lot. The lights were on at Hair

Mavens even though the salon was closed on Mondays. Perhaps Shira was catching up on paperwork or something.

Please, Lord, move her to have compassion for this silly old gal.

She exited her car and locked it. Even though Edna had given her a key to the shop, she didn't feel comfortable traipsing in unannounced. After she rapped on the window, she stepped back so Shira could see her.

Shira's delicate face appeared, a pencil wedged in her mouth. Her expression traveled from annoyance to curiosity. Then, the pencil dropped from her mouth. Within seconds, the door swung open.

"Beulah? What have you done?"

Oh, dear. This was a bad idea. "I'm sorry to disturb you, Shira. I'll let you get back to what you are doing."

Shira grabbed Beulah's wrist and pulled her in, her attention never leaving Beulah's monstrosity.

"Beulah, I love it." She touched the strands then ran her fingers through various sections. "Who did this?"

"Me." Her face warmed.

Shira paused. "You're kidding." Shira walked around her, touching and examining Beulah's efforts. She felt like she was back in beauty school with her teacher grading her.

"Well, you styled it wrong." She stepped back and folded her arms. "I don't suppose you used any styling wax?"

"No." Beulah had never used such a product.

"Uh huh. Round or flat brush?"

"Just my regular hair brush."

"Thought so." Her fingers shifted to her chin. "Beulah, how would you feel about a few lowlights around—"

"Shira, please, I don't want to color my hair." She'd had enough change today.

"Okay, okay." She waved away Beulah's fear then scrutinized the overall style like a scientist. "But think about this." She pulled out the front long strands. "I would keep the front natural, and put the lowlights on the sides and toward the back."

Beulah could visualize the dark brown lowlights mixed with her gray. Very dramatic. "Let me think about that."

"Fair enough." She placed an arm around Beulah's shoulder. "In the meantime, can I clean this up a little and show you how to style it?"

Unexpected emotions welled up in her. All she could do was nod. Beulah had always wanted a daughter. As the only woman in a household with two very manly men, she had spent many lonely weekends while her boys had played, watched, or talked sports.

She loved her son. He was the most wonderful, thoughtful son a mother could pray for—but to share precious times like this with a daughter? Edna had been so blessed.

Allowing herself to relax while Shira took care of her was a blessed treat. She couldn't remember the last time someone else had done her hair.

Shira had taken her time with each stage of the process, teaching Beulah the newest techniques. Shampooing had almost been a spiritual experience. She demonstrated scalp massages and pressure points—to the point Beulah had almost fallen asleep.

Now as Beulah sat at Edna's station—Shira's station—Shira gracefully snipped and combed. She explained how the European greats made hair move and lay just so. The basics Beulah knew well, but these newer techniques, tools, and products were a marvel. Shira patiently answered all her questions, allowing Beulah to touch and try out the products as Shira worked.

Edna's niece moved with precision, while Beulah's attempts had been clumsy and self-conscious. Somehow, Beulah had thought Harriet and she merely needed a little brushing up on their skills. The reality was they were more like country doctors trying to perform heart transplants. There was a whole universe out there, and she and Harriet were still on the farm.

Once Shira shut off the blow dryer, Beulah gripped the armrests of the chair. This was it.

"There." Shira twirled the styling cape off and stood back with her hands on her hips. "What do you think?"

Beulah looked at the mirror. She gasped. It was her, but not her. She tossed her hair and watched it move in smooth waves, only to return to its original shape. There was youth-like sheen and depth.

"This is . . . Oh, Shira, I love it."

Shira radiated delight.

Their eyes connected.

There it was. One of the most sought-after moments of a hairdresser. The magical moment. A sisterhood moment. When a woman and her hairdresser connected over perfect hair.

Men could never have comprehended this.

Beulah bolted from the styling chair and pulled Shira into a tight hug. Shira patted her back, but the young woman felt stiff in her arms. Beulah was a hugger, but she had come to realize not everyone was—like Harriet. Beulah made a mental note: Shira doesn't like hugging.

"Shira, thank you so much." Beulah couldn't help staring at her reflection. "How can I ever repay you?"

"If you're not busy right now." She smiled. "I could use some help answering all these phone messages."

Phone messages?

Shira entered the reception booth and lifted a legal pad filled with writing.

"What's all this?"

"From the newspaper article."

Beulah, how could you forget? "Shira, how selfish of me to take up all this time. You were busy."

Shira winked. "I wouldn't have missed this for the world, Beulah."

"You looked so beautiful in the photos." Beulah took the tablet. "You know, you have always reminded me of Amy—"

"—a Jewish Amy Grant." Shira rolled her eyes. "Yes. Aunt Edna used to say that all the time." She diverted her gaze for a few seconds then gave a half smile. "I used to hate it when she said that. Now I'd give anything to hear her say it again."

In silence, they shared another precious moment—an instant of communal grief and loss. As if orchestrated, they cleared their throats together.

Beulah gave a tight smile. "Okay, my dear. You have me at your disposal. Tell me what you want me to do."

Several hours and a half-pepperoni-half-vegetarian pizza later, the two of them had called back or left messages with over thirty new and twelve regular clients. The appointment calendar for Shira was booked solid, from eight-thirty in the morning to eight-thirty at night, for the remainder of the week.

Panic clouded Shira's countenance as she turned the appointment book pages, curled with the indentations of name after name written in pencil.

"You all right, Shira?" She stroked the young woman's shoulder.

She covered her mouth with her hand. "What have I done?" She blinked back moisture. "Beulah, I can't manage all this. What happens to our walk-ins? I can't stop those, especially since the article."

"I'll help you."

Her head tilted to one side, she reached a hand toward Beulah, not quite touching her arm. "No offense, Beulah, but most of these people will want the more current styles. You're not quite ready for that."

She laughed, despite the sting of truth to the comment. "True. But thanks for the compliment that I will be ready." She pointed toward the shampoo stations. "I'll shampoo, sweep, answer phones, whatever it takes."

A pile of clean towels sat on the shampoo counter. Beulah took one and began folding. "Maybe I could take a couple of Edna's older clients who are accustomed to me. Together with Melly, we should keep you from pulling your hair out. But it's still going to be rough. No question."

"You would do that for me?"

Beulah circled back toward Shira. "Why wouldn't I?"

Shira's cheeks pinked. "I . . . well, I haven't been . . . very supportive." She dropped wearily into one of the hair dryer chairs.

"Pish-posh. You were the most important person on this earth to my best friend. I am honored to do this." She sat in the chair next to Shira. "Besides, you made me look ten years younger."

Her full lips stretched into a smile. "Twenty years."

Beulah nodded. "I rest my case. So, how about showing me how you do that massage thingy when you shampoo?"

25

No. I'm so sorry, Edna. No. Don't go.

Harriet gasped as her body bolted upright. Her heart was either going to attack or jump out of her chest. She labored to slow her breathing.

What in the Sam Hill was that?

The clock read a few minutes after six. She needed to get her bearings. *Just lie back down. Relax.*

She struggled to breathe, forcing her to sit back up. Was this a heart attack?

"Okay, Harriet, old girl. Take a deep breath." But trying to force air into her old, smoky lungs was a challenge. They revolted with a coughing jag.

"Okay, not so deep. Breathe in. Breathe out. The heart is slowing down. Good, good, good."

After a few minutes, Harriet abandoned the thought of dialing 911.

That was scary. All of this because of a dream?

Not just a dream. Part of it was a memory. But before she chewed over the details, she required some strong coffee and a cigarette.

The ashtray was full again. Harriet checked the pack of cigarettes. Four left. It was a new pack when she first sat at the dinette. After the third cup of coffee she could barely control the tremors. At least she hoped it was because of the coffee.

The dream had replayed itself over and over again. After the second time, she began journaling it. She couldn't remember the last time she had pulled out the old leather-bound book. She'd jotted more details in the margins.

She couldn't resist another read.

It began with something that happened a long time ago in the shop. Both Edna and I were doing clients' hair—Beulah wasn't there because it was before she started.

The brat came running into the salon, waving a large piece of paper. Her mother, Aviva, followed her.

Shira must have been six or seven. She ran to Edna and hugged her waist. Edna stopped what she was doing to squat down to hug her.

Shira showed Edna a picture she drew. Edna lifted her up and set the girl on her hip. They walked toward me.

"Look what our girl drew for us, Harriet," Edna said.

Shira held the large paper in both of her small hands. Her broad smile had one tooth missing. Her brown pigtails were sloppy from a day at school.

"See, Miss Harriet?" Her excited voice made me smile. "It's a picture of Aunt Edna and you doing good hair."

Sure enough, there was Edna with her dark brown hair and me with a tall crayon-yellow beehive. Both of us were working on people with curly red hair.

She had drawn little butterflies and flowers all around us.

Edna looked at me. A single tear fell . . .

The pen rolled from her hand. Even after re-reading this thing so many times, she panted, trying to keep the sobs from taking over. No wonder her heartbeat had jumped all over the place.

Calm down, Harriet. She grabbed the smoldering cigarette from the ashtray and pulled the desired nicotine before exhaling.

Finish this, old girl. Then you can move on.

The dream changed. Everything was dark except for Edna's face covered in tears. She held something out to me. As I focused, I saw that it was a large snow globe. She always loved snow globes.

I took it from her and inspected the structure inside.

The globe contained a miniature Hair Mavens. People were inside, moving about, like it was real or something. I got excited. I hugged the roundness to me tightly. Edna said nothing, but her beautiful face showed pain and anguish. I held it tighter until I felt the glass crack and give. The liquid, and all the contents inside, rushed out.

I had broken it.

I knelt down trying to gather the pieces. When I looked up, Edna was shaking her head with her hands over her mouth. She turned away from me.

I knelt on the glass—ignoring sharp pains—and reached out for her. Called out to her. She turned back to me and closed her eyes. Then she lay on her bed where I found her, when she. . .

Harriet shook so badly she had to grip the sides of the tabletop. Even with her eyes shut tight the tears came anyway.

What does this mean? She was no spiritual guru, but all this felt like it meant something important, like she had done something really bad.

She had broken the snow globe. But not on purpose.

It was a dream—that's all. There was nothing she would ever, ever do to hurt Edna.

"I think . . . I think it means Edna wants me to take better care of The Hair Mavens. Maybe?" But wasn't that what she was doing? Trying to protect it from Shira? The brat was the one trying to destroy it. Not her.

Somehow she wasn't so sure about that right now.

The phone rang. It took four rings before she was calm enough to lift the receiver.

"Harriet? You still asleep?" Billie Mae said. "Come on girl, today's the big day. Get your behind in gear. Cornelia and Bernice are chomping at the bit."

"I'm awake, Billie." Boy, was she awake.

"Listen, I want to be there for the bash." She cackled. "Bash. Get it?"

Yeah, Harriet got it. She just wasn't sure she liked it.

"Shira's probably gonna have a bunch of those hoity-toities there today, since you couldn't open your yap and put a stop to that interview."

"What in the world could I have done, Billie Mae?"

"You coulda told that reporter the brat was ruining her aunt's shop. Newspapers love all that junk."

She hadn't thought of that.

"Anyway, our plan will work. Cornie and Bernie will pitch such a loud fit, the whole block will know what an incompetent Shira is."

"Yeah."

"'Yeah.' Is that all I get for my hard work?"

"Sorry, Billie. This is great. I appreciate you helping me get back at the brat." Her words didn't contain an ounce of conviction, because she didn't feel it.

"That's better." She heard her take a sip of something. Coffee, hopefully. "I'll be watching out for any other opportunities. You never know."

"Yeah, you do that." Harriet's gut was doing somersaults.

"Hey, I'll stop by Delicious Bakery and pick up some cherry cheese Danishes to celebrate," she said.

Why was all of this feeling so wrong? Wasn't this what Harriet had wanted all along?

Butterflies apparently had organized a convention in Shira's belly. Originally she had planned to make a trip to Delicious Bakery but she didn't think she could handle the smell.

This was her third walk-through of Mavens. She had folded, dusted, straightened, and fussed with things since six-thirty that morning. The first client arrived in thirty minutes and she was already tired.

The front door opened.

"Good morning, Shira." Beulah—with her new 'do—carried an air of hope and a large pink pastry box with her. "I thought you might need a little help before your busy day begins."

I. Might. Just. Cry. "Thank you."

"My, but don't you look pretty." Beulah patted Shira's shoulder.

What she could really use was a hug. She nodded toward the box. "What do you have there?"

Beulah waggled her brows. "Goodies. From Zaydie's Bakery." She lifted the lid to reveal tiny phyllo-dough turnovers. The savory aroma of garlic and meat rose up. Her stomach actually growled. How was that possible?

Beulah opened her bulky handbag and pulled out hot pink napkins and small matching paper plates. "How about a quick party before the crowd gets here?"

They filled plates with spinach, cheese, and meat-filled goodies. Beulah passed Shira a napkin and shut her eyes. "Thank You, Lord, for this delicious feast. And, Lord, we all need Your strength and wisdom today, but most of all Shira needs it. Help her, Lord. In Jesus name. Amen."

Before taking a crispy bite, Shira winked at Beulah.

Oh, my. The bite nearly melted in her mouth.

As she chewed, she realized the nervousness had left. Beulah would attribute it to the prayers. Maybe.

God, if You are listening, thanks.

One by one the new clients came through the door with great expectations—only a few were somewhat unrealistic—and one by one they left with a smile. The morning was nearly over, and Shira was more energized now than when the first client arrived.

How grateful she was for both Veronica and Aunt Edna's training her in the art of listening. Sometimes the essence of what the client wanted was more important than the actual style. If she paid attention, she could build trust and understanding. This had served her well in New York and now here.

Beulah had made a copy of the day's appointments for her with the full name of each client. It was so much more professional to address each client by name.

Her next client waited in her chair.

"Mrs. Stubbins?" Shira ran her fingers through her new client's thin, over-processed hair. "May I call you Cornelia?"

"No, I would rather you not," she said, reducing the temperature around them by several degrees.

Okay. Someone got up on the wrong side of the broomstick. "Very well, Mrs. Stubbins. How may I help you today?"

She pulled a photo from a grotesque orange pleather purse then pointed a stumpy finger at an image of Jennifer Aniston. "I want her style. Make me look like her."

Mrs. Stubbins could easily have been mistaken for Mrs. Doubtfire, so Shira hoped she was kidding. However, after six years of unpredictability in the hair world, Shira wasn't about to take any chances.

"Mrs. Stubbins, while you have wonderful bone structure," she said, stroking the top of her lifeless shoulder-length hair. "I'm afraid Jennifer's long hair would not do you justice."

She gave Shira an appalled glare, as though she had driven over her kitten. "Are you saying you don't know how to do that style?" Mrs. Stubbins's voice was loud, as though she were talking to the neighborhood. Several women in the waiting area looked up.

"Not at all, Mrs. Stubbins. The style is quite simple, actually. It's that—"

"So what you're saying is, you won't style *my* hair." Her voice rose another decibel.

Now everyone in the salon stared at Shira. Beulah stuck her head out from the supply room.

"Ma'am. I will be happy to do that style for you." Shira gently touched Mrs. Stubbins's shoulder and nodded toward Beulah. "Shall we shampoo you first?"

Mrs. Stubbins knocked Shira's hand from her shoulder. "Don't touch me!"

Several people gasped.

Harriet turned toward the debacle. Great, this was exactly what Shira didn't need. More snide remarks from Miss Beehive.

"Cornelia, cut it out," Harriet said.

A brief instant of surprise passed—for Mrs. Doubtfire and Shira—before the woman sputtered and jumped to her feet. Shira backed up. Mrs. Stubbins clutched her purse to her chest as Jennifer fluttered to the floor.

"How dare you." The wild woman spoke to Harriet. She turned toward the reception area. "Billie Mae, what are you going to do about this?"

Who was Billie Mae? A woman who seemed vaguely familiar stood and leveled an angry glare—not at Shira, but straight to Harriet. The two women were locked in a staring battle, like two rams ready to butt heads.

Harriet took a step toward Mrs. Stubbins and folded her arms across her chest. "I think it would be best if you left now, Cornelia." Harriet shot daggers at the Billie Mae-person. "I think you all should get out of here."

"Well!" Cornelia Stubbins stomped toward the front door. Billie Mae and another woman, threw their magazines to the floor and got up.

"Wait, ladies. I—"

Harriet grabbed her elbow. Shira twisted it from her grasp.

"Shira." Harriet closed her eyes and shook her head.

Shira looked toward Beulah, who mouthed, "Let them go."

The three ladies punctuated their exit by calling Shira a few ripe names then slammed the door. Harriet went back to rolling her client's hair like a full-fledged catfight hadn't almost taken place.

Shira lifted her arms and dropped them to her sides.

The door opened again. Four college-aged girls giggled their way inside.

Later. Shira would have to deal with what had just happened later. She greeted the young women. They twittered louder.

"Are you Shira?" a pretty blonde asked.

"Yes."

Another ripple. Maybe not college girls—these must be high schoolers. A glance at her watch suggested these girls were skipping school.

"We saw your picture in the newspaper," a brunette spoke up.

"Is that a fact?" Shira folded her arms. "Are any of you interested in a new look?"

A few squeals. One of them broke from the gaggle and bravely stepped toward her. "My name is Sarah. Ms. Lowinger is our teacher, and she said you were the best hairdresser ever."

She gave a half-smile. "Does Ms. Lowinger know you skipped school today?"

They gasped in unison.

Brave-girl cleared her throat. "We only skipped gym. We're on the co-op program."

"Is Melissa Cohen in your class?"

Whispers back and forth before brave-girl answered. "Yes, but she stayed for class."

Good for you, Melly.

"Well, I will do your hair—"

More squeals.

"—provided you never skip class again. And—"

146

Feeble promises and dramatic pleas came from the group.

"—you tell Ms. Lowinger that you skipped today." Oh, brother. She sounded so mature. Cari would be proud of her.

Contrite glances passed between them. "Yes, ma'am."

Ma'am? Oy!

"Let's see what I can do for you girls."

Beulah caught her eye and gave a thumbs-up. Why did that simple gesture bring such warm fuzzies?

The door opened again to reveal more walk-ins. The brief respite was gone. Back to work. How was she going to keep up with all this?

Kathy was nearly finished with Mrs. Olsen's hair. It resembled a snow-white bicycle helmet—the style she'd had since before Kathy did her hair.

The laughter of the young girls with Shira and Beulah reminded her of happy times at Gooding's. It had been a long time since she remembered the fun she had while working there. She couldn't stop staring at the girls.

Shira smiled and said things she couldn't hear that made the girls laugh. Two of them stood around and watched Shira style the blonde girl's hair.

Beulah shampooed the girl with brown hair. The girl talked with excited words and hands to Beulah.

When Kathy first entered the salon, she did not recognize Beulah. She looked younger and lighter and happier.

The girl in Shira's style chair said she wanted to look like Jennifer Aniston. She had the picture Mrs. Stubbins dropped earlier. The girl's friends behind her jumped up and down and said, "Yes, yes. Make her look like Jennifer."

Mrs. Olsen's thick hair received one more coat of hairspray. As the mist settled, Kathy had a thought. "Mrs. Olsen?"

The old woman raised her bushy brows.

"I have an idea for another style for you." Her face heated. "Maybe next time we could try something new."

She took Kathy's hand in hers. "Really? Because I love Beulah's hair." She tugged Kathy closer. "I hardly recognized her. She looks ten years younger."

Excitement bumps—Beulah called them goosy-bumps—traveled up Kathy's arms. "Yes, I can do that or something else you might like. I will go through magazines and find some styles so you can choose."

"Oh, yes, Kathy. What fun." She clapped. "I can't wait until next week."

Kathy's face felt tight as a smile stretched to borders it hadn't touched in a long time.

Mrs. Olsen paid for her style. After Kathy secured the cashbox, Mrs. Olsen took her hand. She looked like a cute little girl ready to get into mischief, then pressed not one, but two dollars into Kathy's palm.

"This is too much, Mrs. Olsen."

"No, it most certainly is not, Kathy. Today was so much fun. It was wonderful having young people in the shop again." She smiled toward Shira with all the girls around her. "See you next Tuesday."

Slipping the two dollars into her pants pocket, she returned to her station to sweep up and prepare for her next client in thirty minutes.

"Kathy?" Shira leaned backward as she worked. "There are two gentlemen who need trims. Could you take one of them, please?"

Nyet. Kathy's heart rose to her mouth. The men smiled at her. Both their faces melted into Justin's image. She shook her head, opened her mouth, but no words came out.

Shira's face communicated that she was not happy. "Kathy? Please help one of these gentlemen."

"I cannot, please."

"What do you mean you—"

Beulah scurried over to Shira. She whispered something to Shira. Everyone stared at Kathy. Her feet froze to the floor.

Beulah nodded toward Kathy then stood before the two men. She extended her hand to one of them. "My name is Beulah. How may I help you?"

The all-too familiar, trapped-animal feeling came over Kathy. Her stomach churned the little turnovers she had eaten earlier like a garbage disposal. She did not want to be sick in front of Shira and all these people.

She half-walked, half-ran to the bathroom.

Locking the door first, she hit the switches for the lights and fan. Shaky fingers flung her plastic glasses to the floor. Bending over the sink, she splashed water on her face.

After the sickness left, she raised her head to look in the mirror. A pale, wet face stared back at her. *This is not good, Katya. Shira will fire you now.* Her head dropped.

Shira would fire her for sure.

"Don't fire her, Shira. Please," Beulah pleaded. She wondered how much weight her opinion carried with the young woman. An ounce? A pound?

Shira paced the cramped supply room, her hands on her hips. "Kathy seems unstable. I can't have that right now. She can't refuse to work on clients," Shira whispered then pointed a shaking finger toward the salon area. "Then lose her turnovers in the ladies room."

Beulah watched Shira's agitated movements for some hope of her calming down. "All I can tell you is, your aunt never gave a male client to Kathy. She was adamant about it."

She stopped pacing. "Harriet let that fly?"

"Yes."

"But no one tells me?"

"I'm sorry, Shira. I should have. Honestly, it's something we don't think twice about any more."

She puffed out some air and sat on the lunch table. "You never asked my aunt why?"

"No. She asked us to trust her and not ask questions of her or Kathy. Your aunt required so little from us, of course we respected her wishes."

Shira nibbled her lower lip. "Any clues what might be wrong with her?"

Beulah glanced at the floor and shook her head. "No. I know something dreadful must have happened to her, though. And I know she has no one since Edna passed away."

"So, you don't think she'll go postal on us?"

Beulah chuckled. "No." *But she needed the Lord and others who cared.* How she wished she had the courage to say that to Shira.

Shira pushed away from the table. "I am entrusting her to you, Beulah. Nothing like this can happen again."

"I'll talk with her. You go on back to the giggle-girls."

She walked past Beulah, then turned and touched her arm. "Thanks."

"You're welcome, Shira." Perhaps she had gained a few ounces of Shira's trust.

Beulah exhaled. Kathy was such an enigma. Was it possible to gain a tiny crumb of Kathy's trust?

The clouds rolled in, dark and ominous. Beulah hoped Kathy and she would have a few minutes before the rain started. They strolled down the sidewalk on the west side of the building to a residential area with a small park. Hopefully it would be quiet and afford them some privacy.

The park was empty. The trees had begun to wear their fall colors. What a beautiful, peaceful background for their discussion. Together they dusted off the picnic table and took seats on either side.

Kathy folded her hands and pressed her lips together tightly. "Am I fired?" Her voice was so soft. So hopelessly lost.

Beulah leaned closer. "No."

Kathy seized Beulah's gaze. "No?"

"No. However, Shira wants some assurances that you won't have another panic attack in view of the customers." She smiled. "You can have it anywhere else you like."

Kathy raised her chin and focused on a passing cloud. "I do not understand. Shira does not like us—does not like me. Why is she being so nice to me?"

"Maybe God is softening her heart?"

Kathy shut her eyes and brought her head down. "I do not believe—"

149

"You do not believe in God. I remember you telling me that." Beulah touched her hand. "That's okay, I'll—"

"—believe for me." Kathy gave a half-smile. "I remember you telling me that." She pushed up her glasses.

Beulah resisted the urge to reach over and hug the little waif. She was so fragile. *Lord, help her to trust me.* "Kathy, have you ever spoken to a doctor about these panic attacks? A doctor might help you sort through all these emotions."

Her body stiffened. "No."

Does she think Edna broke her confidence? "Edna never said what happened to you, but whatever it was obviously has caused you great pain. I would like to help. If you ever want to—"

Kathy stood up. "You must please to not ask me of such things."

"I, I'm sorry, Kathy." Beulah reached toward her. "I was trying—"

"No!" She stepped over the picnic table bench and backed away from Beulah. "No." She raised a trembling finger and jabbed it in her direction. "You must please to not ask me of such things. Ever again!"

A lifetime seemed to pass as she stared Beulah into shreds. Something told her to not say a word or move a muscle. Had she been too hasty in telling Shira that Kathy was stable enough to work?

"Ever, Beulah." Kathy's body relaxed enough that she lowered her finger.

"I will not ask you again, Kathy. I promise." Beulah was not moving from this spot.

Kathy released a ragged sigh then pounded her forehead with the palms of her hands. "I am sorry to be mean to you." She took a deep breath. "I am sorry. You are kind, but you are not Edna."

She held her head with both hands. "Shira is not Edna. I do not like all these rules."

Kathy turned away and sprinted back to the shop, as thunder rumbled in the distance.

26

Harriet couldn't believe those fools were eating bugs. What some people wouldn't do for money. The episode of *Survivor* had her thinking maybe her day hadn't been so bad.

The tray, supporting the half-eaten quart of chocolate mint ice cream, wobbled on her lap as she fished for the napkin that had slipped between her leg and the side of the recliner.

It could have been worse. Right? She could be on an island, crawling with bugs, and toasting them over an open flame for supper.

Except, there would be no Billie Mae on the island, madder than a hornet. Maybe eating creepy crawlies wasn't so bad.

The phone rang for the fourth time that evening. Billie had left several messages that would cause the saltiest of sailors to blush. Eventually Harriet would have to talk with her friend, but there were all these bizarre feelings and thoughts going through her brain. She needed time to sort them.

Like, was it possible she was going about this all wrong? Maybe the dream had been some kind of sign from God? She didn't know.

The answering machine clicked. "Harriet, it is Kathy."

The Mouse? Calling her?

She pressed mute on the remote.

"If you could please call me—"

Somehow, Harriet managed to grab the phone without upsetting her ice cream. "Yeah, Kathy, I'm here."

"Oh, I thought you were not home."

"I—uh—no, I'm home. What's up?"

"Harriet, I do not like all Shira's rules. Do you?"

Duh. "Not really."

"I miss Edna." Kathy's voice went soft and gooey.

No mushiness, please. "What's on your mind, Kathy?"

"I want to help you."

"Help me with what?"

"Help you . . . you know."

Was this some kind of set-up? Had Beulah put her up to this? They had been awfully chummy lately.

"Kathy, you need to be more specific."

She gave a soft huff. "I want to help you to make Shira go away. So she is not the owner of The Hair Mavens."

Queasiness settled in her as though she had eaten insects for dinner. "I'm not so sure about this anymore." Had she said that—out loud?

"Harriet, Edna would not want all these changes. What will happen to all our clients? Shira does not care about the nice old ladies we serve."

Shira had passed some of Edna's clients on to Beulah today, so she could work on the hoity-toity customers.

Then there was the shock of seeing the new Beulah when she had arrived for work. She looked—

"Harriet?"

"What?"

"I want to help."

"Why?"

"I, I have my reasons. I do not want her changing Edna's salon into a place with no heart."

Well, Harriet had never thought of it in exactly those terms. The Mouse had something there. "So you have some ideas?"

Kathy sighed. "Yes. I have many ideas."

The Mouse had roared. Harriet placed the receiver back in the charger and lifted the tray with her melted ice cream off her lap. She flumped the recliner into its closed position.

Obviously, she had misjudged Kathy. The Mouse had more gumption and fire in her gut than Harriet had imagined. Harriet's stiff legs ached as she made her way to the kitchen. Kathy was as upset as she about all the changes. And, even though the kid's ideas weren't new, she was no longer alone. She had another insider to help her. Maybe she could tell Billie Mae to butt out now.

The container of ice cream ruined, she dumped the contents into the sink and ran the disposal.

Billie Mae's plan was too obvious and had done the opposite of what she wanted—to turn the clients away from Shira. She had even felt bad when Cornie went off on the brat. *No, they needed to be subtle.* Subtle but thorough.

But maybe Billie Mae could still be an asset. She had some clout with many of the regular clients.

The queasiness returned. She rubbed her midsection. Edna's face from her dream crowded into Harriet's scheming mind. Edna's tears.

She pounded her fist on the counter.

No. This was the right thing to do.

27

Shira pushed the broom around her station for what seemed the thousandth time today.

Melly glanced up from the computer, dark circles under her eyes. "I'm almost half finished with all the data entry." Her sweet smile couldn't mask the exhaustion on her face. "We'll be throwing away the big book tomorrow."

"You, young lady, need to go home and get some rest." Shira swept the clippings of her last client into a dustpan. "It's a school night, after all."

The young woman held up a stack of index cards about an inch thick. "I only have these few left."

This was Melly's second late night inputting the data into Shira's state-of-the-art software. The teenager had taken to it like a credit card at an Estée Lauder sale. But Shira didn't like how pale Melly looked.

"Have you had anything to eat since you started work?"

Melly's wide dark brown eyes gazed toward the ceiling.

"I thought so." Shira rubbed her thin shoulders. "Shut down and go home. You can finish this tomorrow."

"But—"

"No buts. Pack up and go home. It's after eight." For goodness' sake, she sounded like a mother. "Let your mom take care of you. Fix you some chicken soup. And get to bed."

She muttered. Then blushed as she looked sheepishly at Shira. "Can I back up the files first, please?"

"Fine." So this was what it felt like to be a responsible adult. She stroked Melly on the back and returned to her sweeping. Once she finished counting the new product shipment she could finally get some sleep.

"Shira, I'll see you tomorrow." Melly stood at the door. "I promise I'll finish inputting all the clients."

"I trust you." She moved to her side. "You get some rest." She smoothed back a strand of Melly's short hair.

"Thank you so much for this job, Shira." She planted a kiss on Shira's cheek. "Night."

"Night, Melly."

Shira locked the door. Her hand went to her cheek. It felt like an angel had just touched her.

The sweet-smelling suds surrounded Shira's tired body. The mirrors and window were steamy as she soaked in the hot bath. She fluffed up a small mountain of bubbles.

It was time to cut the ties in Manhattan. She had resigned herself to the slower lifestyle in the suburbs of Philadelphia. Besides, shopping here had its benefits. More parking and better prices.

What was she thinking? Shopping? The bags from Crisis113 still sat by the front door. She had yet to inventory, log, and put them away.

She smashed the bubble mountain.

Maybe Cari and Aaron could meet her and Dad in New York to take in a show. Not this trip. Soon, though. Once she sold her apartment they wouldn't have a free place to stay when they were in town. How fun it would be to show them the bright lights. She couldn't wipe the grin off her face as she imagined Cari's reaction to her first Broadway show.

Would Alec ever make it to Broadway? No, his sights had always been set for Hollywood. Alec. She hadn't heard from him in a week. Not since she had hung up on him. Or Fawna, for that matter.

Thankfulness welled up unexpectedly. To think she had almost asked Alec to move in. How much more complicated this moving-on would have been if she had. And having to introduce Alec to Dad? She didn't want to think about that. Alec was everything Dad had warned her about—he had called boys like him bums.

Her eyes scrunched tightly as she shoved away the memories of the long line of bums she had dated over the years. She exhaled loudly, disturbing the airy suds.

Think about something else, Shira.

She ticked off her calendar: Sunday and Monday at her old place. Pack up and move. Find a realtor. That was, of course, if she survived the next two days' schedule.

She wasn't sure she could handle another week at this pace. She lifted a handful of foam and blew them. Two more days of back-to-back appointments. She moaned and sank lower.

What would she have done without Melly, Cari, and Beulah the last few days? Her dad was helping her move. Even Aaron had given his services as a gift.

These people were the real gifts. Gifts she didn't deserve and could never repay. Tears seized possession of her again. *For goodness' sake, I'm a bundle of emotions these days.*

The melodic tone of her new phone echoed in her porcelain sanctuary. She lifted it from the floor. Caller ID read JFOX. Instinctively, she covered herself with bubbles.

"Hello?" The warmth on her cheeks had nothing to do with the temperature of her bath.

"Hi, Shira. Did I catch you at a bad time?"

"I'm soaking."

"Beg your pardon?"

"I'm in the bathtub soaking."

"Oh, uh. I'm sorry." His embarrassment seeped through the line.

Good, she wasn't the only one blushing. She chewed a thumbnail and grinned. "Was there a reason you called, Jesse?"

"I, uh, I brought you some soup."

"Soup?"

"Hot and Sour."

Ah. A peace offering. "Very thoughtful. Thank you."

"Cari told me about your schedule this week. I figured you probably were too tired to fix anything."

Silly man. He thought she cooked. "Give me a few minutes and I'll be down."

"Front door?"

"No, if you don't mind, could you go to the back door?" No sense Main Street seeing her in her robe.

"I'll be there."

Her fuzzy white robe modestly wrapped around her, she shuffled through the apartment, down the stairs, and to the back door in the break room. She flipped on the outside light, taking a quick peek to be sure Jesse was right there. Yes, he was.

Her heart accelerated. She opened the door a crack.

He rested a leather arm on the doorjamb. Dreamy almost amber eyes gazed down at her. Shivers tumbled over her skin like a teenager with raging hormones. "Hey, Jess." She clutched the top of her robe.

"Hey, Shira." That dimple deepened as he gave her his boyish smile.

His full lips, those white teeth . . .

"You want to come in and share the soup?" As soon as the words left her mouth, she knew his answer.

He glanced toward the sidewalk. "No. I don't think that would be wise." He held up the white plastic bag. "Here's your soup."

Holding her robe with one hand, she slipped her other hand through the narrow opening to accept his gift. Their fingers touched. An electric charge passed between them, drawing their gazes deeper. "Thanks, Jesse," she whispered.

Time stood still. She was lost in his eyes and couldn't find her way out.

He blinked and then shut his lids tight, as though forcing her image from his retina. When he opened them, his eyes were shiny with moisture.

"You're welcome, Shira." He shoved off the jamb and stepped back. "Good night."

"Goodnight, Jess." The lump in her throat was the size of one of Aunt Edna's matzah balls.

Jesse walked across the quiet street toward his car. He stopped and turned. "I forgot, your dad asked if I would help you move on Sunday. Is that okay with you?"

She nodded. "Yes. Yes, that would be great. Thank you."

He waved before getting into his car. She smiled and waved back.

She watched as the taillights disappeared into the night. She'd see him again in a few days. Sweet torture.

28

The crystal bowl of potpourri sat on Beulah's shiny coffee table—another of Allison Garvey's how-to-sell-a-house-quickly tips. She had to admit, her living room smelled yummy, as though she had baked an apple pie.

Allison had booked two showings today. She said both were young families. Knowing this took away some of the sting of this new reality. How would she ever be able to say goodbye to years of memories? Every ding on the wall had a story. Every piece of furniture was a piece of their family history. Wil and her wedding photo tugged her to the wall. She lifted the heavy wood frame and held it. These were the people she remembered, not the ones she saw in the bathroom mirror or in the nursing home. What had happened to those people?

She re-hung the picture, entered her bedroom and retrieved the clear plastic shoebox with Edna's jewelry. The night before she had decided to return this inheritance. It didn't fit her, like her wedding dress wouldn't fit her plump body.

Jesse was meeting her for dinner before Friday service at Beth Ahav. She lifted the lid to take the box containing the pearl earrings. Those were for Shira. The remainder of Edna's treasures would go to Jesse. He was the best suited to decide what to do with them. Perhaps give them to a ministry.

Such finery was not for her. She was plain old Beulah. The velvet earring box in her palm gave off an air of royalty.

No, not for me.

She'd held on to these too long. She felt like a thief.

Beulah caught Shira humming a lively tune from the supply room. The young woman had a spring to her step.

"Oh, Beulah." Shira strode toward her. "I didn't hear you come in. I was thinking. Did you know your name is Hebrew?"

"I seem to remember Edna saying something about that."

She placed her arm around Beulah's waist to maneuver her toward the computer. "I Googled your name this morning."

"You what?"

Her chuckle warmed her. "It's a search engine. You know, a way to look things up on the internet." She sat in the chair and moved her fingers quickly over the keyboard.

"Oh." Beulah had heard of the internet, but she'd never used a computer. And she was too embarrassed to tell Shira.

"Anyway, your name means married in Hebrew."

"Married?"

"Yes. See, here's the correct pronunciation. Bay-oo-lah." She pointed to the screen.

"Bay-oo-lah?" A rush of goose bumps traveled over her skin. "How beautiful."

"Doesn't that sound better than just plain Beulah?" She typed more. "See, Israel was called Beulah because she is married to God. That's interesting, isn't—" Shira peered over her shoulder. "Are you okay?"

She took Beulah's hand. "What's wrong?"

"I, I'm not sure." She felt like jumping and dancing. "There is something about that name."

"Your name."

"That's right. My name."

"What are you feeling?"

Beulah stared at her, unsure how to describe what she felt without sounding crazy. "Shira, when I spoke the Hebrew word—"

"Your name."

"Yes, my name. I felt goosebumps. Look, they're still there." She extended her arm. Her skin was like a freshly plucked goose.

Shira nodded and tilted her head.

"I felt like dancing." Beulah nibbled her top lip.

Shira raised an eyebrow. "Do you intend to do that now?"

She laughed. "No, but that's what I felt—feel like doing. This morning I was feeling a little sorry for myself. I needed a hug from the Lord. You gave me one."

Shira stared at her as though she had grown another nose. Perhaps it was best that Beulah changed the subject. "Shira, why were you looking up my name?"

She shrugged a shoulder. "I don't know. I was thinking how your name didn't fit you. Especially with your new look. Your name kind of reminds me of an overweight truck driver." She grimaced. "Sorry."

Beulah laughed again. "Quite all right. Some great-great aunt had it and my dad thought it would be good for me to bear the burden. I've never been fond of my name . . . until now."

Shira tapped her hand. "That's what I mean. When I read the meaning and the way to pronounce it, it seemed to suit you." A few more movements on the keyboard and the Google-thing disappeared and the new software's logo appeared. Shira rose and placed her hands on hips. "So the question is what do we call you now?"

"Beulah is fine."

"No, it's not."

"Really, Shira. Knowing the true meaning matters more to me than how someone says it."

She shook her head. "You look so young and beautiful now. Why would you want that old name?"

"I'm still me, Shira." She went to the mirror. "I love my hair, but I'm still me. I love knowing what my name means. I thank you for this blessing." Beulah took Shira's slim, soft hand. "God used you to bless me."

Beulah couldn't read any emotions on Shira's face. Shira searched her face as one might try to find a destination on a map.

Oh, Lord, let her see You when she looks at me.

Shira gently freed her hand and walked away. "Another busy day, Bay-oo-lah."

"Shira, I have something for you."

She turned. "For me?"

Beulah unzipped her purse and pulled out the velvet box. "This is rightfully yours."

"What's this?"

Beulah opened the box. "Your Aunt Edna's pearl earrings."

Shira bent forward.

"I believe these go with your grandmother's pearl necklace."

"No. I have those." She moved closer to examine them. "I've never seen these before."

"Well, I believe they belong to you now."

"Giving away your inheritance, Bay-oo-lah?" She pursed her lips.

Her inheritance? The goosebumps returned. "What?"

"Those are your earrings. Not mine." She closed the box and handed it back to Beulah. "Aunt Edna wanted you to have them."

"I don't feel right about taking them, or the box of jewelry."

"Why?" Her brow knitted.

"I, I don't feel right."

Shira clasped her hands over Beulah's, squeezing the box into her palm. "Well, my friend, I would feel like a thief taking them from you. And don't you dare think of returning the other pieces."

Thief? "What do you mean?"

"They are your inheritance, not mine. My aunt trusted you to do whatever you need to do with them." Shira patted her on the back. "Besides, Aunt Edna passed on a different inheritance to me."

Shira's eyes rounded. "Look at my arm, Beulah. Goosebumps."

29

Kathy caught up with Harriet on the sidewalk, a few feet from the park behind The Hair Mavens.

"I know how to get rid of Shira, Harriet," Kathy said.

Harriet stopped walking. "How?"

"The computer." She smiled, but did not say that Gooding's had the same software that Shira had purchased.

Harriet took a puff of her cigarette. Kathy tried to get out of Harriet's way before the smoke hit her. "The computer?" She coughed. "I don't know how to work that stupid thing."

Kathy smiled inside and outside. "I do."

"You're kidding."

"No. The place I worked before had the same software."

Her brows came together. "Where did you work before? I thought Mavens was the first job you—"

"It was a long time ago." Kathy's heart stumbled. She had said too much. "I must get the password from Melly then I can go in and delete some files."

"How is that going to help us?"

"Shira will overbook, and people will get angry that they must wait. I will delete only the new clients, not our regular people."

Harriet nodded her head. She seemed pleased. *Harriet sees me now.* "The best part is I can delete from the inventory so we can take product without her knowing."

"Hmm." A frown took the place of the smile. "I don't want to steal, Kathy."

"No. We can hide the product until Shira is gone. Then we can return it when you take over." A little trickle of guilt tried to come into her heart.

"Way to go, Kathy." Harriet shoved her arm.

Kathy staggered and raised her arm defensively.

"Whoa, calm down." She laughed at her. "You sure are a jumpy little thing."

She was still scared of Harriet. If this worked out, she hoped Harriet would know she was loyal and let her still work at Mavens. Maybe Harriet would even like her.

Guilt tugged at Kathy's heart. Now that it was time to do her part, she battled with the maddening questions of whether or not Edna would approve. But then she would look at Shira's new clients and watch as the little old ladies were pushed out of the way. Yes. Sometimes people had to do bad things for the greater good. *Right?*

Melly had sat at the computer since before Kathy had arrived at The Mavens.

"Hello, Melly," Kathy said.

She raised her head and smiled. The circles under her eyes had darkened from when she first arrived. "Hi, Kathy. Do you need anything?"

"No. Well, yes. Could I have your password so I can sign in some of my clients into the new system?"

Her smile grew larger. "Kathy, you know this software?"

"A little."

"Cool."

She moved away so Kathy could get closer. "I can't give you my password, but Aaron has a log-in and password for everyone who works here. Shira wanted to wait until I entered all the files before he taught everyone to use the system."

Nyet. Using her own password wouldn't work—it had to be Melly's.

Melly wrote on a yellow sticky note and handed it to her. "Here's your log-in." She pointed to her first name and initial of her last name. "And this is your password." The next line was long and had letters and numbers. They meant nothing to her.

Melly gave a little giggle. "I know what you're thinking. The password is hard to remember. Aaron said these types of passwords are the best because people can't figure them out." She reached for her purse and pulled out a folded piece of paper. "I keep forgetting mine. I'm always referring back to this."

"I see," Kathy said. A flush of relief.

"Here, let me show you all the stuff this software does. It's great." She twisted in her chair to smile at her. "But only Shira and I will have access to all the modules, like the inventory and ordering stuff."

Melly's fingers moved quickly over the keyboard, showing Kathy all the wonderful features.

Yes, it was the same software. *Kharosho*—good. All Kathy needed to do was get that piece of paper, and their plan would work.

30

The ashtray was full and Harriet's coffee cup empty. What did she expect after two hours of racking her brain—at three in the morning? She picked up the ashtray and dumped the contents into the garbage. For years she had never remembered a single dream. Now, for four nights in a row, that nightmare had woken her up with heart palpitations and a cold sweat.

Was she going crazy? Were they early signs of Alzheimer's? She needed another cup of coffee.

The notes she had originally made about the dream had grown from a few pages to ten. Each night she remembered a little more and jotted it down. Tonight she remembered Edna didn't give her the snow globe. She had been showing it to her. Harriet had pulled it from her grasp.

That's a biggie, old girl. Harriet had taken it from her friend. Had she stolen it from her?

Wait a minute. This is only a stupid dream.

"Harriet, you've never been into this hocus-pocus stuff. It's what you can see and feel that you can count on." She shook her head.

Well, maybe not count on. At least she understood what she could see. Most of the time.

She blew out a smokeless breath. At three in the morning, it was probably best to not lie to herself. She needed help with this. Was there a listing in the Yellow Pages for people who interpreted dreams? A psychic?

No way. She wasn't seeing no charlatan.

Beulah.

Her name popped into Harriet's head as though it belonged there. Where had that come from? What good could she do?

Harriet wasn't speaking to her anyway. She was a traitor. Worse, overnight she had morphed into one of them—the hoity-toities. Beulah must have figured because she looked so good, she was one of them, now. Well, she wasn't—she was traitor to her friend, Edna.

So what do I do? Almost as if on their own, her hands folded. *Pray?*

She shrugged. It couldn't hurt. She cleared her throat and looked up. "Okay, here's the deal, God. If You're there, then I need some help. Tell me what this dream means before I go crazy. Or maybe I'm already crazy and You're letting me know. Anyway, I guess what I'm saying is, I need your help with this one. Appreciate the time. Hope to hear from you soon."

Had that qualified as a real prayer? Seemed like she had missed something.

Oh, yeah. "Amen."

The room was quiet, except for the drip of the kitchen faucet. What had she expected? A burning bush?

"Sunshine today. The high's in the sixties for your Saturday, so enjoy." Harriet slapped off the radio alarm. Sunshine peeked through a small opening in her curtains. For once, the weatherman had spoken correctly.

Despite the two hours of fretting last night—or early this morning—Harriet felt rested. Her feet slid into her slippers. She scuffed to the window and flung open the curtains. A beautiful morning, indeed.

After the prayer, she had trudged back to bed and fallen asleep immediately. The nightmare had not returned. Was that a coincidence? Who knew?

She ran the shower. The Mouse—er, Kathy—was meeting her at Delicious Bakery. She was pretty excited about her plan. All Harriet knew was it had better work.

Harriet hated when people were late and Kathy was late.

It always put her in a bad mood. And she'd been in a good mood, too. A bus paused down the street. Its exhaust burned her eyes. She took another puff of her cigarette to cover the noxious smell. Finally, it pulled away and revealed Kathy. She waved as she walked toward her. About time.

"Harriet, I am sorry I am late."

Yeah. Yeah. Whatever. Harriet opened the door to Delicious. Kathy went in first.

"Hey, Harriet. Where have you been?" Nonni came from behind the counter and pulled her into a tight hug. It felt good to be missed.

Meaty arm still around her shoulder, Nonni nodded toward Kathy. "Who's this?"

"This is Kathy Smith. She works with me at The Mavens."

"Well, nice to meet you, Kathy Smith. I'm Nonni." She offered her other hand. "And back there is my hubby, Frank."

Kathy gave Nonni a limp shake and looked away. "Thank you. Nice to meet you."

"The usual, Harriet?"

"Sure."

"And what can I get you, honey?"

Kathy appeared to be pinching her chin. Her eyes darted back and forth at the display cases. "I do not want anything."

A chortle rose from Harriet. If the kid didn't want anything, Harriet was the pope. She was practically drooling. "My treat, Kathy." She should make enough to afford a measly donut.

"It is okay. I am not hungry."

"I insist, Kathy." Harriet pointed to a pecan sticky bun Kathy seemed to be eyeing. "One of those, Nonni."

Kathy hugged her skinny waist. "Thank you, Harriet."

Minutes later, they carried their breakfast to the little park around the corner. As they passed the shop, the lights went on. Harriet's gut tightened.

"Shira is there already," Kathy whispered.

Once they had settled at the picnic table, Harriet took a small bite from her pastry. Kathy pulled a sticky hunk from her roll.

"So, what's the plan?" Harriet asked.

Kathy chewed a few seconds. "I need to get Melly's password. From her purse."

That sick thing returned. "You're really going to do that? Snoop in her purse?"

She nodded and took another small hunk.

The dream and Edna's disappointed face flickered in her mind. "I don't know, Kathy. This is feeling more like doing something wrong than doing something right for Edna."

Kathy's violet eyes pierced hers. "It is the only way, Harriet."

Just who was in control here?

"Did you tell Billie Mae what we are doing?"

Harriet shifted on the hard bench. "I don't think that's such a good idea."

"But we need her. She can help us keep our regular clients. She knows everybody."

All this still felt wrong to Harriet. "I don't know."

"We must be sure everything is covered, or our plan will not work, Harriet."

Time to redirect the conversation. She took a sip of her coffee. "So, when will you do the computer-thing?"

"Sunday. I will copy the password from Melly's purse today."

"It's Saturday. Melly doesn't work on Saturdays."

Her next bite stopped before it reached her mouth. "No?"

"No. You know, it's the Sabbath. All that Jewish stuff, like Edna."

Her hands dropped. "Then I must wait until Tuesday to get the password." She pounded the table. "This is bad."

"Yeah. Sure is." Harriet hid her relief behind the cup of coffee.

31

Shira's dad reached across the table for her hand. The candlelight flickered with the movement. "You're sure this is all right with you, sweetheart?"

"Sure. No problem." She felt bad not telling her father that Jesse had already spilled the beans about escorting her to Manhattan. But then she would have to tell him that he had stopped by with soup. And she was in her robe. And maybe she should just enjoy the cheesecake they were sharing.

They had just finished a delicious meal at one of Philadelphia's finest restaurants, *Lacoix*. The dessert choice had been his idea, too. Great minds thought alike.

He sipped his espresso. "Jesse will drive the rental truck and follow us. We'll take my pick-up."

The smooth cheesecake nearly choked her. "You have a truck?"

He dabbed his mouth with his napkin. One corner of his mouth lifted. "That's right, missy. I got me one of them bruisers."

She couldn't help snickering. The Texas drawl was a new one. But she had always been a sucker for his theatrics. A couple at a table next to them gave him the stink-eye. "Stop it, Dad. They'll ask us to leave."

Dad gestured his arm, like a cowboy taking off his Stetson. "Everything's fine, folks. My daughter's just having a good time."

I'm going to kill him.

After their hasty exit from the exquisite restaurant—that she would probably never be able to visit again—they strolled toward his Lexus.

"Sorry, sweetie." He tipped his head toward her. "I can't help it. I'll stoop to anything to hear you laugh."

She punched his bicep. "I'll get even with you. Mark my words."

Happiness—no, joy—rose up within her. She felt like a little girl again, walking with her daddy.

He wrapped a muscular arm around her, pulling her tight. Her feet barely touched the ground. "I'll look forward to it, Button."

The ride back to her apartment was filled with comfortable chatter of news about distant relatives and friends she hadn't seen in years. All the tension from the hectic week had evaporated.

As they pulled up to the salon, she sighed. The delightful evening was ending. Her dad parked behind her Mini then turned toward her. "Can I walk you to the door, Button?"

"Sure."

When they had hugged goodnight at the front door, she realized how much she was looking forward to their time together in Manhattan. And almost—almost—wished Jesse weren't going so she could enjoy more daddy-daughter time.

His tall frame tucked back into the Lexus. The driver's side window lowered. He stuck his head out. "See you bright and early tomorrow."

She waved as the car pulled away.

"Goodnight, Daddy."

Shira's *tuckus* regretted riding in her dad's truck, as they hit one pothole after another on New York's streets. *Oof.* That was a big one.

"Dad, is there any way to go easy on the gorges?"

He chuckled but didn't take his focus off the congested road. "Sorry, sweetheart. We're almost there." He checked the rearview mirror. "As bad as we have it, Jesse's got it worse."

She twisted around. There he was, the mensch, driving the rental truck with no power steering. Jesse was going to be sorry he had ever agreed to help her.

The three-hour drive finally ended as they parked in front of her building. Shira kept saying she didn't believe in miracles, but there was enough room for both their vehicles—on a Sunday. Had to make her wonder.

The three of them met on the sidewalk, bending and stretching the kinks out of their bodies.

Dad rested his hand on Jesse's shoulder. "How you doing there, buddy?"

"Okay. My arms feel like gelatin from that steering wheel." Jesse brought an elbow up over his shoulder and pushed it down with his other hand.

"Jesse," Shira said, "I don't know how to thank you."

He shrugged and gave her that smile that sent tingles from her toes to her nose.

"Let's get rolling, you two." Her dad gave them both a gentle shove.

Climbing the stairs to her apartment, she realized any angst she'd had about returning was gone. She never thought she would have said this, but Gladstone was home to her now. The door she pushed open was to the life she had left behind.

The living room and hall lights were on. Great. Her electric bill would be horrendous. Was that water running?

"Nice place." Jesse strolled into the living room. His gaze focused on the fireplace.

The picture of Alec.

"So who's this guy?"

"Uh—"

A loud thump came from the back of the apartment.

Her dad pushed her behind him. Jesse grabbed an expensive sculpture—Crisis109, she thought—from the mantle and held it like a club. They both tiptoed toward the hallway.

Unarmed, she grabbed the heavy lead-crystal bowl off the table and followed the men.

If she weren't so frightened, she'd have laughed at the three of them investigating like some Hardy Boys or Nancy Drew mystery.

"Who's there?" Her father's deep voice commanded respect. From her, anyway.

The bathroom door opened a crack. "Don't shoot."

Wait a minute.

"I have a key. I—" Alec, wearing one of her Egyptian cotton towels, stepped from the bathroom. "Hey, babe. I didn't know you were coming."

"Obviously," Jesse said, lowering his weapon.

Alec sauntered toward her—half-naked—arms outstretched. For goodness' sake, was he actually going to hug her?

"What are you doing here, Alec?" She stepped behind her father.

"Alec?" Fawna appeared—in another one of her towels. She stood behind Alec and held his shoulders possessively. "Shira?"

"Fawna?"

"Babe—er, Fawna, I told you to wait in the bathroom." Alec gritted his teeth.

"Okay, folks, I'm Jesse and this is Sam. Now that we've taken roll call, can we get an explanation here?"

"Babe, you know I got kicked out of my apartment," Alec said.

"No, I didn't know that." The crystal bowl was still in her hand—she could nail both Alec and Fawna in one swipe. "That still doesn't answer why you, and my so-called best friend, are here. Wearing my towels."

"We, uh . . . Oh, man." Alec ran a shaky hand over his face.

Her father pried the crystal bowl from Shira's fingers. "Shira, I think a picture's worth a thousand words." He wrapped his arm around her then leveled a look that turned Alec into a quaking reed. "Both of you will leave these premises immediately, or I will call the police."

"Yeah, and I have my lawyer here who will sue the, the towel off you!" Adrenaline traveled like wild-fire through her body. Her breath came in short rasps.

Alec practically knocked Fawna down as he scurried like a rodent for the bedroom.

Shira stomped to Alec's picture over the fireplace and yanked it down—marquee light and all. The cord tripped her. "Can you pull this light thing off, Dad?"

He pulled it off and dropped it onto the floor.

Jesse glanced at her then turned away and walked toward the windows. She stood close to the front door, holding her birthday gift from Alec. *Hah. Some birthday gift. What a bum!*

She struggled to calm her racing heart, but she wasn't having much luck. Her eyes were glued to her bedroom door. Which was good, because she was too ashamed to look at her father—or Jesse. The humiliation and shame folded together with the anger. She chewed on her lip—first the top, then the bottom—waiting for the two interlopers to appear. The picture became heavier by the second.

Alec and Fawna emerged from her bedroom, holding hands. Seeing them together, the pieces of the puzzle finally came together. Fawna always knowing where and what Alec was doing. Alec always accommodating her best friend—inviting her to join them for dinners and movies. She had paid for their dates. *I'm such an idiot.*

Anger revved up her heart rate again. Her fingers grasped the picture frame so tightly her nails dug into the wood.

Alec stepped closer to her. "Sorry, babe."

"Don't sorry, babe me. You rat." She lifted the picture over her head and in one smooth move—bam. Alec's head popped through the heavy canvas.

Her father chuckled then opened the door. "I think you better leave before she chucks the fridge at you two."

Alec—with his new necklace—and Fawna exited quietly. She slammed the door and fumbled with the lock.

Nervous laughter gurgled out of her. Her body wobbled and her legs turned to gel. Her breath came in short spurts.

"Shira?" Her dad's voice sounded like it came through a barrel. He appeared all fuzzy . . .

Uh oh.

Darkness.

Something wet laid across Shira's forehead. She knocked it off and tried to sit up.

Strong hands pressed her back against the couch. "Shira, you need to lie there a little while longer."

"Jesse?"

He placed the cloth back on her forehead. "You fainted."

"Where's Dad?"

"He went out for some soup."

She couldn't look at him. "Sorry about the drama."

He cleared his throat. "He was your boyfriend, I gather."

"*Was* being the operative word." She snuck a glance at Jesse. He sat on the coffee table, his elbows resting on his knees. "I don't know what I ever saw in him."

"He was the underwear guy."

It took a moment before she comprehended. "You mean the TV commercial?"

He nodded.

"Yes. That was him."

"Nice finale . . . You know, with the picture." He smiled, but not his real smile.

"What's wrong, Jesse?"

"I need to think some things through, Shira."

Her stomach plummeted, like falling off a cliff. "About us?"

He puffed some air. "About a lot of things."

"Fine. Whatever." She snatched the washcloth and covered her eyes. "Take all the time you want." She should have known he was too good to be true. Good riddance, Mr. Goody-two-shoes.

What was she saying? Had she blown this? "Jesse?" She still couldn't look at him.

"Yes."

"I'm sorry I'm not what you expected." He had no idea the girl he kissed and innocently flirted with was in reality a tramp.

"It's okay," he said.

But she didn't think it would ever be okay again.

32

Kathy pulled money from the pocket of her slacks. She had to borrow from her weekly grocery money to accomplish the next step of her plan. Her next client wasn't due to arrive for another half hour. It was now or never.

She made her way to the reception desk. Melly was still inputting data into the computer. Kathy wished Melissa did not look so tired all the time. It made her feel bad for what she was about to do.

"Melly, I am very hungry." Kathy worked her smile to be open and sweet like Melly's. "And you have not taken a break for a long time. Will you go to Delicious Bakery and get a pecan sticky bun for me and pick out anything you want for yourself?"

Melly brought her fingers to her mouth. "I don't know, Kathy . . ." She turned to Shira. "Can I take a little break and go to Delicious?"

"I will watch the phones for Melly," Kathy said.

Shira's brows scrunched together. Kathy's fist tightened around the money. Finally, Shira shrugged. "Fine with me. You could use the sunshine, Melly."

Melly reached down to get her purse. Kathy grabbed Melly's hand. "No, Melly. I am buying, remember?"

"Silly me," Melly said. She stood up. "Thanks again, Kathy. You are so sweet."

No, I am not. She gave the money to her.

Melly waved the four precious dollars. "Be right back."

Butterflies in Kathy's stomach made her sick. She had to hurry. Turning away from Shira, she placed her hands on the keyboard. Shira was too close. Would she see Kathy bend forward and search in Melly's purse?

For several minutes, she could not lift even a finger. She jumped at every sound. Sweat beaded above her lip.

Katya, just do it.

She shoved the purse closer with her foot until she could touch the strap. She tugged. It hit the bottom of the counter. She tugged again until she pulled it onto her lap. The flap had a zipper, but Melly had left it open.

Her fingers roamed the inside, searching for the folded paper.

The phone rang. She startled at the sound. The purse wobbled on her knees. She steadied it with one hand and lifted the receiver with the other.

This was her first time answering the phone, ever. "Hello. This is The Hair Mavens. May I help you?" Had she said it right?

"Sorry, wrong number." Click.

She replaced the phone.

"Who was that?" Shira asked.

Kathy looked over her shoulder. "They said it was the wrong number." She tried to smile, but her lips quivered. It was okay, Shira was too busy to see her.

With shaky fingers, she pulled the purse closer and peered inside. There was Melissa's Hello Kitty wallet, her keys, and . . . a bottle of pills. A prescription bottle. Another one. Three of them. Was Melly sick?

Under the last bottle, she spied the yellow paper. She slipped it out and laid it next to the computer.

She looked over her shoulder again. Shira had her back to her and was talking with her client.

Harriet stared at her with angry eyes. She must have wanted Kathy to hurry. But Harriet did not know she had another plan. A clever plan. Harriet would be impressed when she found out.

Carefully she unfolded the paper and wrote down Melly's password and log-in. Her heart pounded as though it did not like what she was doing. But she had to do this or Edna's salon would never be right.

When she finished, she placed the paper back at the bottom of Melly's purse. Holding the strap, she let it slide down her leg to the floor then pushed it back with her foot. As she stood, she shoved the copy of the password into her pocket.

Melly came through the door carrying two white bags from the bakery.

"I'm back." She lifted the bags in the air. "Thank you so much, Kathy. For my treat and for watching the phones."

Melly passed a bag to her. *I do not think I can eat.*

The door opened again. Mrs. Olsen with her bicycle-helmet-hair waved at her.

"Oh, Kathy. I'm so excited." She brought her hands to her thick white hair. "I told all the ladies of my bridge club that they won't recognize me."

Kathy had forgotten. Today she had promised to show Mrs. Olsen different styles.

"What hairstyles did you pick out for me?" Her face was open and happy. The guilt only built itself higher inside Kathy.

"Mrs. Olsen, I do not have pictures to show you."

Her smile disappeared.

"But I know what style will suit you."

Her smile returned. "What?" She folded her hands and brought them to her chin. "No, don't tell me. I'm so excited."

After her shampoo, Kathy examined her client's face. Her eyes were dark green. Very pretty. Though she had some wrinkles, her skin was not droopy. "Mrs. Olsen, I am going to cut your hair very short."

Her eyes grew larger. "Are you sure?"

Kathy placed her hands on Mrs. Olsen's shoulders. "Your hair is very thick." She ran her fingers through a hunk of thick coarse hair. "With shorter, thinned hair, you will be able to style it in more ways."

Swiveling the chair away from the mirror so Mrs. Olsen could not see, she pulled her favorite scissors and began snipping. Her fingers remembered the art of designing a cut to fit the curvature of a woman's face and the texture of her hair.

With the one-inch curling iron, she curled the top, then finger-raked with a little styling gel. It did not take long. It was a simple cut, one she had done many times at Goodings.

"I am finished." Kathy held her breath and rotated the styling chair.

Mrs. Olsen gasped. *She did not like it. She would never want her to cut her hair again. Shira would fire her—*

"Kathy! I love it!"

"You do?" Kathy's heart skipped.

"Look at me. I'm ten years younger." She moved her head from side to side. "My eyes. They look huge."

Kathy unsnapped the styling cape. Mrs. Olsen slid off the chair.

"Everyone. Look at what Kathy did." Her client almost skipped to the reception counter.

Shira stopped combing her client's hair and went to Mrs. Olsen. She fingered Kathy's client's hair carefully, like a teacher in a beauty school.

Mrs. Olsen clapped. "Isn't it marvelous, Shira?"

"Yes, marvelous." Shira's stare dug into Kathy.

Mrs. Olsen clutched Shira's hand. "Isn't Kathy a wonder?"

"Yes. It would appear she is."

Kathy's breath came in short spurts as she scurried back to her station.

Now, Shira knows about me. She knows I can do hair, like her. She will ask me questions I do not want to answer. I must go on with the plan.

I cannot fail.

"Hello, is this Billie Mae?" Kathy's foot twisted the rug by her bed.

"Who is this?" Billie Mae sounded angry.

"I am Kathy Smith. I work with Harriet at The Hair—"

"Yeah. Yeah." She was drinking something. Kathy could hear ice cubes clinking in glass. "The Mouse. Why didn't you say so in the first place?"

Who was this mouse? "I am sorry."

"What do you want?"

"I was able to get Melly's password to the computer."

"So. Who's Melly?" Another sip.

"Melly? Melissa Cohen. The high school girl Shira hired to help with the computer."

"Cohen, eh. Okay. I'm intrigued. How did you get the password?"

Her face heated. "I snuck it from her purse."

Billie Mae laughed loud. It reminded her of a scary witch. "Good going, Mouse. Very impressive. Tell me more."

Billie Mae liked what she had done. But now she did not know if she liked what she had done. "I know how to use the new computer. I can delete names from the files and—"

"Finally, a plan that can do some serious damage. Does Harriet know you're doing this?"

"Yes."

Another sip. She mumbled something Kathy could not understand.

"I am sorry, I did not understand what—"

"Never mind." Billie Mae coughed very loud into the phone. "What do you plan to do with the files? Delete them all?"

The butterflies appeared in her stomach again. "No. Not all of the files. Only the new clients, a few at a time. Not all at once."

She let out a loud breath. "You going to start tomorrow? Deleting a few at a time?"

Was she making fun of her? "No. I must wait until Shira is gone. It may be this weekend, when she goes out somewhere."

"How are you going to know if she is gone?"

"I can ask her what she is doing this weekend—"

Billie Mae harrumphed. "Your plan seems a bit too flimsy to me." She swallowed, smacking loudly. "We need something else. Tell me about the kid that works the computer."

"Melly?" Kathy did not like that Billie Mae wanted to know about Melissa.

"Whatever."

This was not good. "What do you want to know?"

"I don't know. Tell me what was in her purse."

Her heart skittered. "Why do you—"

"Listen, Mouse, you want to do this or not? You want Shira changing the shop to her way, or you want it to stay the same? Make up your mind."

"I, I want it to stay the same." But do not hurt Melly.

"Okay, then. Tell me what was in the kid's purse."

She clutched the bedspread in her fist. "She had a wallet. Keys." Should she tell her about—

"Come on. She's in high school. There has to be more than that."

"She had medicines. Three bottles."

"Drugs?"

Nyet. "No, prescriptions. Maybe she's sick."

"She must be healthy enough to work there." She laughed again.

Kathy cringed.

"I think we got our plan, Mouse." She snickered. "I don't need anything more than this."

Kathy stood and stomped her foot. "No, you cannot hurt Melly."

"Listen, you want this plan to work or not?"

"No. Yes. I do not know."

"Well, I do know. And another thing, don't tell Harriet about this. She seems to have gone soft on me."

What do I do?

"You hear me? Don't say anything or you'll be sorry."

This Kathy had heard before. The sorry was always painful. She rubbed her jaw where the last sorry had landed three years ago. "I will not tell Harriet."

"You better not." She cleared her throat. "I'll take it from here, Mouse."

The dial tone buzzed loudly. But she could not release the phone.

What had she done?

33

"Shalom. You've reached the Lowingers. Sorry, we missed your call . . ."

Pen poised over her journal, Shira waited until Cari's voice finished her cheery message. "Hey, Care, it's Shira. Tag. You're it. We keep missing each other. I need a friend to talk through the past weekend. My best friend. Talk with you later." She thumbed the off button and laid the phone on her dressing table.

The face staring back from the mirror was tired—weary.

It had been three days since the Alec and Fawna episode. For all the jerky things they had done to her, the biggest jerk ended up being her. She logged Crisis114 in her journal—*Jesse knows who I really am.* The bag from the Cheap Stuff Store sat on the floor next to her. This was her punishment. She inventoried the red plastic, elastic, jeweled bracelets with the matching necklace. Today she would wear them. Her scarlet letter.

Why did she attract the bums? Jesse was as far from being a bum as she was from being a virgin. To make matters worse, her father now knew how sordid her life was. She had cut ties in Manhattan, but apparently there was collateral damage here.

A sigh came from someplace deep in her heart.

Get ready for work, Shira. Another busy day ahead.

The phone rang.

Caller ID said it was the realtor in New York. "Hello?"

"Ms. Goldstein, this is Sarah Edelstein, your realtor. I have good news. We have an offer on the apartment."

Already? "That's great."

"The buyers are in a hurry to move."

"And I'm in a hurry to sell."

She gave a polite chuckle. "I'll email the paperwork today. Just sign and scan it back to me."

"Sarah, I think I'd like you to email it to my lawyer, Jesse Fox."

After giving her the address, they hung up. She hoped she was still Jesse's client. He certainly wasn't interested in her in any other way. Thanks to her.

"Oh, hi, Jesse." Melly held the phone to her ear and glanced Shira's way, smiling. Her adorable face altered from grin to confusion. "Sure, I'll get her."

As Shira made her way to the phone, her heart fluttered with hope. How she had longed to hear his voice.

"Miss Beulah, it's for you." Melly mouthed a sorry to Shira.

Her steps faltered to a halt. Beulah gave her a sympathetic smile as she took the phone.

"Jesse, hi." Beulah leaned on the reception counter. "Thanks for returning my call. I got an offer on the house."

Beulah was selling her house? She moved the broom around her area trying to not be so obvious.

"Yes. That's why I wanted you to review the contract." Beulah smoothed her hair behind her ear and smiled. "Tonight would be perfect. Why not stop by at about seven-ish, and I'll feed you." She giggled.

"Hey, kid, watch what you're doing there," Harriet said.

She had swept a glob of hair onto Harriet's foot. "Sorry."

Beulah laughed again. Jesse must be saying something funny.

Shira, what's the matter with you? Beulah's old enough to be your mother. His mother.

Beulah examined her cuticles. "Don't worry, it won't. I'll stop by Giant's after I visit Wil." She straightened. "That sounds great. See you then." She moved to return the phone to Melly then stopped. "What's that?"

Beulah glanced at Shira. "Sure, I'll be happy to tell her."

Another skip of her heart. He hadn't forgotten her after all.

"Okay. See you later, Jesse."

Finally, the call was over. She went back to sweeping. The cheap red bracelet peeked from her cuff, reminding her of who she was and why Jesse wasn't talking to her.

Beulah turned. "Shira?"

"Hmm." *That sounded nonchalant, didn't it? Like I couldn't care less?*

"Jesse wanted me to let you know he received the email from your realtor."

He couldn't have told her that himself?

"He said he'd get back with you tomorrow."

Great. She was a paying client and Beulah was probably pro bono. "Okay, thanks."

Beulah paused next to her. "Shira, why don't you join us for dinner? I'm picking up some picnic food—fried chicken and salads. It will be fun."

Fried chicken? Didn't she know what chicken fat did to the hips? "Thanks, Beulah. Can I take a rain check? I need to unpack some boxes from the move."

Beulah tilted her head and touched Shira's shoulder. "You sure?"

"Yes. But thanks for the invitation."

She had turned down comfort food for a night alone. Worse, Jesse apparently preferred dinner with Beulah over speaking to her. How lame had she become?

"Dad?" The phone cradled against her arm, Shira lay on her bed. "Am I a horrible person?"

"What?" He chuckled. "Shira, what's going on?"

Yes, the lameness grows. I called my dad for advice. Cari and Aaron were at a prayer meeting. She should be unpacking boxes, but . . .

"You know about Alec and me, right?"

"You mean Towel Man?"

"Dad, I'm serious. I need to talk."

"Sorry, sweetheart."

"Are you ashamed of me?" She chewed what was left of her thumbnail.

"Shira. Why would you say something like that?"

"Towel Man." She may as well go for broke. "Other men."

"Shira, I'm your father. I may not have been the best one, but I have and will always love you."

Where were those tissues? She had two broken tear ducts flooding her face. "Really?"

"Oh, honey. I'm sorry you don't know that." He cleared his throat. "When I saw Alec and put the pieces together, mostly I was glad you got rid of the bum."

"And how do you feel today?"

"Today, I'm really glad you got rid of the bum."

"You said mostly you were glad. What else, Dad? How could you not be ashamed of me—at least a little."

He sighed. "Shira, you were raised in the Messianic community. Your school, our synagogue, and nearly every person you knew as a child brought you up in the nurture and admonition of the Lord."

Shame bludgeoned her. She fought back the urge to end the call and pull the covers over her head, forever. "I'm not following the Lord, Dad. It didn't take."

A soft chuckle. "Shira, the words of eternal life are planted in you. You may think me naïve, but I have faith that someday they'll bear fruit."

There went the goosebumps.

She tried rubbing them away. "Dad, I didn't call you for a sermon."

"Sorry, sweetheart. At least I'm predictable, right?"

And she was beginning to be glad about that—very glad.

Beulah hoped Jesse arrived soon. The delicious-smelling chicken was in jeopardy of being eaten without him.

The table had been set for two. The store had a sale on carnations, so she had splurged. It felt good to add that second plate and silverware—make the table look inviting and special. Meals at home were generally a lonely experience. Meals with Wilbur at the nursing home had become even more sad and lonely. His very presence reminded her how solitary her future would soon be.

An unexpected sigh saddened her. Gone were the romantic, candlelit dinners. Lingering over a meal, listening to Wil talk about his day. More than anything she missed the husky tone of his voice. Her face warmed. No, that wasn't entirely accurate—she missed his knowing touch. His kisses.

Lying on the coffee table, the paperwork for the offer on the house was another reminder life would take a radical change again.

Lord, give me strength for the road ahead.

The doorbell rang.

"Hi, Jesse." They hugged. "Ready for some finger-licking fine dining?"

He gave her a distracted smile.

"Everything okay?" She took his jacket.

"The jury is out on an important case I've worked on for the last two years."

"It doesn't look good?"

"Actually, it's a strong case. But you never know with juries."

Something else was going on. Had something happened between him and Shira?

Jesse's head was buried in the paperwork. His tea sat untouched on the coffee table.

"This contract appears okay, Beulah." He flipped a couple pages and reclined back on the couch. "If you want you could negotiate for a couple hundred more since they want the appliances."

"No. They're a young couple with a baby on the way. I'd like to bless them." She took a sip of tea. "Besides, most condos already have the appliances."

Another distracted smile. Where was that endearing whole-face smile? Beulah snatched the paperwork away. His face registered surprise.

"What are you doing?"

"I'm trying to find out what is wrong with you, young man."

He bent forward, elbows on his knees, and ran both hands through his curly mop.

"Shira?"

He didn't look at her. "Is it that obvious?"

"Did you two have a fight?" She took another sip of her tea. "Sorry, Jesse. I'm an old busybody."

He lifted his head. "No, I need to talk to someone who knows of my feelings about Shira."

"What about—"

"Not Sam. This is a little delicate."

Jesse described the weekend he had spent with Sam and Shira in New York. In between tight-circle pacing and angry remarks about Shira's former boyfriend, Beulah got an earful. He finally paused by Wil's recliner and exhaled loudly. "So, I told Shira, I needed time to think about us."

Beulah cringed.

"What?" As usual, he read her expression well.

"Jesse, can I ask you a personal question?"

He nodded and sat in the recliner.

"You haven't known Shira very long—three weeks, maybe—"

"Twenty-three days."

Oh, my. "Okay, over three weeks. How can you have such strong feelings for her?"

He rubbed his palms on his knees. "This is going to sound a little strange."

Somehow strange and Jesse didn't go together.

"God told me she was to be my wife."

Okay, maybe she had been too hasty. "Can you explain?"

His brown eyes latched to hers. "Beulah, I know it sounds weird. When I first met Edna and Sam at the Messianic Jewish conference eight years ago, they spoke of Shira and how she was in the world and they were worried for her. I asked if I could pray with them."

One corner of his mouth lifted. "I thought I was being polite, since they had prayed for me earlier about law school." He shrugged. "A bond formed between the three of us immediately. It was like an electrical charge. While I prayed, I saw Shira—you know, like in my mind."

She bent forward.

"I saw her, Beulah, but I'd never met her or even seen a picture of her back then. When I did see her photo, I practically fell to my knees." His face was animated. More like the usual Jesse.

"So, the person you saw was Shira?"

"Yes." There was the Jesse smile.

"Did the Lord tell you then?"

"No, it was several years later, during my quiet time when I prayed for her and Sam and Edna." He stared at his hands. "No fanfare. No burning bush. Simply, 'This is your wife.'" He smiled. "It was peaceful. Natural."

"Did you tell Sam or Edna?"

He shook his head. "No. I told Rabbi Joel when I settled here."

"What did he say?"

"He said, 'Time will tell. Test the word and pray.'" He paused as though remembering something. "Frankly, it merely became a part of me—the waiting for her to return to the Lord. The day I would know."

She wasn't sure about all this. Yet Jesse seemed to be a strong believer—mature in his faith. "Do you know now?"

"I thought I did."

"The episode with the boyfriend?"

He pointed a finger. "The ex-boyfriend."

She smiled.

"Beulah." His face reddened. "I've never been with a woman. I haven't dated anyone in six years—not since . . ."

"You heard from the Lord."

He nodded.

She folded her hands. "Jesse, you've known for eight years that Shira was in the world, right?"

"Yes."

"You've interceded on her behalf for those eight years."

"Every day."

"What did you think she was doing those eight years? Working in soup kitchens and saving herself for you?"

His body stiffened.

"Jesse, she's in the world. She's not a believer. Why are you surprised by her actions or her past?"

He gripped the arms of the recliner and stared off. His jaw clenched.

"I'm sorry, Jesse. But if God told you she was to be your wife and you know He would not want you unequally yoked, you better get on the ball and pray for that young woman."

The pounding in her heart almost silenced her. The words she spoke seemed harsh, but she felt the Lord urging her on. "Stop teasing her with your affection. She obviously cares deeply for you. No more late night visits with only the two of you. You are playing with temptation—not a good thing to do. And quit pouting about what she was—"

His chest heaved up and down.

"—and start really praying for what she will be."

His head jerked up. Tears streamed down his cheeks. He fell to his knees. "Dear Lord, please, forgive me."

34

Harriet lit up as soon as she exited Hair Mavens. Although it was dark outside, she stood in the shadows so Kathy couldn't see her or the red glow of her cigarette through the front window.

Kathy had been avoiding her since yesterday. But Harriet was gonna talk to her—she didn't care how long she had to wait. There had been a major change in her attitude. Gone was the lion and back was the frightened-mouse. Something told her she had spoken to Billie Mae.

A chill flowed through Harriet that had nothing to do with the weather. It was the dream. Thoughts of it consumed her. Somehow she had to figure out what it meant.

Kathy opened the door and shouldered her bag. Harriet threw down the ciggy and smashed the nearly whole stick with her shoe. Kathy exited the salon and turned in Harriet's direction, tugging on her coat. She pulled up short when she saw Harriet standing there. Fear practically oozed from her pores.

"We need to talk, Kathy."

Her shoulders engulfed her neck. "I am tired, Harriet. I have to catch the bus."

"I'll drive you home." Harriet grabbed Kathy's elbow and steered her toward the car. "We can talk on the way."

Once on the road, Harriet glanced at her. "You gonna tell me what's going on with you?"

She shrugged.

"You were all excited about getting the kid's password, and now you've clammed up."

"I told you, I am tired."

"No. I think you talked to Billie Mae."

Kathy gasped.

Bingo. "Didn't I say not to talk with her? What did she say?"

Kathy brought her hands to her face. "She did not want to wait for me to delete the files. She has a new plan."

"A new plan?" A burning ate at her insides.

"She would not tell me what it is about. But I am worried about Melly."

"Melly?"

"Billie Mae asked me all sorts of questions about what was in Melly's purse."

Harriet gripped the steering wheel. Dread oozed in. "What did you find in her purse, Kathy?"

"Medicines," she squeaked.

This doesn't make sense. "Is she sick?"

"I do not know. I do not think so."

There was a rat's nest here, and Harriet knew the rat. "Billie Mae will make something of this, you can be sure."

"What do we do, Harriet?"

"I'll call Billie and tell her to mind her own business." She tried to swallow around her own fear. "That we're calling the whole thing off."

"Everything?"

She gripped the steering wheel tighter. "Everything."

"I'm telling you to mind your own business, Billie Mae." Harriet's fist wrapped around the phone until it cracked—kinda like what she wanted to do to her neck if she were there.

"Hah. This was your idea." She slurred her words. Must have gotten an early start on the booze tonight. Billie Mae had changed. When had she gone from fun-loving to cruel?

"Well, I'm telling you it's over. No more."

Her Wicked-Witch-of-the-West cackle brought a fresh wave of chills. "You ain't telling me what to do. It's a free country. You-you watch. You'll thank me that I have the guts to get rid of the brat. You always cared so much for that goody-two-shoes, Edna and her family—"

"What?" Harriet swallowed. "I cared so much for Edna—what, Billie?"

"You ditched me for Miss Perfect Jew, and now you're ditching me for her brat."

"Please, Billie Mae, don't do this."

A string of curses Harriet had never heard before preceded the click.

Dear Lord. What had she done?

"What did she say, Harriet?" Kathy answered Harriet's call on the first ring. She must have been sitting on top of it.

"She said she didn't care what we wanted, she was continuing with her

SHE DOES GOOD HAIR

plan."

She gasped. "What is the plan?"

"She wouldn't tell me, but it's not good, that's for sure." Even the deep drag of nicotine hadn't calmed her.

Kathy whimpered. "I am sorry, Harriet. It is my fault. You told me not to call Billie Mae. I ignored you, and now she will do bad things to Melly."

"Not only Melly." She stamped out the cigarette. "If I know Billie, she'll ruin it for all of us. Once she gets something into that stubborn head of hers, she won't let go. This is just some game to her."

"It is all my fault." A pounding noise came from her end. Was she hitting her head against the wall?

"Hey, listen, Kathy. This whole thing was my idea, not yours." Like a blow to her midsection, she crumbled. "I started this train wreck, not you. Me."

Soft sobs from Kathy knifed her heart.

"Kathy." The words caught in her throat. "If we don't stand together, we could all lose The Mavens."

Oh, God, was there any way to save Edna's treasure?

35

The coffeemaker sputtered and coughed like an old man. Fortunately, the aroma was more appealing.

Sitting at the computer, waiting for it to boot up to retrieve Saturday's appointments, Shira noticed a long note from Melly. Against Shira's better judgment, she had allowed the girl to come back after Friday night services to finish inputting the rest of the inventory data.

Her large, round letters reminded Shira of her own artsy handwriting at that age. She smiled as she read.

> Shira, it seems several people left messages for you after the shop closed. They cancelled but didn't say they wanted to reschedule. Strange, huh? Anyway, there's a report attached. I printed it from the software—O.M.Gosh, so cool! This will give you the names and phone numbers of those who cancelled, so you can reschedule. Or I'll do it on Tuesday.

Cancellations? Well, at least she would have more time for her walk-ins.

A flourish of hearts surrounded Melly's signature. Shira grinned.

"Good morning, Shira." Harriet's face stretched into the largest smile Shira had seen on her in a long time.

Shira repositioned her jaw from the dropped position to respond. "Good morning, Harriet."

"I bought an extra Danish. You interested?" She shook two bags from Delicious Bakery.

This was new. What's she got up her sleeve? "No, thanks, I had breakfast." Was it poisoned? "But thanks for thinking of me." Weird.

As Harriet set up her station, a few details that had seemed randomly strange to Shira from the day before, now grouped themselves together. Little things, like Kathy had swept Shira's station several times yesterday when things were hectic. In fact, she had swept the whole reception area, too.

And even Harriet had done a load of towels.

She didn't know whether to be relieved or worried.

Shira straightened and pushed a hunk of hair behind her ear, to inspect her bed's new location. So much better. This had been her third attempt at perfect *feng shui* for her bedroom. She stepped back and folded her arms.

Wait. Her new furniture bore a striking resemblance to her aunt's. And, her perfect feng shui looked exactly like how her aunt's room had looked before.

"Great, Shira," She muttered. "You worked so hard to be poles apart from her, and deep down you're more like her than you thought."

If only that were really true.

Sandy Brown, her senior-prom date's face appeared like a daytime nightmare. She pulled her sweater tighter as a shiver crawled down her spine. Why had she thought of him?

The memory flickered to life. She and Aunt Edna had had one of the worst arguments ever—in this very room—when Shira said she didn't care what everyone said about Sandy. She was going with him to the prom.

Shira had won that argument. How proud she was. That night had begun as a fairy tale—formals, wrist corsages, and tuxes—but ended in gut-wrenching heartbreak. Sandy had convinced her to leave the ballroom rather than staying with Cari and her date. They had ended up at a cheap motel for a "couple of drinks."

She had lost her virginity that night.

Her journal rested on the dressing table. She searched through the record of her troubled life. A few turns of the worn tear-stained pages and there it was. Crisis87—Sandy Brown stole my most precious treasure. Written next to it in tiny letters: a pair of Seven jeans.

She pressed her fingers against her eyelids trying to wipe away the memory of that time. Sandy had never returned her calls, having moved on to the next in line of conquests. Shira had begged Cari to go shopping a few days later to buy the jeans. Then, she had sat on the changing room floor, pressing the jeans against her mouth to muffle her sobbing.

Sandy had been the first of a long procession of bums.

What had she seen in him? Sandy had been football player, popular, gorgeous. Blonde hair, blue eyes . . . *Alec*.

She stomped to the phone on her nightstand, punched speed call three, and waited. Please, let Cari be there.

"Hey, Shirry."

"Cari, I need to talk."

After nearly twenty minutes of sordid details from prom night, Cari was

189

silent except for the occasional soft sniffing. She blew her nose. Shira rubbed hers on her sweater.

"You never told me this?" Cari honked again. "I wondered where you two went off to."

"I couldn't tell anyone." Another rough sweater rub under her nose— she deserved the discomfort. "Aunt Edna didn't like him."

"Guess she was right. Unfortunately."

They sat in the silence. More than anything, she was grateful her friend wasn't lecturing her. "Care-bear? I think I know why I've dated losers since then."

"Why?"

"I think I was trying to prove I wasn't a loser."

"You?"

"I'm still sorting this through, but maybe I choose guys like him so I can rewrite history. Win them over so they'd treat me nice." She slapped her forehead. "The money I've lost to these jerks!"

"Shirry, that's when you pulled away from me. From all of us."

That sinking-thing, like sitting in the doctor's office waiting for the inevitable bad news, pulled her downward to that dreaded place.

"When you dropped out of college and moved to New York, I felt like you didn't want me in your life anymore."

Shira closed her eyes. Very astute. Cari had only reminded Shira of what was good and innocent, and she was no longer that person.

"I missed you." Cari's voice wobbled.

Big gulping sobs overtook her. "I'm—so—sorry—Cari."

"That's—o—kay."

"I—love—you—Care—b,bear."

"I—love—you."

The sobbing subsided after a few minutes. Cari's voice muffled as though she had pressed her phone against her chest.

"Cari?"

She sniffed and giggled. "We scared Aaron. He's not quite accustomed to estrogen bursts."

"You are very lucky to have someone like Aaron."

"Blessed, Shira. I'm blessed."

I'll give her that.

"Jesse is a good man. And he's interested in you," Cari said.

Shira sighed. How she wished that were true.

36

The plans and small model Steve-the-architect prepared were amazing. The quiet of the closed salon afforded Shira time to examine her vision. She placed the model on the reception counter and bent slightly to peer inside. It was like Barbie's dream salon, with miniature furniture and equipment. Her fantasy was finally being realized.

But had her vision for Hair Mavens changed? She straightened and studied the stations—where each maven worked.

She couldn't fire Beulah. She had become a, a, okay, a blessing to her.

Even Harriet—like it or not—had been a part of her life for as long as she could remember. If she would only readjust her attitude—be like she used to be. An unexpected, vague emotion tried to surface. Shira tamped it down.

She ran her finger across the top of her styling chair. While doing granny hair wasn't her favorite thing, the grannies were. Most of these ladies had known her since she was a baby.

The challenge and thrill of the newer styles were great, but the wash-and-set balanced a world that placed so much emphasis on perfection of the outward.

Why couldn't this salon incorporate both? Shira sat on the cold linoleum. Was she actually considering this? Was she willing to give up her dream?

Or maybe amend it a little?

A quick glance at her watch—she was late. Her appointment with the loan officer at the bank was in five minutes. Grabbing her purse, and Steve's proposal and blueprints she dashed out the door.

All that rushing to get there in time, only to be relegated to a pleather chair for fifteen minutes, depleted her supply of confidence—all that was left was a growing sense of foreboding. She glanced around the bank before looking at her watch again. Where was her loan officer–she read the nameplate on his desk—Bill Henry?

There he was.

"Ms. Goldstein. Sorry to keep you waiting." His tight, square jaw didn't authenticate his being sorry.

He sat on his leather chair and swiveled toward his computer monitor.

That tumbling feeling in the pit of her stomach had become a much too familiar sensation.

Bill Henry cleared his throat and yanked at his collar.

"Is there a problem?"

He shot a fleeting glimpse in her direction then he swallowed. "Ms. Goldstein. There seems to be a glitch with your loan."

"What?" She scooted closer to his desk. "How can that be? I have more than enough collateral. My credit rating is impeccable. I don't understand."

Eyes of gray finally made contact with hers. "All I can say is there's a glitch." He looked down briefly and returned with an intense look of determination. "Please believe me when I say I will do all I can to correct this situation."

Correct this situation? "I don't understand—"

Mr. Henry expelled a long breath. He slanted closer to her. "All I can say is," he whispered, "this is a situation that I intend to get to the bottom of."

He stood and extended his hand to end their meeting. Reluctantly, she took it. His grasp was uncomfortably firm. He stared as though trying to communicate an important message.

"When will you know when you've corrected this situation?" she asked.

He cautiously peered around the room. "Call and ask for me later this week." He gave her his business card. "Don't ask for anyone else."

She left the bank in a daze.

Pulling up to The Mavens, she felt unsettled and questioned if someone had sabotaged the loan. *Don't be silly, Shira.* As she unlocked the door, she noticed something stuck under the welcome mat. A note. She unfolded the paper.

Jesse's handwriting.

Shira, sorry I missed you. I left your paperwork with Nonni, at Delicious—she has done this for Edna in the past. Everything looks good. Mazel tov on the sale. Things are hectic with a case I'm working on, but

will talk with you soon, Jesse·

The good news—he would talk with her soon. The bad news? What would he say?

Beulah entered Mavens—the lights were still off. Shira sat in her styling chair staring off into space.

She shut the door, startling Shira from her contemplation. "Morning, Shira."

"Morning." Shira leapt from her chair. "Caught me lazing, as Aunt Edna would say."

"You okay?" Beulah flipped on the lights.

"Just a lot on my mind." She worked a smile onto her mouth, but it didn't go anywhere else. "Busy day. Mind getting the messages?"

"Not at all."

Shira walked to the supply room like the weight of the world was on her shoulders.

"Shira, I accepted the offer on my house." Beulah didn't know why she told Shira this—except that if Edna had been there, they would have discussed it off and on all day.

Turning back, Shira took a few steps in her direction. "Is this a good thing, Beulah?" Her brows knitted.

"It's a necessary thing."

Shira lightly touched her arm. "Is there anything I can do?"

"Want to go with me to look at condos?" Beulah gave a half-hearted chuckle.

A gentle smile awakened her features. "Bay-oo-lah, I would be honored."

Oh my. Another precious moment between them. *Thank You, Lord.*

Shira resumed her mission in the supply room as Beulah grabbed the pad of paper and pen to record the messages.

Thirteen messages? Generally, the salon might have four or five over the weekend. Apparently, the feature story continued to bring new business. She punched one for the first message.

"This is Bernice Harper and I'm cancelling my appointment with Shira today. I won't be calling again." Click.

My goodness. Where did that come from? Bernice had been coming for four or five years. She wrote down the particulars for Melly and went on to the next message.

"Edna would roll over in her grave if she knew what was going on in that shop of hers. I'll never come back to that den of sin. Cancel my appointment. Wednesday. Two o'clock. In the afternoon. Oh. This is Mrs. Sundergram. Cancel it now. Thank you."

Mrs. Sundergram? A den of sin?

"Shira?"

She emerged from the supply room with a stack of folded towels. One look at Beulah, and she set them down on Kathy's chair. "What's wrong?"

"Listen to these messages." She replayed the first two messages.

"Is this some kind of joke? Play the rest."

One by one, the messages conveyed their clients' disappointment in the—as one client put it—sinful things going on at The Hair Mavens. Long-time customers for Edna, Harriet, Beulah, and even Kathy had cancelled their appointments. More than cancelled—they'd fired them.

Beulah and Shira stared at each other.

"Something's fishy here," Beulah said.

"My sentiments exactly."

Neither of them voiced whom they suspected. Beulah's first thought was Harriet, but many of her clients had called in, too. Even though Harriet didn't approve of Shira's new rules, would she really have gone to these lengths to get back at her?

The door opened. Harriet and Kathy entered the salon together. Shira marched over to them. Beulah held her breath.

"Harriet, what did you do?" Shira's hands were balled into fists at her sides.

Harriet's face turned a bright red. "What are you talking about?"

Shira pointed toward her. "Show her, Beulah."

Beulah lifted the paper half-full of names.

"Those are cancellations." Shira pointed her finger in Harriet's face.

Beulah winced. No one did that to Harriet Schmidt Foster.

"Calm down." Harriet exhibited restraint Beulah had never seen before. "Beulah, can I see that?"

Shira paced in a small circle, her arms wrapped around her waist, as Harriet perused the list.

"Some of these are my clients." Her jaw tensed. She showed the list to Kathy. "There are a few of yours, too, Kathy."

Kathy trained worried eyes on Harriet.

"Well?" Shira stood before Harriet. "Did you do this?"

Harriet shot a quick look to Kathy. Shira didn't seem to notice, but Beulah did. "No."

Shira turned to Kathy. "Did you?"

Kathy's lips quivered. Her whole body followed. She gave an unconvincing shake of her head.

"Somebody did this." Shira threw her arms up. "I can't take this." She stormed back to the supply room.

Harriet glanced at Beulah. Guilt was written all over her face.

The Bible said to forgive and think well of folks, but by golly, as sure as

Beulah was standing there, Harriet had done something.

Question was, what?

Harriet chewed her lip. Shira had watched her like a hawk all day. Frankly, she couldn't blame her. Both Shira and Beulah suspected she was behind all these cancellations. She guessed she was.

Every client that had walked through the door, Harriet had wanted to hug. She was grateful for every white head she set and styled. Did they not receive the call from Billie Mae, or had they received one and had the good sense to know whatever lies that woman broadcasted weren't true?

The front door opened. Melly stumbled in. Harriet glanced at the clock. Past two. She was late. Shame on her with all that was going—

"Melly, are you all right?" Shira dropped her blow dryer and sprinted to Melly.

The kid seemed bad. All pasty white. Maybe she was on drugs or something. *Stop it, Harriet.* That's how they were in the mess they were in.

Melly fell into Shira's arms. Shira helped the kid to one of the reception chairs. "Beulah, call Melly's mom." She shouted.

The kid seemed to be protesting, but Harriet couldn't hear what she said.

"If it's the flu, then you need to be in bed." Shira kissed Melly's forehead. "She doesn't have a fever, Beulah."

Something about Shira kissing Melly's forehead struck a familiar chord. Emotion erupted like a small volcano.

Edna. Shira reminded her of Edna.

Dropping her purse and keys on the desk, Harriet sloughed off her jacket and threw it on the couch. More than anything, she wanted to crawl into bed and sleep a week. The weight of all the guilt had pulled her into a dark hole of depression—a place she hadn't inhabited in a long time. Not since the divorce.

There was a phone call she needed to make.

Sitting at the kitchen table, the third ring was interrupted with Billie Mae's hoarse hello.

"Billie, what have you done?" She pounded the table, causing her saltshaker to tip over. "You tell me now, or I'm coming over there."

"Calm down. It's no big deal." She barely stifled a burp. "I called a couple of people, that's all."

"What did you tell them?" Every muscle in her body tensed.

"I sh-aid that receptionist kid was on drugs. That Shira was selling drugs to all the kids coming there now."

"What? You said what?" If she hadn't already been sitting, she would probably be a puddle of shame and heartache on the floor.

"Ah, come on, Harriet, old girl. All the kids are doing it these days. The odds are in my favor."

"But Shira? A drug-dealer? Melly on drugs?"

"Those old biddies would believe anything I tell them." Her witch-laugh chilled Harriet's marrow.

Old? Oh, no. Her gut clenched. "Who did you call, Billie?"

"The Mouse couldn't give me all the—the hoity-toities. So I called a couple of the regulars."

"You told our regulars?"

"Don't get your girdle in a bind, mishy. I only told a couple."

"How many?"

"I dunno, maybe ten."

Harriet pulled the phone away from her ear and stared at it. With their client grapevine, she may as well have told all of them.

She returned the phone to her other ear, as Billie continued.

"—and Patrick's friend at the bank."

"You got your husband involved in this mess?"

"Why not?" She slurped. "He's as worried as anyone about drugs in our town."

"No one is selling or doing drugs at The Mavens." Billie's slurred words registered with Harriet. "What do you mean about the bank?"

She snickered. "That was a genius idea—if I do say so myself." She sniffed. "Sh-Shira has a loan application at the bank. Patrick's friend is some bigwig. The banker put pressure on her loan guy to reject the loan."

"You didn't." Her forehead dropped to the table.

"Come on. You-you're jealoush coz I thought of it firsht."

Harriet had suspected what Billie Mae had done was bad. But this was so much worse than what she could have imagined.

Harriet ran her fingers through her hair, dislodging her hive. Giving the bad news to Kathy was not a call she wanted to make, but she had to.

"No. No. No." Kathy's whine sounded like a small child being dragged away from her mother. If possible, the news of Billie's terrorism hit her harder than it had Harriet.

"Calm down, Kathy." *Speak for yourself, old girl.* "We have to figure a way out of this mess."

"Nyet."

"What did you say?"

"We cannot clean up this mess, Harriet," she sobbed. "We have ruined Edna's salon." A sound like a kicked puppy came from her.

"Stop it, Kathy."

The howling was replaced by whimpering.

"We'll figure out something. Some type of damage control, and Shira will never know we were behind this."

Damage control? There was no fixing this. There was nothing they could do.

Kathy yanked the suitcase from the closet and threw it on the bed. It had not been opened since Edna had helped her find this apartment. The zipper stuck as she pushed it around. Once opened, a musty smell entered the room.

She grabbed an armful of lingerie from a drawer. The freshly washed delicates smelled of flowers. She paused to take in their fragrance. The closer she brought the clothing to her nose, the less she smelled the stink of the suitcase. The last thing she wanted to do was pack these sweet things in the sour suitcase.

Sitting on the edge of the bed, she held the garments to her heart. The suitcase beside her was from the past—a dark place she had never wanted to return to.

Edna had brought light to her. Even in her death, she continued to shine. She shined in the generosity of her furniture given to Kathy. That had made her barren, lonely apartment a home.

All that Kathy had was because of the love and compassion of one woman—a woman who wanted a crazy group of women to get along and keep The Hair Mavens going. And Kathy may have single-handedly destroyed that.

So, what do you do, Katya? You run away. Nyet.

After returning her things to the dresser Edna had given her, she zipped up the suitcase and shoved it back into her closet. This time, she would not run away.

37

Shira folded towels when the phone rang again. Harriet, Beulah, Kathy, and she stared at each other. No one wanted to answer it. No doubt more cancellations. Some callers were angry, but no one would say why. Shira racked her brain trying to figure out why all of Edna's grannies didn't want to be clients any more.

The ringing finally stopped. Shira resumed folding towels. The rest of the ladies went back to their clients.

Melly was still out sick. Had she been well enough to work, there was no way Shira would have allowed her to take these calls. They were too brutal. Instead the voicemail had taken the bad news all day. She wasn't looking forward to listening to these messages later.

To think only a week ago, the phones had rung because of all the new business. Now they were losing people. Why?

She carried towels into the shampoo area and set a stack in the shelf over each bowl. Perhaps she had been too hasty blaming Harriet. She had lost clients, too. Long-time clients. Had any of them shared with Harriet what happened to cause such a reaction? She wasn't saying, if they had.

Returning to the supply room, Shira grabbed a funnel to refill the conditioner bottles. Two more hours of appointments and then she would drag her exhausted body upstairs and indulge in Crisis115—What the Heck was Going On? a quart of Cold Stone ice cream—and watch a disaster movie.

Her cell rang. She pulled it from her Coach holster. "Hello?"

"Shira, it's Cari," she cried. "Shira, Melly collapsed. They rushed her to the hospital."

"No." She felt lightheaded. She dropped the conditioner bottle and sat on the floor.

Beulah appeared by her side. She squatted and laid her hand on her shoulder.

"Which hospital?" Shira asked, then mouthed, Melly, to Beulah.

"CHOP."

Thank goodness. The Children's Hospital of Philadelphia was one of the nation's best. "Has she been admitted?"

"Yes. She's in room 306." She moaned. "Shira, they think the leukemia is back."

She thumbed the off button and threw the phone, before bringing her hands to her head.

"What's wrong with Melly?" Beulah asked.

Harriet and Kathy, along with their clients, formed a circle around her. "Melly collapsed. They think it's a relapse of the leukemia."

The corporate gasp sucked the life out of her. This couldn't be happening. Not to Melly.

"I have to go." Her legs had turned to rubber. Beulah and Harriet lifted her to her feet. *Wait.* "I have three more clients."

"I'll handle them, Shira. You go," Beulah said.

"Beulah, thank you, but these are new clients. One wants a triple foil." What do I do now?

Kathy stepped toward her. "Shira, I will help you."

"You?"

"Yes." She removed her glasses. "Do you remember me?"

Shira was having trouble concentrating and walking at the same time, and this chick was making like Clark Kent.

"Shira, I worked at Goodings."

What? Kathy had worked for Fidel in Manhattan? Her violet eyes.

The room spun. Beulah held her up until it righted again. *Please, God, I don't have time for this. I have to see Melly.*

"Fine. Do it." Shira couldn't believe she was entrusting important clients to the weird woman at the last station. "I have to go."

"Shira, should you be driving?" Beulah guided her to the door. "Let me take you."

"No, Beulah. We can't both be gone. Things are bad enough here without losing two stylists."

Somehow, she made it to her car and started the engine. She laid her head on the steering wheel.

Please, God, get me there safely. Don't let Melly die.

The phone rang as Beulah twisted her key trying to free it from the deadbolt. She shut her eyes and debated answering the call after this day. She'd had a triple-hitter—salon mayhem, Melly's hospitalization, and Wilbur problems.

But it might be news about Melly. She left the key in the lock and sprinted to the kitchen phone. "Hello?"

"It's me," Harriet said.

Her insides rumbled and rocked. *Lord, I need Your grace with this woman.* "Yes, Harriet."

"Any word on the kid?" Harriet took a long draw on a cigarette.

"Melly? No. I haven't heard anything."

"Oh." She took another drag. A few seconds later, she exhaled. Harriet was stalling.

A nice long soak in her bathtub was calling Beulah like a siren. "What's on your mind, Harriet?"

"Beulah, I had a part in the cancellations."

She dropped into one of the dinette chairs. The nice soak wouldn't be happening any time soon.

Harriet spent the next twenty minutes explaining, sobbing, and apologizing to Beulah for all she had done to Melly, Shira, Kathy, her, their clients . . . the list went on. Beulah curled her hair behind her ear. The situation was far worse than she could have imagined.

To her credit, Harriet had taken full responsibility, but clearly Billie Mae had caused the true damage. Still, Harriet had tilled the soil with her animosity.

Beulah had always felt uncomfortable around Billie Mae. And she had never liked the snide remarks Harriet's friend had made to Edna.

"Harriet, let's talk now. You don't need to apologize to me again. I said I forgive you. You need to repent to Shira."

"I just can't." Her voice came in pants. "It's too much."

Lord, I want to hang up the phone on her. Let her stew in her juices for a while. The twinge of her own guilt halted her cruel thoughts—hadn't she just told Harriet she'd forgiven her.

"My friend, you may think you can't, but eventually it will cause you more problems if you don't. Save yourself the grief."

"Are you going to tell Shira?" Harriet whined like a child.

"I'll give you until tomorrow to tell her. If you don't, then, yes, I'll tell her." She let that sink in. Harriet's sniffling resumed. "Harriet, more than anything I want to see this mess over with. Edna had a vision for the four of us. We have yet to explore it."

"Yeah." She drew the word out suspiciously. "I have one more thing to tell you."

Beulah threw her head back. *No more, Lord, please.* "Is this about what Billie is doing?"

"Kinda. No. Not really."

"Can it wait until tomorrow, please?" Beulah tried not to beg.

"I'm sorry, Beulah. It's late, isn't it? Yeah, it can wait." She blew her nose. "I appreciate you taking time with me. I needed to sort through this. You helped me."

"Harriet, get some sleep. Before we hang up, let's pray."

"Thank you."

Thank you? Harriet willing to let Beulah pray for her? That was something Beulah had never thought to hear from Harriet Foster.

38

Shira cringed as the tone announcing the end of hospital visiting hours stirred Melly from her drugged sleep. The poor child needed her rest. Melly blinked several times to focus on Shira's face. A weak smile formed on her colorless lips.

"Hi, Miss Shira." Her voice was as frail as a thin reed.

Mrs. Cohen smoothed back her daughter's bangs and gave her a tender kiss. "Melissa, Shira hasn't left your side for hours."

Melissa closed her eyes, and her head lolled to one side. Asleep again.

How could Shira leave? She felt responsible for Melly's relapse. The pain of seeing her young body with tubes and monitors was compounded by memories of her mom. Her ever-present child's guilt that somehow she had caused her mother's death intensified her shame of forcing Melly into a relapse.

Her arms wrapped so tightly around her waist, they might leave marks. At Mrs. Cohen's touch, Shira jumped.

"Shira, let me walk you out."

Once outside Melly's room, Mrs. Cohen pulled Shira into a tight embrace. The unexpected hug pushed Shira over the edge. Sobs, deep and painful, surfaced. Mrs. Cohen's body trembled. Together they shared this heartache, this sorrow.

"Sweetheart." Mrs. Cohen stepped back and moved a strand of hair from Shira's face—a gesture her mom had done. "This is not your fault."

"Yes, it is." She crumbled against the woman's shoulder. "Melly was fine until she came to work for me. I shouldn't have let her work so hard."

Melly's mom caressed her head as it rested on her shoulder. Finally, she held her at arm's length. "Shira, look at me. You did not cause this relapse. The doctors say the leukemia is so advanced, it must have been growing for some time."

"Is Melly going to die?"

Fresh tears pooled. "At this point the doctors say it could be a few days or weeks."

She sucked in a shallow breath.

"We're praying that God will heal her. But I don't know."

Bitterness stiffened her muscles. "People prayed for my mom."

Mrs. Cohen took both Shira's hands in hers. "I know. I was one of them."

Shira bit her lower lip.

"Shira, I've witnessed great miracles, and I've mourned other's deaths, like your mom. If you are asking why, I can't give you an answer. I can only say, blessed be His Name."

She smiled and wiped a tear away with her fingertips.

The essence of pure beauty standing before Shira could never be replicated—even in the best salon or plastic surgeon's office. Shira couldn't take her eyes off Mrs. Cohen. She brought Shira's fingers to her lips and kissed them. "Thank you, Shira, for allowing our daughter the opportunity to be a normal teenager. Your gift means more to us than you'll ever know."

Mrs. Cohen accompanied her to the elevator. She waved goodbye as the doors closed.

Thankfully the elevator was empty because the tears flowed again. Once it arrived at the lobby, the doors barely opened before she charged for the exit.

How was it she never had a tissue when she needed it? Her purse seemed to devour every pack she placed in there. She walked past the gift shop. No lights—closed. The automatic exit doors slid open, allowing in a rush of frigid October night air. She hunted for something to blow her nose on.

Pulling her head out of her designer bag, she checked the area. Dark. No one was around. She rubbed the back of her hand and sleeve under her nose.

Yuck. All she managed to achieve was to slide the slimy stuff around her face. She glanced about before she did the unthinkable. Bending at her waist, she pulled the tail of her blouse to her nose and—

Laughter traveled upon the cool night air. She straightened quickly and plastered herself against the wall next to a large potted plant. Maneuvering behind as many leaves as possible, she waited for the people walking on the sidewalk to pass by—her nose getting gooier by the second. A couple, arm-in-arm and in animated conversation, passed without seeing her. Brown curly hair bobbed alongside blonde. She stepped out in the open.

Jesse? With another woman? Their laughter left a trail of gloom for her to follow.

That's it? She was already totally out of his life? Lighten up, Shira. You still technically had a boyfriend when you became interested in the good lawyer.

The gorgeous blonde was probably a nice Jewish girl who attended Beth Ahav, did the Shabbat *bracha*, and danced the hora. And was no doubt ready to be the future mother of Jesse's adorable kids. *I guess it's really over.*

One kiss. One amazing kiss, and he had moved on.

Like all the rest.

By the time Shira entered the apartment, what began as a cloud of sadness that morning had turned into a tsunami of depression. The malls were all closed—but she didn't have the energy to crisis shop had they been open.

She stepped out of her shoes, dropped her coat on the floor, and slumped onto the couch. Her tear ducts were empty, nothing left. Just like there was nothing left for her in Gladstone.

Beulah was waiting for information on Melly. She grabbed her cell from her purse. The red message light blinked. She took it off vibrate mode then Thumbed the caller ID menu. Veronica's number popped up.

She hit redial. Flutters in her stomach brought some color back into her gray thoughts.

"Veronica Harrington."

"Veronica? It's Shira."

"Shira. Thank you for calling me back." Gone was her usual calm, professional voice. She sounded frantic. "Did you listen to the message I left?"

"No. Are you all right?"

She cursed. "No, I am not all right. I need you in Beverly Hills. Now."

The dream job? "What about Nigel?"

She gave a loud ha. "Yes, about Nigel. Biggest mistake I ever made."

Veronica admitting to making a mistake? Shira was going to savor this historic event.

"Nigel," Veronica stretched out the word with disdain, "ran off with the salon's money. He embezzled—I can't repeat how much—and ran off with one of my top stylists." She puffed out air like a deflated balloon. "My top female stylist."

Shira's jaw dropped. "Wait a minute. Nigel isn't gay?"

"No. Not only that, his name isn't Nigel Binghampton. It's Fred Davis."

A geyser of laughter threatened to erupt from Shira. But something told her to put a cork in it. "Is he even British?"

"No." Humiliation laced that word. "He's from Newark."

"New Jersey?" Shira was ready to burst.

"Go ahead and laugh, Shira," she said. "You earned the right."

She grabbed the pillow from behind her back and covered her mouth before letting the hilarity have its way. After a few seconds, and a major abs workout, she gained control. "Sorry, Veronica. This has to be difficult for you."

"You have no idea." She blew her nose. "Here's the deal, Shira. I need you here with me, in California, by Sunday."

"Veronica, I own a salon here. I can't simply leave."

"From what I hear, your salon is an eighties reject in—and I quote—Losersville."

Ah. Alec told Fawna, who must have told Veronica.

"Shira, I'm offering you double what you were earning in Manhattan, plus profit-sharing. Put the place up for sale and hop on a plane."

Double? "Let me sleep on it, Veronica."

"I need to know now."

"I understand your predicament, but I need until tomorrow."

"Fine." If her voice were any tighter, she'd need life support. "I already ordered your plane ticket—first class. As soon as I can I'll email the contract with your salary and profit sharing benefits. Call me as soon as possible."

"I will." Her heart did a happy dance. "Thanks, Veronica."

"You're welcome."

She leapt off the couch and hopped around the living room. The dream job of the century. Beverly Hills. Money. Palm trees. Hollywood. Disneyland. Running a salon that catered to movie stars. Gotta call Cari. She's going to love this.

She hit the speed call. *Wait.* She disconnected the call.

No Cari. No Dad. No salon that belongs to me. No chance to fight for Jesse. No Beulah. No Harriet . . . well, that might not be such a bad idea. No Melly.

She sat on the floor, looking around her. Who was she kidding? Even with all the tzuris she had been through, she couldn't leave. It would be like running away, again.

Moments ago she had thought there was nothing to hold her there, how wrong she was. They would weather the problems with the clients somehow. The money for remodeling would come from somewhere. Her plans to turn The Mavens into a showcase salon unique in its ability to cater to the needs of every age group would be realized.

How all that would happen, she hadn't a clue. All she knew was it would. She snuggled her knees to her chest. The money wouldn't be as good. But the alternative was to leave behind all the people who really loved her. Whom she loved as well.

This wasn't as difficult as she'd thought. *Goodbye, Beverly Hills.*

39

Harriet woke to razor-like pains in her leg. Sweat puddled in her sheets. She threw back the covers and stared at one jim-dandy swollen leg. *What on earth? Dear God, help me.*

She grabbed the phone and dialed 911.

"911. What's your emergency?" Some kid that sounded like a twelve-year-old answered the phone.

"My leg. It's swollen." She gritted her teeth. "I'm in a lot of pain."

"Did you injure yourself?"

"No." She groaned. "The pain woke me up."

"Do you have a fever?"

"I'm definitely hot."

"Any lumps that you can feel in your leg?"

She raised her nightgown higher and ran her fingers lightly over the leg. *Oh.* "Yes." There's another one. "At least two."

"Any shortness of breath?"

"No. I mean, I don't think so." She was bona fide scared.

"Ma'am, we have an ambulance on its way. Are you alone?"

She choked back a sob. "Yes."

"Does someone you know have a key—someone you could call to come over?"

Edna. Billie Mae. She choked back another sob. "No."

"Can you get to the front door to unlock it?"

"I'll try."

Harriet swung both legs out and lowered them to the floor. The pain increased. "It hurts worse."

"I'm sorry to make you do this. They'll have to break down the door otherwise."

No way. She struggled into the living room and unlocked the front door. Her grunts and groans frightened her even more. "I did it. It's open," she panted.

"Ma'am? Are you having any shortness of breath?"

"No. I don't know. Let me sit down." She made it to the recliner and pulled the lever. With her legs elevated, there was some relief. "No. No shortness of breath."

"The ambulance is on its way, ma'am."

"Please, don't hang up."

"I'll stay on the line. My name is Jeff."

"Thanks, Jeff. My name is Harriet." *Dear Lord, what is wrong with me?*

Wake up.

Shira woke to a coughing fit. She must have fallen asleep on the couch. Was that Harriet smoking in her apartment? She shouldn't do that. Aunt Edna didn't like her doing that.

A shrill, pulsating noise caused her to cover her ears. The smoke detector!

Adrenaline ruptured within her. She sprang from the couch and grabbed her purse and shoes by the door. She opened the door. A toxic cloud of smoke rolled in. She covered her mouth and nose with her blouse and sprinted for the fire escape outside, attached to the sidewall.

The cold metal stairs against her bare feet sent another shot of adrenaline through her.

Her salon was on fire.

Flames were visible from the supply room window. She slipped on her shoes as she sprinted to the front. Strange sounds came from the salon, like someone was taking a sledgehammer to it.

Pieces of glass littered the sidewalk. The dry cleaners, under her bedroom window, was billowing black smoke with red flames piercing through. If she had been sleeping in her bed instead of on the couch . . .

She rummaged through her purse until she found the cell and called 911. Between violent coughs, she gave all the pertinent information.

The salon. Aunt Edna's salon. With a shaky hand, she punched her dad's speed call.

"Hello?"

"Daddy?" Shira could hear sirens in the distance. "Daddy, my salon's on fire!"

Beulah awoke to distant sounds of sirens. Her customary prayer for protection for firemen and those in danger didn't calm her enough to go back to sleep.

Turn on the police scanner.

As the wife of a fireman, her home had the continual white noise of the police scanner. Shortly after Wil's second stroke, she had turned it off. Listening to a life he would never participate in was too painful.

She left the warmth of her bed and slipped on her robe. Wilbur's retreat, his study, was located across from their room, next to what had been Tom's room. She rested her hand on the knob for a moment then twisted it. The faint spicy scent of his aftershave, after so long, was still present. She inhaled deeply.

The Uniden scanner sat on the bookcase behind his desk. She turned the power knob, and the crackle of static punctuated the voices of men and women dedicated to service.

Wil's dark brown leather chair bore the faint outline of his body. She sat, welcoming the characteristic squeaks and groans.

"Ambulance enroute to HUP." Someone was being taken to the Hospital of the University of Pennsylvania. Melly was next door to that hospital. She planned to visit her after work tomorrow.

"Three-alarm fire at hair salon located at—"

Shira's address! The Hair Mavens!

Oh, dear Lord, protect Shira and the shop. Protect all those helping her. She bounded from the chair and dashed back to the bedroom.

Shira needed her.

40

The sun rose brightly over what was left of Aunt Edna's salon. Birds chirped as though this was nothing more than another beautiful day; all the while, fire personnel loaded their equipment, stepping around broken glass and wood on the sidewalk.

Shira clutched a plastic bag from the grocery store across the street, to her chest. The kind storeowner had given it to her, along with his sympathies. Inside were the contents of her safe. It was fireproof—she wished her heart were.

The TV news team had packed up and left a few minutes ago. She scooted a few pieces of glass against the building with her foot. Curious residents and business owners still milled about on the sidewalks and streets. She had fielded questions and words of sympathy until her voice was husky.

The bakery couple had brought coffee and donuts to the firemen and police officers. Though they had offered some to her, she hadn't the stomach for it.

Her dad and Beulah had not left her side, but at this point she needed some space as she sorted through her charred reality.

"Ms. Goldstein?"

A nearly bald man with round wire-rimmed glasses extended his hand. He exchanged greetings with her dad and Beulah. Her father wrapped an arm over her shoulder and nodded toward the man. "Shira, this is Bob Henry."

"Ms. Goldstein, I am—was—your aunt's insurance broker." He had this poignant puppy-dog appearance that made her like him immediately—and want to pat the top of his head. "I am so sorry for this loss." His gaze changed to the view behind her.

She couldn't bring herself to look at the shop again.

"The fire marshal informed me the fire started in the dry cleaners next door." He redirected his focus to her apartment window over the dry cleaners, and readjusted his glasses. "With all the chemicals in your place and the dry cleaners, it's a miracle you made it out alive."

Anger rose inside her. Was she supposed to be thankful for this—this miracle?

His blue eyes held hers. "You've suffered a great loss. Fortunately, your aunt's coverage on the building and contents is extensive. Rather, I should say, your coverage. The policy was also in your name. You can rebuild."

Policy? Rebuild?

Beulah touched her sooty cheek. "All those wonderful ideas you had, Shira. You can do them now."

Shira knew she meant well, but it wasn't as simple as that.

Her father studied her. His bushy brows nearly met.

The plastic bag, containing what was left of the salon, crinkled as she unfolded her arms.

Enough. She was tired of fighting. She heaved a loud sigh. "Dad?"

He took a step back, almost as if he knew what was coming. "Yes."

"Veronica called last night. She offered me Beverly Hills."

He stared at his shoes. Beulah released a tiny moan.

"I'm taking the job."

Dad raised his eyes to hers. "Running away, again?"

A new fire—this time inside her—ignited. "Running away?" She stretched an arm toward the scorched salon. "Really? There's nothing here for me anymore." As soon as the words entered the atmosphere, she regretted them. Some mystical fireman had hosed down the anger that flamed inside her seconds ago.

Her dad didn't bat a lash. "There is plenty here for you, Shira. Open your eyes."

The sudden urge to hug him, to have him wrap his arms around her, made her lips quiver. But coldness snaked its way in and squeezed the sentiment lifeless. "I've made my decision."

"Shira, I can't imagine you leaving." Beulah's face was streaked with trails of tears.

The few steps between them disappeared as Shira threw herself into Beulah's embrace. Together they gave in to the sobs of despair. Muscular arms encircled Beulah and Shira. It had been years since she had heard the sounds of her father's grief. They were no less frightening to her now.

"No, Shira." Cari squeaked. "You can't leave."

"There's nothing here for me. I don't fit in." She threw a pile of clothes, shoes, and toiletries onto the counter of Boscov's. Bob Henry had given her cash to purchase what she needed to get by until she flew to LA. He'd also booked a room at a hotel by the Philly airport for her. "I'm too tired to fight any more."

Veronica had graciously changed the tickets from Sunday to Saturday night. She thanked Shira repeatedly that morning and said she would meet her at the airport in Los Angeles.

"Shirry, no. Please don't go away again."

The cashier began scanning her merchandise and placing it in large plastic bags. Suitcase. She tapped the girl on the arm and mouthed, "Suitcases?"

"Care-bear, you and Aaron can visit me. Think of all the fun we'll have. Besides, we can call each other every day."

The cashier pointed her chin over her shoulder to the left. "Suitcases are across from housewares."

Cari sniffed. "That's not what I mean by going away again."

Shira ran down the aisle and skidded to a stop at the display of roller bags. "What are you talking about, Cari?"

"Shira, whatever you're doing *stop*! Please, listen to me."

"I'm listening." She sat on the display and grabbed a purple suitcase testing its maneuverability.

"You are shutting me out again, Shira!"

An invisible fist punched her in the kishkas. Now she understood what Cari was trying to say, she let the bag drop. "I promise you. It's not like that."

She whimpered. "Are you sure?"

"Yes."

"Then why are we having this conversation over the phone? Why aren't we here together, crying into something chocolate, saying how much we'll miss each other?"

Was she shutting Cari out? No, the simple truth was there were too many details to manage. "I have so much to do before I leave Saturday night. Maybe we can get together later. Or tomorrow night."

"Okay." Every ounce of her bubbly personality was absent in her response.

Regret rammed its way into her heart, but she promptly shut the door against it. She grabbed a carry-on, a cute cosmetic bag, and large suitcase then ran back toward the cashier. Later. Tomorrow. She'd deal with her friend then.

The lovely hotel suite quickly soaked up the smoky odor of her clothing and purse. She called the service desk.

"May I help you?"

"Yes, I need to have items cleaned by tomorrow, Saturday morning at the latest. Is that possible?" She yanked the mini-fridge open and snagged a ten-dollar bottle of water.

"Yes, Ms. Goldstein. I'll send someone up. Is there anything else?"

"No, thank you." She took an unladylike gulp of the cool liquid.

"You have a message from an Aaron Lowinger. Shall I relay his number? He said you do not have his office phone."

"Yes, thank you."

Aaron, not Cari? She dialed the number.

"Aaron, this is Shira. Is Cari okay?"

He sighed. "She's pretty upset. We'll miss you, Shira."

Surprisingly, his words distressed her more than she could express. The explanations or justifications she had used earlier evaporated.

"I'm really sorry about your salon, Shira."

"Thanks." Her reply was barely a croak, but at least it was something.

"Listen, Shira, I won't keep you. Did Melly complete the data entry?"

She swallowed back her guilt about Melly—for now. "Yes."

"Did she back up the data?"

"I don't know."

"You have a safe, right?"

"Yes."

"I instructed her to back up each night on the cloud, but also on disc. She would have placed it in the safe with the software."

The plastic bag. "Hold on, Aaron, let me check."

She pulled the bag from her purse. Riffling through the contents, she found a square, black-zippered pouch. After unzipping it, she found a few CDs in several acetate sleeves.

"I found a black pouch with some CDs in it."

He exhaled. "Thank the Lord. That's it. What does the last disc say?"

"It has last Friday's date. That was the night she finished . . . The last night she worked."

"Good girl, Melly," he whispered. "Shira, your files are safe for the most part. The only data missing is anything from Saturday to Wednesday."

Definitely wasn't much going on then.

"I'll stop by the hotel after work to pick up the disks. I can restore everything on my computer at home and print up your client lists."

She hadn't thought about contacting the clients. Yet, here was Aaron—an engineer—covering for her. "See you soon."

He had hung up before she could ask if Cari would come with him. Did her friend even want to see her again?

41

"How long?" Harriet's fingers clutched the scratchy hospital blanket.

The kid-doctor—her comb was older than he was—tapped something on his phone. "At least a couple days, Ms. Foster."

How could she trust a kid-doctor with a Star Trek lapel pin? She wondered if he had Vulcan ears stashed somewhere in his pocket. All the sci-fi gear seemed to fit. Outside her room was a computer thing that looked like a six-foot robot that had been pieced together with spare parts. She'd watched doctors and nurses enter stuff into it all day and night.

"We need to run tests. Thrombophlebitis is serious. If you have clots in that leg, all it takes is one to travel to your lung and you could die."

She froze where she was—afraid to move. Die? Oh, dear Lord, please help me.

"We have you on blood thinners and an analgesic. Are you feeling more comfortable?"

"Yeah." Other than the fact that there might be a terrorist clot with her name on it.

"Okay. I'll check on you tomorrow." He slid the phone into his pocket. "Don't worry. It's good you called when you did. You're in great hands here." His Reeboks squeaked as he walked out of her room.

Why didn't she feel convinced?

Lying in bed had never been her idea of fun. No books or magazines. Only the boob tube. After locating the fat white remote—with the biggest buttons she'd ever seen—she switched on the wall-mounted TV.

The ancient set crackled and displayed a beautiful woman, with perfect hair, perfect teeth, perfect everything at seven thirty in the morning. She didn't need this—

Wait. Was that Shira? She turned up the volume as the news show rolled film of a fire.

"The fire started at Wang's Dry Cleaners next to The Hair Mavens Beauty Shop," the TV reporter said.

Her insides spasmed with fear and dread.

"Fortunately, no one was hurt, but the salon and cleaners are destroyed."

Destroyed? Edna's treasure, gone? This was her fault—she knew somehow this was her fault. All her schemes . . . She had thought she was so smart. She pounded the sides of her head.

God, are you punishing me?

One thing for sure, she deserved it.

Kathy swirled the butter around the iron frying pan with the spatula. She remember how Edna had made the most delicious eggs in this plan. Now it was hers. The eggs spattered and spit as she poured their sunny roundness into the hot pan.

Today, she would work very hard to help Shira. Later, she would visit Melly and see when she would be coming back to work. Everything would be okay. All it would take was time and hard work.

The phone rang. She grabbed the receiver and pressed it between her ear and shoulder. "Kathy?"

Kathy dropped the spatula on the floor. "Beulah, what is wrong?"

"Kathy, I don't know how to break this to you, but there was a fire at The Hair Mavens."

"Is Shira—" Her hand clutched her robe. She could feel her heart thumping like a frightened rabbit.

"No, no. Shira's fine. No one was hurt, but the salon is ruined."

Nyet. "How long will it take to fix the salon?"

Beulah said nothing for a long time. "Shira's going to sell The Hair Mavens." Beulah blew her nose.

This was all her fault. God was finally punishing her for all the bad things she had done. Black smoke rose from the pan.

Edna, I am so sorry. I failed you.

The word HOSPTL came up on Beulah's caller ID. Melly? Hopefully, this was good news. She pulled the towel off her wet head to place the phone to her ear. "Hello?"

"Beulah, it's Harriet." Harriet's voice sounded small and far away. Beulah could barely hear her.

"Harriet, where are you?"

"I'm in the hospital."

That was so nice. She was visiting Melly.

"They admitted me early this morning."

"What!"

"Hey, don't yell at me." She coughed. "I feel bad enough as it is."

"Sorry, Harriet. I'm surprised, that's all. Why are you in the hospital?"

She sniffed and blew her nose. "I don't want to talk about that right now. Is Shira okay? What's going on with the shop?"

"You know about the fire?"

"Yeah." She took a ragged breath. "I saw a news broadcast. How is Shira?"

Twice in one day she had to be the bearer of bad news. "She's having a rough time. She's quitting."

"The salon business?"

"No, The Hair Mavens. Us." Having to retell the bad news made Beulah want to curl up in a ball and cry. "Her former boss in Manhattan called last night and offered her a job in Beverly Hills."

Best to allow Harriet a few minutes to let this sink in. Maybe a little levity would work to lighten this oppressiveness. She gave a half-hearted chuckle. "Harriet, you want to buy a used salon?"

Harriet let go a loud gasp. "How, how could you?"

"Harriet, I'm sor—"

The loud disconnect interrupted her apology. *Lord, I didn't mean anything by that. Please, let her know.*

Okay. She could fix this. She would go to Harriet and make amends. In the meantime, she needed to get dressed and figure out how to contact all their clients.

Lying in a heap on the floor was her soiled clothing, the smoky reminders of the morning's disaster. The cruel and devastating reality wanted to creep in like a serpent. Edna's inheritance to Shira was destroyed. Harriet, Kathy, and she still had what was given to them. But Shira's legacy lay in ruins.

The urge to curl up and cry increased in strength. Instead of succumbing, she went to her knees on the cold bathroom tile. She prayed until she nothing came out, then she was silent.

She can't run from Me.

This was what Beulah needed to hear—feel, deep in her heart. Peace poured over her, like a gentle wave.

Yes. Things seemed bleak. Yes. Shira planned to leave.

But yes, most importantly, God was in control.

Beulah was glad she called Shira.

"Beulah, could you stop by Aaron and Cari's and pick up the client list?" Shira's voice was husky and weak.

"I'd be happy to do that, Shira," Beulah said. "In the meantime, I'll stop by and put a sign on the salon that I'll be contacting everyone."

Shira's news that Aaron would be able to restore all the client files was welcomed—and a praiseworthy miracle. *Thank You, Lord.* Beulah would pick up the list from him after she visited Wil, then Harriet tonight.

"Beulah, thank you for doing all this. You are a true friend." The last word trembled with emotion. "This is harder than I thought."

"It's not too late to change your mind, Shira."

Her silence gave Beulah hope that Shira was still wrestling with her decision. "I can't, Beulah."

"May I ask why?"

"Aunt Edna gave me a treasure. I abused it. I think God is telling me something."

No. "Shira, God is telling you He loves you. He'll help you through this—"

"Beulah, I know you mean well, but I don't want to talk about this. Thank you for all you're doing."

Her cheeks heated. "You're welcome." Would she ever be able to be a worthy mouthpiece for God—or would she forever bungle His efforts?

"You know, Bay-oo-lah, maybe you should think of buying the place. I couldn't think of anyone better suited to take care of Aunt Edna's salon."

Beulah sickened at the suggestion. Was this how Harriet had felt with her feeble joke earlier?

A quiet word came to her. Her arms prickled with goosebumps. "I appreciate the offer, Shira. But The Hair Mavens is your inheritance, not mine. If I bought the salon, I would feel like a thief."

"I have to go, Beulah."

She smiled. *Yes, Lord. This was Shira's inheritance.*

If Beulah hadn't known better, she would have said the salon was a victim of terrorism. One of Maven's windows was boarded up, the other blackened with soot. The dry cleaner's front window and door were completely covered in plywood.

Despair tried to snake its way in again. *I walk by faith and not by sight, so leave me alone, despair and fear.*

Setting her bag of supplies on the sidewalk, she lifted the large hot-pink poster board.

"You need some help, Beulah?" Josie Carter, the owner of the Petal Pushers Florist four doors down, extended her hand toward the sack.

"Josie. Thank you." Beulah lifted the bag. "I have some markers and tacks to put up a sign."

Josie peeked inside the sack then at the salon. "What's going to happen with Edna's place?"

What should she say? "Well. Edna's niece, Shira, is feeling pretty discouraged."

"I can imagine. Where is she staying?"

She told Josie the hotel.

"I think I'll send her some flowers," she said.

"Josie, how thoughtful. I'm sure she would appreciate that very much."

"Beulah, tacks aren't going to hold that sign for long. Let me run back to the shop and get my staple gun."

While Josie dashed for the stapler, several other owners of businesses made their way toward her. As if by divine invitation, they converged on the sidewalk—many bearing gifts.

In no time, with a team of twelve people, they attached two signs to The Hair Mavens. Helen Arnold, the owner of A New Life Antiques, recommended cutting the poster in half. One half stated the obvious, CLOSED. The other a touching note to pray for the staff and that clients would receive calls shortly explaining the situation.

In all the years Beulah had worked for Edna, she had never known that Helen was a strong Christian. Neither of them had taken the time to get to know one another. What a small but precious blessing in the midst of this great trial.

Their little group reluctantly dispersed. Left behind were the sweet gifts—food and cards—and a feeling of community. If only she could take that feeling with her and give it to Shira along with these gifts.

A strange sensation tingled her skin as though she were being watched. She turned. Across the street . . . Kathy. Beulah waved and walked toward her. "Sweetie, I was worried about you."

Kathy resembled a waif in a Charles Dickens novel. Clothing had never been Beulah's thing, but it appeared Kathy threw on whatever was closest to her. A stained sweatshirt, pants baggy enough to fit Beulah, and a pair of sparkly flats. Her hair appeared as though it hadn't been combed in days—or she had been pulling at it.

When the distance between them closed to a few feet, Beulah opened her arms. Without hesitation, Kathy fell into them, sobbing. "It is all my fault."

"Stop that." Beulah lifted Kathy's chin. "You are the third person today to take the blame for this fire. The fire started in the cleaners. It was an accident."

Kathy stared at her with those beautiful violet eyes. Where were her glasses?

"Beulah, what are we going to do?"

"Now, that's a very good question. I think the three of us need to sit down and talk about that."

"Three?"

"You, Harriet, and me."

Her lids lowered. "No Shira?"

Not yet. "No."

"Where is Harriet?"

Beulah, you goose, you forgot to tell Kathy. After she explained what she knew about Harriet's condition, Kathy gazed toward Mavens. "I want to see the salon. Then may I ride with you when you visit Harriet?"

"Yes, but Kathy, we can't go into the salon."

Kathy held her hand. "Then can we stand there a few minutes?"

"Sure." Like a mother and daughter, they crossed the street, hand in hand.

The elevator doors opened. Beulah exited on to the fourth floor of the children's hospital. "This way, Kathy."

Kathy had asked to visit Melly first. As they approached her room, she noticed Deborah Cohen, Melly's mother, resting her head against the doorjamb. She turned and gave a tired smile.

"Beulah." Deborah tightly embraced her.

"Deb, you remember Kathy?"

"Of course." Deb hugged Kathy. "Thank you for coming."

"How is Melly?" Beulah asked.

Deborah nodded toward the room. "She's finally getting some rest. Last night was pretty rough." She folded her arms across her waist. "I'm sorry you came all this way."

Beulah patted her arm. "It's okay. We'll come back again."

Gathering Kathy and Beulah into her arms, she whispered, "Thank you," before releasing them. They backed up a few steps, waved, then turned toward the elevators.

"You did not say anything about Shira or Harriet?" Kathy asked.

"No, she has enough on her mind right now."

Kathy nodded, then stepped into the elevator.

After meandering a half hour, trying to find their way, they finally arrived at Harriet's room. Beulah sighed. She peeked around the door. Harriet stared at the opposite wall. "Harriet?"

Startled, Harriet's face contorted. Her body slanted sideways toward Beulah as though she was going to jump out of her hospital bed. "Beulah, I'm so sorry for hanging up on you. Please forgive me. I've been trying to reach you for hours."

Beulah hurried to Harriet. They encircled each other in a hug. How Beulah had longed for some demonstration from Harriet that they could be friends, real friends.

Kathy stood by—half in the room, half in the hallway.

"Hey, kiddo. Come in here and give me a hug," Harriet said.

Kathy's approach was more guarded. She dutifully bent to allow Harriet to embrace her.

Harriet's beloved beehive resembled a rat's nest. She noticed Beulah's focus. "It's pretty bad, isn't it?" she grimaced.

"It's certainly seen better days." Bringing a finger to her lips, she asked, "How about I trim it up a bit?"

"No way!" She held her head protectively.

Beulah's hands went to her hips. "Harriet Foster, you have to let me wash it, at least."

She harrumphed. "Fine."

She and Kathy worked up a sweat washing Harriet's thin waist-length hair. How did Harriet do that every day—especially shampooing out the layers of hairspray from root to tip? She was exhausted by the time they piled it all back on top of her head.

Still it was a victory. Harriet had never allowed anyone to touch her hair. Not even Edna. Was this a foretaste of more moments—more miracles—to come?

42

Shira couldn't wait to leave. The little gifts Beulah had brought to her yesterday crowded the desk next to her laptop. She was having trouble looking at them without getting choked up. Beulah must have told every business in Gladstone which hotel she was in, because bouquets and balloons had arrived off and on all day, turning her room into something akin to a shrine to friendship.

Why hadn't she asked Veronica to change the flight to tonight? Then she would be on her way and not have to carry all the new emotional baggage from people who cared about her.

She threw her cell phone into her purse and checked her hair in the mirror. The reflection of worry lines, visible beneath her bangs, caused her to pause.

Why didn't you ask Veronica, Shira? Why not leave it all behind? Because staying was the right thing to do. To say goodbye. She swallowed back the rise of emotion. Tonight's good-byes would battle her resolve.

First, Jesse had said to meet him at The Blue for dinner at six. Their place.

Her eyes squeezed shut. It was time to stop fooling herself. There was nothing between Jesse and her, except her feelings for him. It was over.

Finding a parking place wasn't easy. She ended up having to park on the top level of the parking garage, then ride the creepy, dirty elevator to the street level.

The traffic was loud, the sidewalks crowded. So many people.

Inside The Blue, a hostess escorted her through the curtain into the main dining area. Jesse waited for her in a booth, elbows resting on the table. Raising his arm slightly, he gave a brief wave. Once she arrived at the table, he stood until she had been seated.

"Sorry I'm late, Jesse." She accepted the menu from the hostess. "A little trouble finding a parking spot."

He lifted his chin in acknowledgement. "I'm sorry about the salon, Shira." His hand moved toward hers then pulled back. "How are you?"

How am I? I want to fall into your arms and have you console me. Tell me I should stay and try again. Please, can't you read all that in my eyes? "I'm getting by."

He sipped his water. It sloshed over his fingers when he set it down. "Your dad tells me you're moving to California. Got the big promotion." His smile didn't reach his delicious brown sugar eyes.

"Yes." Her heart thundered in her ears. Even as the thought came to her, she knew it was hopeless—but she was compelled to ask. "Jesse, come with me." Reaching across the table, she grasped his hands. "You're a wonderful lawyer. You would have no trouble joining another firm. We could get a place with a pool. Enough room for everyone to visit."

The pain in his eyes wounded her. Mercifully, he closed them. "I can't, Shira." His lids reopened. "My life is here."

Of course. Her. The blonde with the melodic laugh. "Fine." She yanked back her hands. An odd, ugly brew of rejection and anger curdled in her. But she would not cry. "Can I ask you to administer the sale of the salon? Whatever it costs, send me the bill. My father knows how to reach me."

"Shira, please—"

"I can't do this." She seized her purse and scooted her way out of the booth.

Jesse did the same, a lot faster than she did. "Shira, don't leave." He grabbed her arm. His eyes fastened onto hers. An urge to throw her body against his and feel his lips on her own surged through her.

No. She tugged away, shouldered her bag, and turned away from the one real man she had ever loved.

"I see your car, Dad." Here she was, sitting in her car in the hospital-parking garage. She'd been there for nearly an hour, waiting for her father to rescue her because after running out on her dinner with Jesse, she was too emotional to see Melly alone.

"I see you too, sweetheart. I'm hanging up now."

His black Lexus pulled into a spot. Grabbing her purse, she slid out of the car and locked it.

He pulled her into a bear hug and kissed her cheek. "Rough time with Jesse?"

Her lips trembled. She pressed them together, but the quivering shifted to her chin.

He kissed the top of her head and wrapped an arm around her shoulder. "Thought so."

"I'm scared to say goodbye to Melly, Dad." She focused on the stained concrete floor as they walked. "This may be the last time I— What do I say?"

"Sweetheart, I find the best thing to do in these circumstances is to listen."

She leaned closer to him as they made their way to Melly's room.

Outside her room, Shira hesitated. Dad gave her a comforting squeeze before letting go. "Ready?"

Her feet moved in an awkward rhythm—as though they weren't sure if they were moving forward or backward. The room was dark, save the light over Melly's bed. Her small form was still, her eyes closed. Her chest moved up and down like a marathon runner finishing a race.

Mr. and Mrs. Cohen glanced up from where they sat and smiled. Mrs. Cohen touched Melly's hand. "Melly. Shira's here."

Melly's lids opened slowly. She focused on Shira. A sweet smile formed on her angelic face. "Hi, Miss Shira." Her voice was soft and sleepy—like a child waking from an afternoon nap.

Melly's mother extended an arm to draw Shira nearer to her daughter. "Melly's had a much better day today."

Hope trickled in Shira. "That's good, Melly." She tucked her fingers under Melly's small hand. "Pretty soon you'll be shopping at the mall."

Melly slowly blinked. "Maybe."

Mrs. Cohen gently maneuvered Shira into her chair. "Shira, Melly's dad and I could use a cup of coffee. Would you keep her company for a little while?"

Please don't leave me alone. Mrs. Cohen bent to her ear. "She already knows you're leaving," she whispered.

Her dad and Mr. Cohen shook hands, then he hugged Mrs. Cohen. He lowered his chin and smiled as he accompanied them. *He's leaving me here alone?*

"Miss Shira, I already know about the salon and you moving to California." Melly's hand tightened around hers. "I understand."

"Melly, I don't know what to say." Her other hand grasped Melly's lightly. "You did so much to help me. You're very talented and could do anything you want."

Her eyes were the eyes of someone so much wiser than Shira could ever hope to be. "I want to be whatever God wants me to be. Even if He wants me to be with Him now."

A shudder of sorrow flowed through her. "Melly, you shouldn't—"

Her face animated with amusement. "Shira, I'm not afraid of dying. Are you?"

Who wasn't? "Yes. Most people are."

She sighed and closed her eyes. "That's because they don't know

Yeshua. His love. His compassion." Her eyes opened, brimming with tears. "I love Him so much, Shira."

Shira swallowed. Every tube and monitor belied a loving God, but Melly's face tenderly expressed evidence that He was. She only hoped He appreciated this young woman's sacrifice.

"Shira, I've been praying for you."

She stammered, trying to respond. Nothing coherent came out.

"I believe you are supposed to move to California."

Her chin wobbled. "You do?" Then she was right, God did want her to run Aunt Edna's salon.

"Yes." Melly squeezed Shira's hand. "You are on the path God has for you. Just listen for when He tells you to take the next step."

"Thank you, Melly. I'll pray for you."

Melly yawned and shut her eyes. "That's nice."

"No, Dad. I think that would be a bad idea." Exhausted from her visit with Melly, the last thing Shira wanted to do was visit Harriet—even if they were only a few floors from her hospital room.

His bushy brows lowered into his don't-disappoint-me position. "Sweetheart, I know it isn't the most pleasant thought, but you need to allow Harriet some closure here."

Her fists went to her hips. "She needs closure? What about me? She's the one that tried to run me out of town." Her voice rose. People in the hospital lobby stared.

Changing his gaze to let-me-kiss-your-boo-boo, he rested his palms on her shoulders. "I know, Shira. And you have every right to be put out." He exhaled. "This is as much for you as for her. Don't carry the weight of this anger to California. Start fresh." He smiled and jiggled her whole frame. "What do you say? Give the old girl a break."

"O—kay." The one thing in her favor was that visiting hours were almost over. The less time, the better.

Outside Harriet's room, her dad positioned her to enter first—in case Harriet was indisposed, he'd said. She leaned in to see if Harriet was awake. She noticed Shira immediately. Drat.

"Shira?" Harriet repositioned herself in the bed. "I don't know what to say."

That was something new. "How are you feeling, Harriet?" She stepped back to motion her dad to follow her.

"Sam?" Harriet reached for her deflated beehive—it resembled a blonde Leaning Tower of Pisa.

"Harriet." He went to her side and kissed her cheek. "What do the doctors say?"

She folded her arms across her chest. "Kids. They're all kids, here."

That sounded like Harriet.

"I don't want to talk about me." She reached toward Shira. "I need to apologize to you."

Shira shifted back and forth on the balls of her feet.

"Please forgive me for making life so difficult for you." Tears streamed down her makeup-less cheeks. "I wasn't the one who made up and spread that rumor about you and Melly."

Rumor? What rumor about Melly? Did she even want to know?

"But I was the one who got Billie Mae involved in the first place. She just went crazy." One of her beefy hands palmed the tears away. "It's no excuse. And somehow, some way, I'll make things right, Shira. I promise."

Shira sent a pleading glance to her dad. He smiled.

"I forgive you, Harriet." The words felt wooden in her mouth. "And I apologize for giving you a hard time too." There, she said it. Nevertheless, she'd deny it to anyone who asked if she had.

Harriet's mouth scrunched and twisted like she'd eaten a bowlful of lemons. She reached far enough to yank Shira into a hug—more like a death grip.

Once the shock wore off, Shira relaxed. As she rested against the solidness of Harriet, there was an odd sense of familiarity. Shira allowed Harriet to cry for a good long time.

43

Harriet threw the sheet back. *Why was it so hot?* This had to be a new form of torture. Make a person lie in a hospital bed, poke them with needles at all hours of the day and night, then give all sorts of mumbo-jumbo—all to keep a person in a permanent state of confusion. Forget waterboarding. Just admit criminals into the hospital.

She needed to get out of this bed and figure out how to fix the mess at Mavens. All she was doing now was racking up bills.

Where was Beulah? She had said she was going to visit her today. How could she do this to her? The day was half over and the woman was nowhere to be seen. No calls, no—

Whoa. What was she doing? Her heart raced, her breathing fast and shallow. *Harriet, are you trying to kill yourself*

Closing her eyes, she breathed deeply and exhaled. A coughing spell ensued.

Must be time to replace her nicotine patch. She pointed toward the ceiling. "Edna, you'd be proud of me. Two days without a cigarette."

Of course she didn't have much of a choice. She pulled the sheet up to her neck.

"Hello." Beulah had arrived bearing a large plastic bag of something.

Relief and gratefulness poured over Harriet. "How's it going, Beulah?" She watched as Beulah set the bag on the chair and took off her jacket. "What's the weather like out there?"

"Feeling more like October. Brisk." She smiled as she opened the bag. "I brought you some goodies from Nonni and Frank." She opened a white box to reveal an assortment pastries—including her favorite Danish. Harriet's mouth watered.

"Josie sent this little plant." Beulah set an African violet on the nightstand.

The flowers made her grin. She touched the delicate purple petals. *Imagine that.* She had probably said a dozen words to Josie in ten years. She'd never even seen the inside of her business.

"And finally, books and magazines." Beulah pulled at least five books and as many magazines from the magic bag and laid them next to Harriet. "The books are Christian novels I've read. I hope you enjoy them as much as I did."

Holding one of the novels, a lump of emotion made talking difficult for Harriet. "Thank you, Beulah. This is so thoughtful." Her voice resembled a croaking frog.

"Well, you are most welcome." She smiled as she collapsed on a chair. Fatigue had etched itself onto her face. "Have you heard anything from the doctors?"

Harriet pressed her mouth together and looked away.

"I'm not leaving until you tell me what's going on."

This feisty Beulah was fun. "Well, it appears I have thrombophlebitis."

Her brows knitted. "Doesn't that mean you have blood clots?"

How did she know this stuff? "Yeah. But I'm on blood thinners, and they do ultrasounds on my legs to make sure no clots misbehave."

Beulah scooted her chair closer then rested her elbows on her bed. "You need to take care of yourself, Harriet. Let them help you."

"It's tough. I ain't used to being in bed this long. I wasn't in bed this long when I . . ." She couldn't say the word miscarriage out loud.

"How are you doing without cigarettes?"

A snide remark nearly made its way out, but she bit her tongue and shrugged.

"I'm proud of you, Harriet."

Time to change the subject. "What's going on with Shira?"

Beulah reclined against the chair and stared at her fingers in her lap. "She's flying out tonight."

"I—somehow I thought she'd change her mind."

"So did I."

"This is it? The end of Mavens?"

"It would appear so." She blew out a frustrated sigh. "We're broken up and going in different directions."

The dream. The snow globe broken into pieces. This was her fault.

"Harriet? What's wrong?"

"This is my fault."

Beulah stood. "It's not your—"

"No, listen to me. I had this dream."

Beulah paced, but appeared to listen to everything about the recurring dream. After Harriet finished, Beulah sat again. After a while, she moved the books and magazines to the chair, and sat on the edge of the bed. "Harriet, I believe I know what the dream represents."

"Okay." Why did she get the feeling this wasn't good?

"This might be difficult."

"I don't care. I want to know." Still, her gut buckled and bunched.

"I believe God brought back the memory of Shira drawing the picture of you and Edna, because He wanted to remind you of how much Edna loved Shira. But more than that, He wanted to remind you how much Shira loved you."

Harriet swallowed. "Okay, maybe I don't want to hear this."

"I know you think the snow globe has to do with Edna's shop. I don't think it does." She paused. "You said it yourself, Edna loved snow globes. Edna was dedicated to the salon and us, but she loved Shira. It represents Shira."

Something pushed its way up Harriet's throat. She opened her mouth and a wail ripped through her soul. Beulah pulled her into her arms. They rocked back and forth as moans came from somewhere deep inside her.

She sneaked a look at Beulah. "How can you touch me? I'm dirt."

"Shush now. God showed you this for a reason."

"What? To show me what a horrible creature I am?"

"Well, yes."

"Wha—"

"But it's more than that, Harriet."

A nurse scurried into the room, her shoes squeaked to a stop. Her mouth gaped, ready to say something.

Oh brother. When she needed a nurse they were never around. "I'm okay," she waved her away. "Go on."

The nurse studied them for a few seconds then left.

Beulah broke the moment by stepping back. "Harriet Schmidt Foster, it's time you got right with the Lord. You keep fighting Him every time He tries to hug you to Himself."

The tissues on the nightstand were out of Harriet's reach. Beulah passed her the box. She blew her nose and wiped her face. "You're saying that dream was to tell me He cares for me? I thought it was a warning."

"It was a warning. But He warned you because He cares. He had wanted to save you from the pain you're feeling right now."

"I think He wants to get even with me for all the rotten stuff I did to Shira."

Beulah dropped her head into her hands.

"What?"

"Harriet, God loves us. He sent His Son Jesus to die for our sins. Every disgusting thing. What we did yesterday. Today. What we'll do tomorrow."

"But God punishes people."

"Let me ask you this. If a child continually tries to run into traffic, doesn't the parent punish him?"

"I guess."

"Why?"

She'd never done well in Sunday School, and it was painful to be reminded she wasn't a parent. "To keep them from doing it again?"

"Exactly. God isn't waiting around to punish us for every sin. He wants us set free from sin. No matter what we've done, He loves us and wants us as His own."

"Ms. Foster?" The nurse pointed to her watch. "Time for your tests."

What stinking timing. "Now?"

She shrugged.

Beulah picked up her purse. All sorts of racket came from it as she hunted for something.

"There it is." She whipped out a folded blue-colored paper, all crumpled. "It's a little wrinkled." She tried to smooth it then gave it to Harriet. "But the truth in this little pamphlet will change your life."

Harriet took it. A strange sense of awe came over her.

The orderly entered her room, ready to whisk her away for another ultrasound. "Thanks, Beulah. I'll read it."

Beulah kissed her cheek. Adjusting her gargantuan bag—which Harriet now had the utmost respect for—Beulah pointed her finger at Harriet. "See that you do, my friend."

Friend. Harriet liked that.

"Ms. Foster, there are still two clots that I'm concerned about." The doctor had actually pulled the computer monster into her room and typed in something terrible—Harriet was certain—in her record. At least this guy seemed more doctor-ly, and closer to her age.

"What are you saying?"

He finished typing, then stepped toward her. "I'm saying we need to keep you in here a few more days."

She shoved her head back into the pillow and pounded a fist on the mattress. "I don't think I can take much more of this torture chamber."

"Ms. Foster." The stern tone in his voice resembled one of the priests in Catholic school. She gave him her full attention.

"You do understand we are trying to help you?"

"Yes."

"Then, can you do us the honor of cooperating with us? No more picking on the nurses and orderlies. You'd be amazed at how much more pleasant life would be if you didn't fight everyone."

Warmth radiated from her scalp to her toes. She read his name embroidered on his white coat. "I apologize, Dr. James."

He smiled and tapped her arm. "Good. You get some rest. I'll check back in with you tomorrow."

"Thanks."

The room filled with silence. She was alone. Really alone.

God, I'm tired of fighting all the time. I don't want to fight You anymore, either. I want to know You. If You're not running in terror after all the junk I've done in my life, then I'm impressed. I completely understand if there's some lightning bolt with my name on it, but Beulah says you love me . . .

How was she supposed to do this?

Help me, God.

The paper. Where was it? On the nightstand. She stretched until she reached the treasure, then clutched it to her heart.

I'm so nervous.

She patted her beehive—at least what was left of it. Should she put on some makeup or something? She must look a fright. *Okay, Lord. You got me. Not much of a prize, but You got me.*

Scanning the crinkled paper, she discovered a prayer on the last page.

Here goes.

Dear Father, I am a sinner.

Boy, was that ever the truth.

Thank You for sending Your Son Jesus to die for my sins. Please forgive me of all my sins. I ask Jesus to save me. I believe that just as He rose from the dead and lives eternally with You . . .

She scanned the next line. Wow. Was this part really true?

He now lives in me. Thank You. In the Name of Jesus. Amen.

A quiet materialized inside her. Peaceful quiet.

Was this that shalom-thing Edna had always talked about? She tugged the neck of her gown and gazed toward her heart.

Are you really in there, Lord? Inside me?

44

Shira patted her father's arm as he drove. "Dad, you can drop me off at the departure gate." The rain pounded as his wipers struggled to keep up.

He craned his neck to look through the windshield. "No way, Shira. I'm coming as far as I can." He aimed the Lexus into the Philadelphia Airport's short-term parking. "Besides, maybe they'll cancel the flight because of all this rain." He smiled.

This was it. She was really moving to California.

The line to the check-in counter snaked around flat-roped standards. Fortunately an airline rep pointed her toward a much smaller line at the first-class counter. Her father had volunteered to handle her stuffed-to-the-seams luggage. The matching roller bag rested on the floor, her foot shoving it an inch or two every few minutes.

Her dad's moist eyes engaged her. "You know where you're staying yet?"

"No. Veronica is taking care of all that. Probably a hotel until I can find a place." Her smile wasn't convincing, even to herself. "As soon as I know, I'll call."

He nodded. Both returned to the silence of their thoughts—too fragile for any more small talk.

"Shirry!"

Shira's head sprung to the sound of that voice, searching the sea of faces around her. Red curls bounced as her friend raced between people to reach her.

"Cari!" Shira ducked under the rope. "You came."

"I can't believe you were going to leave without hugging me." Cari crushed Shira to her.

The waterworks began. So much for her makeup. "I thought you were mad at me."

Cari drew back and placed her palms on Shira's cheeks. "You schlemiel, of course I was mad at you, but that doesn't mean I don't love you. That I'm not going to miss you. That I don't want to say goodbye."

"I'm sorry, Care-bear." They hugged again.

Cari filled their time with conversation and joy until the trio made their way to security.

Time to say goodbye. She and her best friend faced each other and held hands. "I love you, Cari."

Cari swallowed. "I love you, too." She gripped tighter. "Promise me we'll talk every day."

Words were impossible, so she nodded.

She jerked Shira's arms. "Shira, promise me. Say it."

"I promise." Her voice was mushy with emotion.

Cari squeezed her again then stepped back and looked toward Shira's dad.

He enveloped Shira in strength and warmth and love. "I'm so thankful to God that you are my daughter."

"I'm—I'm glad you're my dad." She didn't want to let go.

He released her first. "I love you, Button."

"I love you, Daddy."

Placing the carry-on and purse straps on her shoulder, she walked toward the security queue. The line was short, and within minutes she was putting on her shoes and jewelry before turning the corner toward her gate. Cari and her dad gave one last wave.

Maybe leaving was a bad idea.

Shira's clients at Élégance had always talked about first-class flying, and about which airlines were the best. This was her first foray.

As she boarded with the first zone of passengers, the flight attendant glanced at her ticket. Her face took on an aura of servitude. "Ms. Goldstein, welcome aboard." She extended nicely manicured nails. "May I help you stow your baggage?"

Wow. "Thank you."

"This is your seat. May I offer you a little wine?"

She sank her tired body into soft, supple leather next to the window. "No, thank you." She fastened her seatbelt.

"Coffee? Tea?"

"Tea. With cream?"

The attendant nodded.

"Our meal selections this evening are beef Burgundy, with baby potatoes and grilled asparagus. Or, blackened mahi mahi in a lime sauce with curried rice and snap peas. We also have a vegetarian plate with roasted vegetables in a polenta loaf, covered in a caramelized onion glaze."

Hmm. She could get used to this. Normally she brought a hoagie on board with her. Cari would have loved this.

A large African-American gentleman made his way toward her. He was dressed in an Yves Saint Laurent suit. Must be first class.

Another flight attendant carried his briefcase. "Bishop Rodgers, shall I stow your briefcase in the overhead compartment?"

"That's fine, son. Thank you."

Great. A bishop. He would probably sermonize her for the next six hours.

She smiled politely.

He extended a beefy paw. "My name is Thomas Rodgers."

Her hand was swallowed in his. "Shira Goldstein."

"Nice to meet you."

"You too."

He nestled his large frame into the seat, fastened his seatbelt, then shut his eyes. He was going to sleep? She should be happy—relieved—but instead she fought disappointment. Why?

Rubbing her arms, she knew why. Because she had a lot of questions she wanted to ask the Big Guy upstairs.

Her row partner continued his nap through take-off and through the violent turbulence as the pilot took them to a higher elevation and, hopefully, smoother air. The bumpy ride felt like some punishment from God. Gripping her armrests, she stared at the bishop, willing him to wake up so he could make amends for them with the Creator of the Universe—in case this was the end.

The smell of their gourmet meals added a new element to her fear—queasiness. She squeezed her lids tight.

"Something smells great," a gravelly voice spoke.

Her eyes popped open. *Oh, thank You, God.*

The big bear of a man stretched and yawned. He beamed a smile as enormous as, well, as he was. "Needed that little nap. Hope I didn't snore." He chuckled. "My wife says hounds bay at the noise."

Despite her rumpled insides, she chortled.

The plane hit a particularly rough patch of air. Instinctively, she clutched the bishop's hand.

He hee-hee'd. "It's okay, Ms. Goldstein."

"Shira." She nodded toward their hands. "Since we're holding hands."

"Shira." He tapped his chin. "That's Hebrew for song, isn't it?"

She didn't attempt to hide her surprise. "Yes. That's right."

"You know, I worship the Jewish Messiah, Yeshua."

Here it comes. The sermon.

He smiled and shut his eyes.

"My father worships him, too." *Shut up, Shira.*

His friendly gaze returned. "That right? Does he attend Beth Ahav?"

"Yes." This was getting weird. "Do you—"

"No, I've never been there, but I spoke at one of your international Messianic conferences."

A girl stops going to these conferences and things get interesting. "Really? I went to those conferences almost my whole life. I would have liked to have seen you."

"One of the most powerful experiences of my life. Rabbi Joel and some other rabbis presented me with a tallit, you know, the prayer shawl, and a kippah. Of course, they couldn't find a kippah big enough for my head." His whole body shook with merriment, like a big brown Santa Claus.

"Shira, you said you went to the conferences. You don't anymore?"

Releasing his hand, she glanced out the window. "No. Not for about eight years."

"Running from God, are you?"

Subtle, Bishop Rodgers. "Why would you assume that?"

"People come from around the world—Israel, Russia, Australia, South America—to that conference, right? Somehow they make their way each year."

"Yes."

"You live in Philadelphia?"

"Actually, I recently moved from Manhattan."

He lowered his chin and looked at her with the tops of his eyeballs.

"Okay, I'm running."

"Are you running now?"

Wait a minute. "You seem like a nice guy." She crossed her legs. "But you don't know me. You don't know my life."

"Fair enough." He folded his hands in his lap. "So what takes you to California?"

"A job. I'm running—managing—a new salon in Beverly Hills."

"Congratulations."

"Thanks."

The flight attendant brought their meals—on real china. Now that the turbulence was over, her hunger had appeared. The mahi mahi was delicious, the dessert of cherries jubilee, marvelous. Was there some little Top Chef stowed back in that miniscule kitchen area?

After the attendant gathered their dishes, she handed them black zippered bags and blankets. Inside were travel-sized toiletries, earplugs, an eye mask, and footies. She stored hers in the seat pocket in front of her.

Shira twisted to look toward coach, but a curtain separated them. If they only knew.

"Nice perks, eh?" he said, eyes closed, ready for another snooze.

"Your congregation must be doing well," she said, cringing at the sarcasm dripping from the words.

He opened one eye. "Frequent flyer miles." He yawned. "But, yes, there are over four thousand precious souls in my church."

She recognized him now. He was that guy—the guy on television. She'd seen him a time or two while channel surfing. "You've written books, haven't you? My dad has a couple." She remembered seeing them in his den.

Both eyes opened. "I'm honored."

Finally, she felt she had his complete attention. She'd probably never see him again, so why not go for it? "Why do bad things happen if God is in control?"

He cocked his head. "Shira, I know your rabbi. I think you know the answer to that."

Games, she didn't need. "Free will. God is a loving God. *Yada, yada, yada.*"

His brows wrinkled. "Careful. Yada is a Hebrew word for knowing someone intimately. Do you want to know God intimately?"

"I—I—"

"There's a lot of rhetoric in this world, Shira. You've been listening to too much of it. Buying the baloney, as I say." He paused, as if listening to someone. "Shira, the words of eternal life are already planted in you."

The hairs on the back of her neck and arms jumped to attention.

"Heed them." He unfastened his seatbelt. "If you'll excuse me." Gracefully maneuvering his large frame out of his seat, he made his way to the restrooms.

She stared at her arms. Still tingling.

Spying the complimentary kit, she yanked it out and unzipped it. Her fingers trembled as she pulled out the sleeping mask and earplugs. Maybe she could sleep—or look like she was sleeping. Anything to keep from those invasive orbs. It was like he had used a microscope to see into her soul.

Snapping the mask in place, she inserted the plugs in her ears. *That should do it. I'm just sleeping here. Don't mind me.*

The leather seat reclined into a fairly comfy bed. The blanket. She removed the mask and snatched the blanket. Tucking herself in, she replaced the mask quickly.

But his and her father's words replayed over and over. *The words of eternal life are already planted in you.*

The seat shifted slightly as the bishop returned to his seat. She maintained her I-am-asleep-because-nothing-you-said-affected-me pose.

Except, it had most assuredly affected her.

45

The heavy glass door closed behind Beulah. She buttoned her coat against the chill. A part of her was relieved, another part grieved. The wind picked up and blew a few colorful leaves around the small parking lot. If it weren't September, she'd have said snow was brewing.

She had a job. Sarah Middleton of Sarah's Family Hair Salon seemed nice enough. She actually had two stations open and was excited that someone might take the other as well. This particular shop would probably suit Kathy better than Harriet—a much younger crowd.

Lord, what will Harriet do? Her health wasn't the best, but she'd need to support herself. She would check with her. See what she'd want to do. All Harriet needed was a station. Her clientele would follow her anywhere.

On the passenger seat was another notice from the nursing home. Franny had discreetly given her the envelope that morning. Once she explained to the nurse that the settlement on the house was next month and she could pay everything she owed in full, the nurse had crushed her with a hug and cried, "Thank You, Jesus!"

Driving home, Beulah made a mental list of all she needed to accomplish for her move. She still hadn't found a new place to live. But she couldn't think about that. Her clients needed her.

First, she would contact her clients again. Let them know she would begin working at Sarah's tomorrow. A week after the fire, she was behind. There was also a growing number phone messages from some very contrite ladies—all had apologized for believing the horrible rumors Billie Mae had spread.

Fortunately, Sarah had extended hours and was open seven days a week.

The light turned red. She clicked down the turn signal to turn left and stopped. From the corner of her eye she saw the hospital sign on her right.

The hospital was another five blocks on the right. Home only a few blocks to the left.

Go see Harriet.

Her forehead rested on the steering wheel. *Lord, I'm so tired.*

She sighed. Yes, Lord.

Laughter emanated from somewhere as Beulah walked the pale blue hallways of the hospital. Boy, she'd rather be in that room. Harriet could be a sourpuss. *Sorry, Lord. That wasn't very Christian of me.*

The gaiety volume increased as she approached Harriet's room. One raspy chuckle in particular was familiar. As Beulah entered, two nurses stood by Harriet's bed, holding their midsections, gasping between fits of hilarity, wiping tears. A third nurse by the door bent forward, her legs crossed. "Stop, Harriet. I have to pee."

This made Harriet and the other nurses laugh harder.

She wasn't sure whether to be concerned or demand to know what was so funny so she could join in.

Harriet finally spotted Beulah.

"Beulah!" She tapped the side of her bed. "Get over here, my dear friend."

Dear friend? Warmth cocooned her from this unexpected greeting.

"Miriam, Jessica, Sue, this is my friend, Beulah." Harriet stretched an arm toward the three nurses.

They shook hands and exchanged smiling greetings.

"Ladies, I hate to break up this chick party, but I've got some serious business to talk over with my friend," Harriet said.

The nurses' obvious disappointment accompanied their good-byes as they exited the room. At that moment, Beulah felt special and honored. Though Harriet's hair had seen better days, her face was radiant. "Harriet, you look great. How are you feeling?"

She clapped once and smiled. "Never better."

"Did you get a good report from the doctor? Will they be releasing you soon?"

"I sure hope so. Still have two pesky clots giving me a hard time. But I'm trying to be a good girl and do what they tell me."

Now, there was something she'd never heard from Harriet.

"Enough of me, Beulah. How are you doing? What's going on with the salon?"

"Well." She sat on the chair next to her bed. "Shira left on Saturday, as you know."

Harriet's eyes clouded for a moment.

"I got a job at Sarah's Family Hair Salon."

"Congratulations." Her wish seemed sincere.

"They have another station open. The owner, Sarah Middleton, seems nice. She's holding it for you or Kathy."

Harriet chewed her lower lip. "Kathy probably needs it more than I do. Give her first choice. I may be here for a few more days and have another week or so to convalesce at home."

Were it not for her cockeyed blonde beehive, Beulah would have sworn she was in the wrong room. "What do you want me to tell your clients?"

She puffed out air. "Beulah, do you think you could take care of some of my clients for me until I can take care of them myself?"

The thought of the extra load weighed on her shoulders. But what was the alternative? "I'll do my best. Maybe Kathy could take some, too?"

Harriet nodded.

"I have to call my clients when I get home. I'll call yours as well and let them know you'll be out for a couple weeks."

"If you give me my list, Beulah, I'll call them. There's not a whole lot for me to do here."

"Sounds good."

Harriet shifted her position and flashed a glance toward her nightstand. Beulah's gaze followed.

An opened Bible? Beulah's eyes widened and turned to Harriet.

She shrugged a shoulder as her cheeks flushed.

"Harriet?" She lifted the Bible. "Is there something you want to tell me?"

Harriet focused on her hands as she folded them in her lap. Her toes wiggled back and forth under the blanket.

Beulah waited.

She shrugged again. "I said the prayer."

"Prayer?"

"You know. The one on that paper you gave me."

"You said the salvation prayer?"

"Whatever you call it. I said it."

Beulah cried out and threw herself on Harriet. "Praise the Lord." What was she doing? She pulled back. "I'm such a goose, Harriet. Did I hurt you?"

She shook her head, her smile wide and eyes sparkling.

Miriam and Jessica ran into the room.

Harriet waved toward the concerned nurses. "I'm okay, ladies. Just some good news."

They fanned themselves with their hands as they left.

"When?" she asked.

"Saturday night."

Beulah took her new sister's hand. "Why didn't you tell me? Call me?"

"I don't know. It felt so private at first."

Harriet's face was clothed in a soft, almost childlike innocence.

She picked up the Bible Beulah had dropped on the bed. "But then I wanted to know more about God. I thought they might have a Bible in the room, like in hotels. I ended up having to ask Miriam. She borrowed one from the chapel."

Lord, this is a miracle. "What have you been reading?"

She opened the Bible to where the tattered tract was placed. "The paper said to start reading in John." Her plump finger pointed to a page. "I'm on the last chapter. What should I read next?"

Lord, if there was any doubt You are in control, it's gone now.

"When can you begin, Ms. Smith?" Mr. Rudolph placed Kathy's application on his mahogany desk. He rested his elbows on the arms of his leather chair and made a tent with his fingers. When he placed them under his chin, he revealed expensive gold cufflinks.

"I can begin right away, Mr. Rudolph." She made eye contact with him. Edna had always reminded her to make eye contact.

"Fine." He glanced toward her application. "We are short-staffed at the salon. Are you sure you don't want to apply there?"

"No." She swallowed. "No, thank you."

He stood. "I'm taking a chance on you. I hope I'm not wrong." He extended his hand. "Welcome to the Hyatt Regency, Ms. Smith."

"Thank you, sir." She grasped his hand then looked down.

"See the housekeeping department on your way to the lower level, they will issue your maid's uniform."

A maid. She pressed the down arrow outside the shiny brass elevator doors. *Mama, I am like you now.* The doors opened. She allowed the ornate box to swallow her and carry her to where she would work out her sentence.

The main elevator stopped at the lobby. She meandered past the check-in counter, the gift boutique, and the hair salon. The tall glass windows of the fashionable salon had etched flowers around the corners. Her feet stalled. The place was exquisite—a smaller version of Gooding's.

But she would not be working to make wealthy people beautiful. She would be cleaning their dirty rooms. It was fitting punishment for all she had done.

The black uniform with starched white collars and cuffs hung on her bedroom door. She lay on her bed, staring at her future. The old life with Edna was gone. Even the hope of a good life with The Mavens was nothing but ashes.

Sadness came, but she had no more tears. She now knew there was a God, because He hated her and wanted her to be punished.

The buzzer sounded.

Lately, kids in the area had rung the exterior security buttons, trying to sell cookies or candy for their school. Ignoring them usually sent them on.

But a few seconds later the buzzer sounded again.

What if they were pranksters—or thieves checking to see if no one was home? She rolled off the bed and pressed the intercom.

"Please go away."

"Kathy? It's Beulah."

Why was she there? "I do not feel well, Beulah. Please go away."

"Kathy, I brought Chinese food. The egg drop soup will cure what ails you. Please let me in. I need to talk with you."

Before Kathy realized what she had done, she released the lock. She remembered too late the dirty dishes on the counter and in the sink. Shame warmed her face.

A knock. "Kathy, sweetie, it's me." Beulah's muffled voice came through her door.

Unlocking the door, she swung it open but walked away as Beulah entered. The last thing Kathy deserved was any of Beulah's motherly hugs. Beulah shut the door and looked around.

"Your home is adorable. I love it." She walked into the kitchen and moved a dirty bowl from the counter to the sink to make room for the bag of food.

Shame now mixed with anger. Beulah should not touch her things—Edna's things.

"I hope you like cashew chicken too."

Cashew chicken was okay. Kathy nodded.

"Where are your—"

"I will take care of this, Beulah. Please go sit in the living room." Kathy pointed to the couch.

Beulah sat as Kathy opened the cabinets and drawers and pulled out the necessary plates, bowls, glasses, and silverware. She set them on the beautiful hand-painted wood tray that Edna had given her. Looping the bag over her fingers, she picked up the tray and took it into the living room.

Beulah jumped up to take the tray and set it on the coffee table. Kathy set the food next to it.

After loading their plates and bowls, they ate in silence. More than anything, Kathy was thankful for the quiet—no questions, no need to not tell the whole truth. When they finished, Beulah helped her clean up and place the dirty dishes and leftover food on the tray. Kathy transported it to the kitchen.

"Kathy, may I help you clean up?"

She shook her head.

"May I talk with you while you clean up?"

She shrugged. Maybe if Kathy were mean enough, Beulah would go home. But no, Beulah followed her and leaned on the counter.

"I found a job at another salon."

She set a bowl down. "Where?"

"Sarah's Family Hair Salon." Beulah only smiled half a smile. "They have another station open, Kathy. Harriet says you can have it, if you want."

Her attention returned to the sink. "I already have a job."

"That's wonderful. Where?"

"The Hyatt Regency, downtown."

"Kathy, I hear they have a beautiful salon. When do you start?"

She turned on the faucet. "I do not work at the salon. I will be a maid."

"A maid?"

The bubbles inched up over the dishes. How she wished they would cover her and make her clean.

"Kathy?"

If Beulah and Harriet knew who she was they wouldn't have anything to do with her. It was better for her to be the one to break things off.

"Kathy, look at me." Her voice reminded her of when Mama had wanted to tell her something important. She turned off the water and focused on Beulah's sweet face.

Beulah's chin lowered. Green eyes went straight to her heart. "God will make a way for all of us."

"God is punishing me for all the bad things I did to Shira."

She placed both palms on the counter and sighed. "Where in the world do people get this stuff?"

"I do not understand what you mean."

"Never mind." She sighed. "Kathy, things seem bad, but I trust God that He will help us. Harriet and I are praying for Shira . . . and you."

Harriet?

As though reading her thoughts, she smiled. "Yes, Harriet."

Harriet praying for Shira? For her?

God liked Beulah because she was so good—like Edna.

He could not like her. But Harriet—she had done many bad things, too. As bad as what Kathy had done. Could God really like her, too?

46

The singer Pink's latest hit played over the speakers of Élégance Salon and Spa Beverly Hills, giving Shira's staff and their clients accompaniment as they went about giving and receiving beauty. Hidden behind the two-way mirror in her second-floor office, she observed what reminded her of a wealthy ant farm.

The antique Dresden china cup resting in her palm held her Starbucks. It felt strange not sipping her mocha mint-latte from a paper cup.

Her assistant, Willow—dressed in Prada from head to toes—scurried about downstairs, taking notes on her iPad. The poor device practically smoked with all her efforts. Shira had sent her on a mission to take a quality survey from random clients.

From Shira's first day, the young woman had followed her like a puppy eager to please. It quickly became annoying. Hence the bogus quality-survey mission. Truth be told, Willow could easily take over as manager. She had been the one to discover the initial indicators of Nigel's misappropriation.

The Beverly Hills' staff consisted of some of the best stylists, masseuses, estheticians, and manicurists in the area. Veronica had been confident they would respect her immediately. Shira figured everyone was simply glad the salon hadn't closed and that product was back in stock.

It only took a few days to figure out what Nigel had done—and hadn't done—and it wouldn't take long to repair the damage. Nigel—Fred, whatever his name—was a potentate corrupted by his new power and girlfriend. Shira had been told that he'd created division in the ranks and a lot of tension by playing favorites with the stylists. She began by creating an equitable division of new clients.

Today's newspaper rested on her antique Edwardian desk. Nigel's terrified face, plastered on the front page of the features page. She twisted to set the cup down and pick up the paper.

Authorities found him trying to cross the border into Tijuana. His girlfriend had turned him in when things got dicey. He was indicted for several counts of fraud, embezzlement, and who knew what else. Apparently, he'd stolen from the Manhattan salon as well.

The face she had loathed in Manhattan looked dreadful. Frightened. Vulnerable. She felt sorry for him. After everything he'd done to her and Veronica, how was it even possible?

She swiveled her pink leather chair around to sit. Smoothing her new Oscar de la Renta skirt, she studied the perfectness of her well-appointed office. Shouldn't she feel happy? Vindicated?

Veronica said she should. She had certainly groveled to Shira for the two days she was there, before flying back to New York. The suite at the Raffles L'Ermitage was the obscenely extravagant evidence of that groveling, as was the additional bonus Shira would receive once she signed the contract.

She sipped her latte. When she entered the hotel's Governor's Suite after her long flight, she had thought she was dreaming. Two bedrooms, living and dining rooms, two and a half bathrooms—why she needed two and a half bathrooms was beyond her. A stocked pantry, four balconies, a fireplace, a huge flat screen TV—Dad would have loved that—and a Bose surround-sound system that would make most men drool.

But the master bath had to be divinely inspired.

She slipped off her pumps and rubbed her toes together, then took another sip of coffee.

Each night she filled the Jacuzzi tub and took in the unbelievable scenes through the surrounding picture windows. The room had been designed to watch the sunset while bathing.

Except she would probably never enjoy the splendor since her whole life was spent at the salon, overseeing the huge conglomerate that Élégance had quickly become.

Since the paper arrived that morning, the phones hadn't stopped ringing. Scandal was the most optimal form of publicity in Los Angeles. They were booked solid. Her days began at six and sometimes ended at nearly midnight.

Two steady streams of tears ran down her cheeks. As perfect as everything and everyone appeared, she knew how hollow and superficial it all was. Aunt Edna had said, "Be careful what you wish for. You may get it." As a teenager, she had thought her aunt's advice came from inhaling perm fumes. Sitting in her pink leather chair in elegance and wealth, she now understood.

There was no time and no one to share it with. No one to snuggle up with after a long day. No one to take to dinner and reminisce about childhood days.

Someone else had also said, "You made your bed. Now you have to lie in it."

Well, this was one big lonely bed.

The keycard to her room slid smoothly, changing the red light to green. Stepping into the living room, she dropped her Michael Kors purse and several bags from Neiman-Marcus on the floor. A few kicks and her Calvin Klein shoes rocketed toward the potted palm tree.

Another successful, predictable day at Élégance Beverly Hills. Leaving the salon in Willow's capable hands, Shira had left early and done a little crisis shopping—even though no crisis had occurred. It didn't matter, her journal had been devoured in the fire.

Tired feet—with a will of their own—led her to the whirlpool tub. By the time she had shed her clothing in a pile, there was enough water to turn on the jets. She climbed in and closed her eyes, as the aerated water tried to perk up her fatigued body.

The phone over the tub flashed a red light. A message. The phone's digital clock read seven. Too early for Cari's call. Besides, it was her night to call.

Wiping her hand on a towel, she reached for the phone then returned to her relaxed position. She thumbed down the caller ID.

Beulah. Hitting redial, her impatience to hear Beulah's sweet voice undid what little tranquility the bath had given her.

"Shira, *Chag Sameach*—Happy Holiday."

Rosh Hashanah. She had forgotten. "Thanks, Beulah. Happy New Year to you." A sudden craving for Aunt Edna's pineapple kugel and tender brisket made her tummy rumble. She was like Pavlov's dog. Holidays came and she salivated for Aunt Edna's cooking.

"What did you do today to celebrate?"

"Nothing. Had to work."

"Oh, Shira. I sure wish you were here. I made your aunt's kugel." She paused. "Edna gave me the secret recipe."

"She did?" No fair. "What was the secret ingredient, Beulah?"

"I don't know if I should tell you . . ." A giggle. She was so cute.

"Come on. Pretty please?"

"Okay. It's yogurt."

"No way."

"Uh huh. Vanilla yogurt."

"Imagine that." Not that she would ever make the noodle delicacy, but still, it was nice to know.

"Your father and Jesse devoured it. I'd have shipped off a piece, but they ate it all." She chuckled.

Shira pinched the bridge of her nose as the burning sensation of tears returned for the second time today.

"Tell me how things are going there, Shira. Have you seen any movie stars?"

Her turn to chuckle. "A few."

They took turns sharing the news of their lives, neither of them speaking of Mavens. The absence practically screamed what their words didn't say. *We miss The Hair Mavens.*

Shira's fingers and toes had pruned by the time their conversation wound down. "Beulah, it was good talking with you. Thanks for keeping me up on all the news." It had probably done more to relax her than the bath.

"God bless you, Shira. You're in my prayers."

Shira disconnected the call and switched off the jets. The spacious room's silence roared. She grabbed a heated towel and wrapped herself in its softness. As she made her way to the bedroom, her feet sank into the thick carpet. On the turned-down bed was the hotel's version of Aunt Edna's hug. She slipped on the white robe and snatched the Godiva chocolate mint on her pillow.

She took the phone from the nightstand to the living room. Though she hungered for human warmth, she had to settle for flipping on the gas fireplace. A whoosh, and flames artfully danced over white crystals instead of logs.

She reclined on the sofa, then punched the number for room service.

"How may I assist you, Ms. Goldstein?" a male voice practically purred.

It was almost creepy how everyone knew her name here. But they didn't know her. "Yes, I have a special request. Does anyone there know how to make kugel?"

"I will inquire, miss." Classical music replaced his impeccable British accent. But in a town of actors, was it authentic? Nigel had sure fooled everyone.

"Ms. Goldstein. I have Chef Rubenstein here. Might he speak with you?"

Rubenstein. He should know kugels. "Certainly."

"Mademoiselle, Chag Sameach." His French accent delivered the greeting with a refined joy.

"Merci, shalom *aleichem*—peace to you, Chef Rubenstein."

"You fancy ze kugels, no?"

"Pineapple."

"Zis ees new to me. Have you a recipe?"

"All I know is the secret ingredient is vanilla yogurt." Sorry, Aunt Edna.

"Aha. I weel do my best, Mademoiselle Goldstein."

She glanced at the ceiling. *Aunt Edna, you have to be enjoying this in heaven—a master chef baking your pineapple kugel recipe.* She tucked her body into the corner of the couch and dialed Cari's number, ready for tonight's tête-à-tête.

"Shirry, Chag Sameach to you, too." Her vivacious personality always managed to travel through the thousands of miles of optical fibers.

Shira's contribution to their conversation was movie stars and directors, opulence and wealth—a sort of Lifestyles of the Rich and Famous via phone. But Cari's offering was better—glimpses into her family, students, her thoughtful hubby, wanting to get pregnant, someone dumping cherry kugel on her white dress after services. Life. Love.

The brief pause between them was as comforting as the discussion.

"How is Melly?" Shira asked.

Cari sighed. "About the same. Mrs. Cohen never leaves her side."

"Does Melly hate me for leaving her?"

"Shira! What a thing to say. Melly loves you. She said the other day that you are on the path God has for you."

"She said that to me when I said goodbye."

"Melly's wise beyond her years."

That she was.

A knock. "Care-bear, room service is here. I had the chef make Aunt Edna's kugel recipe."

"No way. Shira, you live such an exciting life."

If she only knew how Shira envied hers.

She barefooted it to the door and looked through the security viewer. A uniformed bellman was slightly bent over the pushcart. "Hold on, Care." She placed the phone in her roomy robe pocket and pulled the ten dollars she had placed in the other pocket earlier.

The handsome young man pushed the cart toward the dining area.

"Leave it by the couch, please."

He smiled and stepped away, then handed the leather folder for her to sign. She palmed the tip. He gave a short bow before retreating and gently closing the door.

The phone back to her ear, she heard Cari muttering, "Hurry. Hurry. Hurry."

"I'm back."

"Finally. Tell me, what does it look like? What does it taste like?"

How she wished Cari were here. She would have savored this so much more than Shira would. "Well, the cart is covered in white linen. A crystal vase with a perfect red rose stands next to the covered plate."

"Lift the lid. Hurry up, Shira."

She giggled again. "Patience. I can smell the aroma of cinnamon and pineapple. I'm lifting the cover." As though Cari were there, Shira gave a flourish with her hand and removed the silver dome. "It looks like a painting."

"Tell me. Tell me." She practically hyperventilated. "Awk. I can't wait until you get Skype so I can see all this for myself."

"There's a fan of thinly sliced apples, with a dollop of something in the center." She tasted it. "It's whipped honey."

"Apples and honey on Rosh Hashanah," Cari belted out the old song they had sung as kids. She joined her, stumbling over some of the lyrics she had forgotten.

They finished their ditty with a giggle.

"What else is on the plate?"

"Two small stacks of cheese triangles overlapped so they resemble little Stars of David."

"So cool, Shirry. What about the kugel?"

The kugel rested like a golden brick, with rivers of pink flowing over it and onto the blue china. "It's a hunk of noodles, that's for sure."

"Well, that's appetizing."

"There's a glaze over it." She ran her finger through then sucked off the sweetness. "Strawberry."

"Taste the kugel, for pity's sake. You're driving me nuts."

"Okay. Okay." She unrolled the linen containing the silver utensils. "The fork is positioned over the target."

"Stop it."

"I have penetration." Skewering a small bite, she brought it to her mouth. "Ready for landing."

"I'll get you for this, Shira Elisheva Goldstein."

The kugel hit her tongue with flavor and moistness. There was no need to chew. It practically melted in her mouth.

"Shira?" Cari whined. Shira heard a soft stomp.

"It's good."

"Just good?"

"Very good."

"You don't like it?" Disappointment laced her question.

She took another forkful. "Cari, it's delicious, but it doesn't taste like Aunt Edna's. It's a perfect blend of spices and fruit, but . . ."

"You wanted Aunt Edna's."

"Uh huh." The gourmet kugel lodged like a wad of dough in her throat. "I miss her so much, Cari."

"I know." Cari sniffed. And like Pavlov's dog Shira's tears appeared.

47

Beulah's eyes opened. The room was still dark. Boxes she had packed the night before stood as sentries in the corners of her bedroom. The clock read a few minutes before six. But she was wide awake as though she had slept eight hours rather than a few.

Lord, what is wrong?

The phone rang. "Hello?"

"Beulah?" Deb Cohen's tearful voice jumpstarted her heart. "I'm sorry to wake you. Melly's taken a turn for the worse. I know it's early, but could you come and pray with me? You and Edna were such prayer warriors when Melly first—" She was unable to finish her sentence.

"I'll be right there."

Fifteen minutes later she was on the nearly empty streets, making her way to the children's hospital. She found a parking spot and was on CHOP's third floor when she noticed a familiar mop of blond hair on someone struggling with a wheelchair.

"Harriet?"

Her friend stopped and turned to look. "What are you doing here?"

"I could ask you the same thing. Do the doctors know you're doing this?"

"Amazing thing. Last night the doc said there were no more clots. Another doctor was here early this morning and said I could go. I'm already checked out." Her joyful tone seemed out of place right now. "I wanted to check on Melly. Do you think it's too early?"

Beulah pushed Harriet's wheelchair. "No, Melly took a turn for the worse. Deb called me this morning."

"Do you think the Cohens would mind if I came with you?"

They arrived at Melly's room. "I think they would be honored." Harriet struggled to stand as Beulah knocked on the partially closed door.

"Come in," someone whispered.

Beulah's eyes adjusted to the darkness of the room. The lamp over Melly's bed was the only light. Deb and John Cohen sat on either side of the bed, holding Melly's hands.

Deborah gracefully rose and approached her. They embraced. "Thank you for coming, Beulah. Rabbi Joel and Rachel will be here once they get their children off to school." She gulped back a sob.

Such a seemingly mundane task. Getting your children ready for school. Beulah couldn't miss the longing in her friend's eyes.

Harriet sniffed. She had forgotten Harriet was standing there. "Deb, you remember Harriet. She was a close friend of Edna's."

Harriet extended a hand, but Melly's mother pulled her into a tight embrace.

"Harriet was released from the hospital this morning, but she insisted on coming here to see Melly," Beulah explained as the emotional hug continued.

Harriet quietly sobbed in Deb's arms. "I feel so bad about Melissa. She's a good kid. I've never seen someone so pure."

"John." Deborah took Harriet's hand and guided her toward her husband. "This is Edna's dear friend, Harriet. Melly worked with her."

John rose and lightly bussed her cheek. "Thanks for coming. Please, sit here."

A horrified expression appeared on Harriet's face. "I couldn't."

John smiled and steered her to the chair. Deb took Beulah's hand and seated her in the chair across from Harriet.

The activity roused Melly. "Miss Beulah?" She tilted her head. "Miss Harriet?" She closed her eyes, but a satisfied smile rested on her pale lips. "I've been waiting . . . for both of you."

Harriet's eyes widened, her chin wobbled.

Melly took a shallow breath. "I need you both—" She struggled for air. "To do a favor."

Harriet patted Melly's hand. "Anything. Melly, I'm so sorry for being so mean to you."

"I forgive you." She coughed. "Please. Pray for Shira. For Kathy."

"Of course, Melly," Beulah said.

"This. My death. It will be difficult . . . for them."

Harriet's hand went to her mouth.

"But. God has told me." She opened her eyes and turned toward Beulah. "He has a plan. For both of them. For all of you."

"We will pray for them, Melly." Beulah nodded toward Harriet. "Harriet has a surprise."

Slowly, she turned her head to Harriet's side. Harriet's lips quivered. Her eyes blinked rapidly.

"Miss Harriet?"

Her friend's attempt at nodding resembled someone shaking the dickens out of a bobble head.

"You know Yeshua? Jesus?" Melly asked.

More bobbing.

Melly closed her eyes. "I could tell." Contentment rested on her like a bridal veil.

Melly's breathing returned to the restless sleep pattern. Gently, Beulah removed her hand from Melly's, and Harriet did the same.

They met up with John and Deborah in the hallway.

"Are you ready to pray?" Beulah asked Melly's parents.

"Yes," John said.

"I'll meet you downstairs, Beulah." Harriet began hobbling toward the wheelchair.

John reached an arm toward her. "Harriet, please stay. We could use your prayers, too."

Harriet's mouth opened then closed.

One by one they took each other's hands and began their intercessions of hope.

Harriet cracked her knuckles then lifted the papers that might doom her reputation in this city. *Okay, Lord. Here's the deal. I really need You right now, because I want to do the right thing. Beulah says I can just talk to You like I talk to her.*

Beulah had given her a copy of their complete client list, but not before she had tried to get out of her why she had wanted it. Harriet had told Beulah to trust her. Her friend's face had screamed doubt then like magic—or a miracle—it changed to an okay-I-trust-you-even-though-I-shouldn't face.

Lord, I'm calling every single person on this list—people that Billie Mae spread those hateful lies to. I'm going to tell them it was my fault and to please forgive me. Hopefully, I won't be run out of town in shame. Though I should be, I know.

She flipped up the recliner's footrest and dialed the first number. *Okay, here I go.*

"Yeah, Mrs. Taylor, you're right. Edna would have been so disappointed in me." This was the last call tonight. She had put off calling Edna's most persnickety client until last.

"Harriet, you should be ashamed of yourself, lying about that lovely girl, Shira and that Melissa child."

It wasn't actually she who had lied, but Harriet wasn't debating this with her—for the fourth time. Seems she was focused on her own train of thoughts rather than what Harriet had been trying to explain.

"But I must say I'm thankful it isn't true."

"Mrs. Taylor, would you forgive me for what I've done?"

"It's not me you should be asking. It's that darling girl, Shira and that sweet little thing, Melly."

"You're right. I did ask for both Shira and Melissa's forgiveness, ma'am."

"You did?"

"Yes, ma'am."

"And did they forgive you?"

"Yes, ma'am."

"Well, then, I guess I can forgive you, too."

As Harriet hung up the phone, she shook her head. Miracles did happen. So why did she want to celebrate with a cigarette? Though she no longer craved the nicotine, she missed having a cigarette in her hand.

After the miraculous turn of events with their clients, she got a spurt of energy and decided to get rid of any temptation to smoke again. Every ashtray, cigarette pack, lighter, and matchbook clunked around in the thick, black garbage bag next to the front door.

Beulah had bought her some real pretty candles a few months back. Harriet had thought they were too nice to burn, but they were lit all over the house now, sending out sweet fragrances to cover the old, musty cigarette stink.

Time to take out the past. She lifted the bag. It twisted in her hand and hit her bad leg. Pain coursed through her whole body. She really wanted to curse, but instead she gritted her teeth and hit the wall with her fist. Now she wanted a cigarette. *Sorry, Lord. Didn't mean to lose my temper. I don't want to pick up another ciggy. Please help me.*

She remembered another stash and dragged the heavy bag to the bathroom. After cleaning out the medicine cabinet, she slammed the door. Her reflection startled her.

Harriet, old girl, you look ridiculous. Limping back to the phone, she punched in Beulah's number before she changed her mind.

"Hello?"

"Beulah, cut my hair."

"What?"

"I need a change, and you are the only one I trust to help me make it."

"Give me thirty minutes and I'll be there."

Harriet hobbled back to her recliner and dropped into it with a poof of air. She levered herself back. The remote lay on the table. She turned on the TV and flipped through a few channels, watching news, then a reality show until some half-naked people showed up. She flipped to another channel as quickly as possible.

After a few minutes, her heart raced. She craved a cigarette.

No. She grunted her way out of the chair and walked to the garbage bag containing all her smoking paraphernalia. She just wanted to hold one—for a few seconds. She wouldn't light it. *God, I need your help.*

Untwisting the tie, she opened the bag. The stench of her past rose up like a toxic cloud. It went straight to her gut and turned it inside out. She twisted the bag shut and dragged it to the front door. *No more, old girl. Say goodbye.*

Getting to the garbage area was like running the Iron Man Decathlon. Once there, she bent over trying to catch her breath. She flipped back the dumpster lid and readied herself to heft a couple hundred dollars' worth of stuff into obscurity. As tight as she was with money, this would hurt a lot.

With all her strength, she tossed it with a warrior's cry. It hit the metal bin with a clunk, followed by breaking glass. Then sweet silence.

It was over.

She threw her arms in the air. "Thank You, God."

"Harriet Foster, what on earth are you doing?" Beulah stood a few yards away, a hand on her hip, a large bag in the other.

"Saying goodbye to the past."

"Couldn't you say goodbye with your coat on? It's freezing out here."

She limped toward her friend and wrapped an arm around her shoulder. Felt nice having someone care enough to yell at her.

Harriet's kitchen counter looked like an explosion of hair products. Long blonde hunks of her hair were scattered on the floor.

Beulah turned off the blow-dryer and ran her fingers through Harriet's hair.

Her head felt ten pounds lighter. The back of her neck and shoulders were loose and limber, like twenty pounds had been lifted. *At this point, I don't care what I look like. I feel great.*

Beulah smiled broadly. Her eyes twinkled like a little kid. She took the big hand mirror and clutched it to her chest. "You ready?"

Not really. Give me a few days. She touched the top of her head. Nothing was there. *Awk!* Was she bald?

Beulah pushed Harriet's fingers lower. Short two-inch stubs had replaced her beehive. She grabbed the mirror from Beulah and stared at her reflection.

Gone was the bleached blonde. In its place was the chestnut brown hair she'd had as a kid. But Beulah had added a few highlights to some of the tips. The hair was short but layered so that it felt thick and healthy. The ends flicked out in a youthful way that flattered the shape of her face.

Beulah's hands were folded against her mouth.

Rotating the mirror to view the sides, Harriet fingered the strands.

"How did you do this?"

She exhaled. "You like it?"

"I don't like it . . ."

Beulah's face crumbled.

"I love it." *Sorry, Lord, couldn't resist.*

"Shira showed me how to do the point-cut layers." Beulah pulled a tuft of hair and demonstrated.

"Pretty clever." She tweaked a few ends. "Seems like I've got some catching up to do."

"Oh, Harriet. You're going to love it. Gets the old creative juices going again."

A picture of Kathy saying she could handle Shira's clients came to mind. In all the rush and concern for Melly, then the fire, she had forgotten about it until that moment. "Kathy knows how to do all this, doesn't she?"

Beulah nodded as she began cleaning up.

As she remembered watching Kathy style with the same grace and ease as Shira, a feeling of compassion came over her. "Beulah, don't you think it's time we got to the bottom of Kathy's mystery?"

Kathy's shift should have ended over an hour ago. The last room was finally cleaned. Some wealthy college kids had a wild party that covered the whole floor. It took a long time to scrub the rooms. None of the other maids had helped her. But that was what she deserved.

If she were at Mavens, she would sweep hair or fold freshly washed towels—not scrub toilets and clean food off walls. She placed her supplies into their proper spots on the maid cart and pushed the heavy cart down the hall to the service elevator.

Thinking about the long bus ride home increased the ache in her muscles and pain in her feet. By the time she was dropped off at the corner, it would be nearly midnight.

Someone walked toward her, talking. He was alone. Carrying a briefcase and a carry-on bag, he spoke angrily on his cell.

She pushed the cart further against the wall to allow him more room. Snatching a quick glance, her heart thumped. She recognized his face, not his name. He too had been a client at Gooding's. A friend of Justin. Justin, the man who had raped her.

He drew closer.

Squatting behind the cart, she pretended to pull towels from the lower trays.

His expensive shoes came into view. Her ears rang and her breath came in short bursts. *Please, God.*

His shoes were next to her. He still talked on his phone.

The shoes did not stop. They moved past her. Down the hall. She rested

252

her chin on her shoulder and watched him enter his room, then shut the door.

Falling against the wall, she exhaled loudly. She straightened and stood, but her legs and arms quaked. The hallway was empty. She was alone.

Alone.

What if something bad had happened to her? Would someone look for her? Miss her?

Nyet. No one.

It began as a niggling in Harriet's head, now it was a full-blown agitation. Kathy's face kept jumping into her mind. Not even the TV could distract her. She clicked the remote, turning off one of her favorite shows.

What was this? Is this You, God?

The phone lay on the end table. She picked it up as she shoved back the recliner's footrest with her heels. Moving slowly until her circulation activated, she shuffled to the desk to retrieve her phone directory from her purse.

There had never been a reason to memorize Kathy's phone number. Her finger moved down the tabbed letters to S and opened the pages. No, not under Smith. Maybe she had written it under K. *No.*

Shame pressed her heart. She flipped the M tab to her hasty writing. There was Kathy's number, under Mouse. *Forgive me, Lord.*

Resting against the desk, she listened as the phone rang. Finally, a mechanical-sounding man said to leave a message. She hung up—she hadn't a clue what she would have said. *Okay, Lord. I called her, but she wasn't home. Or not answering the phone. Can I rest now?*

Making her way back to the recliner, she remembered when she had called to tell Kathy that Edna had died. The girl had squeaked then disconnected. When Harriet had tried calling her back, the call went to voicemail—with the same mechanical-sounding message.

She sighed and looked up. "You're not gonna let me get a wink of sleep until I investigate this, are You?"

Harriet dialed Beulah's number. Her sleepy hello wasn't going deter her. "Beulah, we need to see Kathy, now. Can you drive us?"

Harriet chewed her thumbnail. Something she hadn't done in years.

Beulah yawned again, as she backed her car into a parking spot on the street in front of Kathy's building. Her attitude had been to kindly humor her. Who was Harriet kidding—Beulah was the spiritual one. Why would God talk to her?

Beulah placed the car in park and twisted in her seat to look at her. "You ready?"

Harriet rubbed her sweaty palms on her pants. "This is crazy. Let's go

TERRI GILLESPIE

back."

Her friend smiled. "Harriet, you felt confident God had told you to check on Kathy." She batted her lashes. "Enough to get me out of bed."

"See? You were sleeping. God didn't tell you anything. I'm sorry to drag you out on a cold night."

Beulah yawned again, making Harriet feel worse. "God didn't need to tell me. He told you."

Harriet scanned the area around Kathy's building. "Do you know which apartment she's in?"

Beulah craned her neck. "Second floor, fourth window from the left."

"No lights," Harriet chewed her thumbnail. "She's not home."

"Maybe she's sleeping?"

"Then she's okay and I'm crazy."

Beulah straightened in her seat. Her lips pressed together. She stared out the windshield.

Harriet knew Beulah—the eternal optimist. She was trying to think of something encouraging to say. Some assurances that she wasn't a loon.

"Harriet."

Here it comes. Some sappy line to make her feel better.

"Harriet, there's Kathy."

"Say what?"

Beulah lowered her chin and pointed. The streetlight revealed Kathy's face. She walked down the sidewalk, toward them.

She and Beulah exchanged an excited glance then opened their doors.

Kathy's head lifted. She froze.

"Kathy, it's us." Beulah waved her arms.

The kid's body shimmied like a ribbon in the wind, before crumbling to the ground.

They sprinted—well, Beulah sprinted, Harriet hobbled—to Kathy's shaking form. Sobs vibrated her thin body. Beulah sat next to Kathy and gathered her in her arms. "There, there. We're here now."

With her bad leg, squatting was out of the question, so she bent over. "Kathy, are you hurt?"

She shook her head.

Thank You, Lord.

Beulah whispered and murmured things Harriet couldn't hear. Kathy only responded with a nod or shake of her head. All Harriet could do was send up a silent prayer or two. She couldn't help feeling left out and useless.

Kathy raised her head and stared at Harriet. "I cannot believe you both came."

Harriet offered a hand to Kathy, who grasped it. With no effort, she was on her feet. They in turn gave a hand to Beulah.

Kathy faced Harriet. "Beulah said God told you to come to see me. Is

254

this true?"

Shuffling her feet, Harriet smiled. "Yeah."

Kathy touched her arm. "Thank you."

She shrugged. "No need to thank me. God was the one."

"Thank you for listening."

This stuff was all new to her. Was there some type of Christian etiquette book? "What say we move this inside? It's getting cold out here."

Kathy and Beulah smiled. The kid took her and Beulah's hands.

A lump the size of Nonni's Danish formed in Harriet's throat. She had heard from God. He had spoken to her.

48

Beulah's eyes popped open to darkness. There was no need to check the clock. The time was the same as it had been the last few mornings. Six o'clock.

Traces of the deep breathing of sleep combined with a radiant atmosphere in her room. She could only describe it as the holiness of God's presence. Like a cloud had settled around her.

The phone rang. Sam's number displayed on the lighted panel.

"Beulah." He drew a ragged breath. "Melly passed on a few minutes ago."

She sobbed. Sam offered up a prayer, punctuated with his own sobs. Together they lifted up John and Deborah and all who had loved this sweet young woman.

They praised God. They thanked Him for His tender mercies.

They sang melodies of worship she had never heard before. Together their voices seemed to meld with other voices unseen. Their prayers touched a pinnacle of purity that kept her prostrate on the floor.

God had gathered home His precious child.

Rays from the sun filtered through the blinds. Beulah rolled to her side, the phone in her hand. She brought the phone to her ear.

"Sam?"

"Yeah." His muffled groan sounded like he was trying to stand.

"What happened to us?"

Silence. "Sam?"

"Beulah, I believe God allowed us to witness Him carrying Melly home."

"I will never think of death the same way again."

"Me neither." Sam sighed. "I need to go online and find a flight to California. Shira will need someone to be with her when she hears this news."

Jesse. "Do you think Jesse should be the one to tell Shira?"

"Why?"

"I'm not exactly sure. Are you sensing anything?"

"Just that it resonated." He cleared his throat. "I will contact Jesse."

Reluctantly, Beulah ended the most amazing phone call ever. What they had experienced wasn't easy to let go of, but God was changing directions fast and she wasn't going to be left behind.

A charge of some spiritual electricity zapped her. Harriet. Melly had instructed both of them to intercede on behalf of Shira and Kathy. She called Harriet.

The first ring didn't finish.

Harriet hacked in her ear. "Is it Melly?"

Beulah had paced, sat, and lain on Harriet's living room floor as they had prayed for Shira, Jesse, and Kathy, as well as Melly's family. Harriet had somehow known to read the Psalms. Each chapter redirected their prayers like a map.

After nearly an hour, Beulah finally made her way to the sofa. Harriet sat back in her recliner. Exhaustion and wonderment had erased years off her face. Beulah hoped hers reflected the same.

Harriet rubbed her chin. "Beulah, I think it's time to call Kathy."

"See if she's home?"

"Yeah."

"Then go over there?"

"Yeah." She placed both elbows on the arms of her chair. "Beulah?"

"Yes."

"I didn't know prayin' was like this."

Beulah leaned toward the apartment intercom. "It's us, Kathy," she said. A loud buzz followed by the unlocking of the heavy door meant Kathy would see them despite hanging up on Harriet when she had called.

Harriet's brows rose as she exhaled.

Beulah's sentiments exactly.

Kathy met them at the door, dressed in her maid's uniform—her face creased with worry. "What is wrong?"

"Let's go inside." Beulah reached for her, but she shied away.

They followed Kathy into her apartment then went to the couch as Kathy locked the door. She stood by it with her arms folded across her chest.

"Come sit with us," Harriet said.

She narrowed her eyes.

Beulah grimaced.

"We have bad news," Harriet said.

Kathy backed up and shook her head.

"It's Melly," Beulah said.

Kathy let loose a high-pitched screech that pierced Beulah's heart.

The young woman covered her ears then ran for her bedroom crying out, "Nyet. Nyet. Nyet."

Harriet's eyes rounded like saucers. "What is she saying?"

"I think it's Russian for no."

Kathy slammed the door, a metal click followed. The two of them jumped off the couch and rushed to the bedroom. Harriet tried the door handle. Locked.

Kathy wailed and spoke more Russian—at least she must have, because neither of them could understand a word.

Harriet rapped on the door. "Kathy, come on, kid, open the door."

The wail only increased, the Russian growing louder.

Lord, what do you want us to do? Beulah hadn't a clue what to do.

Harriet went to the kitchen and dragged over two chairs. She placed them by the bedroom door. Beulah fetched her purse with her Bible.

Making themselves as comfortable as possible on the hard wooden chairs, Harriet squeezed her hand. "You ready for the long haul, my friend?"

Yes, she would love savoring more of the sweet aroma of fellowship and the honor of service shared with a friend.

"I'm ready, my friend."

Beulah pressed her hands against the small of her back and stretched. Harriet strolled around the living room.

For the last three hours they had cajoled, prayed, and read passages of hope to Kathy. Harriet had to change positions every few minutes to keep from another phlebitis flare-up. What a trouper, especially given she was a baby Christian.

Kathy's crying had stopped about thirty minutes ago. Beulah wasn't sure if the poor girl was still listening or sleeping.

The bedroom door clicked and slowly opened. Beulah and Harriet froze.

Kathy appeared in the narrow opening.

Beulah held her breath.

Harriet cautiously approached Kathy. She released a moan and rushed toward Harriet, throwing her slender form into Harriet's waiting arms.

49

For some reason, Shira had felt off all day. Almost as though she had missed something important, like an appointment or birthday.

Perhaps it was just the difference between East and West Coasts. Beverly Hills had a certain rhythm—different than Manhattan's intense pace. It was like she was dancing to the wrong music.

This was her first day on the main floor at Élégance. The last nine she had spent cleaning up after Nigel. Repairing relationships with vendors and staff had kept her mostly in the background. Today she had to schmooze with the clients.

In a town that loved mystery and scandal, the customers were eager to meet the new manager who had avoided the limelight these two weeks. At least that's what her assistant, Willow, kept telling her.

Since ten this morning, a steady stream of unnatural, synthetic faces hoped she would reveal some juicy gossip they could then pass on to their friends. Something about Nigel. Veronica. Anything.

Of course she would share nothing. The games they played sickened her. As she moved on to the next client, out of the corner of her eye she saw several clients whispering. Another two people did not even hide the roll of their eyes in the mirror. She wasn't following the rules. And they weren't happy.

Her stomach clenched. It was fortunate she hadn't eaten that day or she'd have to excuse herself after each conversation.

Be careful what you wish for, Shira. A tumult of emotion built.

She missed doing granny hair. Maybe, not the hair, definitely the grannies. She missed the hugs and home-baked goodies—the sincere expressions of appreciation and awe when they looked in the mirror.

Willow studied her iPad. "Shira, You-Know-Who is with the esthetician.

When she's finished, you'll want to introduce yourself to her. Next—"

Shira placed her hand over whoever was next on her assistant's schedule. "Willow, I think I need a break. I've been on my feet for over eight hours and haven't eaten a thing. I—"

A curly-haired man spoke with someone at the reception counter. Her heart skipped. Shira blinked. She must really be exhausted, because now she was hallucinating.

Before she realized it, her feet had carried her toward the man, a sea of whispers on either side of her. She skidded to a stop on the marble floors, a few feet from the tall figure.

"Jesse?"

The curly head turned. Brown eyes captured hers.

"Shira."

She couldn't budge from her spot. All she could think was, he's here!

He moved toward her. She practically threw herself at him, wrapping her arms around his neck and burying her face in his chest, inhaling his sweet, spicy scent. "Jesse, you're here."

"Shira." He held her waist and pushed her back a few inches. "Shira, look at me."

Lifting her chin, she focused on his face. It had the pall of grief.

"What's wrong?" She stepped away from him. "Is it Daddy?"

"No." A stream of tears escaped. "It's—"

"Melly?"

He jerked her back into an embrace. The familiar shaking and fuzzy aura settled on her. She refused to pass out at a time like this, just refused to . . .

Shira swiped the moist blindfold off her eyes. The hotel living room came into focus. A voice came from her bedroom. Concentrating, she vaguely remembered the cab ride back to the hotel and Jesse carrying her to the couch. Eating a few bites of cheese and crackers.

"Jesse?"

He emerged from her bedroom, a phone to his ear. "She's awake. Yes, I'll tell her." He returned the phone to her nightstand before walking toward her. "Shira, how are you feeling?"

"Stupid." She shifted to a sitting position. "Nothing like drama." The wooziness prevented her from attempting to stand.

Jesse shoved aside all the perfectly placed design elements on the coffee table and sat. He bent toward her.

The real reason he had flown all this way induced a swell of anguish. "When did Melly die?"

Jesse bowed his head. "Early this morning."

Outside the floor-to-ceiling windows, the city was ablaze with lights and activity. "How are the Cohens?"

He rubbed his neck. "Your dad is with them. He said they're doing as well as can be expected." He pointed back to the bedroom. "That's who I was talking to. He sends his love."

She settled into the couch and leaned her head back.

"Shira, I have a roundtrip ticket for you. We can leave early in the morning. The funeral and shiva are in the late afternoon."

She couldn't breathe or think. "Okay."

"I've missed you." He extended his hand, palm up.

As she placed her hand in his, she couldn't help feeling confused. "I've missed you, too."

She searched those light brown eyes for some sign of where his heart was. His head moved toward hers. She waited, resisting the urge to throw herself at him again. The wait was worth it as his full lips brushed hers with the promise of something—and then withdrew.

His gaze burrowed into her heart. She closed her eyes and anxiously— hopefully—waited for the feel of his lips again. He kissed her lips more firmly, as though the slow simmer of the last month had finally begun to boil. Shira wanted more of him and tugged at him to bring him against her.

Suddenly his lips were gone, followed by a thump.

Jesse was on the floor.

She tried not to laugh, but it broke free anyway. He lay wedged between the couch and the coffee table, his chin pressed against his knees. He shook his head and pointed to the ceiling. "Thanks, Lord, I needed that."

"I'm sorry, Jesse." She offered a hand.

He shoved her offer away and braced himself on the furniture. As he made his way to one of the upholstered chairs across the living room, disappointment melted the levity she had felt seconds ago.

"No, I'm sorry, Shira." He scuffed a hand through his hair and smiled. "I can't trust myself around you."

Was that a compliment? Actually, she was feeling a bit like Potiphar's wife, again.

He stood. "I need to go." He marched toward the door. "I'll pick you up at five tomorrow morning."

"Jesse, stay here, please. I don't want to be alone."

His chest heaved. "I can't do that, Shira."

"There are two bedrooms. Please, don't leave me." She hated how desperate she sounded—felt.

He gathered his leather jacket. "I can't betray my first love."

"Oh. Her." She'd hoped the woman she had seen him with wasn't serious. Hadn't their lips been locked a few minutes ago?

"Her?"

"You know, the woman I saw you with a few weeks ago."

"Shira, what are you talking about?"

She huffed. "The night Melly was hospitalized. It was about nine, and you were walking down Chestnut with some blonde."

His face scrunched. Slowly recognition opened his features. "That was Heather Knight."

Heather? How could she ever compete with a Heather? Visions of cheerleaders and prom queens sent the usual wave of insecurities and rejection—and with it the impulse to purchase something expensive.

"She's a lawyer in our firm. We were all celebrating at that Mandarin place down on Chestnut. We won a case I'd been working on for the last two years."

She rolled her eyes. "Celebrating?" Even she cringed at the steeped sarcasm in her voice.

Jesse folded his arms across his chest and gave her a glare that evaporated any other acerbic remarks still in her. "Yes, Shira. The whole office. Heather's husband couldn't be there, and I didn't want her walking back to her car alone. I was escorting her back."

Okay, I'm feeling really stupid now. "I'm so sorry, Jesse." She bounded from the couch but reeled from the lightheadedness. Jesse rushed to steady her. The nearness of him reactivated the desires to have him stay.

"Please, can't you stay?" She smiled and raised her face toward his. "I promise to not take advantage of you."

Pain flitted across his face. Shame roiled inside her.

"I can't betray my first love—"

"Your first love? Jesse, who—" Her eyes shut and reopened. "Yeshua?"

He nodded.

The humiliation of what she had been doing angered her. Jesse offered a pure love and, scum that she was, she had tried to turn it into something easy and cheap. He deserved better. And that certainly wasn't her.

"Get out of here, Jesse." She shoved him hard. Regret and longing fueled more anger. "You tell everyone the harlot isn't coming back."

The sorrow on Jesse's face almost made her relent—but she had to do this for his own good.

"Shira, don't call yourself that."

"It's what I am. Everyone thinks that." She shoved him again. Was she strong enough to do this—to push him out of her life for his own good?

"No one thinks that."

"Oh, really? And you didn't think that when you met my boyfriend?"

He looked away, but not before she witnessed the flush of his cheeks.

"I rest my case, counselor." She swallowed back the sob trying to break out. "Just go."

Jesse rested his hand on the knob. He looked over his shoulder. "Shira, Yeshua loves you so much. More than even I do." He pulled a set of tickets from his coat and laid them on the table by the door.

"I love you, Shira." Then, hands in his pockets, he walked into the hallway and disappeared.

She slammed the door then slid to the floor. Next to her were a half dozen bags from exclusive Beverly Hills stores. She jabbed them with her foot. Their comfort and happiness had evaporated the minute she'd brought them back to the hotel. Now they mocked her.

"Okay, God. I give up!" She hugged her knees and cried big, sloppy, snotty tears. Desperation, regret, sorrow, and other frightening emotions she couldn't name rose to the surface like garbage from a backed up sink. A floodgate of memories from her past opened—she was drowning in darkness and filth. She couldn't breathe. Her heart was coming out of her chest, and her head felt like it would explode.

"God, help me, please!" she gasped.

The gulping sobs quieted. She exhaled.

Peace. She felt the peace.

Comfort. It carried her like cool waves on a shore.

She lay on the soft carpet. Waiting.

He has loved you with an everlasting love.

Calmly, gently the words seeped from her heart to her mind.

Surely He has borne your griefs and carried your sorrows.

The words she hadn't thought of in years—words sown into her as a child—came to life.

He was wounded for your transgressions and bruised for your iniquities.

She drew her knees to her chest.

The words that poured from her heart, then to her mind, now made their way to her lips. "I am like a lamb that has gone its own way." Though but a whisper, the words soothed her. "But He took my sins and died for me. For no one took His life. He has given it freely. For me."

She paused.

Choose this day whom you will serve, Shira. Will you serve Me?

Her chest heaved. Her heart felt as though it would explode into a million shiny stars. It was the question she now knew she could answer with certainty.

50

The metallic Hallelujah chorus awoke Beulah. She pushed herself up off Kathy's couch to pull her cell from her pocket. "Hello." Every muscle in her body cried in protest as she stretched.

"Beulah. It's Jesse."

She glanced at her watch. Seven in the morning. "Is Shira with you?"

"No." He cleared his throat. "She—we argued. She's not coming back. I took an earlier flight last night. There were three layovers, I just got in."

Lord, no. I really thought I heard You correctly.

"Beulah, there was a message on my home phone. The realtor has a good offer on The Hair Mavens."

Her hand went to her forehead.

"Beulah?" Harriet appeared from Kathy's room, looking as disheveled as she felt. She mouthed, Who's that?

Beulah mouthed, Jesse. Harriet nodded then yawned.

"I'm sorry, Jesse. I know you went with high hopes."

"I went to comfort her. But once again, I got in the way." He expelled a frustrated sigh. "All I did was confuse things."

Her insides twisted with guilt. This was all her fault. She had reprimanded him for spending time alone with Shira, and what had she done? Throw them together—and in a fancy hotel room.

"Beulah, I'm exhausted and need a shower and some sleep before the funeral."

"Have you called Sam yet?"

He sighed. "Yes."

"How did he take it?"

"Better than I'm taking it."

"Get some rest, Jesse. I'll see you later." She chewed her lip as she disconnected the call.

Harriet leaned against the wall, watching her.

"Shira's not coming," Beulah said.

"Really?" She shuffled to one of the chairs and sat.

"Yes." Beulah returned to the couch. "She and Jesse got into an argument. He left last night."

Harriet tapped her chin a few times, a faraway look in her eyes.

"What are you thinking?"

She didn't answer right away. Finally, she slapped her thighs. "I think we shouldn't worry about this. God can handle one flighty hairdresser. Goodness knows we've seen Him do enough miraculous stuff lately."

Out of the mouths of babes.

Beulah managed to pull together some breakfast for the three of them. Eggs, toast, and strong coffee, using a French press.

Kathy padded into the kitchen, wearing an oversized T-shirt down to her knees. "Good morning, Beulah. Morning, Harriet." She smiled and rubbed her eyes like a small child. Beulah couldn't resist hugging her. Kathy hugged her back.

Grabbing a plate, Harriet filled it with eggs and toast. "Come on, kid. Let's get some meat on those bones."

Beulah's cell rang again. Sam's ID. Her stomach sank like a rollercoaster ride. He was probably mad at her for recommending sending Jesse—alone. "Sam, how are you?"

"Beulah, I'm blessed." He sounded a lot happier than she had expected. "Shira's on her way. Her flight arrives in about two hours."

"Praise the Lord!" She held the phone to her chest. "Shira's coming."

Harriet gave a celebratory woo-hoo. Beulah brought the phone back to her ear. "Is there anything I can do for you, Sam?"

"Keep praying. It's working great so far."

"You can count on that." She disconnected the call and took a plate. Harriet explained the recent series of events to Kathy between bites. Her violet eyes moved to Beulah's.

"Beulah, may I go with you and Harriet to Melly's funeral?"

"Of course."

A picture formed in her mind of chess pieces moving strategically on a chessboard.

Shira's carry-on droned tonelessly behind her. Lack of sleep and aches from the cramped coach quarters permeated her body. She needed a bath and a bed.

But she couldn't wipe the grin off her face.

"Shira."

There, behind the security guard, her father waved both arms. Warmth and joy deepened within her. "Dad." She waved an arm in response.

He shifted from side to side as though trying to figure a way past security. She picked up her pace—at least as much as her luggage and purse would allow. She finally cleared the security line to her father's waiting arms. He lifted her off the floor.

"Button. I was afraid you weren't coming."

Feet planted on the floor again, she rearranged her purse on her shoulder as her dad took the suitcase. "I'm sorry, Dad. The drama queen struck again."

He draped an arm around her. "You're here now. That's all that matters."

The drive home was quiet. She watched the familiar terrain go by. Should she tell him what happened in California? Part of her had wanted to blurt it out when she had called to let him know she was flying in. She had longed to tell him when she first glimpsed him in the airport.

But she couldn't. *God, this is so fresh and new between us. It's like I don't want to share it yet. You'll let me know when I'm to say something.*

"Dad, how are the Cohens?"

He turned his head briefly. "Pretty torn up. It's like with your mom. You keep praying for a miracle. Then at that last moment when things are bad, you pray that God would take them home, because they're suffering so. But then when He does, you . . ."

He didn't need to finish. She placed her elbow on the door's armrest and cradled her chin in her palm.

"Something amazing happened when she passed on, Shira."

She lifted her chin to look at him. "What?"

He kneaded his lips together. "I don't know how to explain it exactly." His hand reached for hers. "I called Beulah from the waiting room right after Melly—after it happened. As soon as I told Beulah, I fell to the floor. We both started praying and worshipping the Lord. I swore I heard angels. It was like—like God allowed us to witness Him taking Melly home to be with Him."

Goosebumps rippled up and down Shira's arm.

He looked at her with moist eyes then scoffed. "Guess that sounds pretty weird, huh?"

Not as weird as you think.

Shira's dad pulled his Lexus onto his street. A familiar white Volvo was parked in front of his house. A familiar tingle parked itself inside her. "Is Jesse here?"

"Is that okay?" He turned into the driveway. "I'll ask him to leave if you're uncomfortable. He feels terrible about your argument."

She shifted in her seat. "Did he—"

Placing the car in park, he faced her. "No, he did not tell me." He cupped her cheek. "And, believe me, I tried to get it out of him."

She smiled. "I'm okay."

While her dad pulled her things from the trunk, she walked up the sidewalk. Jesse stood there, holding open the storm door. "Hi." Those eyes. That dimple. Maybe she was not okay.

She sighed. "Hi."

They gave each other a platonic side-hug. "How was your flight?"

"Fine." She began taking off her jacket. Jesse helped her.

Dad fumbled through the door with all the luggage. "Don't mind me. I'll just put these in your old room."

"Thanks, Dad."

He winked before climbing the stairs.

She walked into the kitchen and opened a cabinet. Jesse followed. "Jesse?"

His footsteps halted. She pulled out a glass and shut the cabinet before turning toward him. "I'm sorry for my behavior in California. I took advantage of your—"

Jesse took a step toward her, then stopped, as though some invisible barrier kept him from going further. "No, Shira, I took advantage of you."

She smiled. "Trust me, Jesse, it was mutual." She filled the glass at the fridge's dispenser. "I admire you for putting the *kibosh* on it, in any case."

He nodded. "It was difficult. Really difficult."

If it was half as difficult as it was for her, then . . . Wow. She brought the cool water to her lips and took a long drink. Jesse watched her, as though waiting for her to respond.

"Thank you for respecting me." Boy, that sounded corny. *Oh, great.* She was blushing.

Her dad entered the kitchen, wearing a suit jacket and straightening his tie. "Shira, the funeral begins in an hour. Rabbi Joel asked me to get there early. Do you mind riding with Jesse?"

"No problem, Dad."

He kissed the top of her head. "I'll see you there."

Alone again with the man of her dreams. Her heart revved its engines. "Jesse, I'm going upstairs to freshen up. I'll be down in a few minutes. Then we can go."

Shira stayed in her room much longer than necessary, but she knew she needed to put some distance between them. She was tempted to tell Jesse about her decision, about her relationship with God. But she knew she needed to share this news with her dad first.

With a few seconds to spare, she walked down the stairs. He rose from the couch, holding her jacket.

The drive to Beth Ahav was only a few minutes. The parking lot was packed. Jesse parked and shut off the ignition. "Shira, we got a really good offer on The Hair Mavens."

A lump formed in her throat. Was he trying to tell her something? Like, you need to go back to Beverly Hills? "Can we talk about this later? Please?"

"Sure."

Jesse held the synagogue door open for her. As she entered, an overwhelming sentiment of being home rested upon her. Several faces she recognized gave soft-voiced welcomes.

"Shira." An enthusiastic whisper drew her attention. Beulah's lovely face sent a wave of warmth through her heart.

They hugged tightly.

"Hey, kiddo."

Shira knew that voice, but who was this woman? "Harriet?"

She held out her arms. "You gonna give me a hug or what?"

Her hug left her breathless. "You look beautiful, Harriet. Who did your hair?"

She gave a sly smile and raised her chin toward Beulah.

"I knew you could do it."

Beulah blushed. She was so cute, she wanted to hug her again.

"Shira." Kathy appeared from behind Beulah. "I am so glad to see you." She extended a hand, but Shira ignored it and kissed her cheek.

Jesse cleared his throat. "I think we need to go in, ladies."

Beulah and Shira interlocked arms. Harriet and Kathy did the same, as Jesse led them into the sanctuary. They managed to find a few seats in the back, Jesse sitting next to Shira.

A large portrait of Melly rested on an easel on the *bimah*. The sweet mavens' reunion had distracted her, but now Shira choked back a spasm of emotion.

Melly was gone.

Rabbi Joel stood. "If we can begin."

The service was brief but touching. If tears were indication, all had been touched by this sweet girl's life. Shira collected her purse and jacket and tried to compose herself before conveying her sympathies to the Cohens.

"Shirry." Cari wove her way through the crowd.

They met together in a solid embrace that nearly knocked the wind from their lungs. It would have been comical except they were both crying.

"Cari, it's so sad. I loved that girl."

"I know. I can't stop crying." She turned and waved an arm toward a group of teens. "Nearly her whole class is here."

Shira recognized some of the young women who had visited the salon. They huddled together, consoling one another. Shira knew well the pain of losing someone at such a young age.

Melly's family had a circle of people around them so deep that Shira decided to wait until later to give her condolences.

At the cemetery, the plain pine coffin with a Star of David carved on top awaited burial. Lost in the memories of her mom and Aunt Edna, Shira battled the flood of old and new sorrow. Her father enfolded her in his warmth. Of anyone she knew, he truly understood the cold, dark pain. How grateful she was for his warmth. To think she had run from it for so many years.

Rabbi Joel's message of assurance that Melly was in heaven with God reminded her of what her dad had told her in the car. How God had taken Melly home. She snuggled closer to her father.

The funeral over, Shira waited in line to speak with the Cohens. Mr. and Mrs. Cohen stood under the canopy, hugging and shaking the hands of people touched by Melly. A hand touched the small of her back. Without looking, she knew it was Jesse. He shifted to stand beside her.

The couple in front of her moved on. "Shira." Mrs. Cohen held Shira tightly. "Thank you for all you did for Melissa. You brought her so much joy."

She couldn't respond. The words she wanted to say were too large—so heavy with emotion they could not rise past her throat.

Mrs. Cohen kissed her cheek. Mr. Cohen gave her a brief hug and whispered a thank you, as well.

If she could speak, if the words could have made their way past the lump of grief, she would have thanked them. Thank you for raising a daughter who was a pure delight. Who lit up any room she entered. *Thank You, Lord, for allowing me this brief time with her.*

Jesse reached for her hand as they walked toward his car. In the distance, she recognized the old oak tree. While the maples and birch around it had begun to shed their red, orange, and brown leaves, the oak was still mostly green with only a delicate lacing of russet colors. "Jesse? Would you walk with me? I want to introduce you to someone special."

They strolled along in silence until they arrived at her mother's grave. She picked up a small stone from the gravel path and placed it next to numerous others on the headstone that read Aviva Hadassah Feinberg Goldstein. Jesse did the same.

"Mama, this is Jesse." She turned to Jesse. "Jesse, this is my mama."

He made a small bow. "Nice to meet you, Mrs. Goldstein."

This was it. She would tell Jesse about her new faith in Yeshua. "Mama, Jesse is a real mensch. I think you would like him. I—"

A flash of white caught her eye. She looked over her shoulder toward another grave. Aunt Edna's. There was no headstone—that would come shortly before the one-year anniversary of her death—but on the packed mound, surrounded by stones, was a white bakery bag.

She reached over to pick it up, then peered inside. A cherry cheese Danish. Fresh. Her skin prickled as the hair on her arms and neck rose.

"Jesse, can you take me to The Hair Mavens?"

His face registered uncertainty. "Sure, if that's what you want."

"Yes, it is. I have some unfinished business to attend to."

51

Harriet chewed. The kugel Beulah brought to the shiva tasted a lot like Edna's. This was her second piece. She had no idea noodles could taste like dessert.

The Cohens's house was packed. Harriet only knew a couple people, so she had been hanging around the dining room. Eating. Kathy had stuck by her like white on rice. Really, the kid was doing her more of a favor, rather than the other way around. She wished she could get her to eat something, though.

"Harriet." Sam zigzagged his way through the people. "Have you seen Shira?"

She shook her head and swallowed. "No."

"She and Jesse were walking," Kathy said.

Harriet stared at her, surprised Kathy had offered the information. "Where?" Sam asked.

"At the cemetery."

Harriet shrugged. "Maybe she needed some space."

"I guess." He patted Harriet's shoulder. "Let her know I'm looking for her when she shows up."

"Sure." He merged back into the crowd. She turned to Kathy. "So, you saw Shira and Jesse walking?" She took another bite of the noodle dish.

She nodded. "To the big tree where Edna was buried."

The hairs on her arms jumped to attention. "Kathy, do you see Beulah anywhere?"

She stood on tiptoe and searched. "No. Oh, wait. I think. Yes, she is over there by the fireplace."

"Could you get her? I need to find Sam."

After a few minutes, the four of them met by the front door.

"What's going on?" Beulah asked.

"I—good grief, I don't know what to call it." She blew air through her lips. "I think Shira is going to the shop."

"Why would you think that?" Sam's brows wrinkled.

"I don't know. Maybe it's God. All I know is this is the same feeling I got when Beulah and I were supposed to see Kathy."

"Listen to Harriet, please," Kathy said.

The four of them locked eyes.

Sam pulled out his car keys. "That's good enough for me. I'll meet you ladies there."

Shira rolled down the car windows as Jesse drove past the cleaners then The Hair Mavens. The boarded-up windows and For Sale signs tore at Shira's heart. He parked on the street by the side of the building. Up ahead was her red Mini. It needed a bath and some love.

"You okay, Shira?" Jesse touched her shoulder.

She studied the red bricks darkened by soot.

"We don't have to do this," he said.

She expelled the breath she had been holding. "No, I need to do this."

Jesse exited and ran around to open her door. He helped her out and didn't let go of her hand as they walked around the corner.

The Hair Mavens Beauty Shop languished in neglect. As they stood in front of the salon, Shira spotted two homemade hot-pink signs. She read the sun-faded message to pray for all of them. "Beulah must have written that." She wiped the moisture from under her eyes.

She tried the door. Of course it would be locked.

"I have the key." Jesse pulled his keys from his pocket and unlocked the door. "I hired a cleaning service. The glass people will be here next week."

"I need to go in alone, Jesse." She touched his cheek. "Understand?"

He nodded, but she couldn't miss the disappointment in his eyes.

She swung open the door and stepped inside. Gone were all the furnishings and equipment. It had been swept down, the floors mopped, the walls scrubbed. There was still a hint of smoke in the air. But it had been stripped to nothing.

Wrapping her arms around her waist, she shut her eyes and allowed herself to remember. Memories tucked away for so many years came to life on the blank canvas around her.

Aunt Edna placed a stool next to the shampoo station. Shira shampooed her first client's hair, her small fingers intertwined in white strands. Mrs. Sundergram. That's who it was. Although there had been more water on the floor than in the sink, she had felt such a sense of accomplishment. Mrs. Sundergram had given her her first tip . . . a whole quarter.

Another recollection materialized.

Her mama opened the shop's door. Shira ran to Aunt Edna, bringing her the picture she had drawn in school. She had painted pictures for her . . . and Harriet. Harriet had lifted her up and hugged her. "Whatcha got there, kiddo?" She'd oo'd and aah'd with Aunt Edna at Shira's handiwork.

Harriet had loved her. How had she forgotten that? She cringed. The hateful things she had thought about her . . . had said to her.

The journal. Tears fell before the memory crystallized in her mind.

Her mommy's cancer was back. She missed school that day because Daddy and Mommy had been up late crying. Her mom wanted to see Aunt Edna about something, so they drove to Mavens.

As they walked into the shop, Aunt Edna cried out, "Aviva." Her mom and aunt hugged a long time.

"Shira, I bought you something." Aunt Edna had given her a pink digital Barbie watch.

The swirling pink and yellow colors looked pretty. The watch had really big staples holding it to a piece of cardboard. She turned toward her mom for help, but she and Aunt Edna were walking toward the supply room. She didn't know how to get the watch off, or how to fix it so she could wear it. She didn't know how to fix anything—she was just a kid.

A hand rested on her shoulder. "Hey, kiddo." When she looked up, Harriet had jiggled her chin then lifted her up with a groan. Harriet sat in her chair and shifted Shira to her lap. Even though she was eight and too big to be held, she nestled against Harriet's roomy chest. Harriet reached over, opened her drawer, and pulled out a pink tissue-wrapped present with Shira's name written on top.

"Listen, kiddo. I know things are gonna be tough for you and your family for a while." She placed the gift on Shira's lap and looked at her through their reflection in the mirror. "I hope this will help when you're feelin' confused and me and your aunt or your folks aren't around."

Slowly Shira tore away the crinkled paper. It was a book—like the fancy old books in the library. She opened the cover to see it was blank inside, but the pages had straight gold lines for her to write on.

Harriet pointed to the blank page. "This is for you to write your thoughts and stuff that's important to you."

Her thoughts—what was important to her.

When had she turned that sweet, thoughtful gift into an inventory of crises? When had she begun to buy her way out of hurts and rejections.

She stood where Harriet's station once was.

"Shira?"

She turned. Her father stood where Aunt Edna's station once was.

"Daddy." For the second time today, she threw herself into his arms. He held her tight as fresh tears fought for more room on her face. "I miss Mama."

He took a frayed breath. "Me, too."

"And Aunt Edna."

Dad smoothed her hair and kissed her forehead. "Me, too."

Reluctantly, she removed herself from his warmth. "Daddy, I need to tell you something."

He tilted his head and nodded.

"I made my peace with God."

"What do you mean?"

"I mean, I'm His. I asked Yeshua into my heart."

"Shira," her dad choked out. He wrapped her in his bear hug.

The tears they now shed appeared the same as those they had shed earlier in grief, but they were not the same. These were sweetened by joy.

Beulah parked behind Sam's car. He must have broken every speed limit to get there before them. She, Harriet, and Kathy hurried to the front of the shop only to find Jesse standing alone on the sidewalk. His head hanging, his hands in his pockets.

"Jesse?"

"Hey, Beulah. Harriet. Kathy." He began pacing in a small circle.

"What's going on?" Harriet asked.

Jesse sniffed. "I think she's saying her goodbyes."

Beulah stepped closer to the window. Shira and Sam were crying in each other's arms. She turned away. *Lord, is this truly the close of this chapter?*

Harriet's stomach dropped. Beulah's face said it all. Was this the end? No, it couldn't be.

She stepped toward Delicious Bakery and leaned on the brick wall before the bakery's entrance. Her eyes closed. She didn't care if anyone saw her. Still she hoped God didn't mind if she whispered.

"Okay, Lord. Beulah says You are a God of miracles. Now, I've already seen some pretty good ones. And, I don't want to appear greedy, but it would sure be nice if this wasn't the end." She swallowed.

"That maybe there is some hope and life left in the old Mavens. I don't want to bargain or make deals, but I would promise to treat this gift with the respect it deserves. I thank You—whatever You decide. Amen."

"Amen," a male voice echoed.

Her eyes popped open. Bob-the-insurance-guy?

Kathy watched the drama before her. Beulah tried to be a brave soldier and not cry. Jesse looked like a boy who had lost his best friend. Harriet just walked away.

This was bad. Beulah and Harriet said God did miracles. God loved them. But Melly was dead. Edna was dead. The salon was burned down.

Shira was selling The Hair Mavens.

She peeked inside the shop. Shira and Sam were wiping tears from their faces. Jesse said they were saying goodbye. Weren't they all saying goodbye? Beulah would work at another salon. Harriet, too. She would go back to cleaning rooms.

Please, God. I do not want to say goodbye.

Shira and her father were coming out.

Kathy held her stomach. She wanted to go back to the car, now.

"Kathy, don't leave." Beulah put her arm around her waist. "Harriet, they're coming out."

Please, God. Please. Please.

Shira walked out arm and arm with her dad. Jesse's eager eyes searched hers. He wasn't alone on the sidewalk. Beulah and Kathy were with him. As she joined them, she noticed Harriet and that insurance guy approaching.

Shira gazed at her father, then Jesse. "Jesse, about the great offer on the salon?"

"Yes?"

"Reject it."

Beulah gasped.

Jesse stepped toward her. "What are you saying?"

"I'm saying some changes need to be made around here."

Harriet and Kathy lowered their heads and backed away.

She pointed to the boarded-up cleaners. "First, put an offer on the cleaners—I hear they're having a fire sale."

Her dad chuckled.

All Shira wanted to do was to gobble up the smile on Jesse's face. "Got it," he said.

Harriet approached Shira, her lips quivering. "Shira, Kathy knows all the styles and techniques. Beulah has learned some new things, but I'm an old stick in the mud who hasn't learned anything new in years." Her eyes filled.

"Perfect." She placed a hand on her shoulder. "You'll be our first student."

Beulah sputtered. "What do you mean?"

"I mean, we're opening a school with the salon." She took Harriet's hand. "All of us. Edna's School of Beauty."

Someone let out a whoop. Beulah, Harriet, and Kathy pulled her into a group hug. The space filled with squeals, tears, and laughter. Horns honked around them.

Shira lifted her head from the huddle to see Frank and Nonni, Josie from the florist shop, and other shop owners converging on the sidewalks.

Harriet continued walking up the sidewalk toward Nonni, who ran to meet her. Beulah took Kathy's hand and sprinted across the street. A huddle of well-wishers on the other side of the street surrounded them, too. She knew she would join them soon, but first . . .

She sauntered toward Jesse and grabbed his tie. "One more instruction for you, counselor."

"Yes, ma'am." He held out his hands. She fitted hers into his.

She savored the moment. "You must pick me up promptly at seven-thirty on Friday, so we're not late for service at Beth Ahav."

His expressive brown eyes registered confusion. Slowly, awareness sparkled. He looked toward her dad. Her father smiled and winked.

Jesse touched her cheek. He angled his head and brushed his lips on hers, eyes open. He drew back and smiled. She closed her eyes, her invitation to him. His hand moved behind her neck to pull her closer. His mouth found hers and kissed her hard and long.

Whistles, cheers, and horns—the urban love sonnet—sounded around them.

They separated with the unspoken promise of exploring God's purposes for them. Pressing their foreheads together, she wrapped her arms around his neck. Jesse lifted her up in his arms as another round of cheering swelled.

Harriet caught Shira's eye. She winked. "Well, it's about time, kiddo." Harriet's arms rose to the sky. "Hey, everybody! The mavens are back!"

BOOK CLUB
SUGGESTED DISCUSSION QUESTIONS

1.   What do you think Aunt Edna's goals were for giving The Hair Mavens to Shira and not to Harriet? How did making Shira keep all the mavens as stylists possibly play into this?

2.   One of Shira's life goals was to launch her own chain of high-end salons. How did this goal affect her behavior?

3.   Harriet was fine with her predictable life. How did Edna's death affect her behavior?

4.   What were Beulah's goals for the salon after Edna died? For herself?

5.   Kathy/Katya's existence was one of secrecy and solitude because of a painful experience. Have you every isolated yourself after a traumatic event? Was it helpful, or not?

6.   Beulah seemed prepared to sacrifice her job to support Edna's niece. How did that affect Shira? Harriet? Kathy?

7.   The Messianic congregation Edna and Sam attended was called Beth Ahav—Hebrew for House of Love. Discuss how this congregation was a house of love.

8.   Two of my favorite scenes in the book were when Shira styled Beulah's hair and when Beulah cut off Harriet's beehive. These were pivotal moments when Shira and Harriet's hearts were changed. What were your two favorite scenes? Why?

9.   One of the most difficult decisions for me was to have Melly die. She represented the sacrificial death of our Savior. Melly's death had an impact on the ladies. Discuss how this impacted them. How it impacted you?

10.   Have you ever met/fellowshipped with Jewish believers in Yeshua (Jesus)? If not discuss how this might be possible for you in the future. Why might that be a blessing?

11.   Of all the mavens whom do you most identify with? Why?

12.   The women of Hair Mavens are only beginning to realize that their friendships with one another have the potential of changing lives— beginning with their own. How did you see this happening in the story?

13.   One of the first steps for the mavens to develop a relationship was forgiveness. How does forgiveness play a role in unity? How has it played a role in your life?

14.   My passion for nearly twenty years has been unity within the Body of Christ/Messiah—the Jewish people and the nations who worship Yeshua as

Lord, and Savior. A beautiful example is the story of Ruth and Naomi. Ruth sacrificed a life she knew to become a part of the Jewish people (Ruth 1:16). The Hair Mavens series is a contemporary parable of this testimony to unity. Discuss the similarities and differences between the true story of Ruth and Naomi and *She Does Good Hair*.

A portion of Yeshua's prayer to His Abba:
"The glory that You have given to Me I have given to them, that they may be one just as We are one—I in them and You in Me—that they may be perfected in unity, so that the world may know that You sent Me and loved them as You loved me."
John 17:22-23 Tree of Life (TLV) Translation

.

I would love to hear from you. Please visit me at:
www.terrigillespie.com
or write me at:
sdgh@terrigillespie.com

ABOUT THE AUTHOR

Terri Gillespie is an award-winning author and speaker. A member of the American Christian Fiction Writers since 2001 she administered the local ACFW group in Philadelphia for several years. Her other writing credits include: head writer for the Restoration of Israel Minute, heard on 25 stations in 11 states and Canada; *Making Eye Contact with God—A Women's Devotional*. *She Does Good Hair, Book One of The Hair Mavens Series* is her first novel. She lives with her husband of 40 years outside Philadelphia. They have one adult daughter, who lives in Chicago with her husband and son. Terri invites you to visit her at www.terrigillespie.com or Facebook at Terri Gillespie, Author or Tweet her @TerriGMavens.

Made in the USA
Columbia, SC
16 June 2019